D0458536

The Ground She Walks Upon

Other Books by Meagan McKinney

FAIR IS THE ROSE

LIONS AND LACE

TILL DAWN TAMES THE NIGHT

MY WICKED ENCHANTRESS

NO CHOICE BUT SURRENDER

WHEN ANGELS FALL

The Ground She Walks Upon

MEAGAN McKINNEY

Delacorte Press

Published by
Delacorte Press
Bantam Doubleday Dell Publishing Group, Inc.
1540 Broadway
New York, New York 10036

ISBN 0-385-31020-X

Manufactured in the United States of America
Published simultaneously in Canada

For

T. Y. ROBERSON,

my father-in-law.

Thanks for being such a fan.

And thanks for the other

two Toms.

With all my love.

PART ONE

Beltaine

Love, all alike, no season knows, nor clime,
Nor hours, days, months, which are the rags of time.

JOHN DONNE
(1572–1631)

"The Sun Rising"

Chapter 1

T HE DAY had started out like any other. Reverend Jamie Drummond, the only Church of Ireland vicar in the Catholic county of Lir, took a walk with his spaniel after breakfast. By noon, he was in his study reading the Epistles, and he had his tea in the rectory at precisely four o'clock. Afterward, he napped upon the velvet settee while the housekeeper, Mrs. Dwyer, cleaned the woodwork in the church.

Reverend Drummond slept peacefully. He might have wakened past the dinner hour if not for the scream.

"Jaysus, Mary and Joseph! 'Tis the divil at work in the church!" Mrs. Dwyer cried out as she ran into the rectory.

He sat up straight and fumbled for his coat, embarrassed that Mrs. Dwyer had seen him in his shirtsleeves.

"What is this all about?" he grumbled. "You're shrieking like a banshee." He slicked back his gray hair and rubbed his muttonchops as if trying to wake himself.

" 'Tis the work of the divil! I've never seen such a sight in all me days!" The plump housekeeper wrung her hands in her apron. The hem of her dress was wet with spilled washwater and her plain Irish features were pale with fright.

"Mrs. Dwyer, the devil does not reside in *my* church, I can assure you of that," Drummond said with a patient, put-upon tone in his voice, as if he were used to dealing with pagans.

" 'Tis the work of the divil I saw, Reverend, and no one will be convincin' me otherwise. Go look yourself and you'll see what I've seen."

He straightened his clerical collar and took a sip of his cold tea, clearly seeing no need to rush. "Why don't you tell me what you saw first."

" 'Tis the cross. The cross!"

"Which cross? The cross over the altar? Or the one on the steeple?" He scowled. These Irish, they were always so excitable. It was a wonder they could get themselves up in the morning and see to their toils without working themselves into a frenzy. If something was amiss in the church, it was clearly the fault of Griffen O'Rooney. The dull Irish lout tended the graveyard and the church, and things were always going awry beneath the man's inept care.

" 'Tis the cross, Reverend." Mrs. Dwyer's voice lowered to a whisper. "The old druid piece in the case by the font. 'Tis glowin'. I swear it, and if I be lyin' may I burn in hell forever."

Reverend Drummond felt the hackles rise on his neck. Of all the things he'd expected Mrs. Dwyer to say, that surely wasn't one of them. But these Irish, they were always running on about faeries and ghosts. It took little—a flicker of shadow, an unexplained noise—to get them spooked. And Mrs. Dwyer had spooked herself now.

Yet the very fact she'd remarked on the old druid artifact left him a bit unsettled. A flicker of remembrance rallied in the corner of his thoughts.

"The old druid cross, you say? Is that what you saw that scared you?"

The housekeeper nodded, tight-lipped in fear.

Drummond stared at her, his thoughts suddenly very far away.

It simply couldn't be. He had almost forgotten the talk he'd had with his father when he had been but a lad. Now it seemed like a dream, a faded old myth that had eroded beneath the day-to-day living of sixty-three years.

"Now are you sure it was the *druid* cross that looked strange to you? It wasn't perhaps the silver chalice upended on the—"

" 'Twas the druid piece, Reverend. I know what I seen." Mrs. Dwyer crossed herself, twice for good measure.

"All right," he said hesitantly. "I'll investigate." He waved for her to gather her courage. "Come with me and explain what you saw in detail."

"I won't be returnin' there, not with the divil still performin' his evil work!"

"Nonsense!" the reverend interrupted. "The devil is not at work in my church! Come along now."

"Oh, Reverend, please don't force me to go back there!"

She began to wail, and Reverend Drummond was supremely uncomfortable.

"Hush, woman." He took her by the arm. "We will go in there and see what this is all about. Of course it was a trick of the light. You'll soon feel quite foolish. Your superstitious Irish nature has gotten the better of you. I'll prove to you that there is nothing malevolent or otherworldly going on in my church."

He dragged the housekeeper out of the rectory. Crossing the graveyard, a stiff wind whipping at their backs, Drummond was almost relieved to enter the dark, peaceful sanctuary of the church.

From the vestibule, he found the church awash in heavenly light, an easily explained phenomenon with eight stained-glass windows shimmering between bouts of clouds and sunshine. The slate floor was aglow with flecks of sapphire, emerald, and ruby light, also created by the stained-glass windows. The altar and pews appeared in order. The only thing amiss was Mrs. Dwyer's bucket, upended near the christening font, the water forming a gray, soapy lake around the dais.

The housekeeper trembled next to him. Drummond would not admit to it, but even he needed an extra second or two to gather the courage before peering into the glass case.

He kept remembering his father's words of half a century ago: *Jamie, my good lad, remember what I've told you on this day. When I'm gone you'll be the guardian of the cross, and upon your shoulders the burden must fall. In years to come you may think you can shirk your responsibilities, but always remember, you are the guardian of the cross. You must call the council. In your heart you will know when that time has come.*

"Well, I certainly don't see anything strange here." He stared at the small glass case across the room. It seemed perfectly normal, and his relief was a like a blast of fresh air. At least *he* was not a blithering fool. Anglican or not, his father had somehow been swayed by these people's superstitions, but he, Jamie Drummond, had been granted a reprieve from such follies. The moment to act, to obey his own dead father's wishes, had not yet come.

Mrs. Dwyer's voice cut into his thoughts. "If you'll be pardonin' me, Reverend, but you cannot be seein' it from here." She looked at him suspiciously as if she suspected him of being a coward.

He bristled and stepped forward. "No, there is nothing here. The cross looks much the same as it always has." He peered down into the glass case. Nestled in deep purple satin lay an ornate silver druid cross. It was very different from a Christian cross, for the arms were of equal size and set into the center of the Celtic scrollwork was a huge amethyst that glittered, but not unnaturally. It agonized him to have a pre-Christian artifact displayed in his church, but there seemed no way to avoid local tradition. The druid cross had been there at the church longer than he had.

"I tell you, the thing was glowin'! It looked all afire, even though the sun had gone behind the clouds." The housekeeper took a tentative step forward, half frightened, half frustrated that she appeared to be telling stories.

"Well, come take another look, Mrs. Dwyer. There is nothing unusual about the cross." The reverend held out his hand. The old housekeeper took it, holding on to it tightly while she peered into the case.

Puzzled, she looked up and shook her head. "I tell you true, 'twas almost blindin' me. It shot out a purple light that nearly touched the ceiling." She looked up to see if there was any evidence above of what had happened. The tracery on the vaulted stone ceiling thirty feet over their heads appeared untouched.

"The light through these windows can cause trickery, I think," he said gently, wanting very much for this to be put behind him. Anything concerning the ancient druid cross unsettled him. It made him think of things best kept dead. "The colors in the glass shift and sparkle. It's clear now that this was all a mistake. A mixture of odd lighting and too much fiery Irish superstition."

Mrs. Dwyer sniffed. "I saw what I saw, your honor. 'Twas not a result of the Irish in me."

"Now, don't be incensed. Let's just forget this ever happened. Go about your work. I've a funeral tomorrow and the place still needs a good scrubbing."

"If you're forcin' me, I'll go get me mop and clean the place up, but I tell you, 'twas no trick of the light, and I'll not be cleanin' this chapel alone today." The housekeeper stared at him.

He sighed. When would these people behave in a logical, unemotional manner? "Fine. I'll sit right here in the first pew and scratch out some words for next Sunday's sermon. I hope you'll attend it, Mrs. Dwyer. I plan to speak on the ill effects of faerie tales."

He watched her disapprovingly. She gave the glass case one last nervous look, then scurried for the rectory.

Without her, the church seemed to grow unnaturally quiet. He normally preferred the church this way. No unruly children to distract him from his sermon, no blasting organ to shake the windows. No Mrs. Dwyer with her apparitions . . .

But now the silence seemed ominous.

The woman's foolishness was rubbing off on him, he told himself as he settled in the first pew and pulled out a pencil stub and a piece of paper from the pocket of his coat. He tried and tried to think of an opening to his sermon, one that would make the parishioners sit up and take notice, but his gaze kept wandering to the case.

The episode had been nothing but an Irishwoman's imagination gone awry, and he could not let himself be dissuaded from that fact. Still, as he sat in the strange silence of the church, he felt drawn to the glass case.

He stood and walked toward it. Nothing had been disturbed. There was a fine layer of dust across the glass top, unmarred by fingerprints. Mrs. Dwyer cleaned the glass once a week, and otherwise it remained untouched. There was no reason for anyone to open the case and fiddle with its contents. Indeed it was impossible. His father had long ago sealed the valuable silver cross within the airtight glass so that it would not tarnish. Even now, more than fifty years later, the silver glowed as if newly polished.

Drummond stared down at the cross. There was indeed something strange about it today, but he could not quite place what it was. It wasn't glowing, of that he was sure. He studied it a moment, then spied what was bothering him. Twice in the same day, the hair seemed to stand on the back of his neck.

The cross had been moved. The satin had faded in fifty years of sunlight except where the cross had lain and now he could see an impression of where it used to be, exactly the opposite pattern of where it lay now.

His breathing became quick and shallow. There was no way to turn the cross without breaking the glass.

He stared at the ancient pagan cross, mesmerized. It could not be. There had to be a crack somewhere in the glass. A piece had to have been removed and replaced.

He checked, but there were no cracks, no loose sheets of glass, no sign of a glazier at work. Jamie Drummond was stunned. The case had never been opened, but the cross now rested in a new position.

He closed his eyes and slowly reopened them convinced the vision would be gone, but the cross was still in the airtight case, turned as if by the hand of God. Someone could have bumped the case. Yes, he told himself, surely someone could have fallen against the sturdy piece and somehow jarred the cross from its resting place. But he didn't believe it. The cross was too precisely turned. It seemed to be evidence of something he could not let himself dare think.

That it was a sign.

His father's words echoed through his mind.

 . . . *in your heart, you'll know when the time has come* . . . *when the time has come* . . .

"Mrs. Dwyer! *Mrs. Dwyer!*" he shouted, his commanding voice booming through the empty church.

"Oh Jaysus! And what is it now?" her meek voice asked from the doorway.

"Go and fetch young Timothy Sheehan. Tell him I've got a message I need him to deliver at once."

"What've you been seein'! Is the thing a-glowin' once more?" Mrs. Dwyer peeped, not moving from the vestibule.

" 'Tis nothing," he growled. "Just get me that boy and have him meet me in the rectory. I have business to attend."

"Then shall I be cleanin' the church? Alone?"

"No! Get along home with you. Leave the church be for the night."

"Yes, sir." She wrung her hands in her apron once again and departed for the Sheehans'.

Reverend Drummond stared down at the cross one last time. Was it a shadow making him think the thing had been moved? Was he allowing himself to be duped just as he'd come to believe his father had been? He placed both hands on the clear top and peered straight down into the case. No, he would swear the thing had been turned. And the very impossibility of it caused an otherworldly tingle to finger down his spine.

"This cannot be. This cannot be," he whispered as he walked to the altar for the silver chalice. He was still chanting the words when he stepped to the cross's case and swung the heavy chalice into the glass.

The noise was so loud, he would not have been surprised if the sound of glass shattering could be heard in the next county. The shards crunched beneath his feet as he stepped to retrieve the ancient druid cross his father had entrusted to him so many years ago.

You are the guardian of the cross, and upon your shoulders the burden must fall.

He stared at the sublime Celtic treasure. The cross didn't feel unnatural. It was heavy, and like silver, it warmed in the embrace of his palms as it had warmed within other hands centuries past. He knew a lot about it, except how his family had acquired it. That was cloaked in a mystery he knew could never be solved, for any who might know the answer were now long dead.

"Oh, God, help me do the right thing," he whispered. Then he put the cross inside his coat pocket and headed for the rectory.

It was time to gather the council.

Chapter 2

THE YOUNG boy ran out of the rectory as if the devil himself were chasing him. He plowed through O'Shea's carefully cultivated rye in too much of a hurry to hold any reverence for the old man's sweat and toil. There wasn't a stone on O'Shea's soil—the result of years of labor—that might cut a pair of dirty bare feet, but the boy didn't seem to appreciate the velvet earth beneath his toes. O'Shea and his sons nearly died trying to raise the yearly, smooth, shining crop of rye on their field, but in the wake of young Timothy Sheehan, the field was now snaked by a long, narrow ribbon of trampled grain.

"What's your hurry, lad?" called Griffen O'Rooney. The old man's gnarled and bent form mimicked the churchyard yews that surrounded him. He was stooped over, weeding a tombstone, but Lir's Church of Ireland was built on high ground, and even in O'Rooney's position, he could see a fair distance to where Michael O'Shea came roaring out of his house, wielding a hoe, a scowl on his fair Celtic features as he scanned the path of crushed rye.

"I've been sent with a message for the fayther!" the boy

shouted back, redoubling his speed when he caught sight of the hoe in Michael O'Shea's hand. "It comes from the vicar!"

Griffen O'Rooney stared at the boy's retreating back while Michael O'Shea walked unplanted rows of fresh-turned earth toward the grave-yard, the hoe dangling uselessly in his hands.

"Did the boy say what I think he said?" O'Shea asked in amazement. "That he was comin' from the vicarage? With a message for the priest?"

"Did he now?" Griffen answered, wonderment gravelly in his voice, his weathered features in a squint as he kept his eyes on the boy. He was as deaf as a Dublin factory rat though he rarely would admit to it. Still his eyes were sharp. And he knew what he had seen. Better yet, he understood it.

Both men watched as the lad ran through Doyle's vibrant green cabbages, then down into the glen and across Maguire's fallow fields. The Sorra Hills, shadowed in purple, tinted by sunset, loomed in the foreground, their natural grandeur overpowering the group of ancient cotter's cottages—the boy's destination—that nestled at their base. As many things were in County Lir, the low, thatched roofs and wattle and daub walls of the buildings were dwarfed by the consequence of the wild beauty of the landscape, yet by the sheer persistence of the build-ings' age, the cottages stood testament to the power of endurance.

A soft white haze blew in from Carlingford Lough. Suddenly it struck Griffen how strange the townland looked. The four fields of Lir became liquid with the rolling fog, and the weathered gray *ogham* stones, the druid standing stones that separated the four fields, seemed to take shape in the fog, making serpents and elves in his imagination where before there were only rocks.

He knew what was to come. All his life he had waited for this moment. His father had told him about it, like a family rite of passage into manhood, but though his mind had always held out the possibility of it actually happening, never had he thought it would come like this. That it would come with the land. That Ireland herself would tell him. By the eerie way the sun glowed through the mist; the way the Sorra Hills seemed to burn in the background. He had worked the fields all his seventy years, and never could he recall seeing them as he did now with the boy running through them. They were haunting, unnatural, perhaps tainted with magic.

Behind the boy, where the mist rolled in, O'Rooney could still make out the sea, churning and spewing graphite-colored waves against the rocky coast. It would storm tonight. It would happen in a storm.

He looked down at his hands, aged and gnarled from pulling weeds and digging graves. A gold ring so small he had to wear it on his last finger seemed to fire with the light of the fading sun. He'd worn it nearly all his life, and it seemed like an old friend. It was the middle ring of a gimmal, incised with the shape of a heart. His father had bestowed on him the ancient ring when he had told him about his destiny. The groom wore one ring of the set, his father had explained, and the bride would wear another; a trinity of rings so old they were thought to predate Christianity in Ireland.

Griffen turned back to where the small speck of a boy pounded on the priest's door. Lir's fields were indeed strange this evening. Too peaceful by half, now that the sea whispered violence. Even the air was different. The smell of the ocean came in with the saturated fog. The salty, mineral scent hinted of times and places held within unreachable memory. He fought the urge to cross himself.

"The faeries are out tonight, aren't they?" Michael whispered to him as he too marveled at the ever-changing landscape.

Griffen had almost forgotten O'Shea's presence. Too preoccupied now, he didn't answer. Mutely, he watched the boy enter the priest's cottage. The door shut and Griffen looked up. The fog had unaccountably dispersed and the landscape looked as he remembered it, its forty shades of green grayed by an impending storm that still brewed in the Irish Sea.

With the excitement passed, O'Shea apparently put all notions of faeries out of his mind like the good Catholic he was and went back to his cottage. Reluctantly, Griffen went back to his work, pulling weeds around the grave of a woman he used to know. Still, he gave several furtive glances at the landscape around him, as if at any moment he expected to see the strange alliance of light and shadow again. Still, his mind was on the boy and the message the lad was clearly sent to bring.

The council would meet tonight.

⊗

Father Patrick Nolan sat in an old tattered armchair, the note from Drummond in his hand. Moira, his housekeeper, stirred a cabbage and mutton stew in an iron pot suspended on an arm over the fire. The woman's interest seemed to be in the stew, but he suspected by the furrow in her middle-aged brow that she was as concerned as everyone else by the arrival of the letter from the Church of Ireland rectory.

The priest read the letter again, his lined pink lips moving as he read. His aged features, plain, moonfaced, and Irish, filled with the character of six decades of suffering and joy, seemed to grow older as he read. Older and paler. At last, he carefully folded the paper and placed it in a pocket hidden in his cassock.

Frowning, Moira Fennerty set a place at the father's board. She took the cracked Staffordshire plate and set it down next to the single place setting of silver flatware as she had done every evening for the father for almost twenty years. But tonight was different. He could tell she was near to bursting with the desire to ask questions. The furrow was still there.

" 'Tis a right nice stew tonight," she said, clearly hoping to open up conversation. "I've some bread from Mrs. McGrath. She got some white flour on her trip from Waterford. Would you be wanting some, Father?"

"Are you speaking to me, Moira?" he asked sternly in Gaelic.

Moira visibly flinched. "I—I—would you like some bread with your meal, Father?" she repeated, this time in Gaelic, stumbling over her native tongue that, after centuries under the British crown, was now more foreign to her than English.

Father Nolan shook his head and returned to staring pensively into the fire.

"What's in the letter, Father?" Moira blurted out, unable to hide her panic.

"This is not what you think," he comforted her in the language she knew best. "The vicar and I have business to attend to and it is nothing that the gossips of the county need hear about."

"I'll not breathe a word to anyone. I promise."

The priest softened. "Moira Fennerty, I know you're not a gossip. Now don't be as cross as a bag of cats, but I cannot be telling you about it. I gave my word long ago, you understand?" She clearly didn't. He looked around the cozy keeping room as if searching for the words to explain. "Perhaps you should just think of the meeting I must attend with Reverend Drummond tonight a social visit and nothing more."

Moira dropped the stew spoon and looked at the priest as if he were telling her she needed an exorcism. "You cannot mean to pay a social call on that . . . that *man?*"

"That man was once a boyhood friend. Only politics separated us at manhood, and politics must be put aside for tonight."

"Politics! Why 'tis you who insist we all speak in Gaelic. 'Tis what them like you all over Ireland who long ago set up the hedge school so that our young could be taught to spell and write and understand our Irish ways. You're the one to remind us of the English oppression. And now you tell me you must pay a social call on the vicar? The man whose church has no congregation and the taxes from all Ireland?"

The priest gave a mighty sigh. "Reverend Drummond didn't exactly stand by while the English stole our four fields. I remind you, James Drummond was born in Lir. Our Ascendency came here from England before Cromwell. Some before Protestantism. Besides . . . remember, even Lord Trevallyan's mother was Irish. 'Tis hard always to tell the difference. . . ." He waved in the air as if his talk were confusing even himself. "Oh, I know this is difficult to understand, even I don't understand it all the time, but think of it perhaps as our myths of Fenians and the knights of the Red Branch. Some things withstand all of time and politics. And tonight, this meeting, is one of them. You must listen and understand. I have no choice about this meeting with the vicar. We must do what we must do. I promise you, 'twill be the last meeting we have in this lifetime."

"But what are you to talk about? What are you to do?"

The priest had a faraway look in his eyes. " 'Tis a serious task. My own father told me that the future of our fruitful county depends on it."

"And for this we must shove aside our beliefs?"

"Not our beliefs, just our politics."

Moira looked at him, then patted her gray hair as if to assure herself she was still all there in the midst of the unreality of their conversation. For some unworldly reason, Father Nolan was advocating that the lamb lie down with the lion. She would have been less surprised if ancient Sorra Mountain had erupted like Vesuvius. "I don't understand a word of this, Father, but if you must go out tonight and meet with the vicar, I'll speak not a word to anyone. I promise on the everlasting soul of Mother Mary."

Outside, a sudden clap of thunder echoed through the glen. The light, pelting sound of rain muffled on the thatch grew stronger as a storm moved inland.

" 'Tis going to be a foul night. Are you sure you must go out tonight?"

The priest smiled. Moira didn't want to say he was no young colt, but it would be rough going to the vicarage with no more than his pony cart to take him there.

"A long time ago my father told me of my duty. I am part of a council, you see, that meets but rarely. This is the first in my lifetime."

"If the vicar weren't calling you, Father, I'd believe you were trying to resurrect the White Boys."

He looked sternly at her. "I want Home Rule as any Irishman does, but I'm not willing to maim and steal to get it!" He softened. "Now put all your speculations away. I'll go to my meeting and that's an end of it."

He turned to look at the fire, but his attention was drawn downward, to his right hand draped languidly across the worn upholstered arm of the chair. A gold ring that barely fitted on his pinky finger flashed in the firelight. It was an unusual ring, with Celtic tracery forming the shape of a serpent. The bride's ring. He would be giving it away, perhaps even tonight. As soon as they knew who she would be. His father had handed down the ring to him long ago. He'd said, *You are the guardian of this ring, my son, and upon your shoulders the burden of it falls.*

The burden of it falls.

Another boom of thunder shook the windowless cotter cottage.

Moira looked up at the shabby thatched roof as if she expected it to come tumbling down upon her head. " 'Tis a terrible night to go out," she scolded, stirring the stew and clucking her disapproval like a hen. "You shouldn't be going, and I'll never agree that you should."

He opened his mouth to protest, but she raised her hand. "None of your arguing will change my mind, Father."

"Do as you must, Moira Fennerty," he said, his stiff old bones rising from the armchair. He looked at his hot dinner and gave a longing sigh at the warm hearth. "Because tonight I must do the same."

Chapter 3

FATHER NOLAN'S pony cart climbed the high road through driving rain to Trevallyan Castle. The castle had stood since times of old, its very foundation rumored to be built upon Celtic ruins. Irish royalty had once eaten in the great hall, but the English confiscated it in the fourteenth century. The Trevallyans had built the elegant granite towers three hundred years hence, when they were deeded the land by Henry VIII. The Trevallyans were, in the most literal sense, Ascendency, landed Irish peers whose ancestors had come from England. There were some in Lir whose bitter hatred of the Ascendency could not be quelled by centuries of intermarriage and mixed Irish-Anglo blood; these folk kept alive the burning memory of their ancestors' lands—and, therefore, wealth—that had been brutally seized so long ago. But in most, a hatred can go on only so long. After three hundred years of intermarriage to the townfolk of Lir, even Father Nolan considered the wealthy Trevallyans one of their own. Indisputably Irish.

"Good evening, Father!" shouted the Trevallyan coachman, Seamus, as he ran to greet him in the bailey. Seamus held the harness and assisted the aged priest from the vehicle. " 'Tis terrible weather for a visit, Father. What brings you out this evening? I hope it ain't that boy o' mine. The rapscallion! Always in trouble with the girls!"

The frail priest trembled from the cold and rain, yet his voice was as strong as in his youth. "No bad news about the lad tonight, Seamus McConnell, but I've important business with your master. I presume Greeves will show me to a warm fire?"

"Sartinly, Father." Seamus whistled for a stable boy. One appeared and took the pony cart while Seamus helped the priest to the castle's ornate English oak doors. The Trevallyan butler, Greeves, met them at the front door. In seconds Father Nolan was seated before the library fire, sipping a brew of hot whiskey and cream.

"What brings you out on such a night, Father?"

The commanding voice made Father Nolan turn toward the doorway. Shadowed in the archway of aged, heavily waxed library doors, the master of Trevallyan stood. Though but nineteen, Niall Trevallyan seemed much older. The youth had the face of a poet, Celtic fair yet etched with tragedy, and he had the presence of a king, perhaps because, after three hundred years of English-Irish marriages, his blood ran as much Gael as Anglo. The priest had the eerie notion, especially now with the firelight casting the young man's fine, handsome features into sinister shadow, that Brian Boru, the legendary Celtic ruler, must have looked just so before he became High King of all Ireland.

"My lord Trevallyan, how good it is to see you again, my son." Father Nolan tried to stand, but Trevallyan waved him back.

"I'm surprised to see you here, Father. It's not the kind of evening for travel."

Trevallyan entered the library, and Father Nolan was struck how the room paralleled Trevallyan's character. The rich gleam of leather and gilt on the spines of the library's thousands of books matched Trevallyan's intelligent, aristocratic air. Yet the centerpiece of the room was not the endless tomes of modern knowledge, it was instead the portrait of his dead Irish mother over the mantel. The Celt. The progeny of a race born of kings, a race that knew nothing of modern artifice and modern manners. A race of people who could embrace their friends and murder their enemies with the same unrestrained passion. There was an underlying ruthlessness in the gleam of Trevallyan's aqua eyes that Father Nolan knew well. The English-Irish Trevallyan blood was a stunning mix of refinement and savagery.

Niall took the leather chair opposite the priest. Greeves tried to offer the young man a drink on a silver tray, but Trevallyan shook his head and nodded to the door. Greeves discreetly left them alone.

"I've strange business tonight, my son." Father Nolan held out his trembling hand, almost in supplication. The serpent ring on his bony finger glittered in the firelight. "And a strange tale to tell."

Trevallyan's arrogant, well-cut lips twisted in amusement. "You've come all the way here to tell me tales? A funny thing, Father, I thought Griffen O'Rooney was the one in the townland to weave the stories."

"This tale is unlike his many tales. You'd be wise to heed this one well."

Father Nolan studied the young man. Trevallyan was groomed and well-kempt, though he was not dressed for visitors. He wore black trousers, an emerald silk vest, no neck cloth, and a starched white shirt with exemplary points on the collar. He looked at the priest with a superior tilt of his head. Niall Trevallyan's arrogance was notorious throughout the county, but the priest found it easy to forgive in the lad. Trevallyan had lost both his parents to diphtheria when he'd been fifteen. It was rumored the estate was in debt and that the bailiff was stealing funds from the castle accounts—heavy baggage for a boy of fifteen to handle.

But carry the load, Trevallyan did, and well. Now the lands were said to be prosperous, the castle out of debt, the bailiff jailed, and Trevallyan had just finished his second year at Trinity down in Dublin City. The arrogance was well paid for, the priest thought, perhaps even deserved. Nonetheless, Father Nolan believed there was another reason for it. When the boy had placed his parents in the cold Irish earth, he shed not a tear. Father Nolan had come to comfort the lad in his time of need, and he had stood by Trevallyan's side for almost an hour while the boy stared at the two freshly dug graves. Finally, in an effort to help the boy through his grief, he had asked gently, "Shall we say a prayer for them, lad?" Trevallyan had answered in a voice that cracked with impending manhood, with words that still echoed through the priest's heart as a hollow, chill wind of despair. " 'Tis best you save all your prayers for me, Father." The boy spoke no more, and at last the priest was forced by the wind and the cold to leave his side.

Trevallyan was indeed arrogant, but the father wondered if perhaps he used his arrogance like a cloak to cover the lonely, fearful boy who could not cry at his dear mother's grave.

"I've come to wish you well on your birthday, as well, my lord," Father Nolan said, beginning the story he knew he must tell.

An amused, suspicious gleam lit in Trevallyan's aquamarine eyes. "The day of my birth is tomorrow, as you well know, Father. You christened me at my mother's request, though I profess, I find no need to attend Mass."

"Your mother was a good Catholic, and she is in heaven, I have no doubt about it."

"And my father?" The gleam turned a shade darker, a shade more wicked.

The priest shifted uncomfortably in his chair. "The earl was tied to his Church of Ireland roots. But that does not mean I'll forget your soul, Trevallyan."

Niall almost smiled. "Touché, Father, but you still haven't explained your visit tonight. It's not the anniversary of my birth—"

"Ah . . . but it is. The time of your birth was at midnight, was it not? You were born on Beltaine, the most magical night of the Celtic year, on the druid feast of Bel. In a few hours you'll be a man of twenty. More than old enough to take a bride."

Trevallyan finally did laugh. "What *is* this all about?"

The priest shifted forward to the edge of his seat. His serious expression caused Trevallyan's smile to dim. "My son, do you know about the *geis*?"

"I certainly know what a *geis* is, if that's what you mean." Trevallyan pronounced it the Gaelic way, *gaysh*. A unsettling glimmer appeared in his eyes. "How quickly you forget I'm my mother's child."

By the priest's silence it was clear that wasn't what he meant.

Trevallyan chuckled darkly. "What? Are you telling me I have a *geis*? Now, let me see the exact definition . . . it's some kind of ancient bond, or code of honor, or ritual that must be performed or tragedy will fall upon its recipient, am I correct?"

"Correct."

"And I have a *geis*?"

"All the Trevallyan men have a *geis*. 'Tis the price they paid for the land you now call yours."

Niall stared at the priest in amused disbelief. "Come now, Father. Ireland is not quite caught up to the modern age, but surely you don't believe this Celtic tomfoolery?"

"The Roman Catholic Church does not believe in such things."

"And by that, I presume, you include yourself?"

Father Nolan reached for the young man's arm. "I've lived many a year in this Ireland. 'Tis difficult not to believe in ancient things in an ancient land."

"Father," Niall interjected, "The year is 1828. The Gael is long dead. There are no more druids, no more witches. No more *geise*." He gestured to the volumes that lined the library's shadowy walls. "In all these books—and I have read them all—a *geis* is not a natural possibility. I shudder to think what they would say of this at Trinity."

"I know it sounds fantastic, but you must listen."

"But it's preposterous."

"Niall, you're an educated, modern man. But is that all you learned at Trinity? Facts and figures, and everything that is real? I ask you, is poetry real? Is love real? Is the sky overhead real, or is it nothingness? Shouldn't they have taught you to wonder at these things, too?"

The priest's impassioned tone seemed to irritate Trevallyan. He lowered his voice, as if he were speaking to a fool. "There are those things to contemplate as well, but not sorcery, not faeries . . . not asinine Paddy whackery."

Father Nolan drummed his fist on the upholstered arm. "The Otherworld is there! 'Tis imbedded within our Gaelic minds and 'tis a part of our being that no man may take away!"

Trevallyan's mouth formed a thin, straight line. "Keeping these traditions is no cure for the Crown's hold on this isle. If anything, it makes Ireland look ridiculous." He looked at the old priest and softened, but only slightly. "I won't be a part of it, Father. I won't do it to our Ireland.

Would that intellect be valued on this isle as much as witchery," he cursed.

"Niall, you value intellect only because you run from what's inside you, but listen well: No matter how hard you run, one day what's inside will win. Your blood is as Irish as mine. The Gael lives within you, too. Be prepared for its victory, or you will perish."

"State your business, Father. Tell me why you are here and be done with it," Niall growled, his eyes flashing.

"No one knows about this particular business except the council. We will meet with them tonight and that will be it. Hear the *geis,* and then your decisions will be your own."

"Council?" Trevallyan's brows knit together. "Is the Trevallyan *geis* public knowledge to everyone but the Trevallyans?"

"Your parents found each other and fell in love on their own. For them, there was no need for the *geis* so they were never told about it. But you—you are twenty now and still have no bride. And the cross has signaled for us to go forth."

"The cross? What is all this nonsense?"

"Please, my son." Father Nolan's face wore a weary, troubled expression as if burned by the secrets he carried. "Humor a group of old men. Come to the meeting and hear your fate. Then you will have control over it."

Trevallyan stood back for a long moment and stared at the father. He closed his eyes as if in disgust and released a drawn-out sigh. "I'll go and meet with your council, Father."

The priest sat back in his chair, looking even more weary than before. "Good, my son. Good," he said.

"But this should do me for a year of Sunday Mass." Trevallyan pulled the cord for Greeves to summon the carriage.

❊

Four elderly men gathered in Drummond's rectory while the storm raged through the night heavens above. Four elderly men, their faces lined with the burden of their secret. Mrs. Dwyer served them tea and honeycakes at the rector's table while Trevallyan looked on, more as an aloof observer than the subject of the meeting.

When tea had been poured out, Reverend Drummond dismissed the housekeeper and pointedly told her to go home. Mary Dwyer left the vicarage bug-eyed and bulging with gossip. The strange sight of seeing Father Nolan in the Anglican rectory was enough to make her wonder if it were night or day.

From his place at the mantel, Trevallyan studied the group of strange bedfellows, their old, wrinkled faces glowing in the flickering light of one single candle. It was indeed an unholy gathering. Four old men who were as different and disparate from one another as the four fields of Lir. Drummond and the father contrasted as did one of Lir's fields that led to the mountains with one that led to the sea. Peter Maguire, the mayor of the small village of Lir, seemed as common as the field that grew cabbages, potatoes, and rye. Lastly, Griffen O'Rooney sat in their midst, the town's wizened groundskeeper and grave-digger, and sometime storyteller. He was the last of Lir's fields. The field that had ruined many a good Irish farmer. The field that grew only rocks.

And, he thought distastefully, Niall Trevallyan was the *ogham* stone that stood in the center.

"I suppose I should begin." Reverend Drummond looked around the table at the three men. His face was pale and serious, as if he had been asked to give a sermon at St. Patrick's down in Dublin.

"If I may, I think I am the one to explain things to him," Father Nolan broke in, clearly bristling. The dark, wainscotted rectory cast long shadows, and the storm brewing in the heavens echoed the tension between the two men. "Even you must admit, Reverend, the Church of Ireland knows little of the Gael."

Griffen O'Rooney nodded. "It certainly *is* a right fine gale we're havin' tonight."

Peter Maguire's ruddy face turned to ruby as if he were suppressing nervous laughter.

"No, Griffen, I said the Gael. *Gael,*" Father Nolan corrected crossly.

Griffen nodded to show he understood.

"So who is to begin?" Mayor Maguire asked, tucking another honey-cake into his mouth. A crack of thunder broke overhead, and his face drained of color. He looked at the roof as if in prayer. "In truth, I believe *I* should be the one to tell young Trevallyan here. The *geis* was wrought from the four fields, and I am Lir's mayor."

"The wind scared your mare?"

The entire table seemed to shudder.

This time the reverend shouted the explanation. "Griffen, we're off the weather now. We're on to the *geis,* all right?"

"The *geis.* Yes, of course. Let's tell him about the *geis.*" Griffen nodded solemnly, as if what was to come were as inevitable as the death of another old friend. He blew his rather bulbous nose into a faded red handkerchief while all watched breathlessly to see whether his palsied hands would be able to hold the cloth to his nose for the necessary moments. When he was through, he looked around the table at the stares. "I suppose you're all a-waitin' for me to begin, me bein' a storyteller and all. All right, I'll begin. . . ."

"No, Griffen, this should come from his priest," said Father Nolan.

"But I'm the mayor, and the *geis* is tied to Lir," interjected Maguire.

"No, I'm the one to tell him because my family guards the cross," announced Drummond.

"Enough of this bickering like Kilkenny cats." Trevallyan pushed away from the mantel and walked to the table where the old men sat around the one ghostly candle. "No one need take the sole responsibility of explaining the *geis* to me, for I'll ask the questions and each of you will answer in your turn. What is the cross, Drummond?"

Drummond appeared a little disconcerted at the command, as if he weren't prepared to start after all. "It's an old cross, not a Christian cross, mind you, but a Celtic cross, an amulet. It's been in my family since they arrived here." He sniffed. "And I might remind you *all*"—he glanced at Father Nolan—"that the Drummonds have been in County Lir over two hundred and fifty years."

"Fine. Fine. But what does this cross have to do with anything?" Trevallyan asked, growing impatient.

"It moved in the case, my lord," Drummond answered succinctly.

"It what?"

"It moved in the case." Drummond glanced at his fellow council members as if asking them to back him. "You see, the cross was in a case my father had built in the church when he was vicar. The case was impervious to trifling because it was permanently sealed. Yet the cross was moved. It was a sign to begin."

"Begin what?" Niall crossed his arms over his chest. Looming in the shadows, with his blond hair slicked back, wet from the walk to the door from the carriage, he looked darker than he was, and older. He carried the air of an ominous and disapproving master. Suddenly Drummond seemed to lose his tongue.

"The housekeeper Mary Dwyer—Mary—s-said she saw a light from the cross while it was in the case," Peter Maguire stuttered, nervously picking up the explanation.

"Yes, but let's be truthful, the woman's been known to be scared of her shadow," Father Nolan interjected. He looked suspiciously at Drummond as if his worst fear had suddenly occurred to him. "It might have been a signal, but really, how do we know it wasn't a trick of the light? And you—you could be wrong about the cross being moved. Where's our evidence that it was moved now that you've destroyed the case? We might have called this council for nothing, all because of another Protestant error in judgment."

"I did not make an error in judgment!" Drummond rose to his feet and looked as if he wanted to call Father Nolan out.

" 'Tis well you could have!" Father Nolan stood as well. "And if you did, we'll all be feeling mighty foolish!"

"Father," Trevallyan interrupted, putting his hand on the priest's shoulder, "if you have your doubts, why did you summon me here?"

The priest looked at Trevallyan, then at Drummond. His face turned pale and, gravely, he resumed his seat. "I haven't any doubts," he conceded, the fight gone out of his voice. "Reverend Drummond, English land-grabber that he is, is telling the truth. It's time for us to explain the *geis*."

"Then explain it. All of you. This instant," Trevallyan demanded, scowling at each of the four men until they bowed their gray heads in contrition.

"A family of millers had your land before the Trevallyans were deeded it by the English Henry," Father Nolan began.

"When they found out that the land was no longer theirs, they had a sorcerer put a *geis* on the Trevallyan men," said Drummond.

"The male heir of each generation was to marry before his twentieth year or the *geis* would go into effect," finished the mayor.

"And tell me what the *geis* is." Trevallyan looked at each man. They all looked at Griffen O'Rooney.

Griffen eerily began speaking as if on cue. "I'll tell you about the *geis*, me boy." He stared at Trevallyan, his aged and sunken eyes still bright with intelligence. "Your *geis* has four parts because Lir has four fields separated by the standing stone with the *ogham* written upon it.

"The first part is that the cross must pick your bride. The second part states that this girl must be a commoner from our beloved Lir. Part three is that she must be found in the twentieth year of the Trevallyan heir. The story of the Trevallyan *geis* has been kept secret. It's been handed down, father to son, for hundreds of years, and the men you see before you are the only ones left who are descendents of the original council."

The room grew silent as all watched Trevallyan's reaction. The young man looked extremely solemn. Then, all at once, he let out a boisterous laugh. "This is a prank. It must be. You cannot expect me to believe that you four are to pick my bride."

"*We* are not to pick your bride, my son, *this* is to pick your bride." Drummond withdrew the cross from his coat pocket. The men let out a gasp at its beauty. The cross almost seemed alive. It glowed and glittered in the firelight, and the sheer exquisiteness of the scrollwork seemed impossibly fine to have been wrought by human hands.

Trevallyan took the cross and held it at eye level. Purple sparks seemed to shoot from the center of the amethyst, and the scrollwork seemed to turn liquid like writhing snakes. He stared at it like a king meeting his nemesis.

"My lord," Drummond whispered, "in all the years I've kept the cross, I've never seen it so full of fire. The *geis* must be true. This must be a sign."

" 'Tis just the firelight that makes it look strange." Niall tossed the amulet to the reverend. The men gasped. Drummond strove to catch it as if it were a falling babe.

" 'Tis not good to tempt the Otherworld, my son," said Griffen. He stared at the young man, his eyes filled with pity as if he had once peeked into Trevallyan's future and had seen the misery Trevallyan scoffed at now.

O'Rooney's stare seemed to make Trevallyan falter as if he had cut into the young man's arrogance and seen his soul. But ever the master, Trevallyan collected himself, and said evenly, coolly, though his pale green-blue eyes snapped with ire, "I cannot tempt a thing that does not exist. This is rubbish. I don't believe a word. This," he gestured to the cross, " 'tis a beautiful work of Celtic art, but it is not made of magic and it cannot find me a bride. For, tell me, is it to grow wings and fly around the county in search of her?"

"The cross has already found the girl."

All the men shifted to look at Drummond. His face was deathly pale. "It's true. I went out in my hack this evening, thinking the cross might give me a sign of who the girl might be. I told my driver to just go blindly where I told him to go, that there was no definite destination."

"How did you find her?" Peter Maguire whispered.

"I held the cross in my hand and it seemed to work like a compass, its fire increasing when I went in the direction it wanted me to go. When I found the cottage far outside the village in a grove of haw-thorn, I'd never seen it so brilliant. It was blinding."

"You've found the girl," Father Nolan said reverently.

"And who is she?" Niall snapped.

" 'Twas Grania's cottage."

Trevallyan's laughter boomed through the vicarage. "Grania! Old, humpbacked Grania! The crone the townspeople call witch! Why this is rich! I am to marry a woman who is old enough not just to be my mother, but grandmother as well!"

"It could be her daughter, Brilliana, the cross was seeking," said Maguire.

"Who is Brilliana?" Trevallyan asked.

"Grania has a daughter who she had very late in life. The daughter would be your age, my lord."

"That's right!" chimed Drummond.

"We must go to this cottage and see the bride for ourselves." Father Nolan stood.

Trevallyan shook his head. "I'll not bother these women in the dead of night. Not for the preposterous reason of a *geis*."

"I once heard the tale of a young man who laughed at a *geis* placed upon him by an old woman." Griffen O'Rooney's voice issued through the dark room like a shiver. The other old men in the room seemed to huddle together as if they were afraid of the forces they believed howled around them like the wind coming in from the sea. "James Fitzherbert was a fine young man, strapping, tall, and handsome, who lived in this county hundreds of years before you, Trevallyan. He ignored his *geis,* and famine came to Lir, famine we have never seen since. The first to starve was his true love. The lass wasted away until she was nothing more than a skeleton with large, haunting eyes that cried out for food. Some say 'twas hunger made Fitzherbert go mad, but others say 'twas the guilt that robbed him of his sanity."

Trevallyan said nothing. He stared at O'Rooney, anger tautening his lips.

"We *must* go to the cottage, m'lord," begged Father Nolan.

"You turn twenty at midnight," Maguire cajoled.

"Look at the hour!" cried Drummond.

All heads turned to the walnut mantel clock. It was five minutes before midnight.

" 'Tis folly to believe I'll marry this girl. I've never met her. She could be a hag like her mother. More importantly still, I do not love her. I do not know her—"

"Ah, but Trevallyan, you have not asked about the fourth part of the *geis*." Griffen O'Rooney's voice cut through Niall's words like a ghostly howl in the night. All the men turned to look at O'Rooney, each face paler than the next.

"So tell me, old storyteller. Tell me the rest of the tale," Trevallyan mocked, though his cheeks were not so ruddy as before.

Griffen stared at the young man, the pity and the hope still alive in his aged eyes. " 'Tis well you'll hear the story. When we get to the cottage."

Chapter 4

THE COTTAGE was nestled in a gnarled, dense hawthorn grove that had been planted in ancient times. The wind screamed, and the rain fell in sheets, making a rocky creek bed of the road. Reverend Drummond's hack fought its way to the cottage light. The carriage stopped before a low, batten doorway where an old crone of a woman stood, as if she had been expecting them.

Each man filed into the dim cottage. Trevallyan looked upon the interior with disgust. One single oiled sheet of paper covered the small window. The floors were cold earth, and the walls were black with decades of soot from the hearth. Cats were everywhere; fat and sleek, sleeping by the hearth, lurking on shelves, fighting amongst themselves, while rats gnawed and squealed in dark corners, too plentiful even for the pride of cats. There was poverty in Lir, but he had seen none such as this.

"Woman," he said softly, staring at the woman's hands burrowed deep into her apron, hands that were as gnarled as the hawthorns, that should have trembled in the lord's presence, but were instead as still as sleeping mice. "These men have brought me here because they believe I have a *geis*. They think I am destined to marry a young lady from this cottage, and that is why we have come here at this strange hour." Trevallyan watched the woman for a reaction but could find none behind the many wrinkles on her face.

"I know why ye have come," she said, her voice dispassionate, or perhaps disconsolate.

"The reverend told you?"

"He did not."

"But you know of our business here tonight?"

The crone smiled at him, a strangely sad smile, one that showed her only two remaining teeth. "I am Grania, a seer, Lord Trevallyan. I know many things that others do not."

Trevallyan gave the priest a discreet look of disbelief, but Father Nolan was staring at Grania as if he were in awe of her every word.

"Come sit down to the fire." The crone waved to the only chair in the small keeping room. It was a sturdy, oak, three-legged chair black with age and smoke.

Trevallyan refused. "Your hospitality is generous, Mistress Grania, but we won't be staying long."

"This business will not take ye long, I wager." Grania looked at him, studying his face with the same fervor as she might inspect a golden chalice. "Ye be a growed man now, Lord Trevallyan. And ye've come here to seek a bride."

"I've come to indulge my elders," he corrected, his expression lean and rational even in the distorting shadows. "I don't believe in the Trevallyan *geis*."

Grania nodded, as if she understood. "And yet ye are here. And ye want to meet her."

"They tell me you have a daughter."

"Brilliana was conceived of magic. The faeries took hold of my womb and gave me a child when all reason said I was too old to have one."

Trevallyan gave Father Nolan another glance of incredulity. This time the father saw it, and he shifted his feet as if suddenly uncomfortable.

"How old is Brilliana?" he asked, wanting fervently to quit this business with all expediency.

"Brilliana turned twenty a month before."

"Is she here?" Trevallyan's gaze wandered to a moldering curtain that divided the hovel.

Grania took his hand in her own twisted one. He was surprised that it felt gentle and warm despite its knobs and calluses.

"My Lord Trevallyan, let me show ye my daughter. I want ye to see her beauty."

There were tears in the hag's eyes as she spoke.

Niall's expression grew sober. "Introduce me to your daughter, old woman, but don't harbor false hopes in your breast, for I cannot promise to marry her. I'll only marry a woman I love."

The crone smiled. "Have they told ye the fourth part of the *geis*, my lord?"

Trevallyan shook his head.

" 'Tis not ye who have the choice of love. No, the fourth part of the *geis* states that ye must win *her* love. Whether ye love her or not, 'tis a cruelty for ye alone to bear." Her smile widened. She held his hand tight as she led him through the curtain.

One lone candle sputtered in a pool of wax, keeping a weak vigil in the dark bedroom. There was a pile of rotting rags in one corner, the stench of the chamberpot, and a small rope bed shoved into the corner with a woman lying upon it.

"Here is my daughter, Lord Trevallyan. Take the candle and judge her beauty for yeself." Grania handed him the pewter candleholder.

For some strange reason, Niall was hesitant to go forth. The firelight from the keeping room flickered behind him, and he knew the old men had opened the curtain to watch this hallowed meeting. He studied the supine figure on the bed, uncomfortable with the notion that Grania was offering up her daughter for his perusal while she lay sleeping.

Distaste twisted his features. He was not in the habit of disturbing a young woman's slumber, nor to look upon her as if she were a common Belfast prostitute. Not in Lir. He wanted to refuse, but to do so would only prolong this hysteria. And the old crone's hope of a match between him and her daughter.

He stepped toward the girl. She slept with no covers and wore only a sheer oatmeal-colored night rail that molded to her body. She was full-breasted and rounded in the hips. Even in the dimness, he knew she possessed a pleasing female form.

He held the candle to her face.

The blood bled from his own.

"Is she not beautiful, Lord Trevallyan?" Grania rasped behind him.

"Aye," he whispered, truly moved by the beauty of the girl. She was porcelain pale with black hair that hallowed around her shoulders in erotic disarray. Her nose was slim, even regal, and placed perfectly in an oval face of heartbreaking delicacy. Her lips were full, sweetly curved, impossibly red; gruesomely tempting a kiss, even though . . .

Trevallyan crossed himself and stared into the girl's vacant velvet-blue eyes. She was indeed a beauty, an incomparable beauty. No doubt, there had been a time when this woman had laughed and run in Lir's sweet clover. He had dreamed of a woman like her once. She had come to him in the mists, her ethereal beauty untouchable, unforgetta-ble. Still, in his dream, he had reached out his hand to feel her warmth and make her real, but she had hid from him in the mist, and his fury had mounted, for the hand that he so desperately sought was always just out of reach. Never did he imagine he would finally hold it. Only to realize it was stone-cold.

The young woman had been dead perhaps two days.

He touched her cold cheek, running his thumb down skin as smooth as cream, as lifeless as marble. Her unblinking, sightless stare tore at him, and he cursed Death that had laid waste to such youth and beauty. She was perfection; raven-haired and creamy-skinned; the kind of woman praised by the bards. It was difficult to believe she was gone, her eyes never more to sparkle with warmth, to hold a man captive to the gypsy soul within.

Niall hadn't wanted to go along with this foolish *geis,* and yet now, staring at the impoverished beauty, lying like a statue on the pathetic rope bed, he felt an unwelcome and irrational bitterness. As absurd and foolish as it was, he felt a strange regret, as if somehow fate had cheated him. He could now go on with the rest of his life, unhampered by imagined witchery and the silly superstitions of old men, but he had no doubt that the memory of this beautiful girl would haunt him for a very long time.

He stared down at her one last time, unable to drag his sight away. A chill ran down his spine as his imagination took hold. He couldn't shake the vision of her alive, her eyes filled with fire as he chased her through the standing stones, caught her, and kissed her in a shimmering lake of blue flax. The fourth part of the *geis* said that he must win her love, and in Brilliana's case, he could see relishing that task.

And that he would have won her, he had no doubt, for he was young and even he knew he was pleasing to the female eye. She might have been the woman he'd been looking for, the woman to be his wife, his lover, his companion, the woman to carry and nurture his children. He might have had all of that. Instead, he couldn't shake the dreaded notion that it all was taken from him. Brilliana, the woman the *geis* had brought him to see, was dead, removed from this earth forever. All chances, all hope, spent and gone.

Driven by forces he little understood, he leaned down and brushed her cold lips with his, as if for once wishing for faerie tales and the life-giving magic of kisses.

He straightened, and her eyes still stared soullessly toward the leaking thatch. Resigned, he covered her cold, implacable face with a tattered blanket.

"How did she die?" His words were oddly dispassionate. A lie. He looked back at Grania who had started to weep into her gnarled old hands.

" 'Twas a long and suffering death, my lord. I saw it once in a vision, and though I did all to prevent it, her will was her own." She wiped her eyes with her dirty black apron.

"How did she die?" he asked again, his voice emotionless, drained. He longed for the solitude of his library where he could ponder the reasons and toast the poor maid who lay so still beside him. And curse the men who had brought him out this night.

"She was beautiful, was she not? And the lads thought she was beautiful too. So beautiful . . ." The crone began to weep in earnest.

Abruptly Trevallyan turned around. He stared in anger at the four old men who gathered at the grimy curtain, the shock still on their faces.

"Let us leave this woman with her grief. We should not have come." The old woman's tears were like pins in his heart, more powerful than the rain that shook the hovel.

"But—but what of the *geis*?"

"This foolishness is over. The *geis* is no more." The thought should have comforted him. Tomorrow, when he was gone from this wretched place, he was adamant that it would.

"But the cross! It still burns with an unearthly light!" Reverend Drummond held out the Celtic amulet. Lightning seemed to shoot from the large fist-sized jewel. The entire piece glowed, though the cottage's interior was quite dark.

Father Nolan gasped and stepped back from the cross. Griffen O'Rooney shielded his eyes. Maguire genuflected.

Trevallyan watched the men cower before the amulet. In disgust, he grabbed the cross and shook it at them. " 'Tis nothing but the firelight reflecting in the stone! This cross did not bring you here, *you* brought you here! You want so hard to believe in this *geis* that you see signs that aren't there!" He nearly threw the cross on the ground in his contempt for them all. "This Celtic amulet is nothing more than metal and rock, and because of the asinine ideas of men long dead and gone, we've come here on a fool's errand and disturbed this woman's mourning for her daughter!"

"Is this so? Was the *geis* nothing but cruel shenanigans played on us by our fathers?" Father Nolan cried out, fear and confusion in his voice.

"Yes!" Trevallyan raged, soul-weary of the quest that had merely led them to the grave of a woman whose lost, beautiful face he wanted desperately to forget, but seemed burned forever into his memory.

"No," said an old woman's voice.

They all turned to look at Grania. Her eyes were rimmed with red, but she had ceased her crying. Overhead, thunder ripped the heavens and released more buckets of rain. Water dripped from the thatch, forming mud puddles on the floor.

"Your bride is here, Trevallyan. She is here."

Trevallyan looked into the crone's muddy eyes. Slowly he said, "Your daughter is dead. And you, Grania, are not a consideration, for even if our age difference was not an obstacle, you are too old a woman to give me an heir. So who else is there in this bloody cottage?"

The thunder broke anew, and a blast of wind ripped open the hovel's door. The mayor shoved it closed and sealed it with the crossbar. Still, the wind seemed to scream around the cottage, until the thunder and wind turned into a baby's wail.

Grania hobbled over to the pile of rags next to the cold, silent Brilliana. From the midst of the tattered, soiled cloths, she lifted a newborn babe; a small, pink-skinned, raven-haired girl. Grania looked down at the babe with love and sadness. "My good Lord Trevallyan, I've no milk for the babe, and she will die if ye cannot find it within ye heart to help me."

Trevallyan glanced between the dark-haired babe and Brilliana. "Is this her child?"

"I told ye. The men thought my daughter beautiful, Lord Trevallyan. I know not the father. Her death was slow and terrible, but at least she left me this." Grania held the wailing newborn out to him.

Trevallyan did not take her.

Quietly he said, "If you need milk for the child, I'll see to it a wet-nurse is brought here tonight. The Trevallyans have never allowed a child to starve in Lir." He looked around accusingly at the faces of Maguire, Griffen, the father, and Drummond. "I think I understand now. This was a hoax to get me here, wasn't it? But you could have told me the truth—that a child is in need—and I would have seen to it that the babe was well cared for. This theatrical production was unnecessary. So answer me! Was this whole night set up to extract my charity toward this bastard child?"

"I came here because of the geis, Lord Trevallyan," Peter Maguire said, his voice quiet and full of respect. "My father instructed me on the geis when I was a young boy. He pledged my secrecy. If this is a hoax, I played no part in it."

" 'Tis not a hoax, Lord Trevallyan," Grania answered, the babe squalling in her arms. "I have foreseen the future. I knew ye would come here this night. The geis must be fulfilled."

"And how is that to come about?" Trevallyan scoffed. "Would you see me wed to this babe? Is that how you see it? Bloody hell, I will."

"Take her, my lord. Hold this precious babe in yer arms and think no more of the *geis* for now." Grania thrust the newborn into Niall's arms. Trevallyan took the child, if only to keep her from being dropped on the hard earthen floor.

" 'Twill be a while before ye wed, my lord. I have seen it in my visions. If ye ignore the *geis,* tragedy will follow." Grania hobbled over to the hearth and stood by the fire, as if the damp and cold bothered her old bones.

"Old woman," Trevallyan whispered, struggling with the wailing baby. "All of you." He turned to the four old men. "I tell you all that this is folly. I will not be a part of it any longer. You may have your *geis,* but this Trevallyan will not take part in it."

"My son! Look at the cross!" Drummond cried out, holding the Celtic amulet to the fire once more. It released an ethereal purple glow.

" 'Tis all in our minds!" Trevallyan shouted, adamant that they were seeing things that weren't there. He thrust the baby back into Grania's feeble arms and exclaimed, "I tell you, all of you, I will not go along with this any longer. You're asking me to wait almost twenty years for a bride—to wed a woman I don't know and might end up despising. I will not do it."

"Ye have no choice, my lord." Grania's voice sang above the thunder and rain overhead. "The *geis* will be fulfilled by yer will or not. If ye defy it, ye will suffer. The English did not take our lands without a price. This is the price of being a Trevallyan."

"All of you are mad."

"This is not something that must be done now, Trevallyan," Father Nolan said, his frightened gaze darting to the glowing cross. "You've many a year to get used to this arrangement."

"There *is* no arrangement and there never will be. The Trevallyans will not pay for the land by my blood. I swear upon my grave that I'll be wed within the year and that my own children will be not much younger than this babe!" Thunder cracked overhead, making his words even more foreboding than they already were.

"My lord, don't do it!" Father Nolan begged, the rain drumming down upon the thatch overhead like Armageddon.

" 'Twas our fathers that bade us participate, Lord Trevallyan. 'Tis not something to be dismissed lightly. This has been generations in the making!" Maguire interjected.

"I will not go along with this. I shall marry the first woman I fall in love with, and this babe will play with my children." Trevallyan took one last look at the black-haired newborn wailing in Grania's arms, then he swung his cape around his shoulders and departed in the storm for the waiting hack.

"My God, what will happen to the boy?" Drummond wondered aloud when the door slammed.

" 'Tis surely tragedy waitin' 'round the corner," Maguire moaned.

"I'd hoped he would choose to avoid the future I have seen for him," Grania whispered.

"The Trevallyan destiny has always been a dark one," said Father Nolan.

"He has chosen his path."

Ashen-faced, they looked to Griffen O'Rooney.

O'Rooney only nodded and clasped his palsied hands. "So be it."

PART TWO

The Gimmal

I was a child and she was a child,
In this kingdom by the sea . . .

EDGAR ALLAN POE
(1809–1849)

"Annabel Lee"

Chapter 5

H E's A warlock! He sits up there in his castle a-thinkin' of spells to put upon our fair town!" The grubby-faced boy skipped a stone across the small lake in front of Trevallyan Castle. His companions sat upon the rotting trunk of a fallen oak tree.

"Aye. He goes to London nigh every season and he don't come back for weeks." A redheaded boy stood up and looked in the direction of the castle. "Me mam says he's the divil himself livin' in County Lir."

"He murdered his own wife!" A shrill cry came from the rear of the young crowd. A tall, thin boy emerged, his white features turned toward the castle. "He done put her in the grave hisself!"

"That's why he visits her every day!" Another young boy cried out. "The guilt cuts into him."

"Nonsense," said a black-haired girl who sat in their midst. "If he's the devil, he can't be feeling any guilt."

"Still, he murdered his own wife!"

"Grania said she died because she was with child," the

girl retorted, using much better English than the hooligans around her.

"Then why does he scare the townfolk near to death ever' time he comes to town?"

"That's right!" chimed another urchin. "Trevallyan goes a-runnin' his stallion through our fields like he be a-runnin' on the divil's heels. He nigh killed me babby sister, Janey, when he was chasin' that fox with his friends, drunker than a priest on Sunday eve. If he's not the divil, I don't know who he is."

"Grania says not to be afraid of him. So I'm not." The girl crossed her arms over her budding chest and put her nose in the air, as if she were far superior to the ragtag bunch around her.

"Ravenna," the redheaded boy said, "he's the divil, I tell ye, and Grania ought to know 'cause she's a witch."

"She is not!" the dark-haired girl, Ravenna, shouted back, her fine black brows knitted together in a furious scowl. "Grania is no witch! And I know that for a fact."

"You hold your head high above us, and you look down upon us 'cause we don't talk in fine words like yourself, but that don't change the townfolk from thinkin' yer grandmother's a witch."

"The townfolk are fools." Ravenna turned her wrath on Malachi, the redheaded boy. "And what have you to say for yourself that you believe such lies?"

"The townfolk call Grania a witch and Trevallyan a warlock. I'll not be sayin' different without proof."

"Proof! Proof! I'll give you proof! Grania raised me as her own. I love her as I would love my own ma. If she were a witch, I'd be knowin' it. For I'd be a witch, too!"

The gaggle of boys grew quiet, as if Ravenna had just voiced their thoughts.

"Are you a witch, Ravenna?" Malachi whispered. "Me mam says you must be 'cause you've had too much schoolin' for a girl and ye never come to Mass."

"That's right!" Sean, the tall, thin boy, backed him up.

"What's goin' to Mass got to do with being a witch?" Ravenna's scowl grew darker. "And if I know more than you, it's because Grania wanted me to be a fine lady one day and she found me tutors. What's wrong with that? I'm no different than anyone else." She turned and a curtain of jet-black hair hid her hurt expression from the boys.

"Why don't you come to Mass, Ravenna?" Malachi, slightly older than Ravenna's thirteen years and perhaps six inches shorter as well, touched the young girl on her shoulder.

Ravenna stepped away, giving him a peek at her pale oval face. "I'll not be goin' to no Mass. Those old biddies already sneer at me in town. I won't have them kickin' me out of church because I'm a bastard."

The boys silently watched her walk toward the lake. When they grew to be men they would no doubt marvel at her delicacy, but right now, though Ravenna wasn't tall, she towered over the lot of them, her flashing blue-violet eyes terrorizing them, and the mystical, mysterious power of her budding womanhood keeping them in their place.

"Ravenna," Malachi said to her stiff, unwelcoming back, "I don't care if you're a witch. In fact, if you are, I'm glad. For you are the one who can prove or disprove whether Trevallyan is a warlock."

"I'll do no such thing. You think I can put a spell on him, don't you?"

Malachi stepped back from the dark flashing gaze, but his chest puffed with adolescent bravado. "I don't need your help, Ravenna. I can prove Trevallyan a warlock without your magic." He spun around and faced the clan of young, dirty-faced boys. "Which one of you is brave enough to face Trevallyan in the castle?"

"Malachi, what are you thinkin' of?" The thin boy stood, darting glances at Ravenna, who looked down upon them all, her hands on her slim hips.

"I need a man with the courage to get a lock of Trevallyan's hair."

Feminine laughter rippled across the small lake. "What will you do with *that* once you get it?" Ravenna asked.

"You need a man's hair to prove he is a warlock. Why else do you think I need it?" Malachi's sandy-colored brows nearly met from his frown.

Ravenna laughed, the sound as clear as a silver bell. "How ridiculous! Who told you that? I've never heard such nonsense."

Malachi gave her a suspicious look. " 'Tis a fact as old as these fields of Lir: A warlock be known by his hair. Has Grania never told you?"

"We don't speak of such things. . . . the cauldron keeps us busy as it is. . . ."

At the boys' astonished expressions, Ravenna nearly doubled over in laughter.

"Aye, it's a witch you are, Ravenna," Malachi cursed, his cheeks red with embarrassment, "but what kind, we haven't discovered yet."

"I'm no witch, for if I was, I would know how to tell a warlock from a mortal man, and I cannot tell, and neither can you."

Malachi balled his hands into fists and jammed them to his sides. "I can prove Trevallyan's a warlock, and if there's a man here brave enough to get me a piece of his hair, I'll bloody well show you!"

"Fair knights," Ravenna said, circling the cowering young boys, "you've heard Malachi's dare. So is there one here brave enough to face Trevallyan and ask for a lock of his hair?"

The boys stared at her, wide-eyed and silent.

Ravenna looked at Malachi and raised one fine dark eyebrow in scorn. "Sir, your quest is noble, but your knights are weak."

"Why don't you go, Malachi MacCumhal?" chimed the tall, thin lad.

"Why don't you, Sean O'Malley?" Malachi spit back.

The two boys were nose to nose when Ravenna stepped between them. "You war for naught, brave knights, for Sir Malachi, with or without Trevallyan's hair, cannot prove the lord a warlock."

"I bloody curse you, Ravenna! I can do it! Produce the hair, and I will do it!"

"All right. You prove it. *I'll* get some of Lord Trevallyan's hair."

All the boys held their breath as they stared at Ravenna.

"Have you gone mad, girl?" Malachi squeaked.

"I'm not mad," Ravenna answered, her skirts swaying as she circled the lads again. " 'Tis a simple enough task, if you think about it."

"To cut the hair from a warlock?" Sean whispered.

"Nay, I needn't cut the hair from his head. I'll get it from his comb, when I know the lord is away from the castle. Fiona McClew is a servant at the castle. She'll let me know if all is clear."

"You mean to enter the lord's bedchamber?" Malachi asked reverently.

" 'Tis the only way to make you look a fool, Sir Knight. For when I

return with the hair and you cannot work your magic, I will be vindi-
cated." Ravenna's eyes flashed.

Malachi glared at her, his green-gray eyes never leaving her. "If you
bring me the hair, I'll be provin' the master of Trevallyan is a warlock."
He leaned closer to her, butting his nose to her own. "Just bring me the
hair."

"Ravenna, what are you up to, me girl?" Fiona McClew stood in the
Trevallyan kitchen door, yards away from the bailey and the entrance
to the castle.

"I saw old Griffen O'Rooney ranting and raving over in the master's
graveyard again. I thought Lord Trevallyan should know. Is he gone?"
Ravenna stared down at her grimy bare feet. She hated lying. Grania
always told her the elves would come and take away her tongue if she
told too many. The elves would be busy tonight.

Fiona swept gray wisps of hair from her eyes and looked at her. "The
third time this month! Poor Mr. O'Rooney! When will he let the Trevallyans rest?" She made a sympathetic clucking sound and said, "The
master went to Galway. He's not expected back until tomorrow. I'll tell
the footman to inform Mr. Greeves about Mr. O'Rooney."

"Thank you, Fiona. . . . and how are the children?" Ravenna gave
her an innocent gaze.

The kitchen servant looked down at her bulging stomach. "This
makes four. I just hope I don't have fifteen like me mother."

"Grania says children are a blessing from God."

Fiona glanced at her and then away as if embarrassed for her. Ravenna knew the Catholic Church didn't look upon her birth as a
blessing, but Grania did. And that's all she cared about.

"Well, I'll give Grania your greetings—"

"Grania? Yes, Grania!" Fiona's eyes widened, and she disappeared
into the dark recesses of the castle's kitchen. She returned with a small
tin vial. "Here. This is for your grandmother. It's cinnamon bark from
the castle's spice hoards, to bake with or whatever she likes. Will you
tell Grania to send over a potion of clover honey and rosemary? I've

been sick in the mornings, and what with the work I've to do, I just cannot bring meself to face another day."

Ravenna pocketed the cinnamon bark and nodded her head. "Aye. I'll bring it by first thing this evening as soon as I return to the cottage."

"God bless you, Ravenna. You're a good girl, in spite of your mother's sinnin'." Fiona tried to smile and shut the door.

Ravenna faced the closed door, her heart strangely heavy. She didn't like it when people said things like that about Brilliana. Her mother couldn't have been such a bad woman, she was sure of it, but no one in Lir was ever going to take kindly to Brilliana giving birth out of wedlock. Fifteen children were fine as long as the woman was married proper in the church, but one child born on the wrong side of the blanket—even if the woman had died valiantly giving birth to that child—made the woman a harlot, a creature not morally worthy of even a decent burial, a dark stain that must ruin her daughter, too.

Ravenna turned away. She would never convince others that her mother had been no harlot, no matter how she defended her. Especially when even she had difficulty shrugging off the niggling little doubt that her bastardy gave hard evidence to what they believed. The thought, as always, made her melancholy. She was just like her grandmother. She would never really fit into Lir. Lir held no place for the likes of her and Grania. And so it was natural that she and Grania kept to themselves, creating speculation for the gossips about whether or not Grania was a witch.

Her eyes darkened with anger. But her beloved grandmother was not a witch, and Malachi could go to the devil for saying she was. She was going to get that hair for him and laugh while he tried to work his spell. It was foolishness. Children's foolishness that she was beginning to tire of. Perhaps she was growing too old for it. She looked down at the two swelling mounds of her bosom and covered them with her arms, embarrassed. She didn't like her body doing these strange things. Everything was out of control of late, and now her mind was changing, too. She was leaving childhood behind. Going forward into . . . what?

She stepped across the courtyard to the back entrance of the castle, her mind on the future. It was a sore point between her and Grania. All the townfolk said Grania had the Sight. They said Grania could see into the future, but if the old woman could, Ravenna had never induced her to tell her hers. Every time she had asked, Grania had denied she could do it and told her that instead of wondering about her future, Ravenna should mind her studies and wear her shoes, neither of which was a satisfactory answer to a thirteen-year-old who every day found her body undergoing another strange blossoming. Ravenna was desperate to know what lay ahead. Was she to turn out like Brilliana? Or were better things in store for her? She thought of all the tutors Grania had paraded through the cottage while she was growing up. Ravenna was sure her father was paying for it. Grania wouldn't speak of her father, but how else were they getting the money for such frivolities as tutors? It had to be her father. It had to be. He cared for her, and if she could just find him, she knew he would take her as his own. Then she could have a life of carriages, fine dresses, and a father who loved her—like Kathleen Quinn.

Ravenna's expression grew dreamy as she grasped the rough iron door latch. To live the life of Kathleen Quinn had always been her fondest wish. Kathleen's father was Ascendency. The Quinns were members of the privileged Irish class that had land and built mansions and lived in castles. They were all originally from England, or so she was told by Malachi, who professed to hating the Ascendency with all his heart, but she didn't understand how someone could be born in Ireland and still be considered English. The issue invariably confused her. It was even said Lord Trevallyan's own mother was of common Irish stock, but he was the most hated Ascendency of all, for he owned most of Lir and no one spoke kindly of him. Yet Niall Trevallyan was probably more Irish than she was—she, who didn't even know where Grania came from, for her grandmother was a rare stubborn old woman and refused to ever speak of her roots.

Ravenna wondered if she would always have difficulty sorting it out. All she knew was she was not like Malachi and the other townfolk. But neither was she like Kathleen Quinn, who lived in a grand house in the next county over; Kathleen Quinn, who Ravenna spied every Sunday after Reverend Drummond's service, sitting in the Quinn coach with her younger brother and their parents. Ravenna had first spied Kathleen years past in the same carriage sitting between her parents, her girlish hands clasping a velvet-gowned fashion doll with lovely golden tresses. The doll exactly matched Kathleen, right down to its fox muff, and Ravenna had never seen such a lovely sight. She talked about the doll until Malachi fair wanted to sew her mouth closed, but there was no keeping it inside. She had never seen such a beautiful doll. It looked like the imaginary girl Ravenna had always wanted to be, and she had worshipped it and dreamed of it for years.

But now she no longer dreamed of dolls. Instead she dreamed of being a girl like Kathleen; a silk-beribboned girl who sat in a carriage protected by her father. A girl who could afford to turn her nose up at the countryside. A girl who didn't have to walk the rock-strewn paths, or run with the county hooligans, or wipe the splash of mud from her eyes as the Quinn carriage wheeled past.

Ravenna lifted the latch on the ancient iron door. No one was inside the passage, the echoes of servants' voices long dead and gone. A swell of fear gripped her. If she got caught they would believe she was stealing. The master of Trevallyan would see that she was punished. He might even do the punishing himself. She thought of all the talk of him being the devil, but then she swallowed her fear. Malachi's spell awaited, just like her future. But she would show them all they weren't within a roar of the truth. Trevallyan hadn't the power of a warlock and it was up to her, the "witch's" granddaughter to prove it. Quietly, she closed the castle door behind her.

"Griffen O'Rooney is driving me mad. I want you to talk to him." The master of Trevallyan turned a rancorous gaze toward the countryside. The carriage was making good time. They had just passed the standing stone and Lir's four fields spread out below like a marriage quilt. They would be at the castle in minutes.

"Griffen does the best he can, my son. He's gettin' old, like the rest o' us." Father Nolan leaned both hands on a blackthorn walking stick he'd been forced to rely on these years. The glossy Trevallyan brougham was well-sprung, but he grimaced with every jolt as if it pained his bones.

"You speak for yourself, Father. I'm not getting old."

Father Nolan laughed. "No? Why, 'tis must be the light in here that makes me think I see a man before me and not a boy." His smile faded as he watched Trevallyan stare morosely out the window.

Niall had changed in the years since the meeting of the council. Anger had twisted the man's insides like the wind twisted the yews in the graveyard. Happiness was the only balm for Trevallyan's wounds, and sometimes, such as now, the father feared it might come too late. "You're thirty-three, Niall," the priest remarked quietly. " 'Tis young to many, but you look older. The living has made you hard."

Trevallyan's cold aqua gaze settled on the priest. "Just keep Griffen O'Rooney out of my graveyard."

"He feels responsible."

"For bloody sake, he is not responsible!"

The priest, used to the flare of Trevallyan's temper, said calmly, " 'Tis no secret you didn't love the lassie. You went and married her in your haste to spite us and the *geis*. We all feel responsible for that. And you forget . . . Griffen was the one to bury them, to look upon them—"

"Put it to rest, old man," Trevallyan said, cutting him off. "Tell your friends to do the same. My wife died thirteen years ago not because of a *geis*, but from complications of a pregnancy, a pregnancy that you had nothing to do with."

"And a pregnancy that you had nothing to do with."

The frigid silence turned the warm ruby-velvet interior of the carriage into a mausoleum. Trevallyan pinned him with his hellish, cold stare.

"My son," Father Nolan said gently in a voice that croaked with age, "come to Mass this Sunday. 'Twill help with your anger. . . ."

The schooled emotion in Trevallyan's eyes grew hard and distant. "My anger will be duly abated when you manage to keep O'Rooney out of my graveyard."

Grim-faced, the father watched him. Trevallyan ripped his gaze away and returned it to the countryside.

They rode on in silence, until the silence became so thick Father Nolan was compelled to break it.

"Do you still hear her laughter?" he whispered.

Trevallyan closed his eyes, anger chiseling his every feature into stone. He did not answer.

"I remember the anguish in your voice when you told me about the honeymoon. When she could keep the secret no more. She laughed, you said. Your rooms overlooked Montmartre and you told me you felt as if all of Paris rang with her laughter. She knew she was pregnant. She'd known all along. . . ."

Trevallyan's hand slammed against the upholstered wall. "Enough of this."

"But you must listen. You didn't cause her death—*their* deaths," Father Nolan pleaded.

Trevallyan flicked him a glance of ice. "You would know better than I, Father. You gave her last rites. Tell me, when she died, did Helen absolve me of blame?" The words were more cruel than usual.

" 'Twas fate how it ended," the father replied, grief darkening his own aged eyes. " 'Twas a merciful act of God. You must accept it."

Trevallyan's laughter was haunted and lost.

The priest took one hand off the blackthorn—the hand that had once worn the gold ring that was exactly like Trevallyan's—and he reached across the carriage and grasped Trevallyan by the shoulder. "In your haste to find a wife, the girl trapped you into marriage. You could not have known she carried another's bastard. She was a calculating, black-hearted creature, Niall, and only God's love could have saved her. I say prayers for her daily. And the babe."

"I could have saved her," Trevallyan whispered harshly. "I could have made it work. In the end, I would have taken the babe as my own, as that tombstone in the graveyard proclaims."

"You would have done the right and noble thing, my son." The priest's words were heavy with despair. "But try as you might, you're not God, Trevallyan. You can't correct every evil. You can't pull blood from a stone." The priest's lips hardened. "What happened was God's will."

"Was it God's will for me to banish her as I did?"

The question needed no answer but Father Nolan felt compelled to answer it anyway. "You were angry. It was the only thing you could think of to do when she revealed how she had tricked you. Take comfort that you didn't annul the marriage and leave her in poverty as a lesser man would have done. Instead, she had Trevallyan Castle with all the luxuries of London."

"My wife hated this place and you know it. It was her version of hell to be stuck in a desolate Irish county so far from the things she loved. I knew that when I sent her here. And as to the luxuries. . . ." Trevallyan's face became rock-hard. "She had every one except the luxury of a physician to tell the blithering fools attending her that five weeks without a birth is too long to go after the water breaks."

"Even a physician might not have been able to save her."

"Nonetheless, she should have had one. If I hadn't sent her here, she would have had one."

"We have a physician now. You've done that much good for Lir." The priest held out a shaking hand. "My son," he whispered, " 'tis time for healing. The people view you as one of the Ascendency, and ever since Helen's death you've done your willful best to be as debauched and dissolute as possible, but living up to every wicked opinion of you is not the answer."

"What is the answer?"

"My Lord Trevallyan . . . you know the answer."

Trevallyan's laughter was dark and mirthless. "Ah, yes. The geis. My willful flaunting of it has been my damnation. Is that your point?"

"I see a good man in you, Niall. You care for this county. No one starves in Lir. No one lacks a roof over their heads. Your patronage of this county is excellent, too excellent. Some, as you know, would not have it at all. But these villagers in their small little world don't understand that it's mostly because of you that they have avoided the squalor and disease so prevalent in most counties. Because you are not willing to abide such horrors, because you are not willing to look away, these things don't occur in Lir. But they will. Someday, they will come here and knock on Lir's door. If you don't consider the geis."

"I will not consider it. The fate of Lir is in my hands, not the hands of a *geis*." Trevallyan arrogantly, defiantly, resumed his preoccupation with the landscape.

"Your pride is your greatness and your downfall, my lord," the priest said gravely.

"I thought the *geis* was to be my downfall?"

Trevallyan's sarcasm cut like a rapier. Father Nolan saw no point in answering.

The carriage passed beneath the barbican and bumped across the castle courtyard. It rolled to a stop before the doors of the great hall, but no footmen came to open the door until Trevallyan signaled that the occupants of the carriage were through with their conversation.

"Were you walking home when I picked you up, Father, or would you like a drink before my driver takes you where you were headed?" Trevallyan turned to the priest.

"Don't be marrying the girl."

Trevallyan froze with his knuckle poised to knock on the trap for the driver.

He lowered his hand, anger simmering in his eyes. "I'll be married in two weeks. Elizabeth is a beautiful woman. She'll make me a fine wife. I mean to have her."

"You don't love her."

"That is for me to discover on my wedding night, and such things I will not discuss with a priest."

"Four years ago when you were going to marry Mary Maureen Whelan, you got all the way to the altar before I could force a confession from you that you didn't love her. When I asked if you would love Mary Maureen as your wife, you couldn't lie to me. Don't lie to me now, son. You don't love this Elizabeth. You are courting tragedy."

Trevallyan's anger boiled over. "I'm thirty-three years old. 'Tis my right to take a wife and no man shall stop me."

"Love will stop you, Trevallyan. You don't love this girl. She's not right for you and you know it."

"Let's talk about the 'right girl' for me, shall we?" Niall's voice dripped acid. "What is she now? Twelve? Thirteen? Would you have me marry the child and hear her screams on our wedding night? Is that your idea of love?"

"You need to be patient. She will be a woman someday. And when she is, when you win her love, you will see you were waiting your whole life for this one blessed woman."

"If such happiness is to be mine, why not take her now?" Trevallyan said cruelly. "I'll tell the child about the *geis* and force her to wed me."

"Telling her about the *geis* will get you nothing. You must win her love freely, without bonds and manipulations. If you tell Ravenna about the *geis,* she'll marry you only to save County Lir from ruin."

"Ah, yes, the looming fate of Lir," Trevallyan snapped. "Tell me, if this *geis* is true, why has Lir not fallen into ruin? Years have passed, and still the *geis* remains unfulfilled, and yet as you can see all around you, Lir is as bountiful and peaceful as it has been. So where is the truth in your *geis* after all?"

"Luck will hold until Ravenna is of age. Right now she is just a child and a child cannot give a woman's love. You can do nothing now, Niall. You can only wait."

"Let this torture end, Father," Trevallyan said, the old anger seething like snakes in a tarpit. "I've been good to the child. Everything she has, I've been the one to give it to her. Brilliana's daughter would have died had I not taken pity on the child and seen that she lived. Is there no one to take pity on me?"

"You have not been overly generous, my lord. The girl runs with a band of hooligans because the other children look down upon her bastardy. Her face is always dirty, her feet bare. She has but the one small advantage of a tutor, so that she might be educated and keep from becoming like her mother, but that is all."

"The girl could have more, if she likes. The cost is inconsequential to me. If that is all the child has, blame Grania. The old witch won't take my money except enough pennies for Ravenna's sake."

The priest sat back in the plush velvet upholstery and released a sigh. "Call off the wedding, my lord. You must be patient."

"By the time the child Ravenna matures into the kind of woman who would make me a good companion, I'll be in my forties. 'Tis a long time to wait for a maiden who may not want an old man for a husband." Trevallyan knocked on the trap, his lips a taut, grim line. The driver clambered down. The footman opened the carriage door.

"Call off the wedding, my son," Father Nolan whispered, making no move to go with him. "You refuse to believe it, but the *geis* has already proven true. Tragedy will follow you if you wed a woman you cannot love."

"Take him home," Trevallyan ordered to the coachman. He turned to the priest who remained within the carriage. "Hear me and hear me well, Father: The child Ravenna *is not my problem.*" He slammed the carriage door closed and watched it take off down the lane.

Ravenna could barely find Trevallyan's bedchambers in the massive number of castle rooms. There were rooms to display the Trevallyan medieval armaments, rooms for servants, for bathing, even modern velvet saloons for courting, but it took a long climb up a winding stone staircase to the north tower for Ravenna to finally find the master's chambers.

She knew it instantly. The doors were carved with the Trevallyan adder and shield, sending chills through her body. The Trevallyan crest held four shamrocks within a shield that was split with a bar sinister in the shape of an adder, the serpent. St. Patrick had driven all the snakes from Ireland, but the English Trevallyans had symbolically brought them in again in their crest. The Trevallyans had no motto. The crest spoke all.

Taking a deep breath for courage, she opened the doors and peeked inside. The first room was an anteroom, a library actually, the walls covered with mahogany and gilt-bronze-mounted bookcases lined with leather-bound spines. Two chamois-covered chairs sat by the hearth, only one chair showing signs of wear on the bottle-green leather, indicating the room's sole occupancy.

Ravenna felt her heart skip with every damning creak of the hinges as she closed the door behind her. She stepped into the bedchamber. Trevallyan's bed, an enormous four-post cavern carved of black oak and draped in green velvet, was a room unto itself. Scarred from hundreds of years of use, the past was written in its ancient wood, with one especially impressive cut hacked into one of the huge onion-shaped finials. She walked past the bed and wondered if the scars in the bed were caused by invaders to the castle in previous centuries. She was too young to think of jealous lovers and cuckolded husbands.

A small doorway to the left caught her eye. She walked across the lush Axminster carpet, marveling at the way it kept her bare feet and the stone room toasty warm. She turned the brass knob and found herself in the lord's dressing chamber. Inlaid mahogany wardrobes stood sentinel on either side of the room. And beneath a shield-shaped shaving mirror, on a bureau with the carved feet of a lion, lay Trevallyan's comb.

She held the tortoiseshell comb to the light of a small mullioned window high in the stone wall of the dressing room. There were three blond hairs intertwined within the teeth. Triumphant, she pulled them out of the comb and curled them into her palm, marveling at the way they caught the light, like spun threads of gold, so different from her own.

The sound of voices suddenly chilled her blood. She clutched the three hairs and stared at the dressing-room door. The voices came and went and she tried desperately to determine whether they were in the staircase to the tower or were just the echo of passing servants. The voices grew louder, and she was paralyzed by the creak of groaning hinges.

"Kevin, tell Greeves to send up a bath and my dinner. I'll be staying in my rooms tonight." The male voice was well-mannered, even refined, but the underlying anger in it left Ravenna with a fear that stabbed through her like an icicle.

"Very good, my lord. I'll send the footman up to tend to the hearths. Your early arrival was unexpected, or we would have seen to it that the fires were lit."

"Fine. Fine," the commanding voice answered absentmindedly.

The doors creaked shut. There was silence.

Ravenna didn't dare breathe. Her worst terrors had come true. The master of Trevallyan stood in the bedchamber, and she was trapped, hidden in a corner of his dressing room.

She climbed atop a chair beneath the small mullioned window and looked down. It was a hundred feet to the gravel-strewn courtyard, if

not more. Certain death. Silently, she jumped back down to the floor
on grubby bare feet. The only way out of the stone tower was the way
she had come: through the bedroom and the antechamber and down
the steep, winding staircase.

She crept to the dressing-room door, her heart beating a heavy
staccato in her chest. What would he do to her if she were caught?
Thieves were sometimes hanged. Would he hang her, or take mercy
upon her because she was merely a girl? She could feel the blood
rushing from her face. Slowly, she peered into the bedroom to find her
captor.

Trevallyan stood by the bank of windows near his writing desk. She
had seen the master rarely, perhaps only once or twice, but he had
always left an impression. He was not an overly tall man, nor big, but
there was something about him, a wickedness to his slant of eyebrows,
a commanding, even cruel gleam in his fine blue-green eyes, that
convinced her—nay, all the townfolk of Lir—that he could be spawn
of the devil.

His coat and black neckcloth were thrown across the bed. Clad in a
fine batiste shirt, a black figured-silk vest, and wool trousers, he made
a melancholy figure at the window as he stared around across the misty
countryside to the *ogham* stone that stood directly in his view. She
could almost feel pity for the lonely portrait he made: his black-
trousered legs braced beneath him, his arms crossed over his chest, his
profile—when he presented it—refined, yet manly, his nape-length
wheat-colored hair slicked back as if it were common for him to run
his fingers through it in frustration. And the expression in his eyes
. . . bereft.

She was barely thirteen and not sophisticated in the ways of reading
emotions; still Ravenna found herself in the spell of the man's mood.
Power and melancholy made a heady mix. She felt herself drawn to
him. She might have even said, "Please don't be sad," if not for the fear
that froze her voice and the terror of that violent gaze finding her in his
private room and proclaiming, "To the hangman!"

She hugged the dressing-room wall and tried to think of an escape.
The only way was to cross the bedroom and sneak out the door when
the footman arrived to light the fires. The three golden hairs still

clutched in her palm mocked her. It was a meager treasure for so great a risk. She'd been foolish to come here. The days of her childhood were finally drawing to a close. Never again would she stoop to such folly.

She heard a rustling sound in the bedroom, then footsteps.

Panicked, she backed away, her gaze clawing at every wardrobe and bureau for a hiding place. Her hand reached out for the last wardrobe's door latch, and Trevallyan entered.

"God save me," she whispered. Her gaze met Trevallyan's and her back slammed against the partly opened door of the wardrobe.

Ravenna had never seen a man so shocked in her life. Trevallyan looked at her as if she were a shade, a ghost, one of many reputed to haunt the castle. It was a full minute before the stain of anger crept to his cheeks.

"What are you doing here?" His words, deep with fury, gave strange emphasis. It seemed as if he were saying, "What are *you* doing *here*?"

"I—I was not stealing from you, Lord Trevallyan, I swear upon my mother's honor." Her voice trembled. Wildly, she looked past him to see if she could break for the door.

His lips hardened to a straight line, and his gaze pinned her to the wall. " 'Tis a fine thing. You of all creatures to be swearing upon your mother's honor."

"Nay," she whispered, stung by his insult but too frightened to fight him fully. He was master of all Lir. Whatever punishment he wanted to dole out, the county would be hard-pressed to go against his wishes. Tears sprang to her eyes, but she blinked them away as she'd done most of her young life. Malachi hadn't cried when a lord from Dublin shot his father dead right in front of him by outrageously claiming his father was a smuggler in cahoots with Daniel O'Connell. She would not cry either.

"What do you have in your hand?"

Trevallyan's contemptuous gaze lowered to her small, dirty fist and Ravenna's heart lurched as she realized how things looked. If she showed him the hair, he might think she was some kind of witch come to put a spell on him and he would force the magistrate to show her little pity. Yet if she refused to show him what was inside her hand, then his accusations of stealing would be cemented forever.

" 'Tis nothing, my lord. I was not stealing from you, I swear it. By all that is holy, I swear it," she rambled, unsure of which course to take when both seemed to lead her to gaol.

He stepped forward; she backed away. He was not a big man, but to a frightened young girl, he was a giant.

"Show me what you have in your hand."

Witch! she could already hear him cry. There was no way to explain what she had in her hand, except to put the blame on Malachi, which she would never do.

" 'Tis nothing, my lord. 'Tis nothing of any value." Her gaze flew to the doorway behind him. She would have to run. She could flee to the neighboring county and hide. Malachi would help her. There was always Malachi.

"Show me. Now." He took an ominous step toward her.

Her heart was near to bursting with terror. The raw energy of flight took hold of her and she ran out of the dressing room. Her dingy blue gown caught on a chair and toppled it, but still, the carved double doors out of the apartment were almost within her sight. She held out her hands as if to reach them, but an arm lifted her by the waist and slammed her into the down mattress of the lord's bedstead.

"You bloody urchin! Show me what you've taken from here or, by God, I'll bring you and your grandmother in front of the magistrate."

" 'Tis nothing! 'Tis nothing!" she cried out as he grappled with her on the mattress. When he had her pinned, he forced open her grubby fingers and found the three damning blond hairs that clung to her palm.

"What is this?" His eyes were the cold color of the Irish sea. "It looks like my hair . . . ?"

"I'm not a witch. I'm not . . . I'm not . . ." She sobbed.

He looked down at her as if noticing her agony for the first time. The tears on her grimy cheeks left rivulets of clean skin in their wake and her worn blue gown, patched and dirty, seemed to disgust him. "Damned well you're no witch. There is no such thing, you foolish girl."

She stared up at him, not comforted at all by the fact that he believed her, not when his face loomed terrifyingly above her, like Satan come to her in the night.

"Come along. Confess. What were you going to do with my hair?" He shook her as if that would get the truth from her. "Were you thinking in that absurd head of yours that your grandmother could put a spell on me?"

If she weren't so terrified, she'd think he almost looked amused.

"Nay," she whispered, glancing at the palm he held open, " 'tis just the opposite. My—my friends call you a warlock—"

"Your friends. But not you?" He looked closely at her, demanding she speak the truth. He seemed to be truly curious of her answer.

"I—I don't believe you are, but they said they would prove that you were one if I gave them a lock of your hair." She looked at him. Her answer seemed to take him aback.

"You were here in defense of my honor?" he asked slowly.

She nodded.

He lifted his head and laughed as if unable to control it. The sound should have been pleasant, but it was harsh and mirthless, as if he knew no other way to laugh, as if he knew no joy in his life. With the devilish slant to his eyebrows, she suddenly could see how some people had acquired the notion that he was indeed a warlock.

"Tell me, child, who these people are who dare to call me a warlock," he said, taunting her.

She stared up at him, silent, a mutinous set to her jaw.

"Come on, tell me. Otherwise," he drew closer until they were eye to eye; she, locked beneath him on the green velvet counterpane of the bed, unable to struggle. "Otherwise, I'll call in the magistrate."

Her lower lip trembled only slightly. She would be jailed and punished for stealing. So be it. She would not betray her friends.

"I'll not tell you. Hang me if you must," she answered, breathless with terror.

"Hang you," he scoffed as if he found the idea ridiculous. But because it played so well on her fears, he let his gaze flick down to the palm he still held with an iron grip and said, "Confess, you wild creature, or I'll flay the skin from this hand if you don't."

She whimpered, holding back new tears. She would not cry again.

She would not. She glanced at the offending hand, defiance hot on her face. "I will not betray my friends. . . ." The words died on her lips.

His gaze followed hers. She stared at a gold ring that gleamed on his small finger, a gold ring wrought of Celtic tracery in the shape of a serpent. It was the Trevallyan adder, of course. She could see that now. What she could not understand was why his ring exactly matched the one on her hand, the one Grania had given her many years ago at her birth, the one shoved onto her chubby index finger because it was still too big for her other fingers.

"They match," she whispered, utterly bedeviled as to the reason why.

Horror crossed his face as his gaze flickered between her expression and their locked hands that wore identical rings. Suddenly the anger he held in check raged to the surface.

"Get out of here before I beat you senseless and see you most assuredly hanged for a thief!" He clambered from the bed and slammed his fist into one of the bed's thick black oak posts.

"But—but why do I have a ring like yours? There must be a reason . . ." she stuttered, unable to figure out the puzzle of it.

He took hold of her like a rag doll, pulling her to her feet by the rough fustian fabric of her gown. His eyes flickered down at her body and lingered almost imperceptibly at her chest where two small breasts swelled like springtime buds. The fury on his face was a terrible sight. "Get out of here! You're a child! You have no business in my bedchamber! Get out of here before I have the hangman take you out!" He threw her toward the two doors and stalked her as she scrambled to flee. She flung the doors open, a sob caught in her throat. With a renewed burst of terror, she ran down the winding stone steps. And never once looked back.

Chapter 6

ET ME Father Nolan. *Now,*" Trevallyan ranted to the unwitting footman who had come to light the hearths. The young man scrambled to exit almost as quickly as Ravenna had minutes earlier.

An hour later, Father Nolan sat in the Trevallyan library, sipping Greeves's famous warm whiskey.

"She was in my bedroom," Trevallyan announced, his anger barely in check. "Some kind of children's prank. She wanted to know why she and I both have the same ring." He pierced the priest with one of his frigid stares. "Why do we have identical rings?"

Father Nolan took a long, deep sip of his whiskey. His hesitation showed in his eyes. He seemed to brace himself for the other man's anger. "The night we were all at the cottage, I gave the babe my ring, the one that matched yours. 'Tis part of a gimmal that you and the child both wear. A medieval wedding ring."

"Explain what you mean by wedding ring," Niall demanded.

"A gimmal is given out during a betrothal. It is a ring in three sections. The bride and the groom each wear a ring and a third party wears the last one. During the wedding ceremony, all three rings are united on the bride's hand."

"This ring was given to me by my father. My mother did not wear it."

"You forget, Lord Trevallyan, your parents fell in love. Your father married before his twentieth year. They had no need for the *geis*."

Trevallyan glanced at a black Grecian urn on the mantel. His fist shot out and shattered the priceless antiquity into oblivion. "This *geis* is driving me mad. I cannot hear the word again."

The priest watched him, grim and silent. Slowly he said, "What would you have us do?"

"Send her away! Get her out of Lir! I don't want to lay eyes on the child ever again. She's only bound to grow older. I don't want to see her."

"It can be done."

Niall faced the priest as if he didn't quite believe him. "If getting rid of her were so easy, why could I not accomplish this before?"

"I can see to it you never lay eyes on the child ever again, as you wish, but I cannot make the promise that you won't lay eyes on her as a woman."

Trevallyan stared at the ring on his small finger as if he hated it. Slowly he removed it and made to throw it in the fire.

"I would not do it if I were you," Father Nolan whispered.

"My father gave me this ring. He told me to wear it until I was wed. I'll be wed in two weeks. I haven't any use for it now."

" 'Tis only a ring, Trevallyan. Destroying it will not destroy the *geis*. And you will not be wed in two weeks. You don't love the girl. You know it."

"I want a wife," Trevallyan groaned, laying his forehead on the stone edge of the mantel. "I want someone to share my bed and this home. I want someone to dine with of an evening and to help me enjoy the riches this cruel and vindictive God has placed within my grasp only to keep me from sharing them with a mate. You're a priest. Can't you understand loneliness?"

"I understand it too well," the father whispered, "but you shall not be lonely forever, my son, I promise you that—as I promise to send

Ravenna away. But you must promise me . . . no weddings without love. God save us all, tragedy is certain with you, and we have no need for more tragedy."

" 'Tis a curse to force a man to find true love."

"Then you are cursed, my lord, for you *must* find it."

"But true love is for faerie tales. In real life it hardly exists. I would be happy with less, yet you make me scrutinize every woman I wish to bring to the altar."

"The others have failed. The right one will not. You must be patient, Niall. The reward will be worth waiting for."

Trevallyan picked up a shard of the urn and crushed it in his palm. Two crimson drops of blood from his hand splattered on the white marble hearth. "Just send the girl away. Just send her away."

" 'Tis done," the priest murmured.

The tears of fright and anxiety that Ravenna had so bravely held in check while in Trevallyan's bedchamber flowed freely as she ran through the fields toward home. She got to the cottage and ran directly to her bedroom to hide her tears from her grandmother, but Grania, who everyone in Lir believed had the second sight, seemed to see them anyway. The old woman appeared in the bedroom doorway not five minutes after Ravenna threw herself on her bed.

Ravenna looked at her for a moment without speaking. Guiltily she wiped at her tears. Grania merely stared, the lines and sagging skin on her face making her expression inscrutable; her gnarled, aged hands clasped around the fat body of a brindle cat the miller had found abandoned in a granary.

"I—I've done something terrible," Ravenna whispered, her lips trembling with unshed tears.

"Ye went to the castle, didn't ye?"

Reluctantly, she nodded.

Grania moved into the room, using her hands to discern a small walnut chair in the corner. Her eyesight was dimming because of the milky blue shadows covering her irises. Ravenna watched her struggle, knowing how Grania loathed help.

"Me child, 'tis not good for ye to be goin' to the castle. Trevallyan is an angry man."

"He—he thinks I wanted to steal from him. But I did not, Grania! I swear I did not!" Ravenna's tears sprang up anew. Grania reached for her and Ravenna fell to the old woman's lap, sobbing.

"There, there, me child. 'Twill soon pass."

"No, no . . . he—he may bring the magistrate. He thinks me a thief. He thinks all of us thieves." she wept.

"But why, child?" Grania ran her hands lovingly over the jet-black tresses, so much like Brilliana's.

"He caught me in his bedchamber." She told her about Malachi's challenge. "I left without his hair, but Grania . . ." Ravenna's voice grew hushed, "the lord and I have the same ring on our hands. The exact same ring." She held the serpent ring up to her grandmother so she might see it better. "I—I think he believes we stole it from the Trevallyans. . . . Oh, Grania," she cried, "I can't wear the ring anymore if we stole it."

Grania grew still, her milky gaze staring at some indefinable spot across the room.

"Where did we get the ring, Grania?"

"Ye must keep it on, for 'tis to bring ye good fortune. Father Nolan gave it to ye, child, when ye were first born."

"When—when we lived in the hovel?" The cottage Ravenna had been born in was now a fallen-down ruin, inaccessible because of the overgrown hawthorn. She couldn't believe it when Grania told her they once lived there. Their cottage now was perhaps not grand, but it had wood floors, a parlor, a kitchen, and two bedrooms.

"The old cottage was where yer mother died, Ravenna. 'Tis best not to think of it any longer."

Ravenna tried not to, but as understanding suddenly dawns upon a child, she burned with questions that she'd never quite thought of before.

"Grania, we must have been unbearably poor to have lived in that terrible little place. Why do we not live there now? What has changed?

Why can we now afford this cottage when at my birth we were so impoverished, we could not—"

"Fortunes change, me child."

"But there's a reason why they change. What is our reason?" She stared up at her grandmother with curious blue-violet eyes, purple velvet in shadows.

"Child, child," Grania said, appearing almost grieved.

"Is . . . Trevallyan my father? Is that why he looked at me with such loathing?"

Grania seemed to have a difficult time watching Ravenna's expression. "Me darlin' girl, how is it ye think of such things?"

"Then he is not my father?"

"He is not."

"I think of my father, you know I do, Grania. I know he believes me to be an embarrassment, and I suppose that is why he has never revealed himself to us, but still . . ." She looked up at Grania, tears glistening in her eyes. "Does he watch out for us? Is that where we've gotten our money? From him? Does he care about us, even a wee bit?"

The old woman stroked the jet-black tresses beneath her gnarled hands. She didn't answer.

"He does care about us, doesn't he?" Ravenna asked, her child's voice flat, despairing.

"He does not know about us, of that I am sure. Brilliana said he loved her, but she would not tell me his name other than to say he was a titled lord living in Ulster."

"So you do have the second sight! Everyone says you do! Can't you see him so that I might find him?"

"Me child, me dear sweet child, don't think about him anymore. I've seen the visions." She paused as if she knew what she had to say would cause grief. "He is dead, my child. Ye have no father anymore."

Ravenna stared up at her in horror, her smooth, youthful face streaked with tears. The hope that some way, somehow, her father might come find them was put to death as surely as with an executioner. Never again could she daydream with the hope of him rescuing her from her bastardy. Kathleen Quinn would always turn her nose up at her. Forever now.

"Why didn't you tell me about him?" she rasped, her throat raw from weeping.

"There's nothing to be tellin'. Forget about him. Forget about all that is past. Ye should be lookin' to the future."

"What future?" Ravenna asked bitterly, unable to meet Grania's eyes. "I belong to no one, I belong nowhere. The children call me terrible names. And now they're true . . . they're all true . . ." Her weeping began anew. Grania stroked her dark head as she sobbed into her apron. The other questions Ravenna had were temporarily forgotten.

❀

Father Nolan huddled against the Irish Sea wind and knocked on Grania's cottage door. The evening was a chill one, with a storm brewing to the west. Ravenna answered the door, her face and feet now washed, her wild hair combed and plaited down her back. The child wore a brown linen dress a wee bit too small for her blossoming figure. That she was a beauty, there was no doubt. Even poverty could not hide that.

"I've come to call on your grandmother. Is Grania feeling well tonight?" he asked, trying to get the girl to smile.

Ravenna only looked at him with eyes wide with fright. "Come in," she whispered, and motioned to the parlor. The room had only a long bench and two scuffed and battered armchairs, but all were taken up with cats that had been brought to the cottage for want of another place to go. Ravenna brushed aside a large black tomcat that was warming himself by the fire, and offered the priest the most sturdy chair, then left to fetch Grania.

"Have you been keeping well, my fair woman?" the priest said when Grania walked slowly into the room. He took her gnarled hand into his liver-spotted one and pressed it. Grania returned the welcome.

"Ravenna, will ye be a good girl and fetch the father some tea?" she said.

Ravenna nodded and left for the kitchen, her little oval face white with fear.

"The child cannot hear in the kitchen. What have ye come to tell me,

Father?" Grania asked as soon as she was helped to the other chair and the fat brindle cat exotically named Zelda was comfortable on her lap.

"Trevallyan was quite upset to find her in his bedroom today. Did Ravenna tell you about it?"

"She did."

"He wants her to be sent away."

Grania met his gaze, worry clouding her own more than the affliction that left a milky film over her eyes. " 'Tis a cruel punishment for a child's prank. She's only a lass. Where will she go?"

"He'll send her to England to a school for young ladies. There's no doubt at all that she'll be treated well there. 'Tis best, in any case, Grania. The girl is growing up. She can't be running with Malachi and his ilk forever. 'Tis a sure way for her to find herself with a babe of her own."

Grania looked away into the hearth, her stooped figure trembling with emotion. She took a long moment to think about what Father Nolan had said, then she answered slowly, "All right, have Trevallyan send the child away. I could not bear to see her like . . . ." Her words dwindled, as if they were too painful for her to speak.

"Ravenna will have the finest care. Trevallyan can pay for it, and he is willing to see it done. I think he fears her, Grania. Perhaps 'tis best."

Ravenna entered the room with a battered pewter tray, a chipped cup, and the ironstone teapot. She placed it on the table next to the priest and began to pour out.

"Child, the father would have a word with ye. Will ye sit down?"

Ravenna cast her gaze to the floor. Her heart throbbed with fear and anxiety. She knew what this was about. Trevallyan had sent the priest before the magistrate came to take her away.

"Ravenna child, how pretty you've become. You're a young lady now, aren't you?" Father Nolan began gently.

Ravenna could not take her gaze from the floor. She wanted to cry, to run, to scream, but she couldn't. It was all her fault. She had taken Malachi's challenge and she'd known what the price would be if she was caught. And Lord Trevallyan had caught her.

"I wasn't stealing from the castle. I swear I wasn't. I just wanted a bit of the lord's hair to prove he wasn't a warlock," she whispered in so low a tone that the priest was forced to lean over to her.

"I've heard all about it."

Ravenna nodded, her eyes filling with damning tears. They would take her away and then there would be no one to take care of Grania. Perhaps Grania would die because of her stupidity. Suddenly she wanted to die herself.

"Grania thinks it time you go off to school, lass. What do you think of that?"

Ravenna raised her dark head and looked at Grania with eyes full of unshed tears. "Is this to be my punishment?"

"Don't think of it as punishment, me girl, think of it as . . ." the father looked to Grania for help. The old woman's eyes were themselves filling with tears. ". . . think of it as a privilege. There aren't many young girls in County Lir who can go off to a fine school for ladies."

Ravenna watched the priest, taking no comfort in his words. The only schools she had ever heard of were thinly disguised workhouses. There would be nothing but misery there, but she had no choice but to go. She'd been caught and she would have to pay.

"Are you excited about the idea, child? You'll see other young ladies such as yourself and make friends with them—a much better class of friends than these ragtag boys you go running with now."

"Who will care for Grania if I'm gone?" she asked, her voice desolate. Her grandmother was the only one she had ever truly loved and who ever truly loved her. Her whole life had been spent with Grania. They were both outcasts in a hostile land, a land Ravenna now loved fiercely, for Ireland was the only home she knew. So they couldn't rip her from it. They just couldn't.

"Fiona has offered to come every day to see to Grania."

"But who will pay for her services?"

The priest looked uncomfortable. He glanced at Grania. "Child, you mustn't bother your head with pennies and figures. Your grandmother has the means to take care of herself. If she has money to send you to school, then she has the coins to pay Fiona."

"But the money doesn't come from my father, so where does it come from?" Ravenna brushed the quiet tears streaming down her cheeks. Her gaze shifted from the priest to Grania. Neither one spoke.

"Lord Trevallyan is sending me off to punish me, isn't he?"

"Please don't think of it that way." Father Nolan looked at Grania. "Your grandmother was the one to decide to send you to school, and she will pay for it out of her own funds—funds that, no doubt, were given to her by a generous soul who once sought her cures."

Ravenna appeared to accept the explanation, but she did not accept the reasons why she was being sent off. It was Trevallyan's doing, she knew it. Trevallyan was punishing her, and she could not escape the punishment, for she was guilty.

She stood quietly, listening to the priest recount all the plans, but her gaze was glazed and distant as she thought of the man who was forcing her from her home and from her dear grandmother. No matter how she might deserve punishment for her crime, the master of Trevallyan was taking away all she had, and all she cared about.

God save her, how she hated him.

⚯

"Ravenna!"

Ravenna heard her name on the wind as the hired hack pulled out from the lane of Grania's cottage. It was three days later, and all of Father Nolan's plans for her departure had come true. She was dressed in her most hated dress, a dark blue wool with a welting of black around the collar and basque. A corset held her upright, completely flattening any bosom she might have possessed, the laces so tight she could hardly breathe. Her hair, normally a thick black tangle that streamed down her back, was now severely plaited and pinned to her nape. Worst of all, her feet, scrubbed pink, were encased in a pair of black leather boots so new and stiff, every step was agony.

The hired carriage had come, with a dour, black-gowned woman who was to be her chaperone for the trip to the Weymouth-Hampstead School for Young Ladies in London. Ravenna had said a grave, tearless farewell to Grania, forcing herself to be brave and to take her punishment. Even so, it took an extreme amount of self-control not to break down sobbing when Grania hugged her only grandchild to her bosom and looked down at her, pain making her dear wizened face appear even older than it normally did.

The coach departed, and once away from Grania's eyes, the tears had come, Ravenna unable to hide them from the stranger dressed in black. Her heart was being ripped out.

"Ravenna!" the voice called out again.

Ravenna ignored the chaperone's dour, disapproving expression and stuck her head out the carriage window.

"Malachi!" she cried, extending her hand.

Malachi ran behind the carriage looking as dirty-faced and ragtag as usual, his running figure half-hidden in an early morning mist from the sea. "Ravenna! Where are they takin' ye?" he called out, his ruddy expression one of awe at her fancy hired conveyance and of fear that he might never see her again.

"I'm going to England, Malachi! I never got his lordship's hair! Pray for my quick return!" she cried, letting her tears stream into the wind.

"Trevallyan did this to ye?" he called to her.

Ravenna didn't answer. She looked at him longingly just one last time before her traveling companion lowered the shade. The hired black carriage rolled into the mist until Malachi could see it no more. Defeated, the lad stopped his running and stared at the fog-shrouded emptiness of the road, the Trevallyan name on his childish lips, whispered in a curse.

PART THREE

The Geis

A violet . . .
The perfume and suppliance of a minute;
No more.

WILLIAM SHAKESPEARE
(1564–1616)

Hamlet, Act I, scene III

Chapter 7

IRELAND 1847

P ETER MAGUIRE, Mayor of Lir for forty years, died at sunset eight weeks after Lent. He was not a young man, if seventy-five could be considered old, which it was not in Lir. Many a citizen had lived to be near ninety, quite a feat for a poor Irish county, yet Lir was a place of renowned abundance and good fortune. They said the faeries watched out for Lir. Sometimes that was easy to believe.

Peter Maguire was buried in the parish graveyard. Father Nolan held the Mass, and every man, woman, and child left the fields and attended. Almost everyone in Lir was there.

But Trevallyan did not attend, not out of disrespect to the mayor, but because he was in London and word of Peter Maguire's death did not reach him in time to return to Ireland.

Grania did not attend either, for she was becoming too old and feeble to leave her house. She sent another to the funeral in her place.

The young woman came to the funeral the way she had left Lir many years before. She arrived in a hired trap, her face solemn, her feelings cloaked behind a calm, unreadable expression. She kept to herself, standing in the back of the crowd. Her eyes were uncommonly beautiful, the color of violets at dusk as the blossoms become cloaked in blue shadows. But if eyes were truly the windows of the soul, this woman kept hers shuttered, as if she didn't quite trust the world around her.

" 'Tis good to see you again, child, but a child you are no more, I see," Father Nolan said to her when Peter Maguire had been consigned to the ground and the Mass for the dead had been completed. The priest clasped her hand in his and pressed it warmly.

"It's good to be back, Father," Ravenna answered with a poise she had not possessed when she was thirteen.

"What a fine woman you've become. Grania is beside herself with joy that you've returned."

Ravenna looked at the old priest, the one who had sent her away all those years ago. As a girl, she'd cried herself to sleep countless nights at the Weymouth-Hampstead School, fearful about Grania's health, despising the institution's headmistress, who upon Ravenna's first day, had publicly condoned the practice of backhanding "the Irish girl with no proper family" should Ravenna display any of her "inbred pagan defiance." Many a night, she had stared at the light from the gas streetlamp streaming across her blankets, and she had wondered if Malachi had ever lain awake hating the man who killed his father as she hated Trevallyan.

Her punishment for her transgression at the castle had been just and full. The other girls at the school hadn't liked her. She'd been ostracized from the first day, for it was clear even to children she was out of her element. She wasn't used to fine things, nor to servants, and she quickly became a source of malicious amusement on the part of the other young ladies. The night of her arrival, when the servants came to clear the table, she had already taken her plate and saucer to the kitchen. The other girls snickered behind their soft, pretty hands and from that day on looked down their noses at her, all with the blessing of the headmistress, who clearly considered her a cut below the rest of the students. She'd been forced to learn English tradition the painful way, by viewing it from the outside, her nose pressed against the cold glass of her Irishness. Ravenna had no choice but to live with it, for tradition dictated her every waking hour, from her toilet (ladies *never* wore their hair loose) to her meals (the Englishwoman's pasty-faced complexion was best achieved by a diet of cold mutton and gruel; crisp carrots, plump sugar peas, and scarlet love apples that Grania grew in the kitchen garden seemed anathema to a Londoner). She'd been expected to embrace the English life, yet it had been impossible, as it is impossible to live a life one views only from the street.

If she'd ever had the chance to fit in, her schoolmates saw to it that it would never be. The Weymouth-Hampstead young ladies had laughed at the clothes that Fiona had sent with her, clothes that, while new, despaired of any pretensions to fashion; and they laughed at her Irish accent, calling her all sorts of names she still heard chanted in her nightmares. Being a newcomer from another land, she'd never been informed of the singular traditions of the Weymouth-Hampstead School, one of which being that every girl sent to it was expected to have her own set of silver flatware engraved with her initials. The first night Ravenna sat down to supper with the girls, she had discovered to her dismay that she had no eating utensils, and none would be forthcoming until her family sent her some. Meal after meal she sat with the headmistress and the girls, only gnawing on bread and sipping her tea, until finally a servant took pity on her and brought her a battered pewter spoon from the kitchen. For six months, she'd made do with that one crude spoon. She never wrote to Grania asking that a set of flatware be sent to her because she knew they didn't have the money for such frivolity. It was doubtful Grania could even afford the Weymouth-Hampstead School; Ravenna was convinced Grania had been forced to send her there to keep Trevallyan quiet about her crimes. So Ravenna resigned herself to eating every meal with the bent pewter spoon, defying anyone who dared look her way. She held her head high through every meal, but at night, alone in her tiny room, she cried enough tears to run rivers through Ireland. Six months later, a set of silver flatware mysteriously appeared at her place at the dinner table, given to her by an unknown donor. The pieces were engraved with one single initial, the letter R, and nothing else. At first, she had thought there was a generous soul at the school who couldn't stand to see her without. She had hoped that somehow she had a friend sitting at the table who had given them to her, but no friend had ever come forward. Whoever sent them remained anonymous, and perhaps that was best, for in the end the utensils only became another source of torment. The girls were quick to see the lack of multiple initials on her silverware. They tortured her endlessly about not having a father and conjectured that no doubt the man who had spawned her was English and wanted nothing to do with her. The rest of her years at the school seemed to be lived through an endless stream of insults, wounded feelings, and singsong taunts. But now she was free. She had paid her price, and never would she go back.

" 'Tis a shame a funeral's the first thing you see of Lir upon your return, Ravenna."

The priest's words lured her from her dark thoughts. "But it was a fine service. Peter Maguire would have been very happy with it, could he have heard it," Ravenna commented. She studied the father and realized the years had been kind to him. His wrinkled skin was a pleasant pink color, scrubbed by the cold winds of the Irish Sea, and his blue eyes still twinkled with quickness and wit though he had to be past eighty now. He was a right handsome old man for a priest, she thought. Many of the Irish were. Trevallyan, for one. She heard he still had his fine looks though he was almost forty now and led such a debauched life one would expect him to be red-nosed and corpulent. "Will you come to tea, Father?" she asked, ruthlessly shoving aside the past that had been her fault and forcing away all the memories that still hurt her little-girl heart.

"Tea? Why, 'tis quite kind of you, child!" Father Nolan exclaimed, looking as pleased as he was surprised by the invitation. "Peter Maguire has little family to comfort. May I come in an hour?"

"Grania and I would be honored, Father." Ravenna gave him a small, welcoming smile. She picked up her dark blue skirts, and she stepped across a soggy path. Now that she was finally back in Lir, she walked home, no longer bothering with the pretense of the hired trap.

"What are ye to do now, Ravenna?" Grania asked as Ravenna was setting out the tea. "Have ye given it any thought, now that ye be back from the fancy school?"

Ravenna's grandmother was near blind, and she had difficulty walking, but Grania's mind, like Father Nolan's, was as sharp as ever, and Ravenna, no longer a child, began to mourn the waste of youthful souls forced to grow old.

"The first thing I must do is see Malachi. He was not at the funeral." Ravenna inspected a chipped cup, then set it on the tray.

"Ye shouldn't be thinkin' of him, child."

Ravenna glanced at Grania and for once was glad for her grandmother's blindness. Malachi seemed a sore subject. She didn't want to risk upsetting her. "But I do think of him," she said tentatively. "He wrote to me, you know. All those years. He had to have Father Nolan pen them, of course, for he cannot read or write, but they were from Malachi nonetheless." Ravenna smiled. The letters had kept her going when despair and loneliness seemed ready to engulf her like a tide. She kept every single precious letter bundled with a blue satin ribbon and even now reread them. Malachi's veiled references to his ongoing troublemaking still made her laugh, and to this day she wondered how he had managed to pass them by the censorious pen of the priest.

"Ye be wary of him, Ravenna. He be a boy no longer." Grania grew quiet.

Ravenna frowned, arranging a plate of shortbread.

"So what'll ye be doin' tomorrow, child, and the day after that, and the day after that? 'Tis the true question I was askin'."

"Perhaps I'll advertise," Ravenna answered evenly, picking up the boiling teakettle. "Yes, that's probably what I'll do. Someday. I'll advertise for a position as governess . . . or shopkeeper. What do you think of me selling . . . oh . . . shoes?" She arched one eyebrow. The first thing she had done when she returned from England was to remove her shoes and walk about the house barefoot like a hoyden, something she'd *never* been allowed to do at the Weymouth-Hampstead School.

" 'Tis as likely ye to be sellin' shoes as I am to be dancing at a *ceili."* Grania cackled and rubbed her time-ravaged knees.

Ravenna laughed too and missed her aim at the teapot, sloshing hot water onto the tray.

"But, child, have ye really given serious thought to the future?" The old woman's voice grew raspy as if she were speaking a most pressing thought.

Want and worry crept into Ravenna's eyes. Both she and Grania knew she had to do something with her life, but she couldn't see ever leaving Grania again, for she knew the old woman would probably not live to see her return. Besides, there was indeed something she wanted to do with her life, and she had given it much serious thought, though it seemed an unlikely possibility. Amid the harsh, lonely atmosphere of school, she had turned to living in a fantasy world within her head. It was peopled with beautiful princesses, and knights, and dragons, and sorcerers. At sixteen, she had begun to write some of her adventures down, and now she wanted to keep writing them. She dreamed of having them published, but she was only too aware that any Dublin publisher would accept her only if she were a man, and she had too much pride to submit her works under the false pretense that the author was something she was not. Besides, it infuriated her to think a man's story would be judged better than hers simply because a man told it. She was determined that her writing would be judged by content and not by her sex.

"Ye haven't answered me, child."

She looked up at Grania. Hesitating to speak what could only remain a dream, she murmured, "I told you. I'll most likely go to Dublin and advertise."

"And when will ye be doin' that?" Grania sat in a straight chair, leaning on her blackthorn, her old bones uncomfortable in the worn upholstered armchair.

The fragility of her age made Ravenna ache inside. It wasn't fair to know a loved one only at the end of her years. Grania had lived a whole life that Ravenna could know just a small part of. "I hadn't planned on going so soon. Are you chasing me off?" she teased.

"No, child, it's just that . . ." Grania paused.

"It's just that, what? Have we money problems? If so, I will find work at once. But you must promise to come to Dublin with me."

" 'Tis not work I'm thinkin' of, child. Ye be a grown woman now. 'Tis time to be thinkin' of marryin' and startin' yer own family. Have ye given thought to that?"

"Yes." Ravenna looked away. She thought of marriage often in her tales of knights and princesses. But, as for herself, she tried not to think of it, for she had never fallen in love with a man, and her writings made her yearn for true love, or nothing.

"What have ye thought, child?" Grania stared at her with milky, rheumy eyes, her hand shaking on her blackthorn.

"I'm not going to marry for a while. I've just come home." Ravenna prayed that would be the end of it. She didn't want to discuss the subject. Grania was obviously wanting her taken care of before she died, and Ravenna couldn't blame her for that, but instinctively she knew the subject was volatile. Malachi's name might come up, and she didn't want to risk upsetting her grandmother for nothing. Even she herself knew it was an absurd notion to think of marriage to Malachi. She hardly knew him anymore, letters or no. He was indeed a man now, and they would have to reacquaint themselves. But his name was the only one she could think of when the subject of marriage came up. There was no other whom she could even remotely imagine herself with because she didn't know anyone else. Still, none of that was what made her reluctant to speak of marriage. It was instead the fact that she was determined not to marry until she fell in love. She was a girl from the Weymouth-Hampstead School. She'd rubbed elbows with daughters of the peerage long enough to know that love played little part in determining who was fit for a husband. But in her case, it would be different. She would marry a man she loved. And if she never met that man, then she would go to her grave a spinster.

"Ye've just coom home, indeed, but here ye be talkin' of Dublin. Ye can't go there alone." Grania persisted. " 'Tis necessary to have a husband."

"I—I won't be leaving soon, Grania. Not until . . . not until there's no longer a reason to stay here." Ravenna's lips grew taut as she measured tea from a rusty tin. Her education had been superb, but she still made tea her own way, water in the pot and then the tea, the English be damned.

"Are ye sayin', child, that ye'll be waitin' here until I die? 'Tis a foolish waste of time if ye are." Grania cleared her aged, phlegmy throat and placed a gnarled hand on the cat on her lap. In the years Ravenna had been gone, it seemed there was a whole new crop of cats taking the charity to be offered at Grania's cottage. Ravenna petted the fat brindle, Zelda, still Grania's favorite, and wondered if she was destined to be the kind of woman Grania was, to live in a cottage full of stray cats, to weave her tales for the town's children. And to be called a witch.

Grania suddenly pointed a serpentine finger at her and said with a passion, "I'll not be dyin' soon, Ravenna. Not 'til you're wed and taken care of. There's no doubt about that. I failed ye mother. I'll not fail her daughter."

"You didn't fail Mother," Ravenna said quietly. "She loved my father, I know it."

Grania grew still. "I think she loved him too, lass, but I haven't had a vision givin' me the certainty of it."

"Then enough of this sadness. I've come home. For now we still have our house, and *some* money. There's no pressing need for me to be off to Dublin now. I've taken Trevallyan's punishment and wiped the slate clean. Let's begin anew."

"Ye mustn't think he punished ye. He didn't."

Ravenna didn't answer.

"I sent ye to school of me own free will."

Ravenna still didn't comment.

"I don't want ye to be seein' that Malachi again, now that ye are back. 'Twas one of the reasons the father convinced me to send ye off."

"Malachi had nothing to do with what I did," Ravenna was quick to answer. "I haven't seen him in five years. You can't make me turn my nose up at him if I see him on the street. He's the only friend I've ever had."

"He's a rebel. They say he's running with the White Boys. Ye need to make other friends, Ravenna."

She shook her head. "There aren't any more White Boys, Grania. And I can't make other friends. No decent person in Lir will acknowledge me. 'Tis not worth the trouble to try."

"They've forgiven Brilliana by now. Ye'll see."

THE GROUND SHE WALKS UPON

"No. I don't believe it. And they think you're a witch, and you've done nothing to disprove it. I hear you're still mixing brews and potions and selling them to the townfolk. All the fine English schooling in the world won't make them see me as anything but the witch's bastard granddaughter, a girl born too low to be their equal, and now one cursed by an education that makes her all too aware of such things."

"Ye'll fit in one day. I've seen it."

"How?" Ravenna asked, wishing fervently Grania would tell her, because she could never see such a possibility for herself without leaving for Dublin.

"Just ye wait, me girl. Just ye wait. Now here's Father Nolan a-knockin' at the door. Why, ye best be answerin' it quick before he thinks less of our hospitality."

Chapter 8

A PRINCESS had to be very careful in choosing a knight. There were tall knights, fair knights, and handsome knights, but the tallest, fairest, and handsomest were not always worthy of a princess who had grown weary of worldly, physical things. A noble soul in the body of a gnome was preferable to a fair swain who possessed emptiness in his heart and perjury in his mind. The Royal Princess Skya would have to choose carefully her husband.

Ravenna looked up from her scribblings and breathed in the wild salt air of Lir. She had been home less than a week and already the old ways were taking hold of her. Her feet were bare and dusty. She had hung boiled bed linens to dry in the sun and then unceremoniously plopped down in the fragrant grass and begun to write. A breeze wafted from the sea, lifting her tangled black curls from her nape and blowing them gently from her face as she reread her scrawl. There was a smudge of soot down her nose where she had rubbed it after tending the laundry fire. The trappings of her English education were as abandoned as the puddle of soapy water left to drain down the hill toward the thin blue line of the sea.

She was happy. So happy in fact that only Aidan, her faerie tale prince in shining armor, come to take her to his castle, could have made her happier. The Weymouth-Hampstead School was in the past, Grania's knees were feeling better with the mist gone from the glen, and Ravenna had come home. Bother having friends, she thought, holding her arms out wide to embrace the sight of Lir's four emerald fields. The standing stone was like an old familiar, and her feet were finally free of those stiff, terrible boots. Friends were something she had always longed for, and perhaps always would, but in the meantime, she was home. She had her tales of Aidan and Skya for company, and she told herself with utter conviction that there was nothing more in the world she wanted.

"Why don't ye go for a walk in the glen? Meself, I think I'll sit here in the sun and listen to the wind whip the laundry," Grania said, cackling with delight over a batch of new kittens a neighbor had brought them after having found them abandoned in a roadside ditch. Three kittens clung to Grania's apron and one, a black one they named Malcolm, was nestled on the old woman's shoulder, purring so loudly Ravenna could hear it over the wind.

"Do the deer still bound through the clearing where the violets grow?" Ravenna asked, her English-schoolgirl manners fighting the urge to run free through her old haunts.

"Yes, me child. Go see them. 'Tis been a long time."

"It's a glorious day for a walk." Ravenna paused, wondering what Headmistress Leighton would think of a ramble through the forest unchaperoned. It did seem reckless. She was a young woman now, not a child, but the ache to go was almost a physical pain.

"Perhaps I will go." She tied her hair with a glossy purple-satin ribbon, the best she owned, then gathered her papers and wiped her inky fingers on her apron. She was back in Ireland now; back in her beautiful Lir, the townland that she had dreamed of, longed for, forever it seemed. A morning walk while the dew still clung to the grasses was not the shocking, wanton behavior it might have been back in England.

She took one last look at Grania, who was as content petting her kittens as God was at making time. Gingerly, she brought up the topic she was restless to know more about. "I see the townsfolk are still bringing you their unwanted animals. Don't you fear they may become a drain on the pocketbook?"

Grania laughed while the kitten clung to her shoulder. " 'Tis not a fear of that, me child."

"And why not?" Ravenna asked, staring at the old woman. She could no longer squelch the urge to find out the source of Grania's money. With the fantasy of her father put to death before she had left for England, as an adult she burned to understand.

Grania all at once became sober. "I told ye, my child, the money is from a customer who pays me well for me brews."

Ravenna was cursed with no longer being a child and no longer believing everything she was told. "When I was at school, a stranger sent me a set of silver flatware with the initial R on it. I never told you about my need for it because I didn't want you to spend money on such luxuries. But did you send it, Grania? Do you have so much money that you could afford a set of silver flatware?"

"I heard about the way the girls teased ye. It broke me heart not being there to defend ye. But I didn't send ye the silver, Ravenna. 'Twas not from me."

Ravenna took a deep breath and wondered if she was relieved or only more frustrated. She was sure Grania had sent the silver, even though the old woman might have cleaned the cupboards bare to pay for it. She was so sure, in fact, that before she left London, she'd sold the silver in order to be able to give the money back. But Grania didn't lie, and she was certainly not worried about money. Her grandmother had not sent the silver, so Ravenna had only more unanswered questions. There wasn't a soul in the world she could think of who would send her such an expensive gift. Who was the mysterious benefactor? Had her father left her an inheritance that Grania wouldn't tell her about?

"Money is no concern of yours, Ravenna, and we must not talk about it again."

She stared at Grania, who had returned to playing with her kittens. The old woman was never going to tell her anything about their money. Grania was not the eccentric old biddy without being stubborn.

"I'll be back before the sun is overhead," Ravenna said, wondering how she would ever find out about her father without Grania telling her. Resolving to wheedle something out of Grania soon, she stared at her blind grandmother one last time, then picked up her skirts to leave.

"Go quick on the heels of the hunt, Ravenna."

With those strange words following her, Ravenna left for the glen.

"A fox! The hounds are baying like wolves! Hear them, Trevallyan?" The young lord took a swig from a silver flask, pocketed it, then turned to his host.

Trevallyan sat a black stallion with his usual arrogance. His hunting party numbered seven: two London lords, their personal squires, an Italian duke and a French marquis. All were having a bloody good time, except perhaps Trevallyan himself, who appeared rather bored.

"Go after him, then, Ramsay! By all means, I'd like to see that," Trevallyan said under his breath, giving the young man a rather disparaging look. The morning dew was drier than the young English lord.

"By God, I will!" Ramsay thundered in a burst of bravado. He gathered up his reins and kicked his steed to a full gallop, all the while tottering dangerously in the saddle.

"I give him two minutes before he falls on his arse," Lord Chesham said, ruefully watching his partner bounce off his saddle, then luckily bounce back into it again.

"Cousin, you've more generosity than I have," Trevallyan grunted before he and the rest of the party followed the drunken lord in the direction of the baying hounds.

A deer bounded through the woodland, nearly jumping over Ravenna in its haste to be gone. The sun shone gold on its mottled young coat, and Ravenna felt a swell of pity at the thought that it was no doubt frightened by hunters.

Gathering handfuls of sweet fragrant violets to bring to Grania, she raised the flowers to her nose and lost herself in their innocent scent. It was then she heard the hounds.

They were still far in the distance, howling like the savage dogs they were. She gave little thought to them, knowing that Trevallyan was known to frequently run his hounds, but when the sound came nearer, she felt more and more like the young doe that had white-tailed through the glen. She realized it wasn't good sense to be walking in the woods when the master of Trevallyan was out on a hunt. Anything was fair game. Perhaps even a young woman.

She gathered the last of her flowers and stuffed them into the pockets of her apron. The baying grew louder, the sound a sweep of ice down her spine. They had to be going after a fox, but she had no way of knowing if the fox had crossed her path. If it had, she might be in dire trouble.

Half-walking, half-running, she crossed the grass meadow. Briars snatched at her hem and slowed her down. The dogs' baying grew louder.

"Damn," she whispered to herself, cursing the idle rich, and more pointedly the man she remembered from that strange encounter so long ago. "I'll not let them hunt me like a fox."

Still, she picked up her skirts and ran.

⧖

"Trevallyan! Must be a leash of foxes! I've never heard the hounds in such a frenzy!" Lord Chesham called ahead as he cantered through the woods on his hunter.

Trevallyan, Master of the Hunt, galloped hard in the forefront. His scarlet coat made an easy marker to follow as he tried to gain upon the hounds. But all at once, he brought his mount to a stop.

Leaning down, he pulled a long satin hair ribbon from the broken twigs of a bush. Sternly, he lifted one fine eyebrow and shouted to the men riding up behind him, "Fools, the lot of you! Tis not a fox at all! The damned hounds are off their scent! They're going after a girl."

Lord Chesham nearly pulled his mount up in his surprise. "Why do you say that, Trevallyan?"

Trevallyan gripped the purple ribbon. He whipped his horse on, a grim expression lining his handsome face. "Look down, Chesham. Then pray we are not too late."

Lord Chesham look down. The path was strewn with crushed violets newly plucked from the woods.

Ravenna ran until her heart thumped in her chest and her lungs screamed for air. The pain in her side was like a nail being driven between her ribs. She ran and ran until the briars sliced her feet to bloody, stinging agony, but still she couldn't outrun the hounds that trailed her. The baying grew more hysterical. If she was in the path of a fox, she might be torn to shreds by the bloodthirsty hounds before their master could stop them. And if she was not in the path of a fox, if the hounds had mistakenly somehow begun to track her, then outrunning them wouldn't work. She was doomed.

I am not a fox, you bloody curs! she thought, now knowing how it felt to be the fox, stricken with terror as it ran from a pack of obsessed, flesh-ripping hounds. Her skirts caught in the brambles and her ankle twisted in a depression. She righted herself and ran again, the hounds more quick by half.

Branches whipped at her face and clawed at her clothing. Wild-eyed, she searched for a marker or a telltale tree that would give her an orientation, but she could find none. The forest of her girlhood had changed. She couldn't remember the direction of the nearest cottage.

The baying grew louder and more violent. The first bitch hound nipped at her heels. Screaming, she tried to pull herself up onto an oak, but her skill at climbing trees had long ago been driven away in favor of the less useful skills of making tea and embroidery. She jumped, and got a good grip on the first branch, but in her heavy skirts, she couldn't get a foothold on the tree. Other hounds came streaming into the clearing, yowling like Puritans on a witch hunt. Ravenna kicked at them, still holding on to the tree branch. Another second, all she needed was one more precious second, and she'd be up in the tree.

Panting, she swung her feet to get one of them around the thick oak branch. Dogs leapt at her, their vicious teeth ripping her skirts. Two grabbed a fold of her gown and hung on with their mouths, weighing her down. Others followed. Soon, she couldn't escape. Her grasp slipped on the tree branch. She screamed and fell into the pack.

"Hold hard! Hold hard!" she heard a stern male voice shout from above.

But it was too late. Protecting her face with her hands, she waited for the salivating, tearing jaws to clamp on to her.

Dogs were everywhere, bumping her, sniffing her, their tails slapping her, but none of them bit. One command of their master had turned the rabid pack into a tame, even polite, gathering of beagles.

Stunned, Ravenna took a moment to catch her breath. A hand appeared from the pack of hounds and lifted her gently to her feet. Six men on horses surrounded her, but her gaze, blurred with fearful tears, could hardly make them out.

She brushed a heavy lock of black hair out of her eyes and glared at the man standing in front of her. A jolt of recognition passed through her. It was Trevallyan, of course, for he was the only one in the county who owned hunting hounds. He appeared older than she remembered, but he was still fit and lordlike in his manner. Recognition fired in his eyes also. They had both changed since that ill-fated day she had broken into his bedchamber; she had grown from a child into a woman, and he had gray streaked through his blond hair.

"Ravenna."

The harsh whisper caught her off-guard. There was a strange emotion in the rasp of her name, and for several seconds, she could only stare at him, caught like a spider in the web of his shocked stare.

"What are you doing, walking in the woods alone when I'm running my hounds?" he said, wiping all emotion from his face. His words cut the silence like the rip of a bedsheet.

"I—I—" She suddenly boiled with anger. She had paid her price to

Trevallyan. She owed him nothing now. He might be the ruler of the county. Others might fear him, but she wouldn't. She despised him too much. "I could have been killed by these beasts!" She flung out her hand, gesturing to the dozens of hounds that milled at their feet.

"Such hatred in those eyes." Trevallyan's lips suddenly twisted in a dark smile.

She cast her gaze to the forest floor. She hadn't wanted him to know she hated him. Knowing her hatred gave him a power she didn't want him to have. He could mock her with it, and the emotion was too deep for jest.

She glanced at him through tangles of black hair. She might hate Trevallyan, but she would no longer fear him. He was no terrible ogre, she reassured herself, just a man of flesh and blood, a man with human weaknesses and frailties like her own. She looked at him again, puzzled, and tickled by a new fear she had no experience with, one that seemed to grow with every glance at him. She remembered Trevallyan as an old man. Though he had to be twenty years older than she, he suddenly didn't seem so old anymore. She was the one who had fully changed from a girl to a woman with a will and way of her own, but he was the one who seemed different. She couldn't shake the odd notion that he was actually a fair handsome man, and it beviled her as to why, when she'd been a girl, she'd never noticed how piercing his pale aqua eyes were, nor how handsome and hard his lips were. He was only a man. But the way he looked at her now made her feel more anxious than when she'd been caught stealing in his chambers.

His cool aqua gaze wandered down to her ruined clothing. She'd only worn a rough linen blouse and a dark blue wool skirt and apron to do the laundry. Though not valuable, the blouse was ripped on one side, revealing an expanse of shoulder, her apron was long missing, and her skirt was in tatters, punctured and ripped by canine teeth, dirtied with burrs and stray sticks from her gallop through the woods.

His gaze flickered down to her bare feet. She felt like a street urchin. No doubt he still thought her one. The Weymouth-Hampstead School for Young Ladies had failed, and she didn't know if she was happy about it or chagrined.

"Why were you walking on my land?" he asked, any gentleness in his voice gone.

She gave him a poisonous stare, the kind that made the rotten, hurtful little girls at school run away from her and call her a witch. "Your hounds chased me here. I was not on your property."

"Most of this county is Trevallyan land. If you were here in these woods, you were on my property."

She ached to tell him how unfair it was that he, one of the Ascendency, owned so much land when the Celts were in Ireland first. Instead, she kept her mouth closed and looked down at her tattered skirt.

"Trevallyan," a young man on a steed called to him. Ravenna looked up and saw that he was in a group of men who seemed to be chuckling among themselves. They gave her several raw glances, and she could just imagine the lewd comments they were making about her ragtag appearance and her obviously lower class. Anger seethed within her like a slow boiling kettle.

But then suddenly the young man smiled at her, and it was such a handsome smile she had to fight the urge to return it.

"Your unchivalrous nature is showing, Trevallyan," he said, pushing his mount forward. "If these were my lands and I had such a fair damsel in distress chased down by my hounds, I would invite her to the castle for a syllabub and my apologies." The young man doffed his cap to her. He was a blonder, younger version of Trevallyan, yet without Trevallyan's Irish accent. "The Right Honorable Chesham of Coventry, at your service, my lady. Lord Trevallyan and I are fourth cousins twice removed."

She stared up at the young man, wary of his handsome looks and charm. Hardened by her years of English schooling, she'd believed English lords like the Ascendency were the devil incarnate. Malachi had told her so once very long ago. Never had he said they would look like Adonis.

"She's been struck speechless, Chesham," said another man atop a Thoroughbred, flanked by two young squires. He had a drunken gleam in his eyes, and he swayed in the saddle. "Reginald Ramsay, at your service, fair lady. If Trevallyan will not apologize for his ill-treatment of you, then I shall do so for all the good men of England." He bowed to her and almost fell off his horse.

Her eyes widened. Their pretty words flattered her; made her soften. Like Little Red Riding Hood in a pack of wolves, she looked up at the gentlemen, anxious to repel their charm because she knew all too well they liked to have her kind for supper.

"*Bonjour, mon ange noire. Je suis Guy de la Connive, à votre service,*" a third man said in a forced French accent. He was very dark, extremely handsome, and as Ravenna could see, very much in love with himself. Posing on his horse to give her his best facial angles, he said in flawless English, "Is this what the druids call a wood nymph, Trevallyan? If so, then I am suddenly very much interested in Celtic history."

The fourth man grunted his agreement. He was handsome also, beautiful in truth, the very model of manhood. Even without the poses of Guy, who had made a great effort in his introduction to pronounce his name the French way, "Gee," with a hard G, this fourth man was perhaps the most handsome man she had ever seen.

"Is pleasure to meet you," the man said with an Italian accent that was so thick it had to be authentic. He swept back a long hank of blond-brown hair with a practiced jerk of his head. "Long, long time I ride in wood. Wait for girl look like you."

He paused as if waiting for a reply. She merely watched him, mesmerized by his incredible looks, astounded by his bad, inscrutable English, stumped that such a beautiful male creature could have such a dull cast to his gaze, a reflection, she feared, of the intelligence within. He made her recall the bluestocking wit, Mrs. Fitzherald, who once said, "I'm not fond of handsome men—one always fears they'll be dumb."

"Is compliment to girl," the Italian said, prompting her for more of a response than her awestruck stare. He began to look annoyed, and finally she smiled, relieved. If the Beautiful Creature could feel insulted, then at least he wasn't as dimwitted as she feared.

"This is Count Fabuloso," Guy smoothly introduced. He waved back the tall, well-built count, who dwarfed the stallion beneath him. The two men jockeyed forward as if fighting for position in front of Ravenna.

At these shenanigans, Trevallyan's bad humor seemed to get worse. He said in a contemptuous tone, "Chesham, tell your friends that they needn't fall over themselves to ingratiate themselves with this chit. She's unharmed except for some torn clothing, and she's on her way home where she belongs." He looked at her, waiting for her to leave.

She pulled herself upright and stared him in the eyes. If Grania had taught her the Evil Eye, she would have turned him into stone. "My skirt is ruined, Lord Trevallyan. Your hounds did the damage. As I have paid for my mistakes, so must you pay also. You owe me for the cost of my clothes. I'll not be going until you pay me."

He laughed. A rather dark, nasty sound. "What? You think I carry my gold with me when I go hunting? I'll send Greeves over with some coins tomorrow."

"*Tomorrow,*" she scoffed. "You English aren't honorable with your debts. Everyone knows that."

He grabbed her arm with a grip of surprising strength. "To begin with, I'm Irish," he answered, his voice ominous and hard, "as Irish as you and your kind are. The Celts aren't the only ones who've been here for hundreds of years. Secondly, have no fear I'll pay. No doubt the cost of the shabby clothes you wear is less than I pay my sculleries for an hour's time."

"I might not have your wealth, Lord Trevallyan," she spat, "but if you do not make reparation for this wrong, then I declare you a man without honor." She jerked her arm from his hold. Stepping back, she gave him one last disparaging look before she turned to go.

"Wait!" Lord Chesham called out.

She glanced over her shoulder, her expression one of expected disillusionment.

"Niall, tell the girl we must make reparations for what we've done to her," Chesham announced slyly. "I think dinner at the castle might set her a-rights, what do you think?"

Trevallyan stared at his cousin as if he'd just declared himself mad.

Ravenna stood deadly still and glanced at both men. Chesham's offer of dinner was beyond condescending, especially since she could tell by his manner and the way he and his cronies snickered among themselves when they thought she was not looking that they thought her little better than a scullery from the castle kitchen. Still, it amused her to see Trevallyan put in such a tight spot. To refuse Chesham's dare would make him look like an ogre. To accept was clearly his most despised nightmare.

"What say you, Niall?" Chesham prompted.

She watched Trevallyan seethe. If his reluctance hadn't been so insulting, she might have been amused. Finally, wanting to end the whole affair, she turned to go once more, but Trevallyan's voice, devoid of warmth or grace, rang out behind her.

"You would be most welcome to attend dinner tonight at the castle."

She turned, unable to hide the shock that surely crossed her features. Trevallyan looked as if he'd just been forced to stay an execution he'd been wishing for, but Chesham looked as pleased as a cat before a saucer of cream.

With eyes false and pleading, Chesham said to her, "We would be honored, Miss . . . ? What is your name, fair maiden, if I may ask?"

She blushed to the tips of her toes, feeling like the fool Trevallyan thought she was. Defiant about using a trumped-up last name, she stared at the men and said evenly, "My name is Ravenna."

"Ravenna. Of the black hair. Beautiful." Chesham dismounted, every motion a smooth play of seduction. He took her hand and made a grand gesture of kissing it in front of the others. She knew her face had to be the color of cherries. "I especially would be honored, Ravenna, if you would dine with me tonight."

"You're really overdoing it now," Trevallyan said, his expression filled with disgust.

Ravenna looked at the young Lord Chesham and Trevallyan. Both were blond men, but one had the face of an angel, the other the face of the devil. Trevallyan's anger goaded her to defy him all the more. He was clearly most put out that Lord Chesham had forced him to invite her to dinner. To him, she was nothing but a low-born Irish bastard, just as the Weymouth-Hampstead girls regarded her.

So she *would* eat at the castle, she thought rebelliously. She would take them up on the invitation just to prove to the lot of them that she was good enough to do such things. Despite her birth, she was good as anyone else in County Lir.

Then she thought of Kathleen Quinn.

The exalted Kathleen, with her beautifully-plaited blond hair pinned to her nape. Kathleen, in her sky-blue silk dress, she pictured sitting grandly in the banquet hall of Trevallyan Castle, conversing easily with an English lord. Kathleen would have been accepted by the girls at the Weymouth-Hampstead School. A woman like Kathleen was the kind to have dinner at the castle. Not a misfit like Grania the Witch's grand-daughter.

"I must be going," she said softly, ending the matter. She hadn't really wanted to eat at the castle anyway. Besides, she had nothing to wear but the scratchy wool dress she'd worn to Peter Maguire's funeral, and that was hardly festive enough for a dinner party with the peerage.

"Will we see you tonight? At eight perhaps?" Lord Chesham asked, taking her hand and pulling her back. "I'll have Trevallyan send his coach for you."

"Move along, Chesham," Trevallyan nearly barked. "The girl has declined. She has no business at the castle in any case."

Not her kind, she finished his thought for him. Her violet-blue eyes met Trevallyan's; her own sparked with defiance. "I'd love to have dinner with you, Lord Chesham."

Trevallyan shook his head in despair. Out of the corner of her eye, she could see Chesham's face break out in a grin. The others sat their mounts and watched the proceedings unfold like a match between the Christians and the lions.

"Good. I'll have Trevallyan break out his best cognac for the occa-sion," Chesham purred.

"I'm afraid, Lord Chesham," she said, turning to him, "that your host won't be so hospitable. 'Tis fine to chase the people of this county with his hounds. 'Tis another thing altogether to invite them to take bread at the table of the Ascendency."

Her gaze slid to Trevallyan. She waited for his anger.

He hid it well. Calmly, he faced her, and if not for the wicked light in his eyes, she would have never suspected it.

" 'Tis untrue what you say about me, Ravenna. So come to dinner. Let me prove to you the kind of Ascendency you have in County Lir." His gaze flickered over her figure, lingering restlessly on the blouse that was torn and dirty. He lowered his voice until it was for her ears only. "Yes. Come to the castle. You're no child any longer. Come to dinner. 'Tis time you and I have out with it."

She looked at him, confusion flitting across her face.

Trevallyan began to laugh. The men on their horses danced around them as if they were anxious to be a part of the conversation. Ravenna could take no more.

She lifted her chin and looked straight at Lord Chesham. In her best imitation of the Weymouth-Hampstead haughtiness, she said, "The coach may pick me up at eight."

She gathered her torn and dirtied skirt and walked from the clearing toward the main post road. Refusing to even think of Trevallyan, she stared at her angry white-knuckled fists and filled her mind with pictures of Chesham and his unbelievably handsome cohorts. But then she noticed the gold serpent ring, which she now wore on her third finger. Against all sanity, she began to wonder if Trevallyan still wore his ring and if the two rings were as similar as she remembered. She hadn't noticed his ring in their encounter in the woods, but if nothing else, the night ahead promised there would be ample chance to find out.

Chapter 9

W E WILL be having another for dinner, Greeves. Tell Cook to prepare accordingly." Trevallyan shrugged out of his bath and wrapped his hips with a white linen towel. The night ahead would surely prove tedious, but for some reason he was anxious to see it begin. Anticipation hummed in his veins like a narcotic.

"Is the count bringing in one of his *bambini*?" the butler asked drily.

Trevallyan's gaze darted between the butler and his valet who handed him a bottle-green silk dressing gown. "You've been with me too long, Greeves. You're no longer bothering to hide your sarcasm."

"Pardon me, my lord. When your cousin and his friends choose to descend upon the castle, I'm forced to rise at dawn and ring a little bell through the hallway so the "lady" friends might return to their respective beds. The bell tolls and the bodies run through the hall like rats in a dark alley. 'Tis most distasteful."

"Fabuloso isn't sending for any young women on this trip. On the contrary, the girl is Chesham's guest tonight." Trevallyan's gaze caught his image in the shaving mirror that the valet had set before him. Every line seemed to grab his notice, as if he'd just discovered it for the first time. "The fair Ravenna of Lir is dining with us." He looked away from the mirror and grimaced at the girl's lack of a last name.

"Shall Father Nolan be joining you also?"

Trevallyan shifted his gaze to the butler. "Why would we be needing a priest? You expect me to marry the baggage, too?"

Shock slackened Greeves's features but only for a second.

Niall scowled into the mirror. "I know you used to have a drink or two with the mayor. Did the old gossip tell you tales?"

"My lord, Peter Maguire is dead and not long in the ground. If I may, I think it unwise to speak so of the dead."

"Yes, but did he tell you anything—anything of witches and *geise*?" Disgust crossed Trevallyan's expression.

Greeves cleared his throat and did his professional best not to look curious. "The mayor said nothing of the kind. I only thought you might like Father Nolan to attend because he's been at the castle so frequently since you cried off marrying Lady Arabella."

Trevallyan grew pensive. There was an anger within him that festered. "Number four, Greeves. Lady Arabella was number four." He spoke as if in confession. "Four attempts at love. Four miserable failures. That old priest and his searching of my heart. Love has made my life hell when I might have known bliss. Fine. Go ahead and send a note to the father and have him join us. Let's make this whole evening as rich as possible." He lifted his chin, and his valet lathered his face with soap, soap that blessedly hid the lines.

"Very good, sir." Greeves gave a slight bow, shot the valet a rather bemused look, then departed.

The valet shaved. Trevallyan stared.

Above the white lather, the corners of his eyes were rayed with lines. Two fists seemed to take the knot in his stomach and tighten it without mercy. The lines on his face chronicled time and youth that could never be regained. He would never be a young man again. Hope for a future, a future that became more finite with every cursed year was like the sands in an hourglass, trickling away.

He frowned, and the valet stopped the straight razor just before he cut him. Niall relaxed his face and the valet continued. Yes, he was getting older, but women had never complained. If anything, they seemed to be more attracted to him now that he no longered looked the smooth-skinned youth. Helen, his dead wife, had sought a callow face. She had had designs, and she knew all too well that a man of experience would never have fallen for her schemes. It was scant balm for the bitterness that still clutched his heart, but he took comfort in it. Experience and knowledge, he was convinced, could avert the worst disasters. Without a doubt, if he had been older when he'd met Helen, if he had never been told about the *geis,* things would have been different. Certainly the geography of the grave sites.

Helen and her wickedness had scarred him. With every woman after her, each time he became a little more callous, a little more calculating himself. Happiness eluded him, but it had not been taken away by Helen, rather, she and the women who followed merely made him feel its absence more keenly. Now it howled like a wolf on the moor. He wanted what he could not find.

In his youth, his dreams had been simple. He'd desired children to carry on the Trevallyan name and a woman by his side to share the joy and pain of a lifetime. Even the poorest Ulsterman was not denied such things. Yet by fate or God or *geis,* Lord Niall Trevallyan was. It lay just out of his grasp, in the realm of the unreachable. He knew it would come to him if brought by the right woman. So far she was as elusive as the stars that glittered in the night sky.

He turned his head and allowed his valet to work on his other cheek. There were some who would believe the *geis* had cursed him. He knew the old men of the council would say it began twenty years ago when he spurned their wisdom and married Helen. In their minds, his pain had been the price of defiance. His wounded heart and the mocking little grave next to his wife's—his son's grave by inscription, but not by blood—was almost to be expected for casting aside the powers of fate and the Otherworld.

But still, he would not allow himself to fear the *geis.* Intellect was stronger than superstition. Education more powerful than any belief. His rational mind would not surrender to ancient Celtic nonsense. His failures haunted him, but he knew fear of the *geis* was not what kept him alone. On the contrary, if he believed he was succumbing to such foolishness, he'd have married and married and married to prove it wrong. Certainly there was no dearth of marriageable women around him. In his stable of fiancées, there had been Mary Maureen, honey-haired and sweet-tongued; Elizabeth, a hellion from Galway who had amused him to no end; and finally Lady Arabella, gentle, aristocratic, the kind of woman any man would be proud to have bear his children.

But every time he attempted a trip to the altar, that priest erected the brick wall. Love. Had he loved any of them?

The answer sent a spasm of despair through his soul. It was always no, and he had never been able to escape it, because Father Nolan always demanded he see it. Happiness came through love, the old priest had told him again and again, and Trevallyan now knew it better than most after his disastrous attempts at marriage. When it came right down to it, he had had to concede that he could not will himself to love a woman, no matter how hard the lust for her, no matter how sweet the desire. Now, after so many attempts at marriage, it was not fear of the *geis* that kept him alone and unhappy. No, the fear that clutched his heart went deeper than that. He feared he had no ability to love. The old men would say the *geis* had robbed him of that. They would tell him that it was his fate not to be able to find love for these other women. In their narrow little minds, they would believe that destiny had locked his heart away and the only woman holding the key was the girl the *geis* had chosen for him. For her, he would be able to love. Which, of course, he knew was the crux of the Trevallyan curse. He had to win her love, they told him. If he could win her love, he would be free. And what kind of hell could be worse than to be able to love only one, one who might refuse to give her love in return?

He sighed and closed his eyes. The *geis* and its absurdities invariably made him tired. If he could not love, it was because he had not yet found the right woman. In the evening, melancholy and restless, he would prowl the lonely towers of Trevallyan Castle and think of *her,* the nebulous, imaginary woman he searched for. He was convinced he would know her when she came to him, and, *geis* or no, he knew his love for her would be immediate and acute. And why not? He had waited twenty years for it. For *her*. She had become his hunger, and when he found her, he would devour her as a starving man devours bread.

He looked in the mirror once more. The face that stared back had weathered and matured. It showed capabilities a girl the age of Ravenna could not appreciate. The *geis* was wrought of stupidity. He was a man of forty. He deserved a woman by his side, an equal, not some stupid young girl who could not keep up with him. It was obvious beyond even articulating that the only thing he and a girl twenty years younger than himself could have in common was a bed, and he didn't take young girls to his bed. He wanted more than just a mattress binding them together. A woman could satisfy him where a girl could not.

He studied his eyes where the day's sun had highlighted each crinkle. The girl Ravenna might think him old, especially in comparison to his smooth-skinned cousin and his cohorts, but it made no difference to him what she might think. She was not the companion for him. He shuddered just thinking about her, the barefoot hoyden with her ripped dress and dirty face.

He tapped his foot, impatient to be gone from under the razor. He wanted to clear the name Ravenna from his mind.

But she stayed in his thoughts like a haunting melody.

She was just another young woman, he told himself. A babe in many ways. And yet . . .

His eyes darkened. Today, when he had found her in the clearing, there was something about her that belied her young age. There was a sadness, a quiet dignity, that made her seem older than her tender years. Her demeanor had mystified him because it was so unexpected.

So . . . womanly.

He didn't like it. She lingered in his thoughts like a mystery that begged to be solved. And mystery, he instinctively knew, was a dangerous thing. It was the essence of womanhood. It was the thing that drew a man in, left him aching for each new clue until the snare closed, and he was lost in the maze, seduced, vexed, and yet so deeply grateful to be there. To his intense dismay, Ravenna, the illegitimate girl saved from the tavern and the field by his mercy alone, possessed mystery. It unsettled him.

His jaw tensed. The razor paused once more. He made a conscious effort to relax.

A union between them was unthinkable. He was modern, literate, educated. A thinker. Old men and superstition weren't going to rule his life. And even if he had believed in the *geis* and been deliriously pleased with his chosen bride, it would not work. As a wife, the girl would prove to be a disaster. She was not the kind to marry an earl; her class and her poverty aside, she was much too outspoken, much too defiant. Even as a child she had had that defiance. He remembered it well when he'd caught her in the tower. She'd been less than a grubby street urchin, looking then as she had today, with dirty bare feet and a smudged face. But she'd stared at him with those brilliant eyes, like a vixen caught in a trap, just daring him to try and tame her.

He took in his reflection and the face being slowly uncovered by the hand of his valet. Now the child had grown into a woman. There was no doubt about that, he conceded, reluctantly picturing her as he had seen her in the woods, her blouse torn, revealing womanliness in the fragility of her collarbone, a delicate contrast to the full, plump swell of her breasts.

He closed his eyes, shutting out both the view of himself in the mirror and the vision of her in his mind. He wanted no business with her. She'd spent years at a fine English school, but even they had been unable to wring the Celtic wildness out of her. The baggage was a full-grown woman now, and once more he'd caught her trespassing, barefooted, dirty-faced and brilliant-eyed. The thought of a marriage between himself, the scion of intelligence and refinement, and an untamed Irish peasant was beyond the pale. Too, there was no resolving their difference in ages. The girl was nineteen years old, and he was forty. A tender age wasn't his usual fare at all. That she had grown from a foolish girl into a beautiful woman was of no consequence. She was too young and too inexperienced and too raw-edged to interest him.

He gritted his teeth as the steaming towel was placed on his freshly scraped cheeks. An old anger simmered within him. The *geis* could be damned all to hell. He wasn't about to give in to it. To ask him to win this girl's love was ridiculous. Certainly he could marry her, he could bed her, he could lure her with money and status, but taking a young girl to wife seemed only for those out to prove their manliness and youth, neither of which was in question for him. Love was the only question, and he couldn't imagine it. It was rare if not impossible to find a girl of her years who could truly give her love to a man old enough to be her father. He was not going to ever be able to fulfill the command of the *geis,* and deep down he wondered if he wasn't almost relieved by the futility of it. He'd spent twenty years rebelling against the idea of his courtship with the chit, at great cost if the *geis* were true, he thought grimly, reminded of the two gravestones out in the Trevallyan cemetery. He wanted nothing to do with such ideas now.

The valet lifted the hot cloth. Trevallyan stared into the mirror, again watching his face, but thinking of her.

Thinking of the flat, soulless nights that lay behind him, and lay ahead. He wondered if one day the loneliness would become unbearable. Not finding *her* was a terrible secret fear. That it was inevitable was the worst.

Where were the children and noise and happy confusion he'd once thought his due? Where was the life he longed to have?

Ravenna of the black hair and stunning eyes.

Ravenna of the *geis.*

His scowl deepened.

She was baggage. And she shouldn't be allowed to wander through the countryside without escort. He thought of Chesham and the expression on his cousin's fool face when he set eyes on the girl. Chesham and his lackey friends were going to have to leave tomorrow; he would escort them out with an iron fist if need be. He wasn't going to be responsible for the girl being mauled. Hounds were not the only danger in Lir's fields. He'd been pretty loose about letting his cousin and his cousin's friends come and go about the castle, but only because Chesham was brilliant at the hunt. There was still one passion in the joyless Trevallyan existence, and it was chasing down a fox, galloping through the four fields of Lir as if the devil whipped at his back. But the hunt would have to be postponed, and Chesham and his friends encouraged to return to London. The girl Ravenna might think herself more than capable of taking care of herself, with her flashing, rebellious eyes, but an unprotected girl with no title or family was fair game, and no one loved a chase more than Chesham.

Against his will, Trevallyan again pictured the woman they'd found chased down by his hounds that afternoon. The night of her birth rang as clearly in his mind as if it had been yesterday. The mother, Brilliana, had been beautiful even in death, but it would be pointless to deny that the daughter was more beautiful by half. If in her living days Brilliana had been earthy and sexual, her daughter was the antithesis. It rankled to admit it, but now in his chamber alone with his thoughts, he could be truthful with himself. His first glance at Ravenna that afternoon had taken his breath away. She was beautiful. Unutterably beautiful. So lovely that in his mind she seemed a spawn of the heavens, unattainable and wild as the winds that blew across the *ogham* stones.

The valet used the whisk broom on his shoulders. He was finished. Niall looked at his face to see if any spot was missed. The damning lines had returned. The razor had taken away only the hair.

He stood, and his lips twisted in a smirk. It didn't matter. The *geis* would not rule him. He was beyond it; he was above it. It was inconsequential, and it would stay that way if it took all his strength and reason and will.

In fact, he already found his indifference toward the fair Ravenna a comfort. He wished Chesham luck in his courtship of her. The idea amused him. Despite all his cousin's drawing-room expertise, he had yet to meet a man in all of Ireland who could hold the wind in his palm.

Then a darkness fell upon the land.

It was a time of druids and Celtic sorcery, and Skya's people, it was said, were blessed with magic, but only once in many a generation. Skya knew her grandmother had had the powers, yet, she knew also that magic had become the old woman's curse. Her grandmother had died alone, punished and exiled as a witch by the very peasants who could have benefited from her kindness.

One fine, frightening day, Skya knew she was indeed her grandmother's offspring, for she discovered that she possessed the powers, too.

It started in the Royal Garden. Skya and her sisters were admiring the carved yews, just after the harvest rain. They ran and laughed through the copse and delighted in each other's company. Hiding, Skya fled into the Royal Maze. Her sisters quickly followed, and soon, though they found much humor in it, the princesses could not find their way out. They turned one corner after the next, searching for an exit in the perfectly clipped hedge. But every end was a dead one.

Then the giggles quickly turned to screams. Skya was forced to pick up her heavy velvet kirtle and run to her sisters hidden from her in the yews. She found them huddled in one corner, terror etched on their lovely fair faces. Opposite them, a small blue dragon chewed on the bushes, every now and then spewing fire from its long, pointed mouth to char the branches of the hedge, as dragons do, in order to make them more palatable.

"Save us! Save us!" the girls cried out to Skya.

"Begone, you horrible beast!" Skya cried at the dragon.

Her sisters' screams had gone unheeded, yet at the sound of her voice, the creature looked at her.

Skya stared at the dragon, noting everything about it, in hopes that it might give her a clue as to how to rescue her sisters. The creature kept its head below the hedge-line so as not to be seen by a knight who might slay it. The heavy coat of slime on its back marked it as young and healthy, a terrible curse for those who sought to escape it. Its scales glistened iridescent azure blue beneath the transparent slime. Blue dragons were the smallest and least dangerous. Still, they were quite capable of eating young princesses, and Skya knew if she did nothing, her siblings would perish.

"Begone, you most wretched of creatures!" She stepped forward, thinking that if she could divert it, her sisters might flee.

The dragon inched forward until she could feel the heat of its unlit breath. Terror gripped her, and in a mindless moment of panic, her hands unhooked her chatelaine and swung it over her head in the manner of a ball and chain. "Begone from here!" she screamed, knowing her heavy gold chatelaine was a puny weapon against such a powerful beast. Still, she flung it at him, hoping her sisters could find escape while the dragon turned its wrath upon her.

She cringed when the chain and keys lay upon the dragon's jade-colored nose. The creature would be angered and surely take her in its angry jaws. But then the magic happened.

Sparks flew from her chatelaine and covered the dragon's body. The creature glowed as if on fire. In a second, the sparks were gone. And it was the dragon's turn to cower in the corner of the hedge.

"Wh-what?" Skya murmured, her mind unable to comprehend what had taken place.

"Save us, Skya. Save us," her sisters whimpered from another corner, their blue eyes huge as they watched their sister battle the dragon.

The chatelaine had fallen to Skya's feet. She picked it up and wondered how such a mundane article could hold such powers. Turning it over and over in her hands, she thought to throw it again at the dragon, but the creature appeared to be hurting, and she could see the whites of its eyes as it watched her in terror.

"Begone!" she screamed, hoping it would now flee at just the sound of her voice. She threatened with the chatelaine, but the creature didn't move, it remained cowering in the corner. "I said be off with you!" she commanded with a lordly finger. To her shock, sparks flew from her fingertip and hit the dragon anew. The creature made a growling, hissing sound, then it broke through the hedge and fled.

She ran out of the trampled hedge after it. "Begone!" she screamed, shooting sparks at it as it trundled through one of the kingdom's fields of rye. When it was no more than a speck of blue in the distance, she held her finger in the air and stared at it in wonder, amazed at the discovery of her new powers.

"Witch!"

A cry sounded behind her.

"Witch!" Another came from afar.

She spun around in the waist-height grass and found some of the kingdom's field peasants beginning to surround her, suspicion and fear turning their faces ugly.

"Witch!" they chanted again and again, encircling her as if she were a creature they had hunted down.

Skya looked at the finger she held in the air. One little finger. But it had saved her sisters.

And yet, not herself.

Her grandmother's fate now loomed ahead for her. The peasants feared the powers of the Otherworld more than they feared the king. So the girl that loved to laugh and sing and dance with her sisters would either burn as a witch or choose, as her grandmother did, to live alone in exile for the rest of her earthly years.

Skya stared at the hate-filled features of the peasants. With a mournful realization, she knew that to save her sisters, she had just sacrificed herself as surely as if she had given herself to the fiery jaws of a dragon.

Ravenna put down her pen, wishing desperately that she could remain within the text of her fable. Even Skya's tragedy seemed preferable to the humiliation of what surely lay ahead of her during the evening at Trevallyan Castle.

⁂

"I can't wear this. It's so dark, so . . . dull," Ravenna lamented in the mirror. She wore her old blue wool dress with the black scratchy collar. There was no passementerie on the sleeves, no lace accenting the basque. Nothing but coarse dark wool from neckline to hemline, with no dressmaker's touch to break the monotony.

"When ye return from the castle, we'll have Fiona make ye a really fine gown," Grania told her reflection in the bedroom mirror.

Ravenna spun around and faced her, her expression one of horror. "There's no need for that. I won't be going back to the castle. I'm sure Lord Chesham is only a guest of Trevallyan."

"Mayhap, but I think ye'll be seeing more of the castle with or without Lord Chesham."

Ravenna looked at her grandmother in exasperation. She was only going to this dinner because she'd been foolish enough to let Trevallyan anger her into a quick response. Now she dreaded the evening ahead. It would be so much more pleasant just sitting by the fire, spinning further tales of the Princess Skya. If she relented and went, she knew she'd feel as at home in the Big Lord's castle as a beggar would. It wasn't worth putting herself through the agony of it.

She raised her hands to her nape and unhooked the top hook of her dress. She wouldn't go. It was best. She would tell the coachman when he arrived that she wasn't feeling well and to give her sincere regrets to Lord Chesham for his kind invitation.

Resolved to do just that, she unhooked another hook until she felt Grania's hands on her back.

"Ye must go tonight, child. 'Tis important that you face the lion."

"Trevallyan is no lion," she answered.

"Sometimes lions lie within." The old woman laid her gnarled hand where Ravenna's heart beat.

Ravenna turned around and held her grandmother with all her might. When she pulled away, Grania's tears matched her own.

"I don't want to go. You know I don't, but I can't let him win. He sent me away, Grania. 'Twas a just and deserved punishment perhaps, but I've paid my ounce of flesh. I'll never bow to him again."

"Trevallyan waits. The coach is here."

Ravenna heard the squeal of iron carriage wheels as they halted. She glanced at Grania and shook her head. The old woman's eyesight was poor, but her hearing was excellent, almost as if she heard things that no other person could hear.

" 'Tis Lord Chesham who invited me to dinner, Grania, not Trevallyan. As far as I'm concerned, Trevallyan shall be invisible to me tonight." She stared at her reflection in the mirror one last time, dread filling her bosom. She inspected her hair for stray, unruly wisps, and was relieved to find none had escaped the tight, unforgiving bun at her nape. Still, she was less than pleased with her appearance. Her unfashionable hairstyle had no sausage curls, and the plainness of her gown made her feel bland and grim. There was no gaiety in her appearance at all. The night would be torture, as the years had been torture at the Weymouth-Hampstead School. She would feel churchmouse-poor and shabby.

She should not go.

But she would go, she thought with a gleam of determination in her eye. She grabbed her black wool shawl, kissed Grania on the forehead, and climbed into the lacquered carriage before she lost her nerve. They might laugh at her, but she would hold her head up proudly, as she did in the dark carriage with only the swing of the carriage lamps to cast away the gloom. She would go forth with confidence—not because she fit in at the castle, but because she had to show up Trevallyan. He had tried to belittle her, and she had thwarted him. No one had been more displeased at her acceptance of a dinner invitation than he had that afternoon. She was going to the castle because he had thrown down the gauntlet.

Indeed, she thought, the challenge had been accepted.

Ravenna arrived at the castle a little past eight. The carriage pulled up in front of the lichen-covered entrance to the great hall, where not a torch or lantern burned to welcome her. The driver helped her from the carriage and escorted her to the ancient doors framed by a moldering Gothic arch. Without a warning of her arrival, all at once the doors were thrown open from within, and she met with a rigid, stern-faced butler.

He took her gloves and rigolet with utter efficiency, but she couldn't help think he was an odd sort of fellow to be butler to the Trevallyans. The man was stiff and dignified and possessed a certain English-butler stare that went right past her, as if the fingerprints on the windowpanes were far more interesting than her appearance at the castle. He also had his eccentricities. To begin with, he lacked one arm. She hoped she had done well to hide the shock on her face when she realized the sleeve of his black wool coat was empty, for it was unusual, to say the least, to find a man such as he holding the position of butler. But yet another oddity assailed her. While the man almost pointedly refused to look at her, she could have sworn he *was* looking, for they seemed to be playing tag with their eyes—with the old man looking away at the precise moment she turned her gaze toward him—until she felt cross-eyed.

"Lord Trevallyan awaits, miss. I shall escort you to the drawing room. My name is Greeves." Without further notice, he lifted his fine nose in the air, spun on his heels, and walked away.

"But, if I may, I'm Lord Chesham's guest. Is he here as well?" She watched Greeves's departing back and wondered if he was deaf, too. He exited at the far end of the chilly stone hall, and she realized she didn't dare stay behind. If she was forced to go looking for the party on her own, she'd no doubt become lost in the castle's endless number of rooms, as she had so long ago in her unfortunate search for Trevallyan's bedchamber.

"How far is the drawing room?" she asked, nearly jogging to keep up with the tall man's strides. They traversed several dark and chilly passages in their quest for the "festivities"—if such could be had in such a gloomy environment—while Ravenna clasped her shawl to her bosom, suddenly glad for the somber, yet warm, wool dress.

"Not far now, miss."

At that, Greeves stopped by a pair of polished mahogany doors executed in the neoclassic Adam style, a decor toward which she had little goodwill since it reminded her of England.

"Here, miss." Greeves discreetly opened one door. The drawing room beyond looked more dark and uninviting than the medieval stone passageway. The hearth was ablaze, and two candles were lit on the mantel, but they were all ineffective in lighting the enormous cavern of the room.

Ravenna stared at the butler, unsure of what to do next. Greeves motioned her inside with his one good hand. Mutely, she strolled into the room, forcing herself to display self-confidence she most assuredly did not feel, but her upright posture crumpled the moment the butler closed the door behind her and left her alone in the semi-dark.

"Hullo? Is there anyone in here?" she whispered to the dark corners. Scarlet drapery loomed like monsters beneath gold cornices. Two gilt gryphon firedogs gleamed in the sputtering firelight, their evil shadows stalking the door from which she entered.

She shivered and hugged herself. The evening was certainly not turning out as she had planned.

A settee covered in pale gold damask stood near to the fire. She took a seat, but was too nervous to wait complacently until someone came for her. There was a jib door to the left of the mantel, and she wondered if maybe she could find a servant who might help her locate Lord Chesham.

She stood and procured one of the gold candlesticks to light her way. Walking deep into the shadows toward the dark rectangle of a door, she wondered how foolish she would look if she, a guest, did come upon a servant. Willing to take the chance, she felt along the edge of the door for a catch, then realized the door was like those in England. Giving it one good push, it popped open, revealing, to her disappointment, no servant's room, but a musty old stone staircase.

She lifted the gold candlestick and assessed the discouraging amounts of cobwebs. It was a servant's stair, barely lit with gaslights, most likely leading to the kitchen from the keep. She heard a noise, a rather faraway giggle coming from the bottom of the shaft, and she debated whether to call down.

"Looking for my bedchamber?"

She nearly dropped the lit candle. Turning, she looked up the steps and found Trevallyan in the dimness, his face nose to nose with hers as she stood on the step.

" 'Tis right upstairs. How canny you are, Ravenna, to remember."

"I—I *most certainly* was not looking for it," she stuttered with all the indignation she could muster.

He took the trembling candlestick from her hand and pondered it. "Why is it I always seem to find you skulking around my castle with my possessions in your hands?" He held the candlestick up to her, his eyes a crystalline sea-blue in the flames. "I see your judgment has grown better. This candlestick is solid gold. Much more valuable than my hair."

"I was not stealing it, I assure you," she answered, her anger taking away her fear. "Your butler left me all alone back there in the drawing room and I thought to find a servant who could direct me to my host, Lord Chesham."

"I am your host."

She leaned slightly back, uncomfortable with Trevallyan's proximity. "Lord Chesham invited me. Not you."

"But I . . . let you come." The ghost of a cynical smile touched his lips.

She fought the urge to scratch it off. "Then your generosity is only outdone by your arrogance." Ire prickled like heat on her cheeks. "If I may ask, where is Lord Chesham and your other friends?"

"The count and de la Connive are no friends of mine. I tolerate them only because Chesham brings them along and I find it hard to contain my cousin." He looked at her a moment. His words seemed to have grave, personal meaning. "You see, I let him run a little wild here because I have very little family left."

She held his gaze, unable to shake the notion that somehow he was referring to her. Slowly reason returned. "I—I really don't understand why I was brought to this dark, abandoned room if no one is here."

His smile grew a little more wicked. "It seems Greeves has played a prank on us. He knows well enough that in small groups, we gather in the parlor."

"That is not the parlor?" She looked behind her to the exquisite room in shadows.

"That is the drawing room."

"Oh. Of course." She said nothing else, not wanting to look foolish.

"My butler is prone to shenanigans."

"But why would he do such a thing? You could fire him, and the poor man can ill afford to be out a job with his . . ." She frowned. "His affliction."

"He knows I would never fire him." Trevallyan looked at her, his gaze warming in the flickering shadows. "My father brought him to the castle in 1803 when he was still a young man. During Robert Emmet's United Irish rising in Dublin some hard men tried to pull Father from his carriage. Greeves, a bystander, tried to save him. He was shot in the attempt. He lost his arm only because he had helped my father. How do you fire a man like that?"

"I suppose you don't," she whispered, mesmerized by the lord's stare. "Instead you live forever at his mercy."

"Exactly. But we're all at someone's mercy—or some*thing*'s—aren't we?"

She looked into his eyes. Strangely enough, she found no mockery there—only pain—and it bothered her. The pain seemed to carry an accusation.

"I really must find Lord Chesham," she said, her voice low and husky in the intimacy of the darkness.

He nodded, and she felt a rush of relief. It wasn't quite the thing to be a lone woman, standing in an abandoned staircase with the master. She suddenly recalled Sadie, the kitchen girl at the school. Sadie had had one too many visits alone with the stable boy. When she'd been caught, the girl had been summarily dismissed, and later, Ravenna had seen her on the streets, miserable and poor, carrying a newborn babe. The girls had been forbidden to even acknowledge her, but Ravenna's heart had gone out to the poor creature. When she had returned to school, she had scraped together every coin she could find, tied it in a handkerchief, and given it to the cook for Sadie. Days later, Ravenna had gotten a message dictated by the ill-fated scullery thanking her for the coins. Mrs. Leighton, the headmistress, had found it in the waste-bin and had become so incensed that Ravenna had had contact with "the harlot" that she had been jailed in her room for three days without visitors or food.

Now it seemed like a bad dream, but when it had happened, it had been all too real. And the man ultimately responsible for her being there at the school to see such sad tales stood next to her, looking at her for all the world as if she were a stranger to him, not his most bitter enemy.

"I really must find Lord Chesham," she said, her cool words chasing away the intimacy brought on by the shadows and close quarters. "Please. I must ask you to show me to him, or show me the door. I didn't come here to see your empty drawing room."

His eyes noticed her sudden chill, but his expression remained implacable. "Of course. Let me take you to Chesham. He's waiting, no doubt, with bated breath." Abruptly, he grasped her hand and pulled her off the staircase. He shut the jib door with his foot and led her to the mantel, where he replaced the gold candlestick.

She was so stunned to find his hand wrapped around her own that for several unnerving seconds, she couldn't speak or withdraw it. He glanced down at her in the light from the hearth, and she was further shocked to realize that the cold, black-hearted villain of her youth had a most warm, dazzling smile when he wanted to show it.

"You're not what I expected, Ravenna," he said softly, looking right into her eyes. "I have to admit, you've become quite different than I imagined."

"What did you imagine?" she nearly gasped, she was so unbalanced by his strange talk.

"I suppose I imagined you'd be more dismissable. More common. Like your mother."

"You—you knew my mother?" she stuttered, his insults as yet unable to penetrate her shock.

He shook his head. "Not really. I just have an idea how she was and I pictured you that way as well, especially when I found you in the field today, so messy and wild. But now I wonder if you're anything like Brilliana. Perhaps the English school did a good job after all. In many ways, one would find you almost demure. If I didn't know the circumstances of your birth, I'd think you were a lady."

Her earlier numbing shock dissipated like a wisp of smoke. She was left instead with hurt and indignation. She stared at him, hatred burning anew in her breast. Against her better judgment, she let her venom rule her tongue. "You think me not quite a lady, Lord Trevallyan? Then I say you're a fool who cannot see the difference. The girls at the Weymouth-Hampstead School—the gaol to which you sentenced me —were of fine and noble birth, but their souls were shallow and their hearts were cold. If you cannot see such things for what they are, then I pity you."

She tugged her hand to rip it away from his, but he didn't surrender it. Infuriated, she lowered her gaze. She wanted to wound him further by leveling a contemptuous stare at their entwined hands, their unholy union, but to her dismay, she found his serpent ring winking up at her in the firelight, right against her own ring. It was indeed as she had thought: They were identical. The Trevallyan adder.

A moment of stunned silence passed. Their joined hands seemed to draw Trevallyan's attention as well and with a disturbed expression on his face, he, too, gazed down at their matching rings.

By the repressed anger flashing in his eyes, she fully expected him to accuse her at last of stealing the ring from the Trevallyans. She hoped with all her heart that she could summon Father Nolan to verify her story that it came from him, but, strangely, Trevallyan said nothing. The sight of the duplicate rings seemed to upset him. It was he who pulled his hand from hers. He who retreated in anger.

"Lord Chesham awaits," he said matter-of-factly, though his expression said something altogether different. "At the end of the passage turn left, then right. The parlor doors are open. You cannot miss it."

"You're not coming?" she asked, taken aback at how quickly he had twisted the situation. She was the one who had readied herself to pull away, yet he had rejected her. She stared at him, and it was on the tip of her tongue to ask about the rings, but by his stiff demeanor, she knew he would answer no questions.

"I'll be there in a minute. There is some business I want to attend to with Greeves."

She suddenly wondered if the butler was indeed beyond firing. One thing was certain, the noble Greeves was not above a good dressing down by the master, and she'd bet by the look in Trevallyan's eyes that he was about to get one.

"To the left and then right?" She watched him as if he were a little mad.

"Yes. That's right. Go now, before . . ." His words dwindled. He looked at her for a long, intense moment, then he said, "Just go."

She clutched her black shawl to her chest. The room had suddenly grown frigid. It was a pleasure to leave it.

Chapter 10

RAVENNA! THERE you are! We were just about to give up on you and kill ourselves over our disappointment."

Lord Chesham walked from the brightly lit parlor into the gloom of the passage. Ravenna stood in the shadows, unsure how to greet him.

Chesham looked handsome in evening dress—he wore a white barrel-knot tie and a dark blue frock coat that was the perfect backdrop for his blond Adonis features—yet even his warm smile and proffered arm couldn't erase the picture of Trevallyan from her mind, of him staring at their rings. The intensity of it seemed to stay with her like a clinging, invisible cobweb, disorienting her even now.

"Look what I've found wandering in the passage," Chesham announced, not waiting for her to properly greet him. He escorted her into a parlor that seemed to her to be decorated in Ireland's forty shades of green. The windows were hung with lush pea-colored drapery, and the floor was almost completely covered by an emerald-colored turkey-work rug. Horsehair-upholstered chairs and velvet settees were made for sitting and

appeared well-worn. In short, the parlor was a far cry from the calculated coldness of the drawing room. It was a little mismatched and
worn, and she felt better being in it.

Count Fabuloso and Monsieur Guy de la Connive stood near the
pianoforte, each with a glass of cognac in manicured hands. They
bowed to her and quickly assumed their most flattering poses. The
count was a giant in a pale blue cut-in dress coat that fit to his every
bunched muscle. Guy was in dove-gray, calculated to match his eyes.

"Let me pour you a refreshment, Ravenna. Now where is Greeves?"
Chesham commented, for Greeves was not in the room.

He deposited her on a plump velvet couch and stepped to the
mixing table. She watched as he poured her a much-too-healthy
sherry.

"Here you are, my dear." Chesham smiled and handed it to her.
"And I want to say that is a lovely gown you are wearing. . . ." His
gaze dropped so quickly to her bosom she almost thought she imagined it.

"Thank you," she said, a little out of breath, unsure if "thank you"
was really the proper response to that stare.

She took a sip of the sherry and found Guy sitting on the couch next
to her, his gaze filled with practiced poetry.

"Ah, the fair Ravenna . . . as glowing in candlelight as in the
morning's first dew." He took her hand and kissed it. His mouth was
hot and moist in her palm, and the sensation was not unpleasant, but
when he struck a pose as if waiting for her to sigh, she forced herself to
stifle a giggle.

"Butler take long, long time to bring girl." The count broke in, vying
for her attention.

"He's a cunning little fox, that Greeves is. Knows just how to fix
things."

Until he spoke, Ravenna hadn't even realized Lord Reginald was in
the room. He winked at her from in a faded, centuries-old needlework
chair.

"What do you mean by 'fix things'?" she asked, uncomfortable in the
crush of men. "He escorted me to the wrong room and, if anything,
made a muddle of things."

Ramsay's face held a secret smile. "Lord Trevallyan . . . where is he? Our host is certainly amiss in his duties tonight. 'Tis a crime he should be absent from such beauty."

Against her will, Ravenna blushed. She wasn't used to such bald compliments, nor did she consider herself a beauty. Kathleen Quinn was a beauty. The girl was fair as an angel, refined as a queen. In contrast, Ravenna was doomed to be Kathleen's antithesis. She was as dark in appearance as she was in temperament, and no matter how the Weymouth-Hampstead School had tried, her manner was still untamed. Brilliana's blood had proved stronger than the whip.

"The host is absent no longer," Trevallyan remarked from the door.

Ravenna turned. She didn't want to stare, but it seemed as if she were powerless not to. When Niall Trevallyan stepped into a room, he conquered it, overwhelmed it, made it submit; indeed, his sharp, condescending gaze could force a king to feel inadequate. She didn't want to stare at him, but she damned herself and submitted to the urge anyway. And then swallowed the humiliation when he did not return her gaze, nor acknowledge her.

"We were just speaking of beauty, Trevallyan," Lord Reginald prompted, ever the irreverent, "so give us your views on it. Ravenna already knows mine."

Trevallyan walked to the crystal decanters and poured himself a cognac. He glanced at the count and Guy, then seemed to ponder something for a moment. "Of beauty, only one burning question comes to mind: Does the count believe he is more beautiful than Monsieur Connive, or vice versa?"

Ravenna nearly choked on her sherry.

Guy appeared annoyed and the count confused, as if someone had just bashed him over the head.

"You're in a fine temper tonight, cousin," Chesham remarked, irritation etched on his face.

"In a temper? On the contrary. I'm feeling as benevolent as ever." Trevallyan turned to look at his guests, but he seemed to make a point of not gazing at her, wounding her further. She knew he didn't think her good enough to dine at the castle, and it seemed his solution was to treat her as if she were invisible.

"Does that benevolence extend to dinner? I'm famished," said Father Nolan who appeared at the door escorted by Greeves.

Ravenna shot the father a dazzling smile. Suddenly she felt she was in much better company. Father Nolan had never made her feel less than good enough. She was heartened when the priest clasped her hand in greeting.

"Yes, let's have dinner." Trevallyan's gaze swept the room, still pointedly missing her. "Are we ready?"

"And who shall have the honor of escorting Ravenna to the table? Or do we joust for her?" Lord Reginald taunted.

"I have the honor for 'twas I who invited her," said Chesham, holding out his arm for her to take it.

"The jousting has been done, Chesham. I am the host of this gathering. It's my responsibility to escort my guests to dinner." Trevallyan's voice brooked no argument.

Still without meeting her gaze, Trevallyan stepped to the couch and held out his hand. The ring gleamed on his small finger. Ravenna's heart hammered in her chest.

She was insulted and flattered in the same breath. That he could treat her as invisible, then demand the right to escort her to dinner seemed the behavior of a lunatic. And she was as much a lunatic as he, because all she wanted him to do was give her just one look of the admiration that the other men poured upon her like sweet wine, and she would have gladly allowed the blackguard to escort her to dinner.

"Ravenna?" His gaze locked with hers. A long stare that ran the gamut of emotions from confusion to near hatred, crushing her inexplicable desire to gain his admiration.

Manners dictated she should not refuse him, so slowly she forced herself to place her hand in his. The warmth of his grasp shocked her, but the hardness didn't. He made it painfully clear he didn't want her at the castle, and suddenly she had the urge to run home and never return.

He helped her to her feet. She smiled woodenly and took his offered arm, counting the minutes when the dreadful ordeal would be over and she would never have to see the master of Trevallyan again.

The small eating room was done in shades of puce, Prussian blue, and gold. Dinner was course after course of culinary ecstasies. Footmen brought in platters of pheasant, beef, and peacock until Ravenna could hardly bear to look at them. Trevallyan, his cousin Chesham, and Chesham's cohorts seemed unimpressed with the presentation and the amount of food, but Ravenna was beside herself with delight, remembering all the terrible meals she had had back in London. Father Nolan was none too apathetic, either, for she could swear he was on his third helping of trifle.

Conversations with Ravenna confined themselves to ingratiating flattery from Guy or thinly veiled ribald comments from Lord Reginald. Father Nolan attempted to lead them in a discussion of the New Testament. Trevallyan said hardly a word. She did her best to ignore him, yet when the meal was through, and she and the gentlemen returned to the parlor for cordials, she couldn't help but steal glances at him.

Trevallyan stood out from the other men like a stag with a full rack of antlers stands out in a group of young bucks. Yet his presence was more subtle than that and she found she had difficulty defining what it was about Niall Trevallyan that captured her attention. He did not tower over the other men; rather, he was of a good, but average size; and his face, while handsomely wrought, was certainly not as classic-Greek-god-beautiful as the count's or Guy's. Where the count, and Guy, and Lord Reginald wore fashionable white cravats, Trevallyan wore an old-fashioned black one. His vest was not a riotously-colored paisley, it was a somber maroon watered silk. The blush of youth was gone from his face, but perhaps that was what made it arresting. Unlike younger men, the exuberance of stupidity and ignorance didn't hold him in its newborn clutches. With every line on his face, every gray streak of his hair, he stood as a man fully matured, resonating depth. And when she looked into his eyes, she seemed to find a soul even older than his physical self, a man burdened with some kind of inexpressible tragedy, a man pressed by his own mortality. Yet, a man who seemed to understand life as it really was, one who seemed ever more capable of exposing its wonders and limitations than someone of lesser years. All that, Ravenna found when she watched him. And though she wanted to give her attention to Father Nolan, or even Guy, Trevallyan drew her interest even now, as he lounged by the mantel, his preoccupation with some dark thought leaving his cordial forgotten in his hand.

"Ravenna, how have you hidden from my notice all these years?" Lord Chesham said, breaking into her thoughts.

Her gaze darted from Trevallyan upon the dread notion that he might catch her staring. "I've been in England for many years. I left Lir when I was barely thirteen and have not returned since." She hoped she hid the pain in her voice. It wouldn't do to make a gift to Trevallyan of how much he'd already been able to hurt her.

"Ravenna received her education from one of the finest ladies' schools in London," the priest interjected from his seat closest to the hearth.

"London! Huzza! My favorite place!" Chesham brightened. He took her hand and kissed it as they sat on the settee next to the hearth. "And when will you return to England?"

"Never, I should think." She glanced at the father, perhaps a little accusingly. "I'm planning to go to Dublin at some point. Perhaps to find a job with a milliner."

"A *job*? In *Dublin*?" Chesham drew back in mock horror. Even the count was able to rouse himself to stare at her in disbelief.

"My dear sweet girl, surely it isn't necessary for you to leave Lir to go to Dublin to *work*. Whatever would become of you?" Chesham stared at her with such genuine concern in his eyes she was almost touched.

"Lord Chesham, I must make my way in this world, and when Grania dies, my ties to Lir will be no more." She smiled and extracted her hand from his hold. She'd had enough of hand-holding already this evening.

"But that's unheard of. A fine, educated lady like yourself lowering herself to a job in Dublin." Lord Chesham took her hand once more. His eyes twinkled with mischief. "Perhaps I can find you another occupation. Right here in Lir."

It was on the tip of her tongue to ask exactly what kind of "occupation" he meant, when he blurted out, "Or better yet, mayhap I should marry you and make you a baroness!"

Father Nolan gasped and the blood drained from his face. But he seemed the only man in the room able to take the idea seriously. Even the count tittered with laughter. Chesham's comment was so ridiculously false, it was an insult to her intelligence. Still, she bit her tongue to kill her acerbic answer. It wouldn't do to ruffle the feathers of a powerful man, even if she was never to see that man again. "You jest, Lord Chesham," she said calmly, hardly able to look him in the eye without showing her loathing. "I can't be your baroness. You hardly know me."

Chesham laughed. Her play-along seemed to amuse him to no end. "But I would very much like to get to know you better," he whispered for her ears only.

She glanced at him, bemused and irritated by his display. Trevallyan stared at both of them from the mantel, and she could tell by his expression he thought they were behaving worse than fools.

"I'm very flattered, Lord Chesham, but—"

"You must let me call on you. You can't leave for Dublin. Not now, when I've all the world to show you." The earnest expression in Chesham's eyes took her aback.

"Why, how flattering," she murmured, unsure of what to do next. She desperately wanted to leave, but could find no exit. Lord Chesham waited for some kind of answer while she rested her attention on the green damask of a nearby chair. It was an awkward moment. The idea of a courtship might intrigue her if it had come from any man in the room but Chesham. She then glanced at Guy and the count, and threw them in as well. It was a revelation to realize that it would be better to be courted by Reginald Ramsay or Father Nolan than these three fops. Her gaze then darted to Trevallyan. He didn't look at her, and he made her wonder how she would regard a courtship from him.

"Why are you so quiet, my lovely lady?" Chesham whispered in her ear.

She colored forty shades of red to counter the green in the room. Lord Chesham was in no way unattractive. He was a young version of Trevallyan, though Chesham had to be ten years older than herself, and Trevallyan had to be ten years older again than Chesham. Logically, she could see the advantages in having a man like Lord Chesham court her. So why did she wonder what Trevallyan thought of Chesham's offer?

And, worst of all, and most mysteriously, why on earth did she even care?

"Shall I post the banns?" Trevallyan asked dryly, contempt mirrored in his eyes as he still leaned against the mantel, not two steps from where she and Chesham sat.

"Forget the wedding, Chesham, and move right along to the honeymoon," Ramsay interjected drunkenly.

"My son, get hold of your tongue!" Father Nolan exclaimed.

Trevallyan shot Lord Reginald a glance that should have killed the young sot right where he stood.

A thousand deaths were preferable to the blush that crept up her cheeks. "I really should go now. . . ." She glanced at the velvet bellpull near Trevallyan. "Would someone please ring Greeves to see me out?"

"Don't go. . . ." Chesham pleaded softly.

"My grandmother is an old woman. I can't leave her alone much longer," she lied, knowing full well that Fiona was staying with her. She gave the father a piercing stare, praying he wouldn't contradict her.

He didn't.

"Is the evening over so quickly?" The priest put his empty cordial glass down onto a table. "Would you like an escort home, Ravenna?" he asked.

She stood, and watched the gentlemen follow her lead. "Very much," she said, relief in her voice.

"Then it is my pleasure." Father Nolan smiled.

She said her farewells in the parlor doorway. Trevallyan growled something incoherent to Father Nolan, then he mysteriously disappeared, wounding her again with his rudeness.

But there was always Chesham for flattery. He kissed her hand again and again, then his mouth brushed passed her ear and whispered, "Meet me tonight in the back staircase and we can finally be alone."

She must have hidden her revulsion well, for Chesham neatly stepped away and allowed Monsieur Guy to pose in front of her. Deep down, she was probably angry that Lord Chesham believed her so stupid and foolish as to desire an intrigue with him, but she didn't feel angry. It was no surprise what he thought of her. How could he think well of her when his cousin Trevallyan made it clear she was nothing but rubbish, not even worthy of a decent send-off after being invited to dine at the castle.

The count grunted farewell, and Greeves appeared in order to show her to the great hall. Ravenna followed the butler, glad to be rid of the evening's company forever. She wouldn't be meeting Chesham in the back staircase or anywhere else; it had been an insult to ask her. Though she'd been taught well in England how to hide her feelings, the men had raised her ire. Still, she wouldn't waste her emotions on them. All she really wanted to do was go home and never see any of them again, especially Lord Niall Trevallyan.

Nonetheless, she departed the drawing room with a lump in her throat. It hurt her to think that Trevallyan thought so little of her presence that he failed to give her a proper good-bye. He had so rudely exited that she hadn't even been able to thank him for the dinner—not that she had wanted to thank him—but the fact that he didn't even bother to wait for thanks irrationally wounded her.

"The master will see you in the library, miss," Greeves said as she and the father entered the great hall.

"Are you speaking to me, Greeves?" she asked, taken aback.

"Yes, miss. Lord Trevallyan would like to see you in the library. Father, may I serve you a whiskey while you wait?" Greeves bowed to Father Nolan.

"Why, certainly, certainly!" Father Nolan said, taking a seat on an Elizabethan bench by the castle's enormous doorway.

She looked at the priest, wondering what had gotten into him. A man was requesting her presence alone, and the priest was not even offering chaperonage.

"Miss?" Greeves repeated, with increasing superiority.

She stole one last glance at Father Nolan. He merely smiled at her and waved his hands in a motion that said, "Run along with you, child, and *whenever* you should return, I'll be here waiting."

As before, Greeves strode through the great hall, expecting her to follow. With no other choice, she lifted her skirts and walked at a quick clip to keep up with him. The library was only two doors from the great hall. A room warm and slightly shabby like the parlor.

"Greeves said you wanted a word with me before I leave," she said to Trevallyan who sat staring at the fire.

Greeves departed, closing the mahogany library doors firmly behind him.

"Yes. Have a seat."

She bristled. Trevallyan hadn't even stood up at her entrance. She cursed an education that made her desire courtesies that were not given those of her class. He thought her a lowly peasant, and that was all he would ever think of her; still she wouldn't let him treat her like one.

"I should like to stand." She had just the right amount of ice in her voice to draw his attention.

His looked at her, but with a strange, unexpected emotion in his eyes. "Contrary to the end, aren't you, Ravenna?"

She refused to comment.

His laughter was a black, brittle sound. "You stand there in your sorry little gown, looking like a wallflower with no gentleman to sign your dance card, but still you think to challenge me, don't you?" He rose to his feet and took a menacing step toward her. "*Sit down.*"

She wanted to refuse again, but one look at him told her it was pointless. For whatever the reason, he was in a foul mood. It was best to get this business done with and leave the castle with a minimal skirmish.

"What is it you desire to speak to me about, my lord?" She lowered herself to the proffered seat.

"I want to give you a few lessons." His voice was tight with anger. "The first is that you are never to go walking in the woods unescorted again. You were lucky I found you when I did. Something terrible could have happened to you all alone in the forest and—"

"Lord Trevallyan, if I may remind you: The only terrible thing done to me in those woods was the fact that your hounds—"

"That is not the kind of tragedy I am trying to avoid here!"

His shout set her back on her heels. She had never seen a man so angry. "What kind of business is this of yours?" she whispered incredulously.

His eyes flashed with annoyance. "You're a young and beautiful woman now. What do you think a man would do to you if he found you alone in the woods one day?"

She stared at him, her heart beating heavily against her ribs. "I—I suppose he would do what you did when you saw me there."

His grim gaze held her. "I am no ravisher of women. I cannot speak for every man in this county."

"You imply the men of this county are untrustworthy, but what you speak of is a 'gentleman's' problem. Are you accusing Lord Chesham of—?"

"Lord Chesham is my cousin. My own blood relation. But you take him and his group of dissolute friends and put them in a certain kind of mood, throw in a poor, helpless girl like yourself . . . and I cannot say what would happen."

Though she gave no signs of it, she agreed with him about Chesham. Lord Chesham's offer to meet in the scullery was an insult and an affront to her intelligence. Yet, the very thought that Trevallyan believed she needed this lecture was only further insulting. Her simmering anger came to a boil. "What you say about your cousin may be true, but let me correct you on one point, my lord," she countered, lifting her chin. "I am not helpless."

His eyes lowered to her petite, shabbily adorned figure. He was not a giant of a man; still she knew he was thinking even he could overcome her should he ever want to. The message in his gaze was quite clear.

"Why do you make this your concern?" she asked, the look in his eyes making her suddenly desperate to change the subject and even more desperate to leave.

"I am saying this for your own good, you foolish girl."

She stood. "Fine, then. You have said it. Now if that is all—"

"No, that is not all." He stared her down with that unnerving aqua gaze. "Sit down."

Her bottom hit the leather seat once more. She almost hated him. "Are you angry over Lord Chesham's attentions? Is that what this is all about? If so, you needn't be. I have no designs upon anyone in your family as I'm sure you would laugh at the folly of it if I did. So let me assure you that I will be happy to refuse Lord Chesham's call, should he make one—which I don't believe he will."

"He can get you one way or another if he tries hard enough," Trevallyan snapped, then glanced away, as if he were hiding something even from himself. "Lord Chesham is smitten. Even I can see that. But I warn you: Any impropriety will not be tolerated."

Aghast, she just looked at him with wide, disbelieving eyes. His insults went beyond the pale. "Is it because I'm poor that you think I've no honor, no self-respect? Poverty is not synonymous with impropriety, my lord. And only a wretch would think so."

"You misunderstand—"

"No," she said solemnly, cutting him off. "Your meaning really doesn't matter." She stared at him, hurt and confusion written on her face. "Why is this your concern? You aren't my guardian. You aren't my father. My actions don't reflect on you, yet you lecture me as if you have all the right to do so. And you dare to insult me by implying that my behavior might be disreputable. Apologize this instant."

He looked at her as if he couldn't quite believe what he was hearing. Anger crossed his face, clearly a common emotion with him, but another one filled his expression too. It was almost a begrudging respect.

"You may go to the devil, my lord." Hearing no apology, she stood and walked to the door, eager to be gone.

He stopped her, capturing both her arms and holding them in a viselike grip to her sides. "You misunderstand, Ravenna. 'Tis not *your* impropriety I speak of. You've led a rather sheltered life. You're thoroughly alone in this world and you have no guardian. It's not uncommon for an English peer to make free with Irish girls, as you may well know. Any man might be tempted to interfere with you, given the lack of reprisals."

"But there are reprisals! There is the law—"

He shook her until she was silent. "Did the law help your mother? Would you turn out like her? Have you the desire to whelp a bastard like yourself?"

His cruel words sliced her. Tears sprung to her eyes. "What concern is this of yours? Is this only to hurt me? Why do you want to hurt me?"

"Nay, I don't want to hurt you," he whispered. "It's just . . . just . . ."

"What? That you want me gone from this castle and never to cross the Trevallyan path again? Well, I tell you, 'tis done. Tell Lord Chesham I refuse his call. Someday soon I must be making plans to go to Dublin, and I cannot be bothered with him."

The grip tightened on her arms. "Don't you learn, Ravenna? Don't you hear what I'm telling you? You can't go to Dublin. You're a woman alone, unprotected. There's no one to watch out for you in Dublin."

"*I* can watch out for myself," she volleyed.

"You?" he spat incredulously. "You have no relations in Dublin and no means by which to keep yourself. You'll be forced to lodge in some tenement with no lock on your rooms . . . only to wake one night to find a strange man hovering over your bed. Robbing you of what he would have to pay for elsewhere. . . ."

She wished he'd let her go. She began to tremble in spite of the fact that she wanted to show a brave front. "You are not my benefactor, nor my guardian, Lord Trevallyan. I don't have to stay here and listen to these tales." His intensity unnerved her. She could not understand it and so she feared it.

"I'm only trying to give you some worthy advice. Dublin isn't your future, neither are men like Chesham. Chesham is a rakehell. His friends are worse. Just know, my fine girl, that until they offer you marriage and a wedding band is on your hand, you are nothing but a toy to them, and they will treat you like a toy, until you are broken and thrown away."

Unbidden, the tears began to flow down her cheeks. She tried to free herself but he wouldn't let her go. Suddenly she hated Trevallyan at that moment more than she had hated him the day she was sent to school. He spoke a truth she knew all too well, but to have to listen to him say it was like applying acid as balm for an open sore.

Lashing out in the only manner she could think of, she drew herself upright and spat the words at him as if speaking to a dim-witted servant. "My lord, you needn't to remind me of such things. I have my mother as a testament to male heartlessness. And should I need further evidence, I can always remember you and *this* conversation to remind me of pointless cruelties."

She ripped her arms away from him and wrapped them around herself. Uneasily she glanced at the portrait over the mantel of the woman whose son looked so much like her. Trevallyan's own mother had been a Celt, an Irish girl much like herself, but deep in his heart Trevallyan was entirely of the Ascendency. Unlike those Trevallyans before him, this Big Lord felt himself too lofty, with his fine education and polished manners, to mingle with his mother's people. And why should he bother with the likes of her, when he had every advantage? Hundreds of years earlier the king of England had given his family all of Lir's lands and all of Lir's wealth. He had everything and she had nothing. And it was monstrous of him to point out all her misfortunes when he had had so few.

He stared at her. Stunned anger hardened his features.

A wretched silence passed between them.

"Go on. Get out of here. The lesson is learned then," he whispered.

" 'Twas not your place to teach it to me," she retorted.

He looked at her and again she found that strange, humorless smile on his lips. "Indeed, it was my place, because Lir is populated with illiterates and fools. Don't believe what they tell you, Ravenna. I never have. And I never will."

"Now that you've insulted everyone in this county, I can see this conversation has reached its natural conclusion." She gave him a dismissive glance. Trevallyan had proved he was of the Ascendency through and through. The likes of her old friend Malachi would have no love for the man, not if he ever heard Trevallyan speak as he did.

"Remember what I said about Chesham."

She knew it was not even a possibility, but still her haughty English-schoolgirl self wanted to torment him with the idea anyway. "Chesham may one day be my husband."

"In thy dreams. The only thing you both have in common is a youthful age. . . ." Trevallyan's expression suddenly seemed to grow cold, as if he were pondering something that weighed upon him.

She stared at him, hurt by his latest insult, in disbelief over his mercurial mood shifts.

He finally took a deep, invigorating breath and stared back. Cryptically, he said, "I know the truth. Remember that in times to come. I know the truth about all of Lir, and I know the truth about you."

Puzzled, she wiped the tears from her cheek and demanded, "What do you mean, you know the truth?"

He lifted the corner of his fine lips in the mockery of a smile. "All in good time. I just want you to know that I've seen how you've matured, Ravenna. I see the woman before me where there used to be a little girl playing pranks with her friends. That English school has given you a demure, cultured facade. But a facade it is. I see past it. I know the real you. You may cultivate an innocent demeanor . . . but the way you use those eyes, those violet-blue, seductive eyes . . ." A strange, irrational anger shadowed his expression. He touched her face, drawing his thumb gently across the flutter of her lashes. "But just remember, I am immune to it. I *am* immune to it. Yet 'tis no wonder I want to protect Chesham."

Her words were unsteady. His unexpectedly gentle touch left her weak and her emotions in havoc. "You want to protect me, then you want to protect Chesham. Which is it, my lord?"

He dropped his hands as if she suddenly burned him. Refusing to meet her gaze, he said, "As you stated before, I'm not your guardian. What you do with yourself is ultimately your concern. I thought only to be helpful. You're a woman alone, and I've seen what the world does to vulnerable women. Yet, I'm not your protector, nor do I wish to be. The man that desires to protect you, desires to keep you all to himself."

She looked at him for a long moment while seconds ticked by on the mantel clock. He should have met her gaze and announced that she could finally leave. But he didn't. He wouldn't look at her at all. Instead he seemed to be waging a battle within himself and he stared into the fire as if the flames held the secrets of the moon and the stars.

"Good night, Lord Trevallyan," she said softly.

She stared at him, her eyes begging a last look from him, but he wouldn't give her one.

And with no other recourse, she departed the library, numb with the crazy, inexplicable, unsettling notion that the master of Trevallyan, the man who ruled County Lir as if it were his kingdom, was somehow terrified of her.

Chapter 11

THE EVENING ended just as strangely as it had begun. Ravenna walked through the passage toward the candle-lit great hall with her thoughts heavily on Trevallyan. The man was a bit tetched in the head, she concluded. Father Nolan stood at the entrance to the hall, and she found she couldn't help but include the priest in Trevallyan's mad little group as well. To her dying day, she wouldn't understand why the father thought it perfectly fine for her to dally alone with the master of the castle. The final irony had been that she was deposited with Trevallyan only so that he could lecture her on the dangers of being alone with men.

"There you are, my pretty girl!" the priest exclaimed, smiling like an overeager pup. "And how did your little meeting go? Did you find Niall amusing?"

Ravenna noticed for the first time how frail the old man appeared against the black of his cassock. His clerical collar was frayed and poorly mended with blue thread. He leaned so anxiously upon his blackthorn that she was convinced he would topple over if she told him Trevallyan had made her cry.

" 'Twas a meeting of no account, Father. It's done with now. Let's be off, shall we?" She took his arm and led him across the cavernous medieval hall. Greeves stood at the front door summoning the driver. They paused while a servant crossed their path, carrying a satchel of wood for the hall's three room-sized fireplaces.

"Was Trevallyan unkind to you, my child?" the priest asked, walking even more slowly than normal. Ravenna could swear he was trying to pry information out of her about the meeting.

"He was . . ." She thought about it. He had indeed been unkind, but then, so had she. The conversation had heated to an unnatural degree, and she hoped never to repeat it. "He was, perhaps, a bit brusque. But that is the way he is. He did not overly offend me. We rarely cross paths, so, as I said, it is of no account."

The servant spilled the wood at the nearest hearth, making a loud clatter. Ravenna looked over at him, a little surprised the man was allowed in the castle. His back was to her, but she saw he wore field clothes still grimy with the dirt of the stables. He began belligerently poking the fire to reignite the flames and finally she saw him in profile. She gasped. His gaze darted to her, anger and recognition in its depth.

"Malachi," she whispered, taking a step toward him.

The priest held her back. " 'Tis not the time or the place for you to be talking to him, Ravenna."

Ravenna stared at the father, astounded. "What? I may close myself alone in a room with Lord Trevallyan, and yet I may not greet my dear old friend whom I haven't seen in years?" She turned to where Malachi stood far across the hall. He had changed a great deal since they had last met. His red hair had dimmed and he was near six feet tall now, with a man's growth of beard on his face. But the eyes were the same. Hazel eyes, with rebellion like a fire that burned within.

"Malachi," she said, a warm, welcoming smile on her lips. She wanted to run across the hall and throw herself in his arms. All the years that she'd spent in London seemed to melt away beneath that familiar gaze.

And yet, the gaze was not so familiar.

It was a man's gaze now, and it stopped her dead while he stared as

Lord Chesham had stared at her, his eyes lowering to regions of her figure in a manner that was not quite polite.

"Get along with you, Malachi," Father Nolan said, a scowl on his features.

Malachi said not a word. He stared at Ravenna as if she had captured him and he could not move.

"I said get along with you, my boy," the father repeated, more sharply.

Suddenly Malachi's eyes shifted to the left. Trevallyan stood in the entrance to the hall, his arms crossed over his chest, his expression rigid and cold. His gaze leveled at Malachi.

Without a word, Malachi swept up the debris left by the firewood and left the hall. He gave Ravenna not a second look.

Twice heartbroken by their harsh separation, she thought to run after him, but then she quickly realized it would be best to see him tomorrow when they could talk alone. Malachi MacCumhal was the only friend she had ever really had and perhaps would ever have. She longed to cement once more the bonds of friendship, but she knew it was not possible to do it under the circumstances.

She turned and found Trevallyan staring at Malachi's retreating back. A shiver ran down her spine when she found Trevallyan's gaze on her, disapproval etched into his every feature.

" 'Tis best you avoid a character like that." His voice echoed with doom across the rough granite walls of the hall.

She could no longer hide her hatred beneath a civil facade. She gave him such a scathing look she was surprised he didn't roll back on his heels.

Instead, he laughed. "I've just thrown you into his arms, haven't I?"

She didn't answer him. Her retort was lost in the anger that now choked her.

"Come, my child. 'Tis been a long and upsetting night," Father Nolan interrupted, giving a faint hold on to her arm.

She was suddenly shocked at how bad he looked. The priest's face was drained of color, and his hand trembled mercilessly on his cane. If she hadn't known better, she almost could have believed he was somehow grieved by her ill-will toward Trevallyan.

Without pause, she escorted the priest to the bailey and got him settled into the carriage. When at last her attention returned to Trevallyan, she found he had not followed them. Again, he was gone without a farewell.

⚭

The clock struck three in the morning, and Trevallyan gave up on the book he was attempting to read. A fire crackled merrily in the hearth and a full glass of brandy sat on the table next to him, but neither cheered him. The melancholy of the night grew worse by the hour.

He hadn't wanted Ravenna at the castle that evening, but he had allowed it, thinking it would come to naught. But now it was hours past midnight, the girl had come and gone, and he had yet to erase her from his mind.

She was indeed a lovely woman. He could not dispute it. Even in the sorry blue gown she had worn, she was stunning. And her poverty only added to her allure. The worn spot on her elbows, the fray of her hem, cried out for a man to take care of her. Though every fiber of her being seemed to loathe him, even he had to admit it would be a temptation to see her dressed in silks and satins more suited to her exquisiteness. He was quickly discovering that Ravenna had the power to take hold of a man's imagination and never let go.

Already Chesham was a casualty.

He thought back to the moment before he had retired. His cousin had suggested they give a ball for everyone in Lir.

"To celebrate what?" Trevallyan had snapped, irritated by Chesham to no end that evening.

"To celebrate . . . *beauty,*" Chesham had said, and then retired himself.

With that, Trevallyan knew he'd be on a fool's errand to try to remove his cousin from the castle. Chesham would elope with the girl before he would allow himself to be banished from her presence.

And now there was MacCumhal.

Niall reached for the brandy and took a long, burning gulp. Malachi

MacCumhal was trouble. The boy had watched his father murdered in Dublin, and the experience had put murder into his own soul. There was talk Malachi was one of the hard men. There was also talk that the fiery deaths of a wealthy family in Kildonan was caused by mischief-makers setting the house aflame. Three children had died in the household. Three small boys younger than Malachi MacCumhal had been when his father had been unjustly shot.

The brandy glass in Trevallyan's angry grip was near the shattering point while he stared darkly into the fire. Home Rule would come one day; it was as inevitable as the bloodshed that would precede it. Yet, rivers of red would not run through Lir, because he, Lord Niall Trevallyan, eighth generation in Lir, son of a Celt himself, would go to his grave to prevent it. Lir was prosperous and peaceful. After hundreds of years, the Trevallyan roots ran deep in the rocky Irish soil. He could not separate the county from the people any more than he could separate his love for his homeplace from the land that held it. He was Ascendency, but he would not be a foreigner in his birthplace. In ancient times his family had acquired their lands by might not right. Regardless, he would see no bloodshed in Lir. And that was exactly why he had employed Malachi in the first place. He wanted to keep an eye on him. 'Twas better to hold one's enemies close, or so the saying went.

He closed his eyes, disturbed with the thought of Ravenna running to Malachi. She towered over the man in wit and education. It was not her lot in life to shackle herself to a lout, bear his twenty children, and watch him die stupidly, tragically, as his father had died.

His eyes opened, and he looked down at the volume in his lap. It was a treatise on the Wexford Rebellion that had resulted in Ireland being annexed into the United Kingdom. God, how he wanted to prevent the letting of blood. But all his attempts to understand the situation were for naught if he let his passions rule where his mind should. He must handle it like the *geis*. He could do anything, control anything, solve anything as long as he relied on reason. If he ever let emotion take hold, all would be lost.

So he could *not* get involved in Ravenna's life, he told himself. If she should want to follow Malachi, then he must let her. He was immune

to the girl. The *geis* had proved false and impotent. He had no desire to
win the love of a foolish young girl.

He stood and wearily looked around the luxurious antechamber to
his bedroom. His gaze lit upon his favorite leather chair where he did
most of his reading.

The chair was plump, broken-in in all the right places, and well-
used. Yet right next to it sat its shining new companion. A matching
chair that had never really held a visitor to his chambers. He wasn't
comfortable seeing his mistresses in it—though they were more likely
to lounge in the bedstead than aright themselves to read something to
improve their minds—nonetheless, he discouraged its use. Now the
chair remained a virgin, waiting for the day he would marry and had a
wife who, too, longed for a blissful evening of reading.

A knife turned in his gut. Two chairs. One unused, perhaps never to
be. The thought echoed through his mind until he longed to silence it.

He strode for his bed, swallowing his bitterness. He would find a
wife one day, and he vowed she would be nothing like Ravenna. Even
now his mind mocked him with the picture of Ravenna standing in the
hall, hatred for him burning in those bewitching eyes. But he liked her
that way. He couldn't deny it. Her spirit was like a brilliantly lit mantle
she wore around her shoulders. It brought the blush of passion to her
cheeks and the erotic dew of anger trembling on her lips. She was a
sight no man could resist.

His eyes darkened and gleamed with his own anger. Indeed. He
liked the defiance. It was a challenge. It made him want to break it.

⚯

"Is Malachi here?" Ravenna whispered to the batten door, the first
light of dawn graying the horizon. She stood shivering at the entrance
to the MacCumhal hovel, a place she had not been in many years.

The door opened, and a small, dirty face peered out. "Nay, Malachi's
a teh meetin'," the child said in a heavy accent.

Ravenna pulled her shawl more closely about her, fighting off the
early morning chill. "You're little Branduff, aren't you?" she asked. "Do

you remember me? I'm Ravenna, Malachi's good friend. How's your mother?"

"Died," the little boy said in a dull, dispassionate voice, as if he were no stranger to mourning.

Ravenna wanted to put her arms about the thin little shoulders and comfort the lad, but if he was anything like his brother, she knew he would not take kindly to it.

"Can you take me to the meeting, wherever it is? I must see Malachi. 'Tis been ever so long," she whispered.

"I don' rightly know where teh meetin' is." The child's green eyes opened wide at her disappointment. The lad looked so much like Malachi at that moment that as Ravenna stared down at him she felt as if she were reliving her youth. She knew if she removed his torn and grimy cap she'd find a handful of carrot-colored hair.

"But, methinks he'll be a teh market in a wee bit. Why don' you sarch for him tere?"

Ravenna hugged the little boy, despite his protests. "Oh, thank you! I've wanted to see him for ever so long!" With that, she wrapped her black shawl over her head and ran down the rock-strewn path to the market.

The center of the town of Lir was nothing but a large, crumbling barn that had been divided into stalls so that sellers could hawk their various goods. Cabbages and beets filled an entire stall, and on Saturday there was a rag fair where clothing was bartered for potatoes. Ravenna had always loved the market. She had once set up shop there herself. Barely ten years old, she had claimed one dark corner and hawked fortunes all day. It had worked beautifully because everyone in Lir knew she was Grania's granddaughter, and with all the money she had earned, she bought Grania a blue flannel petticoat. But she had never been able to return. Some of the more superstitious sellers banded together and forbade her to enter the market ever again. Now she could laugh at it. It was foolish that any adult would think a person could truly tell another's fortune by reading their palm. Besides, Grania was the one with the Sight—not she. Still, she had never been back until the moment she entered the carriageway.

It was said that the better class of Lir refused to shop there. Many claimed the barn was destined to fall down any day and would surely kill any and sundry who might be shopping beneath it. But others, such as Malachi MacCumhal, frequented it often, not just to sample the crude, cheap wares but to listen to the latest whispers. In that regard, the news at the market was almost as good as the news at the pub.

"Good morning!" A wizened but familiar old man raised his hand as Ravenna sauntered by.

She nodded and smiled and kept going. Malachi was nowhere to be found yet.

"Why, if it isn't Grania's own Ravenna!" Another, somewhat familiar voice cried out.

Ravenna smiled and continued her search of faces. Though barely dawn, the place was filled to capacity.

"My goodness, child, you've grown so!"

More voices cried out to her, and she felt compelled to greet each one. It seemed she nodded and smiled at almost every old man and woman at the market.

Yet nowhere did she see Malachi.

Determined to wait for him should he appear, she settled against a fallen beam and warmed her hands at a small coal fire behind a harness-maker's stall. Daylight crept into the barn like a mist, seeping through the holes in the roof and the carriage doors until all but the darkest of corners of the enormous market were illuminated. Still Malachi did not show.

" 'Tis a right bit of bile you have a-runnin' in your veins," said a whisper behind her. Ravenna turned around and found two men deep in conversation behind the fallen beam.

"Trevallyan thinks to rule like a king. He needs to be reminded that his 'subjects' don't appreciate being subjected." The second man turned his profile toward the fire and Ravenna was shocked to find it was Malachi.

"So how to dethrone him?" whispered his companion.

Ravenna could listen no more. They were speaking as if they were like the White Boys of old. Home Rule or no, she wasn't going to listen in and be a party to their plots, whatever they were. Even the great orator of Home Rule, Daniel O'Connell, did not advocate violence, and so, she believed, neither should anyone else.

"Malachi," she said in a clear voice. She stepped out from behind the beam and stared at him.

Malachi looked up and saw her. The man next to him, a tall, painfully thin man she had never seen before, merely tipped his cap and disappeared into the dark recesses of the barn, and she couldn't help but think of rats exposed in lamplight.

"Malachi, I wanted to talk to you at the castle but—"

"But you could not shame yourself in front of your fine friends," he interrupted, malice in his voice.

"I haven't forgotten my best friend, nor would I if I were having tea with Victoria herself." She couldn't help but stare at him. She was amazed how he had changed, and yet, incredibly, he had remained the same. For the smile that began to grow on his mouth was the same smile she had known in years past.

"Have you come back?" he whispered down at her as if not quite believing she was standing before him.

"No one can send me away again. Not ever." With that she threw her arms around him and hugged him with all her might. Though it was not rational, she still expected the boy with the carrot-red hair, who was smaller than she. It was a bit disconcerting to discover herself in the arms of a man, a very big man, who held her as if she weighed no more than Kathleen Quinn's doll.

"I've not forgotten you, Ravenna. Not ever. 'Tis why I accepted work at the castle. Trevallyan shall pay for sending you away," Malachi whispered against her hair.

"The father and Grania sent me away, too. You can't have revenge on all of them, so forget Trevallyan, Malachi. We've no need to waste time hating him." She pulled back and looked him in the eyes. She was a bit disturbed at the anger still burning in his own.

"Your grandmother and Father Nolan sent you away because Trevallyan forced them to. He is an evil man. He took our land, and we must never forget that. To forgive him his trespasses is to forgive the devil."

She touched Malachi's cheek. It was rough with beard and hard, unlike the smooth one of his boyhood. "I don't want to talk of Lord

Trevallyan. I want to forget him." Truer words there never were. If Niall Trevallyan and his castle were plucked from Lir and whisked skyward, never to be seen again, only then would she be satisfied. For as it was, she seemed to be spending every waking minute either in his company, or analyzing his impossible behavior.

"If you request it, then we'll ne'er speak of Lord Trevallyan again."

The fire in Malachi's gaze burned to coals, but she was not fooled by his temperance. She was further unsettled by the fact that he still embraced her and that his hands lingered at her waist. It seemed foreign to her to think of him as a man, with a man's feelings. But he was one, and the possibilities between them seemed laid right out before her with every touch of his hand and every caress of his gaze.

She stepped away, all at once irrationally nervous. He watched her with a hooded expression in his gaze, one that she had never seen before.

The pandemonium of the market should have diverted her, yet her thoughts clung to him. It wasn't that she didn't like Malachi. She loved him, and she knew she always would. But to love him as a man was something big and rather frightening. She wasn't sure she was quite ready for it, especially now, when he towered above her. She'd been told he had changed, but somehow she hadn't quite believed it. She still thought of him as the scrawny, fighting, muddy-faced lad that she had roamed with all the years before. But that lad was gone, and in his place was a man. A man who in all probability might one day be her husband.

The bustling market with its rough-and-tumble display of goods, its riotous hawking, its burn of smells within her nostrils, of woodsmoke, cinnamon bark, and greasy wool, was still not enough to take her thoughts from her profound realization. She'd always known that she was a girl apart from the rest of society, but now she realized she was worse. Indeed, a freak of nature. To be truthful, she was a female who rarely thought of marriage at all.

Not that she didn't think of love. But love was something separate and sublime, quite different from marriage. While other girls filled their dowry chests or practiced their flirting, she ashamedly admitted she had no interest in either of these activities. Marriage was simply not a goal of hers. She'd been raised by Grania, a strong woman who was independent of men. In Grania's silent code of upbringing, Ravenna had read well the message there: To rely on a man would be to end up like her mother. The love of a man was in reality too fragile, whimsical, impermanent to ever rely upon, so it was best to settle on her faerie tales and repress the desire to fall as desperately in love with someone heroic and strong as she knew Skya was soon to do.

Sometimes Ravenna wondered if she wasn't a silly girl not to be thinking of marriage all the time. If she was not a silly girl, she was definitely a foolish one. A husband would bring her out of the limbo she was in now. If she married, she would not be forced to be governess to a lord's ill-tempered children; she would not be forced to wait hand and foot on spoiled young misses who could not choose which hat flattered them best. No, she could play wife and mother on her own, without being at the mercy of others.

But she would be at the mercy of her husband, and that was where marriage and love diverged. So she would have to choose carefully. But whom should she choose? Chesham? He was rich and amusing. But even if marriage to him were possible for a girl of her social station, she knew instinctively those same qualities would make him a poor husband. He'd stick her at his country home and continue to cavort with the count and Lord Guy. It was one thing for a bachelor to sport a mistress, but the thought of a married Lord Chesham running around Trevallyan Castle after a young woman not his wife made her shudder.

Yet, there were other men to consider besides Chesham. The count and Lord Guy. The very idea made her choke with laughter. The only bride good enough for either one of those two men was a gilded mirror.

As if they would even choose her. She kept her wry little smile to herself. She was dowry-less and untitled, and, worse, a bastard. A girl not even good enough to mingle equally with the people of Lir, let alone the Ascendency. It was as ridiculous for her to think of marrying a lord of the realm as it was for someone to pay to have their palm read by a ten-year-old girl.

Of all the men she knew, Malachi was her most likely match. Per-

haps it would just take some time to begin to accept him as the man he
had become.

"Shall you come to tea this afternoon, Malachi?" she asked, trying to
return some normalcy to their suddenly new and strange relationship.
"Grania's eyesight is fair terrible these days, but still I would like her to
see you. You look so different. . . ."

Malachi laughed. She suddenly saw the boy he used to be. "She'll
knock me on me backside. Your grandma don't like me, Ravenna."

"She hasn't seen you since I left for school. Come to tea—"

"I can't come to tea," he said with finality. " 'Tis busy I am, Ravenna."
He put his hands on her waist—hands that were large enough to span
it—and drew her near. "But I want you to promise to meet me tonight.
I'll come by your cottage and pick you up at midnight—that way old
Grania won't know you've gone."

"Midnight!" she gasped. "What are we going to do at midnight?"

He smiled. "Don't tell your grandmother. Promise me? If you don't,
I'll show you a good time. I promise I will."

Ravenna suddenly had the idea that Malachi thought her a simple-
ton. He was up to no good, and he believed for some reason that she
couldn't figure that out.

She smiled at him, willing to play the game until she could twist it to
her advantage. "I'll go with you at midnight, but first you must tell me
what we are going to do."

"We'll be doing what every woman likes to do. This. . . ." he whispered. He pressed his lips to hers and drove his tongue deep into her
mouth.

Ravenna was appalled at the unaccustomed familiarity. She might
have actually struggled against him except that surprise had bolted her
feet to the ground.

He kissed her, driving his tongue deeper and deeper until at last he
seemed to derive some satisfaction. Then, pushing her aside, he picked
up the cap he had laid on a bale of hay and sauntered out of the market
without another look back.

She just stared at him, unable to even draw her hand across her
mouth to wipe away the kiss. It was a shock to discover in the years
since she had been gone that Malachi MacCumhal had become just like

any other man. The boy who had so painstakingly written her through the parish priest, the boy who had made her laugh and through his mischief made her forget she was not Catholic, and not legitimate, and not good enough, was gone. Disappointed and confused, she left the market with shoulders slumped in depression, and wondered about heroes who had fallen to the earth.

Chapter 12

SKYA ACCEPTED her banishment to the Dark Woods of Hawthorn. Her father wept as she walked away from the castle, but she knew if she were to stay, all her family would be suspected of witchery, and she could not allow that to happen especially when her father, the king, was busy defending his lands from the neighboring warring kingdom. It was a fact that the only way the king could save his daughter would be at the expense of the entire kingdom.

So Princess Skya walked into the Dark Woods of Hawthorn, every owl, every mouse on the shadowy woodland floor sending lonely shivers of fear through her heart. She was fortunate to find an old, abandoned cottage deep in the tangle of hawthorns. And there she lived in exile, crying sad, silent tears for a family she could have no more.

Ravenna looked up from her small oaken writing desk and became mesmerized by the random flickerings of the candle that lit her work. Her bare feet were tucked beneath her, and she wore only a loose, flowing white night rail with her black wool shawl draped over her shoulders to protect her from the chill night air. Grania was snoring in her room across the hall. It was eleven o'clock.

The chair scraped across the waxed floorboards as she pushed away from her writing and drew the candle to the window. The town of Lir was only a speck of waning yellow firelight in the distance. A storm spit froth over the Irish Sea, erasing the horizon. Lightning flashed, and a minute later the thin rumblings of thunder rolled over the cottage.

"I'm sorry," she whispered to the cold, wind-battered panes of glass, feeling bad that Malachi might be waiting for her in a storm. But she refused to shake the notion that it was his due for his bad behavior. He'd hurt her with his kiss. Not physically, perhaps, but her feelings were wounded that he could treat her so casually. She was not a loose woman, and she was not a piece of property for him to ply and mold as he wished. He had not asked her to meet him, he had demanded it. She had had a choice in the matter, and he seemed to have forgotten that.

"So sorry," she whispered again, blew out the candle, and crawled into bed.

❦

"Speak not a word," a harsh, raspy voice said in her ear. Ravenna struggled to sit up in bed, but a sooty hand clamped over her mouth and held her down. Her heart drummed in terror as her gaze clawed at the darkness to see who it was who held her.

"Why did you not meet me?"

Her fear seeped away like the ebb of the tide. She pulled at the fingers on her mouth and said, "Malachi?"

"Why did you not meet me?" he demanded again, his dark figure smelling like the inside of a smoky tavern.

" 'Twas not a proper meeting, now was it?" she whispered back, her deep blue-violet eyes, if he could have seen them, expressing her anger most eloquently.

"Bah! What have you become? The posh young miss? You're no Kathleen Quinn, Ravenna, and you needn't act like one."

"How dare you!" She would have slapped him on the face if she could have taken good aim in the darkness.

"Now don't you be denyin' it. You're no Kathleen Quinn and you know it."

Ravenna lowered her threatening hand. She knew she wasn't Kathleen Quinn, and he was right, there was no point in saying otherwise. "Still, I won't be having clandestine meetings with you. Grania would die if she was to waken and find me gone."

Malachi swept back her hair, his hand strangely tender. " 'Tis just that I want to be with you, Ravenna. I want to know again the times of our sweet childhood."

She stilled, unable to reprimand him when he spoke what she also wanted so desperately.

"Come," he coaxed, pulling her hand, "walk with me to the Briney Cliffs, and see the moon vanish behind the June thunderheads, as we did when we last knew each other."

"Nay. 'Tis not right—"

"Come. You know you want to. Even in this dark, I can see the wildness in your eyes, the wildness that aches to go with me."

She felt him throw a man's heavy coat over her shoulders. She pulled back, reluctant. He nearly dragged her across the floorboards.

"We're not children anymore, Malachi. This is not right," she hissed, pulling away.

He touched her, gently holding her against him. "We're not children anymore except in our hearts. Come, let's be children just this once more. . . ."

She stared up at him in the shadows. Lightning lit the sky, and she found his eyes. The same eyes that she knew. The ones she pictured every time she read and reread his letters.

She knew she shouldn't go with him, not in the middle of the night, but as much as she hesitated, his draw was stronger. It was a chance to regain the past, to find the Malachi she sorely missed.

Before she could utter a protest, he led her down the dark staircase and out into the cold sea wind. He took her hand and ran through the night-shadowed fields of green-gold rye. And suddenly she began to laugh as she had not laughed in years, the sound bubbling from her chest like the raucous giggles of children. A stiff breeze cut through her night rail, but she didn't care if she was cold. She only wanted to remember a finer, more innocent time, and enjoy the company of her very best friend in the world.

"Is it the way you remember?" he asked when they reached the top of the Briney Cliffs. The sea swirled and swished at the base of the rocks, releasing a salty mist that she could taste. Behind her, the moon sat atop Lir, its white, unearthly glow casting blue shadows in front of them while storm clouds inked the watery horizon and bled slowly onto shore.

"Yes, it's beautiful," she whispered, hugging herself, her plaited hair flying behind her like a black banner. "Just as I remember."

"Then kiss me," he rumbled against her nape, his lips buried in the tender flesh of her neck. Slowly a hand crept up her waist, reaching . . . reaching . . . for parts she kept private.

"No," she whispered, and stepped away from him. The winds suddenly became icy. He offered warmth, but for some reason she didn't want to accept it. By all reasoning, she should desire him to kiss her. Nonetheless, she didn't.

"I remember a fiery creature from days of old, not this prude you've become," he said, shouting over the increasing blasts of wind.

She didn't answer him. Instead, she stared at the storm, wondering when she would feel the first cold drops.

"Kiss me, Ravenna," he said, his arms clamping around her like a bear's. His lips dragged down her neck, and she trembled within his warm embrace.

There was something terribly wrong with her. She spent hours day-dreaming about love, and now, when she had someone to love, she was rejecting him; her very own friend, Malachi.

Whatever was wrong with her? she asked herself while he nibbled on her fragile earlobe. Was she repulsed by him? On the contrary, Malachi was a fine specimen of a man; he was tall, strong, and his face —while perhaps not the godlike visage of Count Fabuloso—it was most certainly pleasing to the eye, and doubly so to her for he was her friend.

So why couldn't she give herself freely to him? The question tortured her as his arms tightened, and he pressed himself against her form, which was clad in only a thin shift of linen.

"Stop, Malachi. Please stop," she found herself saying, though she cringed at saying it.

His lips turned cold, and he leaned against her impatiently, as if he were unused to such a reluctant female. "What is it?" he almost snapped.

"I—I just don't know." She turned away and hugged herself, staring far out at sea. "It's just that we're so different now. So different. . . ." She bit her lower lip. What she couldn't say was that *she* was so different now. She hadn't grown up by his side and seen how the other girls in town accepted his kisses. While he was at the stables bussing the girls, she had been practicing the useless skill of pouring out tea at the Weymouth-Hampstead School. She knew she was just a bastard. He long admitted his mother had never approved of her, for she was not even saved by attendance at Mass. And yet, here she was, unwilling to take his kisses because his crudeness and lack of guile shocked her educated mind.

"Now that you've your fine friends at the castle, I suppose a gent like me ain't good enough, is it?" He took her roughly in hand.

She released a small cry. He frightened her, but she couldn't bear the thought that she might have hurt him. "No. You must not think such things," she gasped.

"Then what is it? Are you looking for a proposal before a man can kiss you?"

"Nay. I don't want a proposal." She struggled to be free. He wouldn't release her.

"You mean you don' be wantin' *my* proposal." His anger turned on like a spigot. "You want a big, rich man, isn't that right? It's what all you lassies want. A bloody gent to buy you nice things and set you up fancy."

"I don't want those things," she confessed, panting. "They offer no guarantee of respect and love. And that is what I want most, Malachi. I want respect and love, and you aren't giving them to me!"

"I'll respect you with this!" He raised his hand as if to strike her.

She faced him, her stance frozen, her eyes daring him to do it.

They stood there, poised on the cliff like statuary until a flash of lightning crackled across the water. The violence of it seemed to waken Malachi to what he'd been about to do. In horror, he glanced at his raised hand. In the same fury, now of contrition, he pulled her to him and buried his face in her hair.

"Forgive me! Forgive me! My God, I would never hurt you." Now it seemed his turn to tremble. " 'Tis just I saw you in the castle and I . . . I could not bear it. You're mine, Ravenna. You always have been. Don't go to the castle anymore. You must not do it."

Suddenly he froze.

"Oh, Jaysus," he rasped. Quickly, he let her go. She nearly stumbled over the rocks.

"What is it?" she cried out. Then she saw the reason. In the distance, streaming out of Lir was some kind of search party. The men carried torches and there looked to be nigh twenty of them.

"What on earth is that? They can't be looking for me," she whispered. "Grania couldn't get to town that swiftly. . . ."

"Listen, Ravenna, I must go—" He grabbed the coat from her shoulders. Without it, she realized how bitterly cold the night really was.

"Malachi—" She hugged her chest and turned to look at him. The tone of his voice had told her everything. "Have you gone and done something bad? Are they looking for you?"

"Ravenna. Just kiss me once, for you may not see me again for a while." His voice shook. In the fading moonlight, she could see his gaze shift to the stream of torchlights running over the hills.

"What have you done, Malachi? Oh God," she whispered, staring at him. "Is Home Rule worth this violence?"

"Yes," he rasped, pulling his hair in agitation. "The Big Lords are not our kings. We had our own kings before they sent these English dogs to command us. Trevallyan sits in his castle while I fetch his coal for his hearth. Me! A descendant of Celtic warriors!"

She took a deep breath. Her heart felt as if it were being ripped from her chest. "But you haven't hurt anyone, have you?"

He stared at her while the storm battled behind him. She could hear the rain fall on the sea beyond like the coming of troops.

" 'Tis just been mischief, Ravenna. You must believe me. The boy-os and me haven't hurt anyone . . . intentionally."

She saw the gleam of tears in his eyes, and she longed to hold him, but there wasn't time. The men streaming from Lir were spread about the countryside. Already they could hear their shouts above the screams of wind.

"Go," she said to him, afraid of him and for him at the same time.

" 'Tis a war we're fightin', Ravenna. Just keep that in mind and don't judge me harshly." He held her close, but his embrace was as quick and ethereal as time. In seconds, he disappeared into the rocky outcrops of Briney Cliffs.

"The memory of you was my only friend in England," she cried into the shadows of the night, but she knew he had not heard her.

The trip back to the cottage was cold and terrible. The wind brought rain, and the path became obscured with mud. Her thin linen night rail was no protection from the elements, and the freezing downpour soaked her to the bone. She might have regretted the trip, but though the rocks cut her feet and wind drove through her like icicles, she was glad she had gone. Malachi trusted her enough to reveal to her what he was up to. Perhaps one day, she might get him to see that destruction and violence weren't the answer to Ireland's problems, as Father Nolan had said so many times.

Her shawl caught on a hawthorn. She tugged on it but it was no use; the thing held fast. "Bother it anyway!" she cursed in the howling wind. She'd return for it in the morning. A sodden shawl wasn't going to keep her warm tonight.

She slid down the hill and into a field of blowing ryegrass. Covered in mud, she had to fight the tears that sprang to her eyes. Life was too difficult sometimes, she thought.

Bitterly she picked herself up and slashed through the tall grass as it cut at her ankles. Seeds and burrs clung to her muddy wet gown, increasing her agony. Why did they fight, anyway? she asked herself, trudging desperately through O'Reilly's fields. Malachi fought for his precious Home Rule, but he had raised his hand to strike a woman. Was Home Rule going to help her? Was it going to make Malachi and men of his kind see her as a person and not just a young woman for the taking? He would never admit it, but Malachi was in some ways no better than his English counterparts. Lord Chesham had prettier words and far better skills at seducing a woman, but in many ways he and Malachi wanted the same thing.

So were all men the same? Did lust drive all of them?

She wiped the rain from her eyes and searched for the beginning of the road. By her calculations, she should have found it by now, but she was not as canny about the geography as she had been as a child.

" 'Tis the bride. The bride!"

The voice made Ravenna nearly jump from her skin. It was Griffen O'Rooney. He stood in the middle of an iron fence. It took her a moment to realize that the iron fence was the same one that surrounded the Trevallyan family cemetery.

" 'Tis the bride. Ye've finally come to save us!" he shouted to her.

She stared at him, his face lit by a feeble lantern he held up in his hand. Everyone called the old man mad, and he had had a penchant for the Trevallyan graveyard for as long as she could remember. On a cold, rainy night, she had no desire for a conversation with him.

She backed away, wondering how the old grave-digger had become a lunatic. O'Rooney's rantings about a bride made no sense, but she didn't expect them to. All she wanted was to find her cottage, dry herself by the fire, and crawl beneath a heavy woolen blanket.

"Doan' go!" O'Rooney shouted, his aged, unsteady form remarkably impervious to the lashing torrent around him. He began to walk to her, all the while saying, "See what tragedy we brung . . . we killed her . . . the lass and her child. If we'd only listened to the *geis*. . . . I had to bury her all alone, for Trevallyan could not bring himself to come to her graveside. 'Twas you he was waiting for! We should have stopped the wedding! We should have stopped the wedding!" The old man suddenly began to sob, and the sound sent shivers down Ravenna's spine. She might have tried to help the old man to his caravan, but despite his frailty, he was larger than she, and she didn't think she could handle him.

"Come back! Come back! Don't leave us!" he called to her, exiting the cemetery.

Ravenna knew she could outrun him, nonetheless, his strange words sent terror through her heart. She looked back, and O'Rooney stood in the downdrafts of rain, reaching out for her hand as if he wanted to take her somewhere. She was cold and exhausted, and susceptible to rash action. She ran blindly in the direction of her cottage, her hands tearing at the windswept night as if it would get her home faster. Suddenly, out of the black night carriage lanterns flashed before her eyes, sending the rain down around in a golden glow. She fell into what she thought was a mud-filled ditch. Horses' hooves flailed above her. She screamed. Then all went dark.

⚘

"What the bloody hell's going on out there, Seamus?" Trevallyan barked from the interior of the carriage.

"We've hit something, me lord. I—I think we've hit a girl. . . ." The carriage driver struggled to hold the horses to keep them from bolting.

"Christ." Trevallyan thrust open the carriage door and braced himself for the cold, pelting rain. "I don't see anything—"

"Over there, I think. In the ditch," Seamus called out from the driver's perch.

Niall drew up the collar on his greatcoat and stepped to the ditch. He nearly choked when he saw a body, muddied and crumpled, and drowning in the water that gushed from the roadside.

He slid down the embankment and gathered the small figure in his arms. A wet hank of hair hid the girl's face. That she was a girl he had no doubt when he took her in his arms. The softness was unmistakable, but in the dark and the rain there was no way to distinguish who she was until he could get her to the lantern of the carriage.

"Get to the castle in double speed," Trevallyan ordered, the girl limp in his arms, the rain running in rivulets down his face. He pulled the wet, dirty form into the carriage, and the vehicle took off at breakneck speed.

He turned up the carriage lantern, heartened the girl was breathing deeply and well. Shrugging out of his heavy wool greatcoat, he wrapped it around her sodden figure, the lamplight revealing all too well how female she was. She wore nothing but a thin, translucent night rail, and though grimy with mud, it was wet enough for him to be able to gauge a small waist and shapely hips. The gown clung lithely to one of the girl's thighs and her chest left almost nothing to the imagination. He pulled the coat over her full breasts, her chilled nipples like buds straining to bloom against the thin, dirtied linen.

Leaning her against the upholstered back of the seat, he swept away the muddied curtain of dark hair. A feeling of intense anger and unease swept over him when he saw who she was. The face failed to surprise him. Somehow he knew it would be Ravenna. He had warned her not to do foolish things, not to get into trouble, and now here she was, thrown into his arms once more. She was lucky to be alive, and—his eyes swept her disreputable state of dress—she was shameless. A sickening emotion akin to jealousy seeped into him when he thought of the few possibilities for her being out in the night in such a state of undress.

He laid his head against the leather seat-back and tried to cool his temper. The girl was a hellion, and he'd known that ever since he'd found her thieving in his bedchamber. He'd hoped the English school might have tamed her—after all, she had acquired some polish there, given the chit's stiff behavior at dinner—but somehow he might have known it never would. The granddaughter of a reputed witch had to be one of the few females in Lir a man could count on to be running about in the rain in only her nightclothes.

He heaved a strangely burdened sigh and appraised her condition, doing his best to ignore the picture she had made before he wrapped her in his coat: the way her breasts rose and fell with each rhythmic breath, the way the sodden fabric caught between her legs, outlining a dark, seductive triangle, tantalizingly veiled. He did his bloody best to force it all from his mind and assess the damage.

There were no bones broken. When he had assured himself of that, he drew his attention to a small red gash on her forehead. It was the only mark on her, and where, no doubt, one of the horses had nicked her with an iron shoe. She moaned as he touched it, a very good sign, and he decided it was not likely to be serious.

She fell against him as they clambered over the old moat bridge and entered the bailey. He stared down at her red, moist lips parted in unwilling slumber. Limp in his arms, she slept like a princess waiting for a kiss.

Of course, the girl would be Ravenna. He knew it not so much because she was one of Lir's truly unpredictable creatures, but because destiny seemed to be throwing her at him whether he wanted her or not. He didn't believe in the *geis* and he never would. Still, there were times such as now when he wondered if there wasn't an odd little force at work in Lir.

" 'There are more things in heaven and earth, Horatio, than are dreamt of in your philosophy,' " he whispered to the still girl in his arms.

Then he tipped his head back and laughed. He had almost had a moment of weakness, but it wouldn't signify. He was a modern man who would defy that stupid *geis* to the end. He would never fall victim to it. There wasn't a woman in all of the United Kingdom fine enough for him to beg for her love, and this wounded, bedraggled, disgraced creature certainly wasn't the one to make him do it.

With malicious glee, he threw a gauntlet to the gods.

Chapter 13

RAVENNA DREAMED of Malachi. She lay in a bed of blushing rose petals as soft as silk pillows, and her childhood friend stood over her, watching her as she slept.

"Drink this," he whispered. "The doctor gave you some laudanum for your aching head. You must take some more."

She raised herself up on one arm and took the heavy silver goblet. It occurred to her that Malachi owned no silver goblets, but she wasn't bothered by incongruities in a dream.

"Now rest," he told her, his accent more refined than she remembered.

She lay back against cushions she had mistaken for rose petals. Malachi still watched her, this time from a seat on the edge of her bed. He was and had been her only friend. In school, she had clung to his friendship as a child clings to an old, worn-out rag doll. He'd changed, but now he had returned, and she was glad that this Malachi who sat near her was unlike the Malachi on the cliffs.

He took the goblet. His head close, too close, to hers.

And suddenly the kiss she hadn't wanted on the cliffs she

now seemed to desire. Forgotten dreams of this man returned to her, and she ached to feel hard lips pressed upon her soft ones; yearned for a strong, gentle hand to run down her back and take her by the waist and pull her against him. In her own penned tales, she told of sweet love, but in her reveries, as now, the need for it burned like a fire tame innocence could not extinguish.

She needed one tender kiss. But it had to be from the right man. It must come from the right man.

Was Malachi that man? If not him, who other would there be in Lir?

She gazed at his face, amazed at the planes and lines she didn't remember him having before. But they were handsome planes, and the lines were cut deep with character. They drew her to him.

He was not the Malachi she remembered. Though he had grown to be a man, Malachi had spoken on the cliffs like a child. He had raised his hand to her like a man of no account. Yet she knew the Malachi before her now would not do that. There was wisdom in his eyes, an intelligence wrought of emotional pain that would dictate his behavior. This man was, in truth, a man fully matured. One which she had feared Malachi hadn't yet become.

She reached out from the haze of her drugged sleep and touched his cheek. It was smooth, well-groomed, warm. Sensuously hinting of beard.

He watched her, not moving. And perhaps because he wasn't moving, and forcing things upon her she wasn't ready for, she found herself riding with the impulse. She took his jaw in her weak grasp, raised herself up, and pressed her lips against his.

His reaction pleased her. His body went rigid and his lips turned wooden and implacable, but as she crushed her lips over his in an ever increasing amount of passion, he seemed to melt like an icicle in the spring sun. After a long, almost painful hesitation, his hand deliciously entangled itself in her hair, and then her kiss became more fervent, and she thrilled with the power of turning stone-cold lips warm and pliable with desire, letting them sip from hers until his greed widened like the rings from a stone dropped into a pond.

Slowly, slowly, he kissed her back. Kissed her until she again fell asleep atop the rose petals, her thoughts, her dreams, on Malachi MacCumhal.

⚯

Trevallyan closed his eyes, no longer able to look at the sleeping girl in his bed. The shock of what had happened still left him immobile, as if a net had fallen from the heavens, capturing him. What the bloody hell had happened? He hadn't even seen it coming. One second, he was helping her sip from a goblet and the next, he was on her like a wolf, taking her mouth as if he'd never kissed before.

Against his will, he forced himself to look down at her. Ravenna slept in the ancient Trevallyan bedstead, the mud had been gently wiped from her face and her hair had been toweled dry. The physician had heavily drugged her.

Hell, he thought, clawing for any source of comfort, she probably hadn't even known whom she'd been kissing.

But he knew, came a little voice. Because he'd done it. Allowed it. *Participated.*

The very idea was like a kick in the gut. Of all the girls he should find himself kissing, this girl was the last one he wanted. When a man was bound and determined to thwart his "destiny," it certainly seemed a fatal error to take destiny in his arms and kiss her as if he'd been aching to do it for days.

His ire increased with every slow, peaceful breath that issued from her parted lips. He'd told Greeves he felt responsible for the accident, which was why he had insisted she be put into his rooms so that he could personally keep an eye on her. Now he wondered about the elaborateness of the lie. In truth, he felt no guilt over what had happened on the roadside. By all sanity and reason, he should have hauled her back to her grandmother's house and let the old witch tend to her aching head. But he hadn't, and the reason eluded him. Vexed him. He still didn't know why Ravenna had been out there on the road. According to the messenger he'd sent to the cottage, Grania hadn't even known the girl was gone. Ravenna had not been running around at night in a rainstorm, half naked, because she was seeking help for her grandmother. She'd been out there because she had gotten into some kind of trouble.

His angry gaze turned to a stray black curl that had slipped across her forehead, making her look vulnerable and even younger than she was. Against his will, he reached out and caressed it. Again he wondered at the insanity that had made him bring her to the castle. The idea brought a thunderous furrow to his brow.

If he'd believed in *geise*, he might indeed believe he and this beautiful sleeping girl were meant for each other. After what had transpired this night, he had no problem envisioning himself with her. Her nubile charms, quite deliciously exposed beneath the mist of her wet night rail, had found an appreciative audience. It was said lust and love were inextricably intertwined. If he lured her to his bed, would he find the magic of both in the *geis*? He smiled a little wickedly, a little wryly. Lust he'd known before. And while it was a strong and pleasant instinct, it held no magic. It needed love.

So it was love or nothing. Lust would bring him about as far as his marriage and all his attempted marriages had brought him.

He frowned, the lines deepening on his cheeks. He could get Ravenna into bed and to the altar. Money and power had historically made it easy to throw aside the smooth skin as Count Fabuloso possessed and create instead the desire for an older face. Arabella, his last fiancée, had never mentioned their age difference. She'd been clearly well-schooled by her mother, and if love could be faked, Arabella had performed well.

But love could not be faked. That was the essence of its definition. Love was real; it could not be bought nor manufactured. In the end, neither he nor Lady Arabella could keep up the pretense.

So he could capture Ravenna, he could seduce her, he could marry her. Regardless, the *geis* stated that it was she who should fall in love with him, a troublesome idea even if he did believe in *geise*, for in his mind was the inescapable truth that had left him empty-hearted all these years. He wanted to love and be loved in return.

This time, falling in love himself might not be so difficult, he thought darkly as he stared down at the lovely young woman asleep in his bed. But inducing the same sentiment in her could be problematic.

He could give her expensive baubles and dresses that might win her affection, but they would never win her love. With love, all the obvious methods were doomed to fail. Even the idea of becoming a countess couldn't make her give her love to him. He was all too familiar with the type of woman who could do brilliant portrayals of "a woman in love" in order to acquire such things.

And then there was Malachi MacCumhal.

Unwittingly Niall's eyes flashed with jealousy. He'd seen how she had looked at the lad as soon as she recognized him in the hall. There was a softness in her eyes he could never imagine her turning toward him. If she wanted a lout such as MacCumhal, he was at a loss as to what might turn her head.

Anger gripped his insides with all the strength of an ironsmith. The *geis* was utter nonsense, and he could not be dictated by it. Even now, when he thought of the night of Ravenna's momentous birth, he cringed at the stupidity of the old men who still believed they saw things when all that they saw was lightning and shadow. Slowly the fury eased from his body like an outgoing tide. The girl sleeping in his bed was not his concern and never would be.

But what ebbs must flow once more, and again he felt the anger rising in his chest.

He should get rid of her. He should send the pest away, he thought, his gaze resting on her damp, parted lips.

She had kissed him and made him feel things he had not wanted to feel. He should banish her from the county, transport her to Antrim to work in one of the Great Houses there. . . . But she had kissed him. And suddenly the thought of sending her from Lir was becoming untenable.

His finger traced her fragile jawline and moved downward in a line between her lightly clad breasts. It stopped at her belly and he drew imaginary circles over the silk counterpane, moving in a spiral down to her blanketed hips. He lusted after her. There was no point in denying it, for any man would lust after such a creature whom he'd seen wet and nearly naked. He longed to sink sweetly between her thighs and taste once more her honeyed lips and skin.

But he wouldn't. It was best that he had no business with her. He wanted a woman to love. A wild creature such as she was no kind of woman to make him a companion.

"My lord . . . ?" A cough broke out behind him. Niall turned and found Greeves in the doorway.

"What is it? Has the doctor returned already?"

"No, my lord . . ." Greeves looked almost pained. He made a sad, stately figure when he grabbed the empty sleeve of his frock coat as if for security. "It seems there's been mischief in the next county. Lord Quinn is here along with several of the townsfolk. I believe this needs your attention right away."

Niall glanced down at Ravenna one last time. Her color was good and she slept with long, even breaths. There was no urgent need for him to stay in attendance.

"Get Fiona to come here and watch over her. And tell her not to talk," he snapped as he grabbed his waistcoat and jacket.

"Very good, my lord. I hope . . ." Greeves looked behind him as if spooked. "I hope there isn't too much trouble."

Niall tossed him a look of agreement, then glanced back at Ravenna. He thought about that stupid *geis* and then, like a train helplessly bulleting in one direction, he thought about the kiss.

Bother the girl anyway, he thought, and all the silly superstitious requirements of the *geis*. He'd gone this long without begging a woman to love him. He was damned if he would begin with Ravenna.

⊗

The blinding glare of morning poured through an enormous window in front of the bedstead. Light hit Ravenna's head like a ball peen hammer. She squeezed her eyes closed and burrowed once more into the comforting darkness beneath the satin quilt like a bat seeking its cave.

Then memory assailed her and she released an audible groan. She wasn't home. Home didn't have satin quilts and lavender-scented sheets. Her cottage also didn't have windows that went from the floor to the heavens, letting in an abominable amount of sunshine.

She recalled her disappointing meeting with Malachi and the subse-

quent encounter with Griffen O'Rooney in the Trevallyan graveyard.
She'd run from Griffen into . . . a carriage. That was it. She hadn't
seen it, for she would have avoided the thing if she had. She'd been
disoriented and she'd slipped beneath the horses' flailing hooves. And
whoever had found her had brought her to his or her home for recov-
ery.

She slowly took her aching head in hand and crept again from
beneath the covers. Grania had to be worried sick about her, and if
strangers had found her on the road, they might not know whom to
notify.

She eased herself to a sitting position and prayed for a gun that
could shoot out the light. But no matter the physical pain, she knew
she had to gather herself together and return to Grania. Grania was too
old a woman to take the strain of fearing for her only kin.

Using care in her movements not to jar her throbbing head, she
leaned back against a mountain of downy pillows and willed her eyes
to open despite the assault of sunlight. Slowly, she raised her eyelids
until the room no longer appeared as if she were viewing it from the
bottom of a pond. The bedstead, the brocaded green curtains, the stone
walls, all came into focus at once, and realization dropped on her like a
net. Her breath caught in her throat. She was back in Trevallyan's
bedchamber.

She remembered all too well this room from that fateful day of her
childhood. The Cromwellian doors still gleamed with beeswax, the
windows of the tower still pointed at the top in Gothic tracery. In the
antechamber beyond, one chair by the hearth looked well-used—even
more worn than she remembered—while the other, though it had been
years since she had laid eyes on it, still looked as if it had left the
cabinetmaker's yesterday.

Her eyes closed with the horror of it. Lord Trevallyan's coach must
have been the one she had encountered on the rain-swept road. Frag-
mented pieces of memory came back to her. She'd been hurt, and he
must have brought her to the castle. Now she was in the last place she
had ever wanted to be again. In his bedchamber. And not only a visitor
to it, but an intimate one at that, for she lay in his bed, as she had no
doubt lain for hours, and she wore only . . .

She forced her gaze down at the foreign garment covering her. Of course her own clothes would have been too wet and muddied for her to be put to bed in them. She lifted one arm and saw how the sleeve extended way beyond her fingertips. The garment was sheer white batiste with mother-of-pearl buttons down the front. A man's shirt. Trevallyan's shirt.

A hot, sickly blush crawled up her cheeks as she remembered what she had been wearing when Trevallyan must have her found her. She had been wearing nothing but her night rail. She could just picture the ladies at the Weymouth-Hampstead School, or the Catholic matrons of the parish, dropping dead of mortification. She couldn't even blame them. Her own constitution was much more sound than those sheltered English roses, and even she felt ill with shame.

"And forgive us our trespasses as we forgive those who trespass against us. . . ."

At the sound of Trevallyan's voice, she jerked her head to the right. There sat the reason for her humiliation, watching her, his eyes as cool as the ice from the winter Boyne.

She met his gaze, for the moment forgetting the blinding white pain in her head. He sat in an elbow chair with his black-booted feet crossed in front of him. He was dressed in black trousers and a starched shirt much like the one she wore. His black neckcloth nearly covered his fashionably turned-out collar, and his figured-silk waistcoat, the color of crushed grapes, lent him an air of wealth that seemed in marked contrast to his dark, somber gray frock coat. He looked down at her, with an air of disdain. His face was freshly shaven and smelling of vetiver soap, while she, on the other hand, looked a mess.

Shrinking inside from humiliation, she pictured herself as she sat in the bed. Her hair hung in a curtain of black knotted hanks, and she was hardly bathed since her encounter with all the mud.

She waited for him to say something cutting, but he didn't. He merely glanced at her and said obliquely, " 'Tis a good motto for life, is it not? 'Forgive us our trespasses as we forgive those who trespass against us.' "

She opened her mouth, quick to explain that she had not meant yet again to be trespassing on his land, but her gaze fell on his face.

Beneath all the polish, he appeared worn. There was a tiredness around his eyes that she hadn't noticed before. He looked as if he'd been carrying a terrible burden that had now been lifted. In the back of her mind, she wondered if perhaps it was she who had burdened him, but the idea seemed so absurd—the Lord Trevallyan sitting vigil at the bedside of a woman little better than a street urchin—that she couldn't quite believe it. There was no reason for him to care for her; more so, in her every encounter with him, he'd gone out of his way to make sure she knew what little value she held in his esteem. If there was something troubling him, it surely hadn't been her health. Then her gaze lowered to his lips. A terrible, downright sickening thought occurred to her. She had dreamed she had kissed Malachi, and it was a dream so real she could still feel the press of warm lips on her own, feel the hard, strong hand cup the back of her neck and pull her farther into his embrace. She would swear on her grave she had kissed someone and that it hadn't been entirely a dream. If all along she'd been in Trevallyan's possession, then she might have actually kissed . . .

Her hand clamped over her mouth that was now open wide with shock, not retort. She met his gaze and her eyes burned with guilt. It couldn't be true. She couldn't have kissed him, but the discomfort she found in his own gaze damned her more than her own foggy remembrance.

"Did—did . . . Did I kiss you?" she whispered, agony in her voice.

"Yes," he answered coldly, suddenly unable to meet her eyes.

She cringed at his stiff, disapproving countenance and wondered how she could have become such a trollop. Perhaps she was cursed by her mother's past after all. Perhaps it was something she could not control, like the funny, hot feeling she got whenever she thought of the men who bathed nude in the River Lir. So was her life over? Was she now going to have the urge to kiss every man? Even the good father and Trevallyan's old, one-armed butler? God save her.

" 'Twas not *that* unpleasant, I wager."

Her gaze flickered back to his. If she didn't know better, she'd believe there was a tiny, so-small-if-you-blinked-you-would-miss-it, glimmer of amusement in his blue-green eyes.

Stupidly, she stuttered, "Wh-what was not that unpleasant, my lord?"

"The kiss."

"But I didn't mean to kiss you," she blurted out, backing away from the topic like a wet cat running from a bucket. "Please believe me, I thought you were someone else."

Trevallyan stared at her so pointedly he seemed to be drilling holes right through her. "I see," he said, his voice tinged with a strange anger. "Was this man, perchance, the criminal who burnt down the Quinn barn last night?"

She felt a knot tighten in her throat. Malachi had been in trouble when she'd seen him last. She didn't want to hear tell of crimes. "Was anyone hurt?"

"The barn couldn't be saved." He quieted. "Nor could Kathleen's prize mare."

Ravenna stared at the rumpled sheets, sickened by the picture of a terrified mare burning up in flames. She couldn't believe Malachi, the boy she had known and loved, would do such a wicked deed, but deep in her heart she knew it was probably true. Something had happened to him. Growing up poor and resentful had turned Malachi's mischievous tendencies into criminal ones.

"Do they know who it was that burned the barn down?" she asked, her throat dry and fiery from withheld tears.

He gripped her jaw and turned her head to face him. "A man said he saw the criminal's face lit briefly by the barn fires. He said he thought the lad looked like . . . Malachi MacCumhal."

"A scant sighting in the dead of night is not evidence the fire was set by him." She bit her lower lip and her forehead lined with worry. "Besides, I can't believe Malachi would *purposely* do such a thing. Nobody loves horses as much as he does. Why, he sneaks old Reverend Drummond's mare an ear of corn every time the old man isn't looking."

"Malachi will hang if he doesn't quit this White Boy nonsense."

"He didn't burn that barn down, I tell you!" She thrust her jaw from his grasp and stared at him with eyes that glittered with anger. Her behavior was contrary to her thoughts, but as irrational as it was, she still couldn't accept Malachi's blame. And especially not from Trevallyan. Niall Trevallyan had never known hardship and loss. He sat in his fine castle all day, counting his riches and devising the next pleasure, like all the rest of the Ascendency. At the moment, the wife and baby buried in the Trevallyan graveyard didn't seem to mar her picture of him one bit. The man before her had been born to every privilege and fortune, and he could never know how Malachi felt. Never.

"You defend him?" Trevallyan asked coolly.

"Yes," she snapped, though she was no more sure of Malachi's innocence than Trevallyan was.

Trevallyan screeched back his chair and rose. He crossed his arms over his chest and peered down at her as if she were a hapless child. "So you claim he's not guilty. I trust you can back up that claim."

She stared up at his grave features, fear for her dear friend twisting in her heart. "I—I *know* he didn't burn down that barn. You must understand, I know Malachi. He's a good lad. I *know* he is."

"What you think of his character is irrelevant to the magistrate."

"Oh, please, *please* don't take this to the magistrate. You must not get the magistrate involved in this petty mischief."

"Ravenna," he tipped her chin up so that she would look at him, "this is not petty mischief and it is already in the lap of the magistrate because *I* am the magistrate."

She gazed up at Trevallyan in shock. She'd been away so long in London she had forgotten the hierarchy. It was easy to understand why Malachi hated Trevallyan so. Malachi always referred to Lord Trevallyan as if he were king. If Niall Trevallyan owned all the county and was the magistrate too, he might as well be king for all the difference it made.

"Fifteen people came to the castle this morning demanding Malachi be hanged. They want the lad's politics put to rest once and for all."

"Have they caught him?" she whispered, her voice wan and hollow from grief.

"No. He's hiding. But when they do catch him—"

"When they catch him you can tell them he is innocent."

Trevallyan raised one faded gold eyebrow. "How so?"

"Because he was with me last night," she uttered, her face still as stone. Lying was a sin, but she couldn't believe all the terrible things said about Malachi either. Besides, it was true. Malachi had been with her last night. At least part of the night.

But, just as she had dreaded, when the alibi was out, she saw on Trevallyan's face what everyone would think of her story. All would say that she and Malachi had met on the bluff because they were lovers. Her reputation, if she ever had one anyway, would be ruined.

"By the clothing I found you in, I needn't ask what you were doing." The lord's expression seemed to grow hard, as if he were fighting the urge to slap her.

"Tell Lord Quinn that Malachi didn't burn down his barn. He's not a White Boy. He would never hurt anyone intentionally."

"His politics are bad, Ravenna. It's rumored he's hurt—no—*killed* people, whether he wanted to or not. He seeks justice with injustice. You're a fool if you cannot see that."

She stared at him for a long moment, then crumpled to the bed, defeated. "I don't know if he burned the barn down or not. I only know that I was with him last night. And I shall say so if I must in his defense."

Suddenly she was grabbed by force and shoved against his chest. "You are never to see Malachi MacCumhal again, do you hear me! You are to stay away from him. Stay away from him!"

She released a muffled sob and looked wildly into his aqua eyes. She had never seen anyone so angry. Not even Malachi had looked so murderous. "What right do you have to order me about like this and tell me who will or who won't be my friend? You act like a jealous . . ." *Lover,* she'd almost said, and she might as well have, for the word stood between them as clear as if she'd spoken it.

He released her as if he had suddenly discovered she was anathema. She fell against the satin coverlet and pillows in a heap of white batiste shirt and jet-black hair.

He stared at her and said, "I do *not* care for you."

"Then why do my affairs concern you in so passionate a manner?" she retorted, brushing a knotted tress of hair out of her eyes.

He looked away as if he despaired of answering. "This *geis,* it's destroyed my life. . . ."

"What are you talking about?"

"Do you know what a *geis* is, Ravenna?" He turned and looked at her with the same cold expression she knew so well.

"I know what a *geis* is."

"The Trevallyans have a *geis*. I've defied it." His gaze traveled to the window where the graveyard could be seen beyond. The black, crumbling tombstones jutted through the low-lying mists, which the sun had yet to burn away. She shivered at his expression.

"Some in this county would say that beyond in that grave lies the proof of my defiance," he whispered.

"What is your *geis*?" she couldn't stop herself from asking.

He looked at her and a fearsome smile twisted his lips. "The day I believe it will be the day I tell you."

"But . . . you must believe it a bit or you wouldn't be behaving this way. . . ." Her words dwindled as he drew closer. His expression was hard and somewhat mirthful. She didn't like it at all.

"I'm an educated thinker. A modern man of the nineteenth century. The coincidence of this *geis* bedevils me, I'll admit it. But believe it, never." He sat down on the edge of the bed and clamped his hand at her nape. She stared up at him, frightened and yet intrigued by his strange moods.

"You've grown into a beauty, Ravenna, and don't think I haven't noticed. It's just one other thing that bedevils me." His gaze slid downward to where the shirt parted, revealing a healthy portion of her breasts.

Embarrassed by her loss of modesty, unnerved by his challenging stare, she struggled to clutch the shirt together, but with his remaining hand, he held hers to her lap.

"What do you see when you look at me, Ravenna?"

Her eyes locked with his. The pounding of her heart grew fierce. "What do you mean?"

"Out of curiosity—if I were to come to your bed—how would I fare against your young stallion MacCumhal? Would you look at me and find me a good and worthy partner?" He drew her closer until their noses almost touched and she could feel the heat of his breath on her cheek. "Or would you just laugh at me and call me a lecherous old man for chasing such a sweet young skirt?"

A red-hot blush prickled her cheeks. He had a right to think her a loose-moraled woman after how he had found her and after her confession that she had been with Malachi last night. Still, rational thought didn't squelch the fire of anger burning in her chest. His insulting talk was too keen to ignore.

"My lord, I would not reject you for your age," she looked at him hatefully, "but for your wit."

He laughed. It was a deep black-humored chuckle that rumbled up from his chest. She thought he might let her go. Instead, he held her tight and whispered, "If you had answered any other way, I might not have wanted to do this." Slowly he lowered his face. In a warm breath, he murmured, "This time there is no laudanum. This time you will know whom you are kissing."

She gave one jerk of her head for him to release her, but his hand on her nape was too strong. His mouth pressed down on her own, beckoning her to succumb. She refused, fighting the kiss with every grain of her strength; still, he was winning. His lips still held hers in a warm, hungry kiss, and moment by moment, his hold on her softened as his seduction grew more powerful and she began to melt in a slow surrender.

Malachi's attempted kisses had never been like this. There was a calculation in Trevallyan's movements that strangely thrilled her. Where Malachi's brusque lovemaking had been like the rut of an animal, Trevallyan's was like being wooed ever so gently, ever so smoothly, ever so blindly, over to the devil. He was manipulative, as complex as a spider's web, and with every repeated pull of his lips upon hers, she wondered how she was going to escape the maze of his weavings.

In the end, the choice was not her own. As slowly as he had begun the kiss, he pulled back, making her wallow in every strange, mixed-up feeling he had given her. He fingered her kiss-burned lips as if his touch were salve. She wanted to spit on him, slap him, anything that would make him feel as damned and confused as she was feeling now.

But she tried no retaliation. Anything she could do would look child-ish. He would only laugh at her, increasing her humiliation. He was king in Lir. He was God. He was even magistrate. She had no power over him. Only the power to reject. And reject him she would, for she despised him. Never more than right at that moment.

"I sent Grania a note telling her about your accident," he said softly. "The physician said you should have bed rest for a week. I've informed your grandmother about all of this. She knows when to expect you back."

Ravenna was suddenly glad for one thing. Trevallyan's vileness had diverted her from her aching head. But now she felt the room spin and she began to realize that her eyes squinted from the pain in her head.

"I won't endure your hospitality for that long, I assure you." She rubbed her temples and looked around the room for her clothes. Then she remembered again she had worn nothing but a night rail when he'd found her.

Feeling cursed, she drew back onto the pillows and said, "If you would be so kind as to have Grania send me some clothes . . ."

"She'll send you a gown when the physician says 'tis time for you to leave. In the meanwhile, I believe you look rather pale. I suggest you get some sleep," he stood and walked to the door, "and pray for Malachi MacCumhal's soul."

She opened one eye and glared at him. Like a fencer who wished to be the last to parry, she said, " 'Tis your soul you should be concerned with, my lord. You may be meeting your maker sooner than you think." She wiped the back of her hand across her mouth as if it had left a bad taste there. "Especially if you try to kiss me again."

His lips curved in an angry smile. "I don't like this *geis*." His gaze lit upon her lips as if in possession. "No, I think I'll wait . . . and next time let you be the one to kiss me." With that, he turned and departed.

She fell into a fitful sleep. Greeves entered the chamber at one point with another servant, who brought her a tray of food, but the tray remained untouched as Ravenna dozed in the enormous four-poster bed, the darkness of closed eyes the only balm for her aching head.

When she fully awoke, it was night. Candle shadows danced from the lit lusters that had been placed upon the caryatid mantelpiece, and the leaded glass of the huge windows were moist from the heat emanating from the fireplace. A servant had come and gone once more, for there was a hot pot of tea on a tray lined with pristine linen, and her pillows had been fluffed and placed in order behind her still aching head.

She wanted to get out of bed and stretch her sore muscles. She was pleased and disconcerted to find one of Trevallyan's Kashmir dressing gowns laid across the foot of the bed, should she care to use it.

"Bother him," she grumbled, and reached for the black dressing gown. Its softness amazed her, and when she wrapped it around her body she was further bedeviled by the fact that it smelled faintly of vetiver soap and something else . . . or rather, someone else.

She rolled up the heavy emerald-green satin cuffs and touched her bare feet to the cold stone floor. Thick ruby-colored Persian rugs with birds and the Tree of Life design were scattered across the floor, and she used them for stepping-stones to the antechamber, where a pleasant little fire burned at the hearth, and the chair-side table was stacked with ancient, well-read tomes.

After pouring herself a cup of tea, she sat in one of the two chairs. It was habit to take the lesser of two things, perhaps because of her days at the English school, so she sat in the used, worn chair first, pointedly avoiding the newer one. Yet, no matter how she tried, which way she shifted, she couldn't get comfortable. The chair had been broken in in all the wrong places. Where she needed give, it bumped out, and where she needed support, the upholstery was worn down into a hollow. It should have been a comfortable chair regardless, for even in its age, it was a fine chair and well-made, but for some inexplicable reason, it proved nothing short of medieval torture for her. Unable to bear it, she lifted herself from the seat and stepped to the newer adjoining chair. She sank into it and released a sigh of exquisite comfort. It fit just right.

With her thoughts again able to return to the situation at hand, she snuggled down into the chair and searched the room. Undoubtably, her dignity would be salvaged if she opened the door and trotted back to Grania's right now, but her forehead still ached abominably, and she couldn't summon the wherewithal to plan an escape. Short of one stolen kiss, Trevallyan had been more than generous with his hospitality. He had procured a physician and had even allowed her the most luxurious room in the castle in which to recuperate. She had nothing to complain about except for her host's rather boorish behavior, and it wasn't likely that Trevallyan would be visiting her often. It was probably wise that she stay a few days. The walk home seemed interminable and would probably only do her further harm. Besides, her head still hurt abominably and there was a tender red welt across her temple where one of the horses' shoes must have met with her head.

She sank further into the chair and made the decision to accept her temporary quarters. In a few days she would feel more like herself and would be able to return home on her own. For now, she would rest, and keep her mind off Trevallyan, the thought of whom made her head pound even more.

Sipping the tea, she stared into the fire until she felt sleepy again, but unwilling to let herself go, she straightened and reached for one of the books beside her. A large piece of blank paper fell out where Trevallyan had marked his place. She made a halfhearted attempt to find the page the paper had meant to mark, then wickedly closed the book and replaced it on the table, the bookmark still in her hand. She felt the urge to write and was pleased to find an inkwell and a Venetian glass pen on Trevallyan's nearby desk. Curled up in the unused chair, she began to scratch out Skya's next adventure:

The years went by. War with their neighbors dragged on, moving painfully on bloody, battled feet. Skya's sisters grew into women, and Grace, the younger and more headstrong of the two, was the one to first ask about Skya.

"Papa, I remember the dragon," she said one day while her father, the king, was busy with his war minister.

"My good, fair daughter, there, there, how nice. Now move along," the

king answered distractedly. " 'Tis been a year since Prince Aidan has disappeared and King Turoe has just sent a note citing heinous retribution if we don't surrender his son."

"Why don't you surrender him, Father?" Grace asked with an innocent's logic.

"We haven't got him, my sweet. We don't know where the man has gone off to. Prince Aidan may have died on his travels, but his father, King Turoe, believes we hold him captive. I fear until he seizes our castle and searches it himself, he will not believe us."

"Have we sent a messenger and told King Turoe this?"

The king rubbed his finely bearded jaw in frustration. "My dear, it's not as simple as all that. I have sent messengers. For a year, I've done so, but in war one isn't always believed. Prince Aidan was last seen to the north of our kingdom, and so his people have concluded that he is held captive here at the castle. All we can do now is defend ourselves against these new attacks. Now you can see Papa is very busy, so be a good girl and—"

"Papa, did the dragon kill Skya? I had a dream about her. 'Tis been so long since I saw her—I was a child when we encountered the dragon—is that why she is no longer with us? Is she dead?"

The king looked down at his youngest daughter, who had grown into the full bloom of womanhood. He looked damned, cursed, as if he didn't know how to explain anything of the confusing world to so pure a creature as Grace. "Child—oh, if only you were still a child—your sister is gone because she had powers our people little understand and greatly fear. She lives in isolation, and there she must live until . . . until"—the king seemed to find a strange lump in his throat—"well, for a very long time. Until our people understand her and accept her as one of their own." He looked away as if hiding something wet and sad in his eyes. "Go along with you, Grace. I'm very busy now."

"Where does she live?" Grace asked as she picked up her velvet kirtle and headed for the door.

"Somewhere in the Dark Woods of Hawthorn. Somewhere quiet and lonely and unmarked by human hatred." The king released a deep sigh, then he dismissed her and turned his attention back to the war minister who was telling him how many fires would be needed for all the cauldrons of oil. . . .

Ravenna grew more and more sleepy until the glass pen went limp in her grasp and its point wept black ink onto the bottom of the page. Her head lolled back onto the plump, like-new leather chair, and she had one last thought before slumber took hold. 'Twas a curious shame so beautiful a chair had gone unused, lo, these many years.

Chapter 14

TREVALLYAN ENTERED his apartments with a candelabra in his hand to chase away the shadows. He walked through the darkened antechamber, and to his surprise, he found his bedstead empty, the covers thrown aside in a haphazard manner as if the occupant had been in haste to leave it.

A thin light sputtered from the mantel where the luster's flames were drowned in a pool of beeswax. He raised the candelabra to better illuminate the room, but she was nowhere to be found. Ravenna was gone as if spirited away by the moss faeries.

He looked toward the antechamber doors. The glow of coals dying in the hearth painted the small room an unnatural devilish red. When he entered it, he was unable to put his finger on exactly what was out of place, on what was bothering him. Then he froze in his tracks.

The chair. There it was. *The* chair. The one that had never been used. *She* was in it.

He stared, unable to summon the force to propel himself

forward. His urge was to snatch her from the seat and shake her until her head spun. He didn't want her in that chair. The chair was special. Waiting. But not for her. *Never* for her. Yet he knew he couldn't do anything rash. If he forbade her a seat in the chair he might reveal himself to be a lunatic. And he didn't want to do that. He was a rational, intelligent man who rarely got bested. Even now, he told himself it shouldn't bother him what chair she chose to sit in.

But it did. It did.

She sighed and snuggled deeper into the upholstery, appearing completely at ease. As if the chair had been made for her.

He scowled and eased himself down into his own chair, staring. She was Satan's angel, asleep in *his* chair, her black tresses falling across the leather-upholstered arm like a widow's veil. In the demon light, she looked wickedly beautiful, incongruously innocent. Everything about her tempted him.

He squeezed his eyes closed. He would not be bested. He would not succumb. Superstition and fate, they were nothing but the products of coincidence. Intelligence was what mattered. Using his brain and not his loins would win him this fight against stupidity. And he wanted to win, didn't he?

He growled an oath.

Then his attention was blessedly distracted by the sound of paper slipping to the floor. He looked down at Ravenna's dangling arm and found a loose sheet with her practiced scroll covering almost every inch of it. He wondered if she was penning a letter to MacCumhal, and though he knew it was ungentlemanly of him to read it, he had never professed himself to be a gentleman. He leaned forward and retrieved it. He read it all the way through. Twice.

Grace took the news of her sister's exile very hard. At night she found she had difficulty sleeping because her mind pictured Skya alone and weeping into her apron. She heard the sound of human wails in a dark woods where no human sounds were ever heard.

She awoke one morning with the determination to seek out her sister and rescue her. If that was not possible, if Skya refused to return, then Grace

wanted to at least bring her sister a stein of red wine and some occasional
company.

The battlements of the castle were crenulated with the silhouette of
soldiers. They waited in silent agonies for King Turoe to begin his long-
promised siege to find his son, the prince they did not hold. Grace veiled her
long blond hair with a crude piece of fustian she had "borrowed" from one of
the kitchen workers, then, looking like a common serving wench, she stole
out of the heavily guarded bailey. She ran down the promontory on which
her father's castle stood and lost herself in the Dark Woods of Hawthorn
below.

Niall replaced the paper on the table beside Ravenna's sleeping figure. A little begrudgingly, he had to admit her writing was a fine piece
of work. One that showed skill and imagination, and the ability to take
its reader by the hand and lead him into another world. Indeed, he
wanted to read on, but he knew there was no more. The story was now
just a fragment; the rest had yet to be written, but what little he had
read proved an intelligence and sensitivity he didn't want to grant
existed in a girl he had found running shamelessly in the night.

Reluctantly, he forced himself to look at her. He'd been rather
shocked by the sight of her in the chair, but now the shock was
lessening. He had bought the chair for his wife long ago, before he even
knew who his wife would be. There was irony in the *geis,* if nothing
else. The thing was beginning to have a personality of its own, mocking
him at every turn.

He looked down at the sleeping girl. Her pink lips were parted in
slumber and her heavy black lashes created smudged shadows beneath
her closed eyes. She looked pale and vulnerable and in need of protection. It rather irked him to see her that way. Pale and vulnerable.
Trustingly asleep in his chamber, in *his* chair, as if there were no such
things as big, bad wolves.

A bit more roughly than needed, he placed his hand beneath her jaw
and pushed her head up.

Slowly, the glorious black lashes fluttered open. She met his gaze
with a steady one of her own. He was pleased to see the slight glimmer

of fear in the violet depths of her eyes. Think what he might of the girl, he had to admit she was not unintelligent.

"You should not be out of bed," he said brusquely.

"I was not only out of bed, but on my way out the door." She pulled back from his touch, irritation enlivening her dark-angel face.

He glanced with amusement between the bed and the massive carved doorway. "And you needed a nap in between? Methinks you tire easily."

She didn't bother to answer; instead, as if a dread thought had just occurred to her, she straightened in the chair, swept back her hair, and covertly searched for the paper. When she saw it on the table, she seemed to relax.

"What have you been doing all evening?" He was pleased how the question seemed to unnerve her.

"I—I was reading. I didn't think you'd mind. You've so many books." With apprehension in her eyes, she stared at him like a mouse waiting for the barn cat.

"What have you been scribbling over here?"

He nonchalantly reached for the paper on the table. She leapt out of the seat like a wraith.

"Don't look at that! 'Tis mine!" She snatched it from his hand. To her obvious chagrin, he began to laugh.

Glaring at him, she said, "You read this while I was asleep. How dare you! How rude!"

"I thought you might be penning inflammatory pamphlets. One can't be too careful with the likes of your friends, me girl," he said, unable to stop the black laughter that emanated from his chest.

"You thought no such thing. You were snooping. At least admit your crime."

"All right. I was snooping. So what exactly are you writing? I couldn't decipher it."

She appeared wounded. "I'm writing a novel."

His laughter broke out anew. "Indeed? That's rich." He could see she despised him. Her venomous stare could kill a boar.

"And why do you mock me? What's wrong with my becoming a

novelist? 'Tis a fairy tale I'm writing. I think it most suitable for
women."

"You'll never get it published. Why don't you spend your time
sketching, or improving your needlework like any other gentle-
woman?"

"Give me one reason why I shall fail at this." She placed her hands
on her hips and dared him to answer.

He stared at her, dismayed at her spirit, beguiled by her appearance.
"I can give you one reason, and then a multitude," he said slowly.
Despite wanting to appear aloof, he couldn't stop his gaze from flickering down her figure. Admiration—and something not nearly so pure—
crossed his features as he regarded the way her curves wore his dark,
masculine dressing gown. What was it about a woman in heavy masculine clothes that made her seem five times softer and more curvaceous
than in her own clothes? Looking at her, he knew he would be forever
vexed by the question.

"You won't get published," he stated, "because you're a female. Pub-
lishers just don't publish novels by a woman."

"They've published some women. And women may like to read what
I write. I write about heroines."

"You're ignoring the fact that the chaps in London aren't going to
take you seriously. Publishing is an ancient business, run by men. They
don't care to read what women like. All that romance. Why, I shudder
to think about it."

"But if there was money to be made, they would publish a woman."

He heaved a sigh, wondering how he could make this small, fragile,
bulldoggish female understand. "Women may indeed want to read
novels such as yours, but they'd best settle on penny gothics because
that's all there will ever be for you ladies. No man wants to read about a
woman. That is, unless she's the victim of a tragedy."

"I've tragedy in my novels."

"Then why don't you take a *nom de plume*. Niall Trevallyan is a nice
name."

Her expression seemed very far away, as if she were already having
reveries about her success. "No, I shall write under my own name,
'Ravenna.' I shall become a great novelist, and if the literary community

laughs at me and disparages my work because my heroines triumph
over their tragedies, and over men, then so be it. I shall be beloved by
my readers."

"Silly girl. You will lose that battle."

" 'A wild wish has just flown from my heart to my head, and I will
not stifle it. . . . I do earnestly wish to see the distinction of sex
confounded in society. . . .' " Ravenna stared at him, and added,
". . . and in publishing."

He groaned. He couldn't believe it. Where had this child been
spawned? He couldn't quite pin her down. Just when he thought he
had her character assessed, he discovered another facet of her character
he'd never counted on. "Don't throw Mary Wollstonecraft at me. And
where did you read all her nonsense anyway?"

"One of my teachers had *A Vindication of the Rights of Woman* in her
room. She let me read it whenever I was invited to tea."

He stared at her, confounded. Ireland was rumbling with rebellion
for the Home Rule, and yet, here was this little ember of a woman
talking of equality between the sexes. Perhaps 'twas a good thing she
was a bastard and not raised papist. He couldn't wait to see what
Father Nolan would have to say about her outrageous thinking. Wickedly, he made a mental note to invite the father and Ravenna both to
tea. Already he had several incendiary comments tucked away in his
head to ignite that little tête-à-tête.

"I shall get published, just you wait, Lord Trevallyan."

Her determination impressed him. "They will never accept you."

"Perhaps not men. But that's only half the population."

" 'Tis the only half that matters."

"Now."

She tossed him a quiet, secretive smile that could have seduced Saint
Patrick to stroll through the fires of all hell. His stomach rolled into
strange knots as he watched her clutch the satin lapels of the dressing
gown to her breasts and walk to the coal-lit hearth.

She was nothing like he had thought she was. Every time he had her
caged, he only had to look behind him and she was there, taunting him
to capture her once more.

"Is this career as a great novelist going to save you and your grandmother from poverty, or will you marry Chesham instead?"

She extended her hands toward the glowing coals, her composure unruffled by his thinly veiled insult. "What business this is of yours, I shall never know, but since you insist upon prying into my life, I will tell you. I pray my work gets published, but Grania and I do not depend upon it. We receive a stipend every month from my father."

"Father . . . ?" He nearly choked. "But you don't get that money from him. You don't even know who he is." He could have kicked himself once the words were out.

Her eyes glittered like a cat's. Angrily, she said, "My father loved me dearly, Lord Trevallyan. Though he hadn't the chance to marry my mother, he nonetheless saw to my care and upkeep. Grania won't admit where the money comes from, but I know just the same that it is my father who has provided for me. He loved me."

Now that's a *real* fairy tale, he thought, silently watching her, but she was so poignantly defiant about her father's love, nothing short of a pistol to his head would have made him admit at that moment that it was he, not her disreputable father, who had paid for her upkeep all these years. "My guess is that he did not deserve such a devoted daughter," he said softly.

She seemed pained, as if struck by regret. "No. I think he must have deserved much better."

There was a long moment as they both stared into the fire, each seemingly absorbed in his or her own thoughts.

Finally, she whispered, "Have they caught Malachi yet?"

Niall looked at her melancholy profile until it was burned into his mind. "They say he has escaped into another county. No doubt his cronies'll get him shipped to America. You'll probably never see him again."

The pain in her eyes made him suck in his breath. Anger grew and consumed him. It licked like flames at his heart. Especially when he saw the crystalline sparkle of tears in her eyes.

"What do you see in MacCumhal?" he demanded cruelly. "He's a rotten character. He'd only have gotten you into trouble; worse yet, he might have gotten you killed. He's gone, and I say good riddance. He

saved us the length of rope we might have wasted to see him hanged."
He stared at her, oddly exhilarated by the anger in her gaze. When she
said nothing, he couldn't resist the temptation to push her over the
edge. "I see you sorrow at his departure. You cry because you did not
have an end like your mother's."

"Malachi is my friend. If you were something other than the devil
himself, you would know what it is like to lose one's friend."

She leashed her fury well, and he was sorely disappointed. He
wanted to see her lose control. He wouldn't have even minded if she
had tried to slap him because he would have enjoyed the tussle. Better
yet, he would have won.

She looked up from the fire, giving him that steady, composed gaze
he knew she had learned in the English boarding school. For the first
time ever, he regretted having sent her away.

"If you would excuse me, I'd like to be alone now," she said.

He cursed himself for forgetting her fragile health. Suddenly the
shadows beneath her eyes, her pale, drawn face, gave him a small stab
of guilt. "Of course. You must not be feeling well."

"I'm feeling fine, Lord Trevallyan." She stared at him in a rather arch
manner. " 'Tis just that I would like my privacy to pray that Malachi
reaches his destination with God's speed. To pray for his soul and his
safety."

Jealousy struck him like a hot poker. Before he could stop himself,
he released a bitter laugh. "It's pitiful that you should pray for him.
What? Has your literary soul taken with his rebellious impulses? How
cliché, how stupid."

"Stop it." Her English facade finally began to crack beneath her Irish
fire. "I won't take this. You're not my father, and you're not my lover.
You cannot scorn me and tell me what to do. I won't listen to you."

"I'm not your father . . . but I would be your lover." He stared at
her, shocked by the truth that had come from within. "Oh, yes," he
whispered, his voice hushed by the revelation. "That I would be."

The sheer, unadulterated horror that crossed her features would
have made him laugh had it not been for the fact that it bruised him
sorely. Covering over his vulnerability, he sneered, "So, shall we all
queue up? MacCumhal, Chesham, and now me? You could have us all,

you know. Each in our own way." The words felt like bile on his tongue.

"I hate you." Tears of hurt glistened in her eyes. "No man has ever made me hate like I hate you."

He stared at her, wondering if he was pleased the *geis* would now never come true, or torn apart that this woman who was slowly winding him around her finger despised him as she despised no other on earth.

Numb and silent, suddenly longing for his whiskey decanter, he bowed and left her in peace.

Ravenna slumped to the chair as soon as the door shut behind him. In tearful agony, she wondered how he could treat her so viciously one minute and so tenderly the next. As she sat hugging the arm of the chair, it crossed her mind that Trevallyan might be a lunatic. It was possible he was the product of decades of bad English breeding. But she knew if Niall Trevallyan was insane, he hid it well behind an intelligent, orderly, mature facade.

She closed her eyes, her injured head and pride draining her of energy. She did hate him. He made her feel like a whore. He made her feel loose and dirty and stupid. He'd done worse than even Malachi had done.

And yet . . .

And yet, he had spoken to her about Mary Wollstonecraft. He had rooms full of books that few in her world seemed to appreciate. She could talk to him when he wasn't being cruel, and she felt he listened —a strange and unique trait in a man. In some ways, Niall Trevallyan had many of the characteristics that she wanted in a man. His company offered not just the flattery of male desire, but a man to talk to, to read with, to walk with in the garden, holding hands. Were there no other men such as he? She recounted in her mind all the men she knew. When she got to the picture of the count and herself walking in the garden and talking about Mary Wollstonecraft, she suddenly choked on a giggle. The sad truth was there seemed to be no man out there for her. She wanted a hero; she dreamed her father had been a hero, she wrote about heroes, but where was the one for her?

Against her will she stared at the massive carved double doors where Trevallyan had exited.

Chapter 15

ORNING TEA was carried into the private apartment at precisely eight o'clock the next morning. A small, gray-haired, sweet-faced Irishwoman whom Ravenna thought was named Katey brought it to her on a silver tray with hot crumpets wrapped in lacy white linens. Too officious for questions, Katey addressed Ravenna's bleary-eyed countenance with a pleasant "good morning," then briskly screened off the bed with the bedcurtains.

From behind the green damask walls, Ravenna heard the noise of a stream of heavy-footed servants bringing hot water up from the kitchen. Her nerves were set on edge by the screech of a copper bath dragged across bare stone and filled with bucket after leather bucket of boiling water. Unsure what was expected of her, she pulled the covers to her chin and waited for Katey to come fetch her. The desire to bathe was strong—she still wore the mud that she had fallen in so many nights ago—but her desire for privacy was stronger, and she was certainly not going to trot nude to the bath before what seemed to be a dozen servants.

Katey, in her exceedingly cheerful manner, solved the dilemma. She dismissed the lead-footed army, and when the last had begun the descent down the tower stairs, the maid drew back the bedcurtains, sprinkled French rose petals into the bathwater, and disappeared herself, leaving Ravenna astonished at the almost mechanical efficiency by which the household was run.

Of course, the servants would be *forced* to be exacting in order to meet Niall Trevallyan's arrogant expectations, she thought crossly. She stared at the tub for a long time, convincing herself that if she had the energy to make it to the tub, she had the energy to find her way home. Her head still hurt, but not nearly as acutely as it had the day before. But there was no solving the problem of clothes. She had none other than Trevallyan's batiste shirt. Even Trevallyan's dressing gown seemed to have disappeared with Katey.

With a weary sigh, she drew away the covers and climbed down from the bed's high mattress. She unbuttoned the shirt and trailed it on the ground behind her, dropping it before the tub, then she sank within the sweet warmth of the water. After pouring herself a cup of tea from the nearby table, she sighed again, this time for another reason entirely. For the first time in her life she was experiencing true luxury.

Dreamily, she sipped her tea and blew at the fragrant, rising steam of the tub water. The copper tub's contents heated and soothed her sore muscles. Soon, she thought she would either be fit enough to run home, or would fall asleep.

"Hullo, what have we here?"

She nearly leapt from the tub and plastered herself on the coffered ceiling. A man had entered the antechamber. She didn't dare turn to see him, but she knew he stood directly behind her and she recognized his voice instantly. It was Trevallyan's cousin, Lord Chesham.

"My fine cousin coaxes me to return to London, and yet here I find his reasons for staying behind . . . a young lass in the master's chambers . . . and who are you that Trevallyan has found you worthy of sharing his bed?" Chesham took two steps farther into the room. Ravenna crossed her arms over her chest and turned her head as far from him as she could. She wanted to cry out for him to be gone and spare

her further shame and embarrassment, but her voice would not coop-
erate. Mortification choked her.

He chuckled and took another step. The sound left her uneasy. It
made clear there were other issues suddenly at play besides her lack of
modesty.

"Let me see your face, lass, and I'll bring you a pretty trifle from
London. Would you like that? A pretty trifle for a pretty face. Come.
Turn around and look at me."

A terrified sob caught in her throat. If she looked at him, he would
never leave her alone. The situation damned her. He'd already jumped
to all sorts of incorrect conclusions; if he discovered her true identity,
he might be so jealous over what he believed to be the master's conquest over her that he could be capable of any kind of retaliation.
Trevallyan should have never been so outrageously courteous as to
allow her the use of his room. Chesham would now think she was the
lord's mistress. And no matter how she might word her denials, she
knew from Chesham's predatory tone he would never let her out of the
bedroom before all his questions were answered.

"Come, tell me your name. . . ."

He stood almost behind her. She shivered and wished she could curl
into a ball and drown herself in the rose-scented bathwater. Anger fired
within her, but she shunted it aside. The heart-pounding fear of his
discovering her identity took all her attention. If she could not make
him go away before she was forced to turn around, he might take
advantage of her and no one would see fit to punish him. She was a
naked, unmarried woman in the master's chambers. There would be
no one to stand up in her defense.

"Please—" She shuddered as he placed his hand on her back.

"Turn around—"

"What the bloody hell are you doing in here?" another male voice
boomed from the doorway. Ravenna grew weak with relief. It was
Trevallyan's voice.

"I came here looking for you but found . . . this." Chesham
paused. He removed his hand from her back, and she could hear him
step away. She heard him whisper, "Who is she, Niall? She's got to be a

servant from the looks of her dirty hair. Since when have you taken a liking for servants?"

"Get out, Chesham." Trevallyan's tone brooked little discussion. Every word was tight with barely leashed anger.

Footsteps went to the door, but before Chesham left, she heard him say, "When you're through with her, tell her she might perhaps find a place in my bed. I've never been privileged enough to have a go at your leavings."

"Get out!" Trevallyan growled. The doors were promptly shut behind him and she heard the fading sound of boots tap on the winding stone staircase.

Ravenna didn't move in the tub. She sat in it, frozen, holding her arms over her breasts in a pitiable attempt at modesty. She didn't know what she had expected in Chesham, but his crudeness had shocked her. Trevallyan had told her she would be nothing but a toy to him, and though Chesham hadn't known whom he was toying with, Ravenna saw miles into his character from this brief episode.

Her cheeks hot with anger, humiliation, and the struggle to keep herself from crying, she finally turned her head to look at Trevallyan. He stood grimly by the closed door, his arms folded across his chest, his gaze pinned on her own.

"Thank you," she whispered.

He smirked as if in apology. "Love and Chesham. It's not a pretty sight. I hope you finally see his offers for what they are."

"No one took his offers seriously but you, my lord."

She stared at him. He nodded as if absorbing this little bit of information. He seemed to be doing his damnedest not to look at her, but every few seconds she could see his eyes flicker downward toward the tub where her figure dissolved in blurry pink tones beneath the water. Her back was to him and her arms were crushed over her breasts, but even so, she had scant coverage. No matter how she tried to cover herself, her breasts spilled out the side, offering him a healthy look at her nudity. And by the light in his eyes, she could see he held a most manly appreciation for it.

To her relief, they heard the sound of a door opening in the dressing room. A servant bustled around, and though they couldn't see who it was, Ravenna thought that perhaps Katey had returned through the servants' stair.

Ravenna looked at Trevallyan expectantly; he gazed back, seemingly reluctant to go.

Katey began to hum loudly in the dressing room, banging drawers and opening wardrobes. Without another word, Trevallyan placed a book on the nearby table. He gave Ravenna such a strange, piercing look it seemed to stop her heart. Katey entered the bedroom with an armful of soaps and linen towels, and when Ravenna turned back to look at him again, he was gone.

"Here we are! A fresh bar of soap for your hair, and Himself's finest pig-bristle brush to brush it dry by the fire." Katey puttered to the tub, handing her soaps and rosewater. The servant was clearly oblivious to the master's quick exit and to the tensions that seemed to still linger in the room.

Ravenna lowered her arms and allowed Katey to assist with washing her hair. The servant poured warm water over her head and began to scrub with a pink cake of soap. The ministrations were just what Ravenna needed. She felt tense and soiled. A good hard scrubbing seemed to wash away both sensations.

When she was finally clean, Katey wrapped Ravenna in another of Trevallyan's dressing gowns and placed her by the restoked hearth. Then the servant ran the pig-bristle brush through her clean hair until each black strand was shiny and dry.

The bath and her "visitors" had so exhausted Ravenna, she actually looked forward to returning to Trevallyan's soft bed. She truly wished to go home, but the fight had been more than she could stand.

"There you are, miss," Katey said, standing back and looking at her work. "You look right as rain, but perhaps a little weary around the eyes. Let's get you back into bed. Here, we'll fetch you a good book to read." The servant walked with Ravenna to the bed and helped her up the little stool that assisted her onto the high mattress. "What will you read, miss?"

Ravenna looked across the bedroom into the antechamber. She remembered Trevallyan had placed a book on a table. "That one, over there." Ravenna pointed to it. "Will you read me the title?"

Katey walked to the book and picked it up. "I can't read rightly in English, miss. If it were Gaelic or the Church's tongue, Latin, perhaps . . . but there was only the hedge school for me and then only for a few years." Katey brought her the book. She plumped the pillows, then retreated from the chamber with the tea tray.

Ravenna fingered the embossed leather. She was speechless with surprise when she read the title: *A Vindication of the Rights of Woman*.

She flipped through a couple of chapters, such as "The State of Degradation to Which Woman Is Reduced," and "Writers Who Have Rendered Women Objects of Pity," the subject about which she was most impassioned. The book was an original printing of the 1792 edition. She closed it and studied it in her hands, still unable to believe that Trevallyan even possessed a copy, much less that he had brought it to her.

The book flipped open on her lap. She could see a scrawl inside the front cover. Amazed, she read

To Ravenna,

"It would be well if they were only agreeable or rational companions."

> Niall, eighth earl of Trevallyan
> on WOMEN
> (in the words of Mary Wollstonecraft)

A sleepy smile crossed her face. As infuriating as the man was, she found herself looking forward to thanking him. Trevallyan had too many facets to his character to hate all of them at once. And there was no denying that he had wit. The exact kind of blackguard's wit that appealed to her own.

She closed the book and fell into a dream-filled sleep, already planning her repartee for when she would see him next.

Ravenna was reluctant to admit to the disappointment she felt when she didn't see Trevallyan all the next morning. Noon came and went and led into a sleepy afternoon. By evening, her supper having been served by Katey in the antechamber, she sat in the lonely chair next to the hearth. All day Trevallyan had yet to show and now into the night. She had yet to thank him for the book. Ravenna fell asleep, her thoughts captivated by him.

Convinced that he would arrive in the morning, she asked Katey to dress her hair into something other than the wild tangle that fell freely down her back. Katey obliged, almost forced into sorcery in order to tame the coal-colored tresses into a respectable chignon. The maidservant even went so far as to pin small shamrocks to her handiwork, but as the hours ticked by, the effort was for naught. Trevallyan did not show.

Two days passed. The second evening, Katey arrived with Ravenna's clothing from the cottage, and Ravenna was told that she would finally be allowed to leave in the morning. Ravenna should have been ecstatic, but she was oddly disconsolate. He'd made no attempt to visit her, and now she even doubted that he would see her off in the morning. She didn't know why his disappearance bothered her. She didn't expect to be in his thoughts; in truth, she didn't expect him to act as anything other than the rude beast he was, but somehow, every time she looked down at her book, she couldn't stop herself from wondering what had kept him away.

"You didn't eat a morsel of your supper. Is your head still a-hurtin'?" Katey asked softly as she looked down at Ravenna's untouched tray.

Ravenna gazed at the kindly woman. Suddenly she realized how indebted she was to her. Katey had tended to her with all the care of a mother. Ravenna knew she wouldn't be feeling as well as she did were it not for Katey's constant attention.

"I'm not very hungry this evening." Ravenna pressed the servant's hand in a show of affection, "I've never quite thanked you for all the time you've given to me. It's just occurred to me that I may never see you again unless I pass you on the road going to market. I hope that you will always remember how grateful I am for your care."

"Why, 'twas nothing, miss. I'm always glad to help Lord Trevallyan where I can." Katey smiled and patted the hand atop her own. "Ever since me poor Eddie died of the drink, and he took in meself and the babe, there's nothing I wouldn't do for the master. When Himself told me about you lying up here, all hurt and dirty and wet, with no one to ease the sufferings of your poor head, I was quite glad to be able to lend a hand. Especially knowing who you are, miss, and all the need for secrecy."

"Secrecy?" Ravenna asked, rather surprised.

"Why yes. Of course. 'Tis why you haven't seen nary a servant but me. Himself wouldn't allow it. Even tonight when he was taking his whiskey in the library, he was still concerned that no one know you spent all these days under his care."

"Well . . . who am I, then, that Lord Trevallyan has taken such great care with my reputation?" Ravenna stared at the servant, waiting for an answer. She was disappointed to see Katey begin a retreat.

" 'Tis up to the master to decide that, miss," the maid said, a little nervously.

Confusion crossed Ravenna's face.

Katey seemed to take pity on her. Pensively, she wiped the table with her apron and explained, "The lord is a lonely man, miss. You must understand that. He's not in the habit of bringing home waifs in need of care. In truth, Himself doesn't bring too many people to the castle at all. Oh, you may hear about the routs and such, but those are all Lord Chesham's doing. Usually the master takes his drinks as he may, and then he retires to his chamber to sit in the chair opposite yours, and he reads all through the night. An educated man, Himself is. I've heard he's read all the books in the castle and then some. He lives in his library."

"Is that where he's been . . ." *sleeping* she almost blurted out, but the question was even too improper for her, ". . . where's he's been all this time?" she corrected.

"Himself's got County Lir to look after and look after it he does. Not much time for visiting, that one. 'Tis partly why he is lonely." Katey sauntered toward the servants' door in the dressing room. In a pleasant voice, she said, "Just you rest now, miss. I'll bring you a toddy from the kitchen before bedtime."

"Thank you, Katey," Ravenna said, her thoughts very far away.

Katey tried to hide her enigmatic smile. "My pleasure, miss. You know, old Peter Maguire was quite a gossip. God bless you, miss. And God bless our Ireland." With that, Katey disappeared into the dressing room and the servants' passage beyond.

Boggled, Ravenna stared at the dressing room. She rose from her chair to call Katey back and have her answer all the questions firing in her mind, but when she reached the dressing room, the servant was gone, escaped into the medieval labyrinth of the keep.

She knew a better source for answers anyway. Trevallyan. As Katey had implied, he was even now in his library sipping a whiskey. It was only proper for her to thank him, and she didn't know if she would see him in the morning to be able to do so.

She ran to the shaving mirror over the bureau. Her hair was presentable, if not exquisite; her cheeks were pale, in fact she still looked a bit ghosty with her large eyes and dark hair, nonetheless, she pinched some color into her face, straightened her bodice, and left for the Trevallyan library.

To find one room in the midst of two hundred was a daunting task. It took more than a quarter of an hour for Ravenna to even make her way to the newer portion of the castle, but once there, she found it was not difficult to detect which room was the library. There was only one light burning beneath the elaborately carved and gilded doors in the new wing. Unless Greeves was up late polishing the silver, the occupant of the room had to be the master.

She placed her hand on the gilt doorknob and experienced a sudden attack of nerves. He might not be pleased to see her. In fact, he might be quite displeased to find her intruding upon his private life. She pressed her ear to the mahogany door. No voices. Whoever burned the candles was alone.

Slowly she opened the door.

She remembered the library well from their last conversation in it. Trevallyan sat in a chair facing the hearth beneath a portrait of a woman to whom he bore a distinct resemblence. The woman had to be his mother. The Celt.

"My lord," she said in a low tone.

Slowly he turned his head. If he was surprised or pleased by her appearance, he didn't show it. Instead, his features hardened into an implacable, unreadable expression.

"What are you doing here?" he said.

Her nerves caught on fire. "I—I came to tell you farewell. I'll be leaving at first light." She met his gaze but didn't enter the room. There was no point in running into the dragon's lair.

"You don't look well enough to be leaving." He rose from his chair and walked over to her. Taking her arm, he led her to the chair opposite his. It was a large, old fashioned wing chair from the previous century, and it enveloped her within its needlework.

"I—I really didn't mean to bother you here in your library," she said, becoming a bit unglued by his intense gaze.

"Then why did you?"

The question seemed unanswerable. Even she wasn't sure why she had sought him out. She wouldn't have minded a pleasant chat before retiring, but one didn't have pleasant chats with Lord Trevallyan.

She clasped and unclasped her sweaty hands. "I told you. I came here to say good-bye—"

"No."

His answer left her with little leverage. Slowly, she added, ". . . and to thank you for the book."

"I see."

He stared at her from his chair, so far away, more than an arm's length away, but still close. Close enough so that she could see the color of his eyes. Green stones awash in deep water.

She met those eyes with all the bravado she could muster, but they were terrible, disapproving eyes. He had always disapproved of her, and with every attempt to win his regard, she had seen the disapproval grow deeper, had felt it sting more. It had intensified with every encounter, until now, when she was as polished and educated as she would ever be in her life, the disapproval cut a path through her self-worth like a scythe through O'Shea's rye.

"What's wrong with me that you look at me the way you do?" The whisper may have left her mouth, but it came from her aching heart.

"There's nothing wrong with you. You're beautiful. So beautiful that . . ." His gaze flickered down her face and figure. She wore the old scratchy blue dress she had worn to Peter Maguire's funeral. It was not a dress to win beaux, but he seemed to hardly notice what she was clothed in. He looked too deeply to notice the superficial. ". . . so beautiful I'd like to . . ." His gaze locked with hers. The message in his eyes scared her. And the excitement she felt from it, even more so.

"Shall you be my lover, Ravenna?" he said with words what had already been spoken.

She took several deep breaths and stared at him. Everything should have been so simple now. It was the point where a maiden should renounce the cad and stomp from the room in righteous indignation. Kathleen Quinn, no doubt, would have leapt from her chair, cracked Trevallyan across his face, and sent her brother to the castle at dawn to cut him down.

But she had no such option. Try as they might at the Weymouth-Hampstead School, they could not turn water into wine. She understood all too well from years of grinding repetition that she was poor, orphaned, Irish. Her education had not elevated her. It had only tortured her further by creating dissatisfaction with her lot in life. With no family or friends to protect her, she could no more take Trevallyan to task for his offer than she could keep Malachi from the hangman should they catch him.

Quietly she stood and then walked to the door.

"You haven't answered me," the voice boomed from behind her.

She turned to face him, wounded not only by the insulting offer but by the fact that she almost longed to accept it, and if not for her heightened sense of self-preservation, an instinct born and bred from her lowly beginnings, she feared she might have.

"No. The answer is no." She gave him a steady, diligent stare.

He stared back from his place in the chair, a strange frustration on his face. His voice became quiet, almost ominous. "I'm not making you an offer, Ravenna, I'm asking you a question. Are you to be my lover?"

"What would make you ask such a question?"

An unholy glint appeared in his eyes. "I've been told there is no choice in the matter. For years they've been telling me that my world and its circumstances are preordained." He nodded to the portrait of the beauty above the mantel. "She was much like you, Ravenna. My mother was a commoner, Irish and poor, but my father was captive to her love until his dying day. They needed no *geis*. They married, and it's been said that is why there's peace in Lir. The Trevallyans must marry commoners, and they've a *geis* to make sure they do it."

He stood and stepped toward her, his intense gaze staring right into her soul. "So the question keeps running through my mind until it's fair driving me bloody mad: Will you be my lover, Ravenna? Is it as certain as the fact that the moon will rise above the *ogham* stone on *beltaine*? And if not, how shall I win you? Have I enough money to cloak my age? Have I the charm to seduce you where Chesham and his amateurish efforts have failed?"

"Do you love me? That's the only chance a man will ever have." She raised her chin, pride building a fort around her fragile emotions.

He shook his head and looked at her as if she were a stupid child. "Do I love you? How absurd. That's not it at all. For you're the one who's to love me. This *geis* that has damned my very soul says I am to win a woman's love. And they say that woman is you, Ravenna."

She looked at him. A slow shock seeped into her. His talk mystified her, even frightened her, but it made such insane sense. He had a *geis*, and she was entwined in it. That was why even now, she wore a ring with the Trevallyan adder on it. There was a *geis* driving all this madness, and no doubt it had been for years. Perhaps even before her birth.

Her hand went to her lips in dismay and horror. So many questions flitted through her mind. Why hadn't Grania told her about this? Grania knew all the sorcery that went around Lir and she wouldn't have kept her granddaughter stumbling around in the dark, unforewarned. Or did Grania know it all along and keep it secret from her? Had all of Lir and the heavens above known about it and kept it from her?

The thought left her unbalanced. She didn't quite believe it; she didn't *want* to believe that Trevallyan's actions so far had been at the prompting of a *geis*. But still, there could be truth in his words, considering the fact that their rings were alike. And she now understood Trevallyan's inexplicable interest in her. Fate and a few old men of the county were trying to drive them together, but the *geis* had not figured on her resistance. Nor, obviously, had it figured on the elusive nature of love.

"Where are you going?" he said to her departing figure.

"If you have a *geis,* then perhaps you'd best hold to it or suffer the ill fortune it brings."

"You agree to be my lover?"

She wouldn't turn around and meet his stare. "If you have a *geis* that says you're to win a woman's love, then that is your *geis.* And if I'm that woman, then you must win my love."

"They say all of the county will suffer if I don't fulfill this thing I curse and despise. There's famine to the south. I can't bear the thought of Lir, our beautiful, abundant farmland, turning into a graveyard like down in Munster. Does that make you understand my offer?"

"If you must win my love, then you must win it. There is no other way to fulfill a *geis.*"

"Do you believe in *geise,* Ravenna?" he said a little desperately.

Her voice was hollow with tears. "No," she said. She didn't know why she wanted to cry, but she suspected it had something to do with the futility of the conversation. She now understood all the cryptic behavior of those around her. Trevallyan's regard and attention had only been the result of a doubt planted in his educated mind that the *geis* might be real. Now that they had discussed the idea, it would be dismissed as the folly it was. As she would be.

There was an extended silence, then the room crackled with harsh laughter.

She turned to look at him, feeling the wet, acid etch of tears down her cheeks.

"Don't you see how absurd this is?" He reached her and took both her arms in a grip. "The ancients of this county have devised all these plans, and yet not even you believe any of it."

"Yes. It's absurd." But she didn't feel his apparent joy. She didn't know when she had become attracted to him, or how to define the attraction she felt. Niall Trevallyan was certainly not the impressive physical specimen his cousin's friends were. In fact, she wondered if she passed him on a crowded Dublin street if she would even notice him. He was not a particularly tall man, nor was he a man of bulging muscles. But as she stared up at him, she decided that without a doubt she would have noticed him anywhere. His piercing gaze left an indelible mark on her memory. His face was handsome in detail, his lips and nose clearly carved of noble ancestry, but what set him apart from other, more common men was the acute Celtic slant of his brows. It made him look wicked, a progeny of the devil. And all Trevallyan's altruism couldn't erase the feeling one had when one looked at him that he was a man who held the power to destroy and create as a birthright.

"Please . . . let me go. I'm tired. I need to rest." She lowered her gaze to his hands that held her.

"Stay. Have a drink with me and celebrate."

"No, I'm not feeling well."

He dropped his hold and watched her step away.

"Ravenna?"

She paused.

"You seem almost depressed. What makes you so?"

She didn't answer. She thought he might finally leave her in peace, but instead she found his hand at her waist.

"Sit down and have a drink with me. Come celebrate my victory over darkness and stupidity. The *geis* is done with." He led her back to the wing chair and forced her to sit.

Mutely she watched him as he stepped to a table where several decanters sat upon a silver tray. In one fluid motion, he poured a drink, bent to give it to her, and, almost as if he had forgotten who she was and believed he was having an evening in the library with his mistress, brushed her lips with his as if about to kiss her.

Shocked, she opened wide her eyes. Their faces were only inches apart. A sheepish smile crossed his face, and she saw the ghost of the young man he used to be.

"I forget myself in my delirium." He flashed white, even teeth. "I remember I vowed that you would be the one to kiss next."

Damning him, damning herself, she licked her lips that ached for the unconsummated kiss. He was about to straighten and something tugged at her heart, almost as if she physically mourned the aborted kiss. She knew she would never understand what drove her to it. It might have been despair, or even exaltation, or merely the urge to reenact her dream. Whatever the reasons, she lifted herself to him, and with all the willfulness in her orphaned soul, crushed her lips to his.

She half-expected him to pull back as if burned. Unsure if her kiss was welcome, she placed a trembling hand on his cheek. To her intense pleasure, he broke from her lips and kissed her hand, hotly pressing his lips and tongue to her sensitive palm. Then, he pulled her hand to her side and buried his face in her neck, his mouth making an unholy trail across her vulnerable throat.

Moaning, she gave him the response he seemed to seek. She threw back her head and silently begged for more. Expertly, he complied. His fingers wound in her hair, releasing it from the ebony pins. Tilting her head back even farther, he kissed her mouth in so desperate a manner he didn't seem to care whether she could keep up with him or not. The jolt from his invading tongue sent her soul heavenward. Deep inside, she almost feared his rough, intimate kiss, but she had to have it. It seemed as necessary as her next breath and soon she grew to like it—too much—betrayed as she was by the melting of her thighs.

"What a spell you weave, witch," he groaned while his hand slid up her waist. She whimpered a futile protest, but he took possession anyway. He cupped her corseted breast, silencing her words with another soul-devouring kiss.

The heat between her mouth and his seemed to outburn the hearth. Her wool dress which had been inadequate in the cold stone passageways of the castle now seemed to itch and burn, fairly shrieking to be cast off. He bent and kissed her breasts beneath her clothing. She nearly sobbed with relief when she felt his hands at her back, inch by torturous inch, releasing the hooks that held her dress together.

"Promise me . . ." he whispered in deep gasps, ". . . you will renounce MacCumhal . . ."

She barely heard him. Her head nestled against his chest and her entire being filled with his scent. Malachi had smelled of perspiration and the lingering muskiness of arousal. There was no such earthiness about Trevallyan. He smelled clean and wealthy like the scent of newly bound leather books and V.S.O.P. And there was another scent as well, one more subtle, but unquestionably more powerful. It whispered of things ancient, dark and mysterious. The smell of soot from a druid fire. The lingering bite in the air of gunpowder after a duel. It was dangerous, seductive, unnatural. And she found she could not get her fill of it.

"No more MacCumhal . . ." he rasped. His hand slid beneath the parting of her dress and caressed the warm skin of her back. A hook or two popped as he reached for more of her, and insanely she wondered how he was going to be patient enough to extract her from the intricate armor of her clothing.

He undid five more hooks. Her dress began to gape in front as the back parted more and more. With studied slowness, he grasped the neckline and shoved it down to her bust. The fabric pinned her upper arms to her sides and exquisitely forced her to receive his kiss without the ability to push him away.

She was almost grateful to feel the release of her corset hooks, allowing her breath to come easy and fast as his teeth grazed her collarbone and his tongue burned in the valleys of her throat. The corset fell away and her dress fell with it, settling around her waist. She wore only a flimsy chemise, and he wasted no time before he pulled it off one shoulder to expose the half-moon sliver of a pink nipple.

He bent to her. His palm rested on her bare shoulder, then slid slowly downward seeking its treasure. "Promise me . . ." he whispered.

She moaned, confused, unsure.

His hand slid farther. Her heart pounded in her chest, drumming for his touch. Still, she prayed he would slow down. Anxiety shot through her at the thought of him touching her breast. No one had ever done such an intimate thing before.

He lowered his head and tugged on the chemise. He tugged again revealing more crescent of nipple. "Renounce MacCumhal," he black-mailed. "Tell me of his crimes and renounce him." His mouth opened, and she gasped. Panic ran through her heated, thrumming veins like cold mercury. By instinct, she knew the point of no return had arrived at her doorstep, but she could not renounce Malachi, she would not. Not even by the means of this sweet torture.

"I was with him. 'Tis the truth and I can't say otherwise," she moaned softly.

He looked at her, his face taut with lust.

She held his head, begging for him and pushing him away at the same time. She didn't want them to quit; in truth, the thought made her want to wail with the injustice of it. If he would only take her swiftly and hard, she wouldn't be forced to think about all that was wrong in what they were doing. With an overwhelming awe, she finally understood why Sadie had let the stable boy have his way with her. There were some people in the world who drew hapless others to their sides. It was inexplicable, but nonetheless real. She wondered if she had just discovered Trevallyan was the light and she, the doomed moth.

"Renounce him. Tell me you had no part in his crimes. Or I'll find him and see him hanged." He held her gaze, violence in his own. He fingered the edge of her chemise and his knuckles dug into the flesh of her breast. She despised the way her chest rose and fell with an un-ladylike passion. Any second, he looked as if rage would make him tear her clothes off and shame her to the core of her being.

Half-sobbing, she pulled back, clutching at her gown to keep herself covered. "Are you so vengeful you would see a man hanged because I did not do your bidding?"

His breathing was hard and angry. "I would have you erase these pictures in my mind—these pictures of MacCumhal taking you on a hilltop—"

"No! 'Twas not like that!" She pushed him away, holding her un-hooked bodice to her chest.

"Then what was it like?" He began to stalk her, unfettered rage and jealousy twisting his features. "Did he take you in a barn, did he whisper pretty things to you in the hay? Or did he steal into an alley and lean you against the wall and . . ." His voice began to falter.

"Why must you make me sound so unclean?" She wiped tears from her cheeks. "I'm not a whore, yet you want to force me to admit I'm one."

"I've tried to protect you. I warned you about Chesham. I've tried to make you worldly and educated . . . still you take up with the likes of MacCumhal." He ran an angry hand through his silver-blond hair. ". . . and I find you running nearly naked through the rain after a rendezvous with him . . ."

"We were children—"

"No longer, no longer," he cursed as if damning his own misery even more than hers.

She covered her face with her hands. "I abhor what you've made me. I see that I'm nothing but an underling to you, a pauper who's been placed in your path at every turn." She looked down at her unfastened bodice and began to weep. "One who you've finally found some use for. . . ."

Coldly, he stared at her, at her mussed hair, her raw, kiss-roughened lips, her loose gown. He seemed to enjoy every punishing word, as if it cemented his own wavering convictions. "You might be right."

She shook her head, hurt as never before. Through her misery she heard him whisper, "Just take the pictures from my mind, Ravenna. I see you with MacCumhal and I despise it."

Sobbing, she pulled her gown into some semblance of modesty. Then without a look back, she fled the library, and ran until her side ached, until her breath grew tight and painful in her lungs. After a few moments, the door in the keep loomed before her. It was the same one she had used to flee Trevallyan so long ago. But she was now no longer a child who could run from her troubles. Her heartache would go with her, and she knew it. Still, she opened the door and with a gasp of freedom, she ran into the night, and toward home.

Chapter 16

WHEN RAVENNA arrived back at the cottage, she found Grania by the fire, warming her stiff old bones. She entered the keeping room quietly, glad that Grania couldn't see her disheveled appearance, nor the hurt in her eyes.

"Ye've come back!" Grania exclaimed, her hand shaking with excitement and age as she reached out for her granddaughter. "I've longed for ye, child. 'Tis been lonely here . . ."

Ravenna dropped to the floor and placed her head in Grania's lap. "I'll never leave again, I promise." She did a poor job of hiding the tears in her voice, for she could see Grania's expression turned mournful.

"Malachi sent ye a message, child. He wants to see ye. His friends at the market will take ye to him."

Shaken by this news, Ravenna grew silent. Finally she whispered, "Is he the one for me, Grania? Malachi's in bad trouble. He's hiding—I fear he's done something terrible. Tell me, I must know." She clutched at Grania's skirts waiting for the answer.

"The man for ye is the man ye love."

"I love Malachi. I would do anything for him, as I know he would do for me. But still . . ."

"Ye are not in love with him."

"I don't know." She lifted her emotion-ravaged face. "Lord Trevallyan told me about his *geis*. You knew it all along, didn't you?"

"Yes, child."

"Am I the girl?"

Grania did not answer.

"I don't believe in superstition. They call you a witch, Grania—they always have—and I laugh because I know you are no witch, that there are no witches. I just want to know, whether the *geis* is fulfilled or not, do you think I'm destined to love Trevallyan?"

Grania laid a gnarled, beloved hand on Ravenna's face. "Child, I cannot tell ye sooch things. I have me visions and many times they come true, but I cannot will them to come to me when I need them. If ye are destined to fall in love with Trevallyan, then ye will do it."

"And can nothing change the path of destiny?" she almost sobbed.

"The will can change destiny. If you do not want to love Lord Trevallyan, then you will not."

"Thank you, Grania," she whispered, burying her head in the old woman's lap. "Thank you," she repeated, feeling as if she had just been saved from drowning.

⚭

Reverend Drummond looked out at the church's summer fields of potatoes. Lir was beautiful at this time of day. The land was cast purple and green beneath the haze of a Celtic twilight. Atop the hill of the rectory, Drummond listened for the roar of the sea in the distance.

Millie Sproule, a maiden cousin who had taken Mrs. Dwyer's position when the old woman had died, had dragged his favorite armchair out onto the rectory lawn. There sat his ancient figure, taking his tea, enjoying every moment. He was a man in the sunset of his life, watching the day disappear beneath the Sorra Hills.

In pastoral harmony, the form of Michael O'Shea appeared in the distance, hoeing and tending to his plants with all the care of his father.

His four brothers had long since departed for America, but now six of Michael's sons worked the fields, as Michael had done before them.

Reverend Drummond had found peace. The emerald splendor of the landscape was balm for his Ulster soul. Nothing was more satisfying to a loyal subject of the Crown than to see his land tilled and fruitful. Donations would be good this year from the looks of the abundant landscape.

"Wha's he doin'?" Millie Sproule whined, still not adjusted to the quirks of the people though she had been in Ireland more than five years now.

"What's who doing?" asked Reverend Drummond, cursing his age. His eyesight wasn't worth a damn these days, and every time Millie had to raise her annoying voice in order to explain something to him, he felt as feeble as Griffin O'Rooney.

"Why, Mr. O'Shea. 'E's on his knees, diggin' up all his potatoes. I daresay they haven't gotten big enough for him to start harvestin'. Why . . . Go on! Look at him! He's running around like a madman, diggin' up them potatoes!"

Those potatoes, Drummond thought, fighting the urge to correct her. Millie Sproule, to his familial shame, spoke like a tavern wench.

"He's shoutin'! Go on with you, look! They're all a-runnin'! Even McKinnon is dropping his hoe and comin' 'round the *ogham* stone."

"I can't imagine!" Though his eyesight wasn't what it once was, Drummond could make out the blurry figures of men running toward O'Shea. They were in a panic. "Get me out of this chair. I've got to find out what's happening." The reverend held on to Millie Sproule's arm. He rose from the chair and forced her to lead him down the rectory lawn to the tilled fields below.

Slowly they made their way through a furrow of potatoes. Men were running to Michael O'Shea. When the reverend and Millie reached his side, they found Michael on his knees, his head bent low in defeat.

" 'Tis the blight, it is," someone in the crowd whispered in despair.

Reverend Drummond broke through the crowd to see the plants. They were dusted with a downy mildew. The tubers in Michael O'Shea's hand that should have been the size of rocks were instead the size of acorns.

"Famine is come to Lir," another man announced, his voice full of doom.

There was a long, oppressive silence, and then Michael began to weep.

"My good man," Reverend Drummond put a hand on Michael's shoulder. " 'Tis only a bit of blight. All is not lost."

"Famine is everywhere in Ireland, why not in Lir, too? We're just as downtrodden by the English as in Derry," an angry man spat at the reverend.

"See here now," Drummond defended himself. "The famine is not England's doing. And it is most certainly not *my* doing. The crops are not all doomed. Harvest what you can, Michael. I'll see that your family's fed."

"Blight can't come to Lir. It can't," McKinnon keened as loud as if he were at a wake.

"We've been lucky here in Lir," Drummond said. "The famine has not touched us. If we see a bit of what the others see, we should count our blessings it's not worse."

"It's not over yet, Reverend." The angry man looked at Drummond.

Drummond didn't recognize him but thought he was one who ran with Malachi MacCumhal. "Sir," he said coldly, "if blight has come to Eden, 'tis best to go to the serpent with your complaints."

"You are the serpent, Reverend."

"Nay. I am not." Drummond leaned on Millie Sproule's arm. He turned to go, but before he did, he said, "We were born of Eden. But no more. You men take to the serpent if you must, but I shall denounce it."

"What's he saying?" one man mumbled in Gaelic.

"He's a crazy old Anglican. Leave him be," McKinnon answered in the same language.

Meanwhile, Drummond took the exhausting walk back to the rectory, his every thought consumed by the Trevallyan *geis* and the babe, Ravenna, Niall had held in his hands so many years before.

It would be the last in his lifetime. But he knew, without a doubt, he must call another meeting.

⚭

"My Lord Trevallyan, you know why we're here." Drummond sat stiffly in the Trevallyan library, flanked by the aged, bent forms of Father Nolan and Griffen O'Rooney.

"The blight has come to Lir. Famine awaits at our doorstep. Have you made any progress with Ravenna?" Father Nolan's hand trembled on his cane as if it were a sign he feared the answer.

Trevallyan agitatedly ran a hand through his hair. "Enough of this. I beg of you. Are you to blame this entire famine on one girl?"

"Not on the girl! Never on the girl! 'Tis our fault. We never should have let you marry," Griffen O'Rooney chimed in. He sat a bit away from the group. His clothes were dirty and tattered, and his nails were bloodied where he had dug in the graveyard, attempting to plant flowers where no flowers would grow.

Trevallyan watched him with unease. It was clear he thought the old man mad and didn't want him in his library.

"He's right," Drummond broke in. "Ravenna's not to blame. You are the one who must win her love."

"She knows about the *geis*. I told her. She doesn't believe it and neither do I." Niall poured himself three fingers of whiskey. He meant to sip it, but the next time he looked down, the glass in his hand was empty.

"Can you not win her love, me boy?" Father Nolan asked softly. "With all your money, have you not the means—"

"My money be damned, 'tis not enough." Trevallyan laughed, bitterly. "The task is impossible. I'm twice the lass's age, not a boy to be begging for favors. She's taken up with MacCumhal, and there's naught to be done about it."

"But have you really tried with her?"

Trevallyan looked at Drummond with ice in his eyes. If the minister had known him better he might have thought the ice was hiding hurt. "I have approached her. That is all I will say. I've done my part. She doesn't want me. Let us go on without this *geis*."

"But the blight—" Drummond interjected.

"The blight has nothing to do with this." Niall refilled his glass, his jaw set in anger. "Besides, no one in Lir shall starve. We'll destroy the potato crops and use the land for cattle if we have to, until spring, when we can replant corn. You know I'll use all the Trevallyan lands and money to protect the well-being of this county."

"But who will protect you, my lord?" Father Nolan asked.

"Why do I need protection?"

"Your money is not limitless. You will lose thousands of pounds on your crops alone if the blight continues. Too, there are rumblings of rebellion. Some in this county would see you dead."

Trevallyan met the father's gaze with a steady one of his own. "If you're speaking of MacCumhal and his ilk, then let it be said right now that I am not afraid. If they're thinking of lynching Ascendency in Lir, let them think again. I will not be lynched. I am as Irish as they, and I've the God-given birthright of this land."

"Centuries ago when the Trevallyans took this land, their payment was the *geis*. You have not fulfilled yours, Niall," the priest said softly.

"She does not love me." Fury stained Trevallyan's cheeks. He looked at the priest with eyes that gave away no emotion. "What else is there to say? She's given her heart to another."

"But I hold the heart—I hold the heart—" Griffen began to rant in the corner.

Disgusted, Trevallyan rang for Greeves.

When the butler arrived Trevallyan pointed to Griffen and said, "Take him to the kitchen and see that he is bathed and fed. I do not want to see him in the graveyard anymore tonight. Lock him in one of the servants' bedrooms if you must, but see that he is taken care of."

Greeves nodded and motioned for Griffen to follow him. Griffen did, but before he left, he turned to Trevallyan and said, "I hold the heart. If you need it, 'twill be yours." Mournfully, he followed the butler out of the room.

"Christ," Trevallyan muttered, disgust and despair etched on his face.

"I must be leaving too," Drummond announced. "Millie is waiting in the carriage and it's grown cold this evening." Wearily, he reached for Trevallyan's hand. Trevallyan helped the old man up. "My boy, 'tis doom I fear I see. I do not want to trust superstitions, but so much has happened . . . I cannot help but believe them sometimes." With a sigh, he picked up his shawl and slowly crept from the room.

Trevallyan was alone with the priest. A silence passed between the two men like the silence of father and rebellious son.

"There will never be another meeting of the council. Peter Maguire, rest his soul, should have been here tonight," Father Nolan commented softly.

"What you've held on to all these years is gone. I'm sorry, but 'the truth will out.' " Trevallyan leaned his head on the mantel. He looked tired, as if he'd been fighting a war he could not win.

"Have you fallen in love with her yet?"

The question seemed to startle Trevallyan. His head shot up, and he stared at the priest. "Why do you ask me such an inconsequential thing?"

"Inconsequential? No. It is anything but that."

"Why do you ask?"

"Your anger makes me think it, that's why. If you didn't care for the girl, these questions, this *geis,* would leave you dispassionate. You're far from that, my son."

Niall turned away, as if he didn't want the priest to read the expression on his face.

"What say you, my lord? Do you think of her often? Does the thought of Malachi MacCumhal kissing her make you feel murderous? Does she appear in your dreams when you long to forget her?"

Trevallyan would not turn to face him.

That was all the answer Father Nolan needed.

The old priest leaned shakily on his cane and made to depart, but before he did, Trevallyan asked in voice hushed and solemn. "If it's true, if I do find myself falling in love with the girl, what do you make of it?"

"It fills me with pity, my lord, and it makes me believe in *geise.*" The priest stared at him. Slowly, he said, "They may take away the Trevallyan riches and the Trevallyan lands, but there is no greater curse than to love someone you cannot have. We Celts are a strange people, as you know from your own flesh and blood, Niall. If we wanted to curse the Trevallyans, we could have found no better way." He nodded to the morose figure standing at the mantel. "God bless you and keep you, my lord."

Chapter 17

RAVENNA DID not sleep for two days. Her anger simmered beneath a calm facade like a pot of water on the edge of a boil. Fury turned to hatred, then cooled to a false, self-induced detachment. Deep down, she knew she was not indifferent to Trevallyan, but she made a deathbed vow to herself that from now on she would show nothing but dispassion toward him.

Grace and Skya were her only escape. In the wee hours of the morning, when the hurt threatened to erupt in tears, she stumbled to her battered old writing desk and scrawled by the thin light of a puddly candle.

Grace found the cottage as if led by the hand of a faerie. She reached the copse in the woods where the cottage lay just when the last beams of sunlight filtered through the dense canopy of tree boughs. Darkness carpeted the forest floor like a moss. The only light was from clusters of mushrooms that seemed to glow as if sprinkled with enchantment. In just one visit to the old woods, Grace understood why her Celtic people weaved the tales they did.

An old bridge built of gnarly, petrified wood stood between her and the cottage. Below, she could hear the singing of a brook as it skipped across smooth stones. A candle burned in the cottage beyond, and Grace felt a flood of excitement pulse through her at the thought of seeing her long-lost sister once more.

"Who goes there?"

The voice brought Grace upright. The horrible croak was most certainly not her sister's voice.

"Who may ye be?"

There it was again. A wretched, annoying, whiny sound like fingernails dragging across slate.

"Tell me, or ye will not be crossin' my bridge."

Grace looked down. Way down, to where the brook flowed beneath the bridge. There in the dank, shadowy cover stood a troll no taller than wheatgrass. He wore grimy, patched braies the color of mud; short, pointy-toed boots, and a wretched, filthy bliaud that had once been the finest velvet but was now crushed and soiled. He stared at her from the darkness, his pale knobby nose a blight on his face, his stringy black hair falling across piggy, malevolent eyes.

She cleared her throat to hide her fear. "I—I am Princess Grace. I've come to see my sister Skya who lives in the cottage."

"She is yer sister?" A pudgy shadow of a thumb jabbed in the direction of the cottage.

"Indeed." Grace nodded. "I've come a long way to see her."

"If ye be that one's sister, then ye will not be crossin' my bridge."

To her dismay, the creature crossed his arms and stared at her, a mutinous jut to his horrible little chin.

Ye will not be crossin' my bridge, a little voice inside her mimicked. This little troll was like a crotchety old woman. "Surely you don't hold the power to keep me from crossing the bridge? Why, you barely reach my hips." She stifled a small giggle.

The troll jumped up and down in a display of fury, and she heard water splash beneath his little boot-clad feet. "You will not cross my bridge! You will not cross my bridge!" he ranted.

Grace gathered the fabric of her kirtle and stepped onto the structure. The bridge gave an audible moan beneath her human weight, a thing for which it was clearly not built. She took one step and another. The other side, where her sister's cottage dwelled, loomed ever closer, but beneath her, she heard the ominous sounds of the troll rummaging around in a container as if he were desperately searching for something. He must have found it, for he released a vile little laugh.

She placed a foot on the other side and began to run. In her mind, she thought she heard the sound of hundreds of tiny feet running behind her, but she discounted it. Until a creature grasped on to her linen kirtle and clawed its way onto her shoulder.

Screaming, she looked right into the face of a huge, ugly rat. Behind her, an army of them ran toward her, so many that they were tumbling from the bridge into the shallow brook. The troll's laughter rang through her ears with the lyrical sound of sweet revenge.

"Help me! Help me!" Grace cried, and ran to the cottage. She pounded on the door, and when it opened, she ran inside, rats and all, not even bothering to acknowledge the sister whom she hadn't seen in years.

"Grace!" Skya exclaimed, running to her to give her a hug. The rats did not seem to bother her at all.

"Skya . . ." Grace croaked, limply holding out her arms for her sister's embrace. Rats fell from her head and shoulders as Skya held her tight.

"Come have food and drink and tell me of home." There were tears in Skya's eyes as she gazed at her little sister, but this was not the kind of reunion Grace expected. Mutely, she watched Skya clear a place at her board and set down a clay pitcher and a plate full of sweet biscuits.

Grace wondered if she were living a dream. Rats streamed in the front door unnoticed, but when one shimmied up the table leg and scurried for the biscuits, she couldn't muffle her gasp.

"Rats! Rats! Why does he always send rats!" Ignoring her sister, Skya picked up the offending creature that was just about to feast on the biscuits. She held the rodent up as if to study him, then she gazed around her cottage. Grace looked too, cringing at the hundreds of ugly gray-brown rats that haunted the corners and cabinets.

"Oh, bother it! He'll pay." Then to Grace's amazement, Skya snapped her fingers. The rats suddenly turned into brilliant white doves, hundreds of them. They flapped their wings and flew from every window and door,

leaving iridescent feathers in their wake. Without comment, Skya blew the
snowdust of feathers from the board and bade Grace sit down and enjoy her
refreshment.

"Tell me of home. How is Mother? And Father?" Skya asked.

Grace's ears still rang from the coos of the doves as they fled the cottage.
"Skya, you're really a witch, aren't you?" she said in awe.

Hurt and discomfort crossed Skya's beautiful face. She sat down with her
sister at the board and said in a sad little whisper, "Yes, I am really a witch.
And to pay for this magic means to never fit in." She took Grace's hand and
squeezed. Every melancholy word echoed in Grace's heart. "How I wish I fit
in."

⧟

Griffen O'Rooney had finally found a home. He had a warm, dry
bed, the first he'd seen since the madness struck years ago, and three
fine, healthy meals a day in the castle kitchen with the company of
more servants than he could talk to. In the mornings, when he awoke,
Fiona gave him his breakfast beside a blazing hearth.

"Heat's good fer the bones," he said to Fiona while she punched
down a yeasty dough at a marble-topped kitchen table.

She smiled absentmindedly at him. No one at the castle seemed to
mind the old man. Even the lowly sculleries thought it better to have
Griffen in the kitchen, warm and dry, than out frightening them all in
the cemetery.

"I've got to be speakin' with the master today," Griffen announced
with self-authority.

"Ah, the master's quite busy, Mr. O'Rooney. Perhaps I can send
Tommy James here to give you someone to talk to. . . . now let me
see, where did I see that boy last? He was helping in the stables, I
think. . . ."

"I must talk to Trevallyan today," Griffen insisted, clearly not hearing
her. "I must tell him the story of how I come by the ring. 'Tis time, I
think, for him to marry. Why, the lass is all grown up."

"I really can't say if the master will see you," Fiona said, a distracted, confused expression on her face. She picked up an armful of laundry and made to leave.

Griffen's mood seemed to just skirt panic. "I must be tellin' the master the story today. You will tell him for me, won't you?" He looked at her.

Sighing, Fiona nodded her head. "I'll see what I can do for you, Mr. O'Rooney."

The room was like an abandoned tomb when Trevallyan finally made his way to the kitchen. The old man sat in a black-painted Windsor chair by the fire as if trying to escape the chilly stone walls around him. His eyes were dreamy, his face serene. An old man waiting to be called home.

"How many years are you now, Griffen? Into your nineties, I would imagine," Trevallyan said at the doorway.

Griffen looked at him. If he could not make out the words, he at least still heard the sound.

"Fiona said you needed to speak with me." Trevallyan's face took on a patronizing expression.

"I've a yearnin' to speak with you, Lord Trevallyan," Griffen repeated, clearly not hearing a word.

For some reason, he was in the mood to indulge the old man. Trevallyan eased his form onto a nearby bench. He remained silent while O'Rooney began to speak.

"Me lord, I've the third part o' the gimmal." Griffen's rheumy gaze stared at Trevallyan's hand. He touched the ring on the master's last finger. "You cannot be marryin' the girl without it, and I'm feared I may be dyin' soon."

The muscles in Trevallyan's jaw hardened. He knew the old man was going to bring up this nonsense, and after the last meeting, he didn't want to talk about it.

"You must know where it is. The ring, the third part of the gimmal, be put in the graveyard fer safekeeping. Your wife is sleepin' beside it. She guards it in the vault."

Trevallyan nodded. The situation couldn't be worse in a penny Gothic.

"Me father gave me the ring when I was a young man. He told about the *geis,* and he told me his father before that gave him the ring."

"You mean it didn't come from a faerie who lured him into a forgotten wood and plied him with drink?" Niall could have bit his tongue after he said it.

"Drink? I'd like a drink," O'Rooney echoed, obviously hearing only half of what he had said. Niall smiled. He rose and searched a cupboard. The servants would deny until their faces were blue that they kept spirits in the kitchen, but he'd bet his castle that they did. He came upon a bottle of whiskey jammed behind several crocks of dried apples. He poured O'Rooney a healthy drink, then placed the bottle within easy reach of the old man.

"Ah, nothin' like a good gargle, eh?" Griffen smiled. He hadn't a tooth left.

Trevallyan nodded. He stood up to leave, but O'Rooney kept him with, "There's one last story I have to tell. 'Tis the story they tell near Antrim way about a man . . ."

Trevallyan sat down on the bench once more, growing impatient but unwilling to be rude.

". . . A fine young man he was, rich and powerful. He could have any young lass in the county fer his wife. . . ."

Niall shifted on the bench. Any more parables about his life and fate, and he was going to have to use Herculean measures to stop himself from wringing the neck of the bastard who recounted them.

". . . But instead, this young man—this viscount, he was—found a girl in Dublin who caught his eye. She was a beautiful girl, with raven-black hair and breathtakin' eyes, eyes that should have been laughin' but weren't. . . ."

The feeling of déjà vu crept into Trevallyan. Slowly he gave O'Rooney his attention.

". . . He didn't take the girl to his bed at first, because she was such a sad creature. She had followed a man to Dublin and had been discarded. Men had been cruel to her. It took her a long time to be trustin' the viscount, but he vowed to make her trust him, because he found himself in love with her. Despite her past, she was the girl he wanted to be marryin'. When she laughed, his world was filled with birdsong, when she cried, he mourned as though the banshee was at his door."

Trevallyan didn't move. A thousand questions flitted through his mind, but he remained silent so the old man wouldn't lose track of his story.

"He sent the girl home with the promise of a weddin'. He should never have done it. He feared she was goin' to be havin' his babe and he had nightmares o' losin' her. O' losin' his babby." Griffen looked at him and Trevallyan felt shivers run down his spine. The story was inversely parallel to his own life. In many ways it followed, except that the tragedy he knew Griffen was about to relate was, unlike his own life, softened by love.

"He did lose her," Griffen whispered. "Near Antrim way, 'tis said this young man met his fate before he could fetch his bride. He died with her name upon his lips and the promise that he would meet her in the hereafter."

"Antrim, you say he was from?" Trevallyan belted out in an attempt to get Griffen to hear him.

"Aye. Antrim. I've heard said the castle is named Cinaeth."

Trevallyan nodded. He was about to ask further questions when O'Rooney began to speak once more.

"I should have been tellin' Grania, but the story was old. It went through many a mouth. I don't know the truth of it."

" 'Tis all right, old man." Trevallyan placed a hand on the fragile shoulder. Griffen seemed to take comfort from it.

" 'Tis your tale now. I couldn't let it die with me."

Fiona entered the kitchens at that moment. Both Griffen and Niall looked up at her as if they were astonished where they were.

"Oh! Am I interruptin'?" she asked, blushing to the tips of her toes to find the master in the servants' domain.

Trevallyan stood and looked down at Griffen. "Nay, 'tis all right, Fiona. We're finished with our discussion. Leave Griffen to the bottle. Tell Greeves to replace the one I took."

Fiona looked at the green bottle next to the old man, her eyes wide and innocent. "I can't imagine what you mean, my lord. What bottle? Not here in the kitchen."

"It suffices to say that you heard me." Trevallyan looked down at Griffen. The old gravedigger looked tired. "Enjoy yourself, O'Rooney. Take my hospitality and heed Fiona's care. If you need anything, tell Greeves."

Griffen nodded, and Trevallyan wondered how much he had heard. Leaving the old man content by the fire, Trevallyan left the kitchen, his mind, his plans, already centered on a trip north to Antrim.

⊗

"My lord, there has been mischief done to the keep. It seems someone tried to start a small fire there. The south door is charred. Curran saw the flames and put it out. We're fortunate it was not worse." Greeves handed Trevallyan a gold salver with a note upon it.

Grim-faced, Trevallyan looked up from his library desk and took the note. He read it and put it down.

"May I be of assistance, my lord?" Greeves asked, tucking his one useless sleeve into the pocket of his frock coat.

"What a day this has been. . . ." Trevallyan stood. "I'll be going to Antrim, if not tomorrow, then the day after. Right now I have the need to go into Lir. Tell Seamus to ready the carriage." Almost as an afterthought, he said, "Oh, and give Curran a gold piece for his loyalty, and have the damage to the keep repaired."

"Yes, my lord." Greeves paused at the door. "May I ask . . . was the fire expected?"

Trevallyan released a long, melancholy sigh. "Not the fire, but the mischief. Yes, I would have to say it was expected. Thank you, Greeves. That is all."

"Thank you, my lord."

When Greeves had gone, Trevallyan picked up the note and read it once more.

Meet me at the market today.
Ravenna

He balled the note in his fist. Damned if he could tell whether it was Ravenna's handwriting or not. He had read the fragment of her story, but her script hadn't left as much an impression on him as the words.

His eyes darkened as he thought of the fire in the keep. It was obvious the note could be a ruse. Malachi and the rare lot of slummy bastards he ran with were not beyond such diabolics. If it was a fraud, it was a good one, for he was driven to meet her. As much as his instincts told him to stay at the castle, he knew he would go to the market. He would do it only to hold on to the slim thread that Ravenna —the beauty he had dreamed about last night with erotic fervor—had truly desired to summon him.

Chapter 18

RAVENNA HADN'T wanted to walk to O'Shea's for their potatoes, but word was out about the blight. O'Shea's crop had to be eaten or it was forever lost. As many a soul had tragically learned, once blight took hold of a field, even the apparently healthy potatoes could not be stored, for they, too, would mildew. Thousands had starved in dear Ireland learning this fact.

So she and Grania had decided to throw their lot in with the other townsfolk and buy out O'Shea. Even if they never got around to eating all those potatoes, O'Shea would be salvaged and, if they were lucky, the blight could be stopped at his field. If they all stuck together, Grania had sagely advised Ravenna, the agony that had occurred elsewhere might not happen in Lir.

With several silver coins in her purse, Ravenna struck out on the high road to help bail poor Michael O'Shea and his sons out of their misery. The day was appropriately gray and misty, befitting her mood. Yet for all her preoccupation with the news of the blight in Lir, for all that she deeply empathized with her neighbors' sufferings, she couldn't shake her despondency over what had transpired several nights before at the castle.

Trevallyan.

She couldn't even think the name without feeling a jab to her heart. On the outside, she had vowed to present a cool crust of dispassion whenever the master's name should be mentioned, but inside, with every passing hour, she knew she was lying to herself. She felt anything but dispassion. He had humiliated her. In as many words, he'd all but agreed that he viewed her as little better than a possession to him. And the rancor over Malachi, it was nothing more than jealousy that someone lower in status than the great earl of Trevallyan was sampling his wares.

She thought of her kiss and died a little more inside herself at remembrance of the display she had made. It boggled her now why she had kissed him. At the moment, she had wanted to kiss him desperately, but now she could see it had been stupid, dangerous, and altogether utter folly. A man such as Trevallyan would never love her. She had surrendered to the honesty of her emotions, and he had slapped her in the face with the pretensions of the Ascendency; she had melted for him, and he had told her she was a loose woman.

Even if there was a *geis* and all of Lir was to fall prey to blight, famine, and anarchy without her following its command to marry Trevallyan, she now knew she could not love the man. She couldn't see being able to love someone who had treated her as he had, who had toyed with her life and her feelings as if she were nothing but an expendable peasant girl whose use was physical and not spiritual, never spiritual. After all, it was surely his belief that only the Ascendency had souls and desires and feelings above those of an animal.

She felt tears sneak up on her. Trevallyan seemed to have broken her. She'd outlasted the torture of the years at the English school, but Trevallyan's treatment, while much more brief, had scarred her more deeply. To kiss a man, to trust him and desire him so intimately she wanted to submit body and soul to his every wish, made a woman too fragile. He should have trod softly, with care; instead, he'd been callous, and brutally forthright. It was like a knife to her gut to think that even after their kiss he viewed her no better than those terrible girls at

Weymouth-Hampstead had. She was mere Irish, of ignoble birth. And somehow that gave all and sundry the right to flay her feelings the way a whip flayed bare skin.

She wiped her tears with the corner of her shawl. She was not like Malachi, ready to die for Home Rule and fight the Ascendency at any cost, but she had a better understanding of the Malachis of her oppressed land with each year that she felt the sting of her lowly status.

At the crossroads to O'Shea's field, she looked down the opposite road toward town and toward the castle beyond. People were gathering around a cart or some kind of vehicle in the center of town, a strange occurrence, but not so unusual if a tinker had come to town. The castle stood in the backdrop. She didn't want to look at it, but she did.

Almost nothing was visible in the mist except the crenelations of the old keep. One single light in the window that said someone, perhaps the master himself, was in the master's bedchamber. What was he doing, she wondered, as she stood-stock still in the road, her gaze fixed to the distant keep as if it—or its occupant—held a mystic power over her. Was he sitting in his chair with a blazing hearth chasing away the gloom of the day? Was he reading a novel, a glass of cognac held lazily in his hand? Or was he thinking? Did she cross his mind? Or did the memory of their encounters go with her when she fled the castle?

Tears threatened again. With an iron will, she forced them back and her face grew placid, as placid as the marble face of the Virgin Mary. Vowing to forget him, she spun on her heels and turned toward O'Shea's.

But then she stopped.

Her brow furrowed. The group in the town. There had been something not quite right about the gathering. From the corner of her eye, she'd seen a figure rush to the group. What was it about that figure that disturbed her? She grew still.

It was the black bag he held in his hand. The man was the physician.

A black, terrible foreboding engulfed her. Someone had been hurt in the middle of town. Someone who had driven through in a cart . . . or carriage. There weren't many who owned such vehicles in Lir.

She clutched the willow basket to her chest and began an anxious run-walk in the direction of Lir. The closer she got, the more she could see the cause of the gathering was indeed a tragedy. Men with grim, lined faces looked on while women held their children in shacklelike grips so they would not disturb those who were assisting.

She roughly pushed through the crowd without thought or bother of manners. A strange panic gripped her, as if she knew whatever she might find in the middle of the crowd was somehow inevitable. Like sorrow amidst a plague.

"Is he is dead? Is the poor boy-o dead?" she heard several call out. She pushed through some men, and with a sickening lurch to her heart, she realized that she stood in front of a black carriage with the Trevallyan crest lacquered on the door.

"Easy with him. . . . easy there, lads," a man said softly next to her.

Trevallyan, her mind cried. Desperately, she clutched at the men who had moved in front of her. She again pushed her way to the front of the carriage. A body was being lifted from it, scarlet drops of fresh blood spattered across the chest.

Trevallyan, she moaned silently, not yet able to see the face, unable to see whether he was dead or alive.

Numbness crept through her. Above, the body moved from one set of hands to another and another and in the background, somewhere, a woman wept. The scene seemed to play out in minutes instead of seconds, as if slowed by the hand of God. It took every bit of her strength to push through the crowd one last time.

The men lowered the figure onto a wagon. She pushed through to the wooden sides of the vehicle, her heart pounding like a hammer. The face. She had to see the face.

"Seamus! Seamus!" a woman behind her wailed. Ravenna looked down at the wounded man. It truly was Seamus, Trevallyan's carriage driver, who lay in the wagon. His face was deathly pale, his mouth slack, his eyes squeezed shut. He'd been shot through the chest and now clung to life by the thinnest of threads.

The crowd thronged around him, easing him out of her view. For a long moment, she simply stood where she was, unable to move. It wasn't Trevallyan. *It wasn't Trevallyan,* she kept telling herself, despising the odd relief she felt every time she repeated the realization. Yet, horribly, another thought came to her.

She turned around and stared at the abandoned carriage. With renewed anxiety, she saw the holes and raw wood where shots had entered it. The door was off its hinge and the interior was dark and despairing, as if no life lingered there.

Was Trevallyan still inside the carriage? Had he been left in there, because . . . he was now beyond human help?

Choking back the sudden rush of emotion, she stepped to the carriage to peer inside. Her mind rebelled at the thought of what she might find in there, but she still clawed at the door to open it. She had to know what had happened to him. She had to see for herself. There was almost a spiritual need to see him. If he was dead, she would always wonder whether in some mystical realm, the realm of *geise,* she hadn't been the one who had somehow gotten him killed.

"He's no longer there, miss," Drummond, the Anglican minister, told her as she twisted the metal latch on the carriage door.

"Where—where is he?" she stuttered, staring at the old man. Had they already taken him away? He couldn't possibly be worse off than Seamus and still be alive. So had they laid him out alongside the road? And was there anyone at his side? To hold his hand, a hand that might soon grow cold?

The panic inside her swelled. She didn't love Trevallyan. Indeed, she had vowed to never bother with him again. So perhaps it was the sight of Seamus, or the blood, or the terrible notion that Malachi, even if he was not the triggerman, surely knew who the man was that sent this scene into such a spiral of despair. But deep down, she knew it wasn't any of these things. *Trevallyan. Trevallyan.* His name kept ringing in her mind like a druid chant, beckoning her to find him. She must find him.

"Look yonder, miss." Drummond pointed behind her to Doyle's tavern.

Sickened, she turned around.

Their gazes locked instantly.

Trevallyan stood beneath the tavern sign with Father Nolan. He held his right arm to his side, and she could see blood on the makeshift bandage. The wound was obviously superficial and didn't seem to hurt him. Indeed, there was not pain in his eyes, but anger. Fury. She pitied those who had done this to him.

Every man, woman, and child in the crowd fell silent as they watched them. She looked away from Trevallyan for a second and found all eyes turned on her. The townsfolk were gauging her reaction. Even Trevallyan, she thought, as she stared at him once more, was assessing her. Did everyone in Lir know about the ridiculous, trumped-up *geis*? And did they blame her for what had happened? Did Trevallyan believe the *geis* now, and believe her to be the indirect cause of this mischief the boy-os had done?

She turned away and abruptly began to walk out of town. It was all she could do not to run. The strange urge to rush to Trevallyan, to touch him, feel his warm arms and see the life still in his clear blue-green eyes was like a fire burning within her, a fire she couldn't under-stand and wanted desperately to extinguish. Now she just wanted to go home. The potatoes and O'Shea forgotten, she now just wanted to forget her fears and the confusing flood of emotion that had surged when she thought Trevallyan murdered, and she never wanted to think of them again.

"Are you sorry they didn't get me?"

Trevallyan's words were spoken evenly, with perhaps only a hint of malice. A strong hand gripped her arm. Right in the middle of the road out of Lir, he forced her to look at him. She wanted to pummel him with her fists, her fears, her shame, her relief, made her hate him anew.

"I had nothing to do with this and you know it. You know it!" she fairly screamed at him.

"I know."

Only two words, yet they instantly disarmed her. She looked up at him and fought the desire to bury her head in his chest and have a good long cry.

"Who did do it?" she whispered, afraid to hear the answer and yet desperate to know.

"I don't know. I didn't see them," Trevallyan whispered, drawing her near.

" 'Twas not Malachi. I know he could not—"

"Quit your blathering. He doesn't need your excuses." The anger flared in his eyes once more. She could see the old Celtic blood-lust had been ignited in him. "If he did this, I shall see that he pays."

"And if he did not do this?" she choked out.

"Then I shall make him tell me who did."

She stared at him, unable to think of a defense. Even she believed Malachi would know who had staged the ambush.

She gazed down at the hold on her arm. Suddenly flustered, she said, "Please—let—let me go. I'm glad that you weren't hurt—truly— and I shall say prayers for Seamus. Now you must let me return home." She tugged on her arm. He dropped his hand. With fire in his eyes, he watched her leave.

"Griffen told me about your father. Things you don't even know."

The words stopped her. She glanced at him and saw the sincerity on his face.

"Tell me. What did he say?" she almost gasped in her haste to know.

A wicked little smile turned one corner of Trevallyan's mouth. "All in good time. I shall expect you at the castle for dinner tonight so that we may discuss it."

His ploy was ingenious. If there was one thing that could bring her back to the castle, it was news about her father.

In awe and frustration, she stared at him. He'd just made a mess of all her plans. She had vowed never to see him again, yet now she was expected for dinner. He didn't care about her, save what information he presumed she could give him about the boy-os, but she wasn't going to be able to turn him down, for she would do almost anything to find out about her father.

"I don't wish to see you anymore, my lord," she said, her words stiff, helpless.

"Come at seven o'clock. We can have a sherry in the library before we eat." The wicked smile still shone in his eyes. "Now you'll have to excuse me. I must find out how Seamus fares." He bowed to her as if he were in court dress and not standing on a boggy road, his shirt and coat torn at the arm where a bright red bandage signaled his wound.

Infuriated, she ran back to the cottage. She threw herself on her bed and begged for the courage to spurn his knowledge of her father. Yet she knew, most painfully, that she would be at the castle gates well before seven o'clock.

⚭

Ravenna walked the dark and lonely road to the castle even though she had no doubt Trevallyan would be sending a carriage for her. The outing was a form of rebellion, of independence. She had kissed Grania good night and struck out on her own, half hoping the Trevallyan carriage would pass her along the way so she could stick her nose up at it. But before long, she regretted her decision. A quarter of the way to the castle, a large shadowed figure crossed the road and blocked her passage. A salt wind kicked up from the east, blowing her hair and the hood of her cape into her eyes, and making it difficult for her to distinguish who it was who stopped her.

Her throat was dry and tight with fear when she called out, "Who goes there? What business have you with me?"

"Why do you head to the castle at this hour, Ravenna?" the man said. His voice possessed an aching familiarity.

"Malachi," she whispered. Running to him, she was glad there was no moonlight to reveal the suspicion and fear that crossed her face. "What are you doing here? Everyone is looking for you—they think— well, they think you've been up to something terrible."

"I've been hiding. But I had to see you. It was worth all risk."

He touched her face, and his gentleness moved her. He wanted so much to please her, yet nothing he did pleased her.

"Do you know who tried to kill Trevallyan, Malachi?" She knew her voice was cold. It seemed to bring him upright.

"I wouldn't be shootin' Seamus if I were wantin' to kill Trevallyan." Bitterness ate at each word.

"Well, someone made a mess of it, to be sure. So tell me who it was? You must tell me."

"I can't be doin' that."

She slumped in despair. His reaction was not so much unexpected, as disappointing. "Please, Malachi, in the name of God, you cannot be doing such awful things. The men you're with are killing innocents."

"The Ascendency have no innocents."

"And Kathleen Quinn, is she not innocent?"

His silence grew ominous. "What does she have to do with this?"

She took his rough, work-worn hand in her own soft one. "I remember how you were once. She passed in her carriage. We all admired her, but you—you wouldn't even look at her—it was too painful. I could tell you worshipped her."

"It's you I worship. I only worship you." He hung his head. "Why do you go to the castle, Ravenna? Why?"

"I . . ." She lost her tongue. There didn't seem any way to explain it all to him, about her father and her long stay at the castle while she recuperated, and the way Trevallyan looked at her that made her want to flee and succumb at the same moment. "I don't love him," she finally whispered. And it was the truth. She didn't love him. There was only a strange growing attraction she felt for him, and she was determined to overcome it.

"Then come with me. I want to marry you. We can go to Galway. Me uncle lives there—I can be a fisherman, and we can forget all about Lir and the Ascendency . . . and the boy-os."

"Tell me who tried to kill Trevallyan. They should be brought to justice, and you know they should be," she pleaded.

"Justice! There is none here!" He raised his fist to the window-lit castle in the distance. "And all because that man has taken everything that should be ours! But tell me he won't take you. You must tell me so, Ravenna."

"He may only take what I choose to give," she said softly.

"Then give him nothing. Come. Go with me now."

She was at a loss. Her friendship with Malachi would always exist, no matter what, because of their childhoods, because of the letters that had held her together in London. But she didn't love him. She had no way to explain to him that she was changed from the girl he used to know. Her education had ruined her, exiled her from all the expectations of her class. She would be unhappy being a fisherman's wife, and yet she knew in her mind that his offer was the best a girl such as she could hope for. She couldn't accept it, however. It was now not enough. So her only choice was to do nothing, to be no one, to live in the limbo of her self-imposed exile forever.

"Trevallyan says he knows information about my father. That is why I'm going to the castle and why I must go now." Unshed tears caught in her throat. She was hurting him, and the last thing she had ever wanted to do was hurt him.

"He lies. He only wants to—"

"No!" She fought the urge to cover her ears. "No, Malachi, it isn't like that. He's been a gentleman. Always a gentleman."

"He can afford to be." The hatred in his voice was clear.

"Please, you must go." She looked both ways down the darkened road. "If someone should come and recognize you, the peelers'll put you in the gaol. I don't want to see you come to that." She turned to him. "Please stay out of trouble. And tell them to leave Trevallyan alone. He's done nothing wrong but be born to a legacy you cannot abide."

"If he takes you from me, I'll do him."

She gasped. "Don't say such things."

"Aye, but it's true." His voice was hoarse with emotion. "I'll not abide him takin' you from me. I love you. I've always loved you. You're what I live for, Ravenna. You're me beautiful girl, and I pined for you all the years you were at the English school. He cannot be takin' you away from me. I can't live with losin' you to him."

"You aren't losing me to him," she said.

"But I'm losin' you, and if not to him, then to who?"

She released a small sob, knowing he wouldn't understand. Knowing she would hurt him. "To me, Malachi. You're losing me to me."

His silence gave testament to his pain. A light broke the hills in the foreground, and Ravenna wondered if it was a carriage from the castle, come to pick her up at the cottage.

"Be off now, before they find you." Her voice wavered with tears. She touched his face in a tender gesture of farewell.

"I'll win you. Whatever it takes."

His words sent a chill through her blood. "Don't do anything foolish, Malachi. If you picture Trevallyan's blood running, then remember that his is no different from Kathleen Quinn's. I don't believe you could hurt her."

"She was an angel. With her clean face . . . and her velvet dress." He crushed Ravenna to his broad chest. His voice was hoarse with pleas. "But don't you see? Kathleen Quinn is not real. You are real. You're the earth that I walk upon, the ancient *ogham* stones that cross Lir's fields. I worship you, Ravenna. Don't you see it? Don't you care?"

The lights from the carriage were growing stronger. Fear and concern caught her breath. "Please, you must go—"

"Then meet me. After your dinner with Trevallyan. There is a servants' passage from the drawing room that is hardly used. Take it, and meet me at the bottom of the stair. All that I ask is that you meet me."

"All right. I'll meet you. But now you must fly."

Before the words left her tongue, he was gone, merely a shadow in the night.

Chapter 19

THE COACH drew near, and she was caught in the light of its lanterns. As she thought, it was the carriage sent from the castle. Ravenna allowed the man who had replaced Seamus to help her ascend the vehicle, and before she knew it, Greeves was showing her to the library.

Malachi's encounter left her rattled, but she was more so within the castle, in the clutches of Lir's esteemed member of the Ascendency, magistrate and king. She had wanted to forget him, and yet if what Trevallyan told her proved to be the truth, if he did truly help her find out who her father was, she would be indebted to him for the rest of her life.

She warmed her hands at the fire, refusing the chair Greeves offered her. He bowed and left. When Trevallyan didn't show, it occurred to her that the mischievous one-armed butler might have played another trick on her and put her in the wrong room, but then she heard a noise at the entrance, and Trevallyan was there.

He gave little indication he'd been wounded. The bandage, if he still wore it, was hidden beneath the arm of his frock coat. He looked fit and rested, dressed in his usual somber attire, dark coat and trousers, relieved only by a glimpse of stark white shirt that peeked through a black neckcloth. Miraculously, he had eluded death, a fate Seamus now wrestled with.

"Sherry?" He raised one aristocratic eyebrow.

"Yes," she answered, irked that he always deemed it acceptable to dispense with a proper greeting and farewell in her company. She was nothing but a peasant to him, and would always be such. She marveled at how infuriatingly supercilious he could be. To him, the attitude was clearly a birthright.

He walked to the mixing table and handed her a tiny glass of the amber-red liquid. She took a sip, willing it to have quick effect on her nerves.

"How is Seamus?" she asked quietly.

His eyes hardened to ice. "He is barely alive. I fear only a miracle can save him."

"Miracles have been known to happen."

His gaze slid to hers. Without premeditation, he reached out and ran the back of his hand down her smooth cheek. "Yes," was all he said before he turned away and sat in the large leather chair by the fire.

"So tell me about my father. That is, after all, why I've come." She walked toward him, again irritated that he would seat himself before seating her.

"I fear if I tell you now I shall be lacking company at dinner." He glanced at her, the same old disparaging, amused glance that was somehow inbred into the peerage. In one lightning moment, he'd expressed disdain for her cheap clothes, her low social position, and her suspect manners.

Bristling, she said, " 'Tis unfair of you to keep me on tenterhooks, waiting to hear—"

" 'Tis unfair of you," he interrupted, "to be . . . to look . . . so . . ." His angry gaze drifted to her figure. He became inexplicably angrier.

"You must tell me about him. I need to know," she implored quietly.

"After dinner."

She stared at him. He watched the flames in the hearth, his posture implacable.

"You know I desire to know about my father. You leave me no choice but to wait." Her voice never wavered. "It seems I am at your mercy."

"How quickly you forget it."

She forced herself to swallow the scathing comment on the tip of her tongue. Instead, she said, "This pretense is preposterous. Shall I return when you are feeling better, my lord?"

He finally looked at her, and there was a slight quirk to his mouth, as if he enjoyed her standing up to him. "No, stay. Forgive my ill temper. 'Tis not every day I am shot. Especially by a felon who would as soon see me hanging by the neck from my own tree as lying by the roadside in a puddle of blood."

"I promise you and Seamus that I'll do my best to find out the man who did this."

His eyes gleamed more dangerously. "Indeed?" He took a small folded piece of paper out of his jacket pocket and threw it on the table beside her.

She reached for it and read it with a slow, building horror.

Finished, all she could do was leave it on the table and place her shaking hands in her lap. "You know I didn't send that message to you," she whispered. "I don't know why they used my name."

"Because they knew I would come," he said quietly. He watched her, and his mood turned morose. "My man O'Donovan saw you talking to MacCumhal. Were you with him, perchance, before you went to town today to find Seamus carried off like a corpse?"

"Malachi didn't do it, I know he didn't do it."

"How do you know?" he challenged.

"I just know, 'tis all. You must take my word for it."

His lips twisted in an all-knowing, cynical smile. The contempt in his glance was like the flick of a whip. She knew he was remembering the night she'd gone with Malachi to the Briney Cliffs; the night he'd found her lying in the road in her sodden night rail.

"I do believe I hear Greeves's footsteps." Coldly, he stood and offered his arm to her. "Come, dine with me."

Being without recourse, she allowed him to escort her.

Greeves took them to a small, cozy eating room off the parlor that she had never seen before. It was hung with threadbare medieval tapestries of indigo and gold. Long ago, it must have served as some sort of dressing room for the Celtic king who had built the castle. Now, since it was off the modern kitchen, it was furnished with a small mahogany table and old-fashioned Chippendale chairs from Trevallyan's ancestors. Trevallyan, no doubt, took most of his meals in this little room. It both pleased and chagrined her that he felt no compulsion to entertain her in a grand, distant manner. She wondered why he was so comfortable with the intimacy of her presence in his lair. Especially since he didn't seem to be able to make up his mind how he felt about her. He was either angry at her, lusting after her, or mercilessly reminding her of her inferior social position—all of which managed to inflict pain.

With little conversation, they sat and ate Fiona's tempting meal. The mutton was delicate, the peas fresh, the bread white and crusty. Afterward, they were served an exotic drink made with mint, sugar, and whiskey called a julep. Trevallyan explained that the recipe had come from a plantation in Mississippi where some Ulstermen he knew had struck it rich in cotton.

She sipped her drink, sated on the good food and watched him from across the small table. The places Trevallyan had gone, the world he had seen, she envied it. She might have even told him so, except that Greeves entered the room and told him the physician would like to speak to him.

"Would you care to retire to the library while I check on Seamus?"

She stood and clutched her napkin. "All right. Then will you tell me about my father?"

"In good time. He might not be your father, you know."

"I know he is. I can feel it."

He quirked his lips, then departed.

She told Greeves not to bother escorting her to the parlor, that she could find it on her own. Greeves nodded and began to clear the table for Fiona. He didn't watch her as she left.

In the passage, Ravenna decided to take the moment to meet Malachi. It made her nervous thinking of him waiting for her inside the castle while Trevallyan blamed him for the shooting. Determined to tell him to leave before Trevallyan returned from Seamus's, she darted past the parlor to where she remembered the drawing room to be. Opening one door after another, she finally stumbled upon the correct room, but this time there wasn't a fire in the hearth to light her way.

There was a lamp on the table outside the door. Retrieving it, grateful that it was lit, she scuttled back into the drawing room, making sure to close the door behind her.

The jib was easy to find from memory. The door sprung open and she descended the damp, winding staircase, her nerves rattled by the sound of tiny feet that scurried below.

"Malachi?" she whispered to the darkness.

Not a sound answered.

"Malachi?" she said again, this time much louder.

"Aye," came a voice, muffled by distance. She took the stairs two at a time and descended far enough into the earth so that she could see the light of his lantern.

"There you are," she exclaimed, relieved to see his familiar face.

"Ravenna. How goes it?" His mouth was hard and disapproving. He was clearly jealous.

"We'll be done soon. Trevallyan had to leave me to check on Seamus."

"Seamus is dead."

His words froze her. The shock of it felt like the sting of ice. She knew the man had been terribly wounded, but somehow she couldn't believe the incident had ended in a death. She had always hoped the boy-os would see the trouble they were entering into, and quit before something this terrible happened. "How—how do you know?" she asked numbly.

"Everyone knows by now."

She detected his own horror and fear in his voice. Weakened, she lowered herself to the stairs, unmindful of the damp ruining her best wool gown. "Why did they do it, Malachi? Why? Tell me why?" She couldn't run from the question. The incident had gained nothing; it had only lost. No one was better off for it. No one.

"You know why it was done," he answered distantly.

"But what did it accomplish?"

His silence was testament to his own confusion. Finally, in a shaky voice he said, "Come with me to Galway. We'll forget about the boy-os and put this mess behind us. You can dream of Trevallyan all you want, and I'll never complain, just come with me, Ravenna, come and be my wife and . . . and . . . and . . . save me . . ." He grew deathly silent. Then she heard the harsh, raspy sound of a man's sobs.

Her heart seemed wrenched in two. Malachi had grown into a man, but here, weeping at her feet was the young boy she had known, the little urchin who had stood up to others in her defense, who had in his noble, childish way, clung to the shreds of honor his father had left him before he had been killed.

Slowly, she put down the lamp and wrapped him in her arms. He cried on her breast for a long time while she held him and pressed her smooth cheek to his wet one. He quieted finally; the grief purged. Yet in the absence of tears was a silence that spoke of confusion and blame and death.

"You must leave here," she said softly when he raised his head.

"Aye, but not alone. . . ."

"Yes, alone. I've got to stay and find out about my father. You must leave the county and never see the boy-os again. You can go to Galway without me."

"I won't."

"You must."

"I love you."

She closed her eyes. Slowly she lowered her head to his shoulder, despair eating away at her insides. She didn't love him in return, and the words to tell him seemed unspeakable.

His brawny, meaty arms wrapped around her like steel bands. They alone seemed enough to protect her from the storms seething around her, but as she was coming to find out, brute strength lied. He couldn't protect himself, let alone her.

"Go to the next county, at least. Perhaps one day—if things change —I will join you," she whispered at last, unable to offer him anything better.

"But what must change?" he asked, dragging his lips across the top of her head.

My feelings, my desires, for you, for Trevallyan. "I don't know," she fibbed.

He held her close, as if unwilling to let her go, as if he somehow knew they might never be together again. Gradually, she succumbed to him, holding him close as well, enjoying the bittersweet kinship, if only because she knew it was destined to be so brief.

And brief it was.

A shuffling noise startled them. They looked up the winding stairs. The shadow of a man loomed over them.

"Get up, MacCumhal, so that I may see your face when I kill you."

The voice shattered the tender moment. Terror traced through her veins as she lifted her head from Malachi's shoulder. Trevallyan stood above them on the staircase. He was all but hidden in the darkness save for the gleam of lamplight on the pistol he held tightly in his hand.

"No—this is all wrong—" she stuttered, gasping for the breath to still her pounding heart.

"You killed Seamus, you bloody, incompetent bastard, and you shall pay for it." Trevallyan lowered himself to another step. Then another. The light played off his angry features. "He worked for me all his life. He was like my own family, and you murdered him. . . . And for what? What?" His shout echoed through the stone staircase like the moan of a phantom.

"He didn't kill Seamus. I told you that," Ravenna pleaded, still clutching Malachi.

Trevallyan reached the step just above their entwined figures. He gazed down at their embrace. Even in the flickering shadows of lamplight, she could see the rage burn in his eyes.

Slowly, deliberately, he placed the pistol to one side of Malachi's head. Slowly, deliberately, he pulled back the hammer.

Malachi stiffened within her arms. She released a ragged gasp.

"Stand up so that I may kill you like a man. I'm not like the coward who killed Seamus."

"Trevallyan—no! My God, no!" She reached up and grasped the pistol's muzzle, turning it toward her.

"Would you have me shoot you both?" Trevallyan asked. Too quietly.

"How did you know I was here?" she cried out, searching for any delay.

"The lamp was missing on the table outside. When I entered the drawing room, I saw light beneath the jib." His face bore pain. "These stairs lead to a cave beneath the castle. That was how I knew you were meeting . . ." he growled some unintelligible oath and pointed the pistol back toward Malachi, "him."

She pressed her cheek against the muzzle. When the initial surge of fear ebbed, she whispered, "Would you shoot me too, Niall?"

She had never before used his Christian name. It seemed to move him. She prayed it moved him. The seconds passed.

He caressed her hair, wrapping a lock around his palm like a bandage, the black tresses in stark contrast to his strong white hand. She watched him closely in the darkness. A bitter smile touched his lips. "I think this *geis* might make me shoot myself before you, Ravenna."

She stifled a bout of nerves. "Then let Malachi go. I promise you he did not pull the trigger this afternoon." She held Malachi tight. He felt like a fence post in her arms, as tense and straight-backed as a wooden soldier. He was terrified. Even in the cold damp of the stair, she could feel the perspiration drip from his temple.

The pistol was a rod of cold death against her cheek.

"You beg for his life, my love?" Trevallyan whispered.

"Yes, yes. Let him go and I swear you shall never see his face in this county again."

"Promises that are never kept."

She leaned the pistol to her cheek, terror locked in her heart. Malachi had begun to tremble, but he said not a word in his defense.

"Let him go," she pleaded. "I would rather you kill us both than see him die for a crime he didn't commit."

"Do you care for this bastard that much?"

"Yes," she said truthfully, unable and unwilling to explain where her feelings for Malachi began and ended.

Trevallyan's anger broke free of its chain. He unwound his hand from her hair and shoved a booted leg at Malachi. Entwined as they were, both she and Malachi tumbled down several steps. She felt Malachi scramble to help her to her feet when Trevallyan butted the pistol point right in the young man's face.

"Don't touch her," he growled. "Leave this place and never *ever* return. Do you hear me, boy-o?"

Malachi nodded. Even in the darkness Ravenna could see he was white as a sheet.

"You're not worthy of her regard," Trevallyan spat like a curse. "So begone. Run like the spineless cur you are, and know that I'd have seen your brains dripping from these walls before I'd have let you go, if she had not begged me to spare your wretched life." He booted Malachi once more and sent him tumbling farther down the stairs.

In the cover of shadows, Malachi stood. In his shabby clothes and shabby dignity, he raised his fist and clear voiced, said, "This isn't over, Trevallyan. You can't take everything from the likes of me without paying a price. Just you wait. There'll be many a dry eye at your funeral." With that, he took his leave. He jumped down the stone treads three at a time and disappeared in the blackness below. Deep in the darkened bowels of the keep, she heard him curse like a hell-bound sinner.

And then there was silence in the tower, and the patter of rats' feet echoed once more off the walls, and the metallic drip of water on stone continued as if there had never been an incident.

Painfully, Ravenna clawed at the damp stones to aright herself. She rose to her feet, her heart heavy with dread. Now she had to face Trevallyan all alone. Now she would feel the brunt of his fury over Seamus's death.

"Come here," he said hoarsely.

As if she were Grania, she took the two treads slowly, each reluctant movement costing her in strength and resilience.

In the light flickering from Malachi's abandoned lantern, she found his expression dark with betrayal, and something else, an emotion that exquisitely straddled love and pain.

"I only came here to find out about my father, not to meet Malachi," she whispered futilely to him.

As if it caused him untold agony, he took her by the waist and pulled her against him. In a raw, low voice, he said, "Did you know they were going to try to kill me?"

The question hit her like a slap across the cheek. "No. I didn't know about it. On my mother's grave, I swear to you I didn't." She stared at him, her heart drumming in her chest. It looked bad. There was no denying it.

From his waistcoat, he removed the small note he had shown her earlier. Further damnation. "Do you know anything about this? Any-thing?"

She shook her head, unable to accept that her name on that small piece of paper had become the vehicle of the day's tragedy. "I know nothing about any of this except that I know Malachi is not capable of killing. He is simply not capable of it," she whispered, her voice qua-vering with fear.

A repressed rage contorted his features. "You're all blameless, isn't that right? The whole bloody lot of you. And you, *you,* claim the most innocence of all. Yet time and again, I find you in a clandestine meeting with MacCumhal. I find you holding him and probably even . . ." He didn't seem able to finish.

"I wouldn't hurt anyone, my lord." Her entire body trembled. "Mala-chi was my friend from childhood. I understand him, 'tis all."

"But you refuse to understand his need to destroy me." His voice lowered to a growl. "To murder Seamus, God rest his soul."

"No." She grabbed the lapels of his topcoat. "Malachi wasn't the triggerman. I know he's sorry for what happened to Seamus. He was not the man to kill him, and I'd lay down my life to prove it."

He stared at her. With a surge in her stomach, she knew he didn't completely believe her. Finally, in monotones, he spoke as if tired of fighting a war he could not see, nor understand.

"When I was a young man, I held a babe in my hands—a beautiful baby—a child who held nothing but promise." He rested his cheek against the top of her head as if he were praying for her soul. "I was told this child was to be my bride and I ridiculed the idea. But I found I couldn't abandon her. She was a life to be molded, her promise had yet to bloom. Even though I didn't want her, I was compelled to help her. I saw to it she had everything. . . ."

Her breath caught in her throat. His words hypnotized her. He couldn't be telling her what she thought he was saying, but the shocking truth of it seemed like the final piece in a long-held puzzle.

"The babe grew up to be a woman. A beautiful woman. And even though I had provided her everything, shaped her life as I wished, I told myself I didn't want her." His cheek was warm against her hair, his embrace warm and almost comforting. "Yet one day, as fate threw her at me time and again, I stumbled upon the fact that the beauty had a soul. She possessed a wit that I found distracting, and a heart that seemed as lonely and wanting as mine. I found myself thinking about her, worrying about her, wondering about her. Soon she was all I thought about."

The embrace turned into the cold steel bands of a trap. His hand clamped in her hair and she cried out more from the shock of his revelations than from the roughness of his touch. What he was saying couldn't be true, but deep in her heart, she feared it was. He was her provider, not her long-lost father. It had been Trevallyan all along.

He tilted her head back so she'd be forced to look up at him. Behind her, she could hear her wooden hairpins scatter down the stone stairs like grapeshot. "But here I find she is in thick with murderers and thieves. All my schooling," he shook her, "yes, *my* schooling, and *my* cottage, and *my* silverware, and *my* money, has not kept her away from the wrong kind. I thought to make a lady of her and here I find instead . . ." He couldn't seem to speak the word.

"Don't," she begged in an anguished whisper.

"And the thought of him . . ." His voice trembled. "The thought of *him* . . ."

The idea seemed like a dagger twisting in his gut. He closed his eyes as if shutting out the pain. ". . . the thought of MacCumhal . . . *fucking* you is enough to kill me."

A sob caught in her throat. Writhing beneath the shame of his words, she couldn't even look at him.

"No more thoughts, however. No more." He held her hard, ignoring her struggles to be free.

"Don't ever speak such terrible words to me again," she cried, fighting off tears and struggling with his unwanted hold. It shocked and hurt to think his money had been governing her all her life without her ever knowing it, but it hurt worse that he thought her nothing but a whore in need of salvation.

"Terrible? Terrible?" He seemed to laugh. "Nay, words are not terrible. Seamus being murdered is terrible."

His anger erupted, and his dark, furious expression was a fearful sight in the suffocating dimness. She yearned to run from him and return to the warm safety of her cottage, but it was impossible to flee him now. His angry grasp was like an iron shackle. He had stolen everything from her this night, even her home. The cottage wasn't hers to run to anymore. It had been his all along. Her world had been ripped apart.

With a moan of defeat, she quit fighting him. Despondent, she murmured, "I only came here to find out about my father. You must believe me that I had nothing to do with the shooting today. I promise you that if you tell me what you know about my father, I will leave here and never bother you again."

"Griffen told me the story about a man who died twenty years ago in Antrim."

"Who was this man?"

His expression turned hard. "Who? I'll tell you who. But not here. Oh, no, definitely not here."

She nodded, then came upon a cold realization. Her gaze locked with his. "I won't—"

"You won't, eh? For him, but not me." His laughter rang in her ears. "No doubt the thought of this old man pushing up inside your young sweet flesh is too distasteful."

"How you *speak* is distasteful," she said violently.

In an ominous tone, he said, "Distasteful or not, it's time. They threw you at me. Well, I'll tell them all: I've caught you. Do you hear me? I've caught you."

Panic made her mouth go dry. She stared at him, unwilling to accept the meaning of his words. "I'm not a prize you've finally won," she whispered.

"No?" His lips twisted in the mockery of a smile. "But what are you then? A princess? A peeress? A fine lady whom I should court on bended knee? You're a fraud. *My* fraud. Your education—or rather *my* education—enlightens you, but not well enough. You seem unable to grasp the fact that you were born a bastard child, alone and penniless, who'd probably be dead by now without my tender mercies."

"Tender mercies," she accused softly. "Is that what you've shown me?"

A tiny glimmer of guilt flashed in his eyes but he seemed determined to ignore his better self. In a husky voice, he said, "Without me, you'd be digging the fields for praties . . . or worse. I'm your salvation and always have been. You fail to understand that."

"I understand everything too well, my lord. I've no delusions. How can I, when you've always seen to it that I be made brutally aware of my lowly circumstance?" Tears came unbidden to her eyes. "Fear not that you've *ever* mistaken me for a lady, for you haven't, but still I'm not your slave. You can't do with me as you wish. If you are my salvation, then I'll defy all those who would have me saved."

"But who's to stop me, Ravenna?" He calmly looked down into the black hole of the bottom of the staircase. "Your one mangy knight has fled. Your meager protection is gone." He looked back at her, his gaze burning. "Now it is time."

"I'll tell you only once: I want nothing of this and nothing of *you.*"

"Ah. 'Tis good to finally hear the words you should have told Mac-Cumhal."

She released a moan and ground her fists into his chest. He took her waist in a viselike grip and again pushed her against the stair wall. With excruciating slowness, he lowered his head to hers.

"Don't do this." Her voice quavered with sorrow. "Don't take everything from me in the name of salvation because you fear a *geis* and want to prove it wrong."

His breath was hot on her temple. "I'm not afraid of a *geis*. The *geis* is only words and I damn them." Slowly he caressed her face, his own a dark shadow. "There's only one thing I have learned to fear in this world: It is the inevitable."

"And is this inevitable?" Her words choked on tears.

He didn't answer her; he only stared.

The question bore down on her like a lead weight. She began to weep. No woman had ever wanted to be free of a man more than she did at that moment; nor had any woman desired one as intensely. With every insult that cut her, she longed for his approval that much more. Caught between desire and despair, she found herself trapped with only two choices: She could flee him now with a broken heart, or she could hand her heart to him and watch him break it.

The decision wrenched her very soul.

He waited in the silence for further protest, further struggle. None came. Slowly, relishing every touch, he lifted her chin and crushed his mouth over her parted lips.

She closed her eyes, allowing him to take of her mouth what he would while she cursed him with all her might. Countless times she had told herself she hated him; now her hatred had betrayed her. It had left her weakened where she should have found strength. But his hold was more than she could fight because it was not just physical. He kissed her with an anger and passion that she had never felt in her life, and it only made her ache for his love. Ache to see the gentle side of him hinted at beneath his roughness.

She didn't want to believe that there were powers beyond her control making her feel things she didn't want to, but as he took her face in his palms and kissed her again and again until her back met roughly with the stones of the stair wall, until her lips seemed to yearn for him of their own free will, she knew there was no denying it. Surrender was an impossible choice, but it happened anyway. Because the lies were sweet and the emotion overwhelming. Especially when his mouth, his lips, his touch, seemed to reach into her soul until her mind whispered, "At last. At last. I have found you."

He broke from the kiss and began to drag her up the stairs. Her lips were raw and her mouth felt empty. Hating herself, she pressed the back of her hand to her mouth, as if holding the feel of his lips; a poor substitute for the kiss she really wanted.

He pulled her up the stairs to his bedchamber above, and she offered no protest. Somehow he'd spun a web around her that took away her abilities to defend herself. The pitfalls were all too evident; he was an older man, wise in the ways of seduction, and she was merely an innocent girl, too naive to completely understand the danger, too entranced to stop him. And there seemed no way to stop. It seemed destined that they be in his bedchamber. Inescapable that he be kissing her again, by the chairs in the antechamber, against the carved oaken bedpost, on the satin counterpane that covered his mattress. And she couldn't lie to herself. She wanted his kisses. They were long and sweet and erotic. More than that, they were water for the desert of her lonely soul. She had no one in her life; no lovers, no friends. Grania was old and not long to remain in this world. There were no real prospects for marriage, and the future was just a dark maw where nothing seemed destined to grow.

Indeed, she yearned for his kisses. For the false promises they fooled her into believing. He was of the Ascendency and she was nobody, someone even shunned by her fellow villagers. Trevallyan would never stoop to her social level to make a lady of her. Men of his stature didn't marry women like her, not even with a *geis* and all the county praying for that marriage.

His hand cupped the back of her head as if he were drinking from her mouth, releasing a brilliant joy within her even as doom shadowed her path. She would have him. Even though alarms were sounding when all she wanted to hear was music. Even though he had yet to speak of love. He was carnally obsessed with her, she knew that, and that was all it was. But when he unhooked the old blue woolen dress for the last time, she offered no more protests. She only stared at him in longing and pain, tortured by the impossibility of a strong-willed, powerful man such as he surrendering so completely to a low-born woman that he would beg for her love.

"I'm a virgin," she whispered as he kissed her bare shoulder, the woolen dress this time slipping ever so softly off the heavy silk of the bedcoverings.

He paused, her words seeming to barely sink in. "A virgin," he murmured, scorching the hollows of her throat with his all too warm tongue. "Good, good," he grunted, continuing the hot path with his tongue.

"Are you listening? Have you heard?" Her voice was thick with repressed passion. She didn't know what part of her was still fighting him, still clinging to sanity, but perhaps her self-preservation was stronger than she realized. She was convinced she should feel more gratitude for it, but her thoughts were clouded, and, strangely, she felt only resentment.

He pulled her onto his lap and his hand captured a chemise-covered breast, sending a fire of sensation through her loins. "I've heard you," he said softly in her ear. "I'll believe you soon."

"Are you . . . ?" She could barely form the words. His mouth found her nipple even through the fabric of her clothing. She moaned and said almost drunkenly, "Are . . . you . . . so much a devil as to . . . make me prove it?" The argument was weak. He'd never had any trouble admitting he was a devil.

"You were meant to be with me." His breath came quick and hot. "Being a virgin is irrelevant; it's just a function of your body. I don't want your body." His voice grew tight as he shoved away the straps of her corset and chemise and uncovered one plump bare breast. "I want your soul," he whispered before his lips covered her nipple.

She helplessly entwined her fingers in his hair and prayed for a bucketful of cold reason to fall down upon them. She should run, she should reject this madness, but she knew she wouldn't. He drew her to him by an inexplicable magnetism. The need to be with him pulled on her like an otherworldly force, as if fate and the universe had deemed it inescapable. *Inevitable.*

"Please . . ." she whispered, unsure of what she even wanted, her eyes growing dark with female arousal.

His boots made a doomed sound as they each dropped to the rug. His shirt and trousers lay in a pile on the floor, and his black cravat was draped over the bedpost like a mourning armband.

Please. The word echoed through her mind as he covered her, taking away the last bit of clothing she wore. She couldn't even articulate what she wanted. Did she want him to let her go? Or did she want him to kiss her and again use his tongue in that wicked way he had just demonstrated?

His mouth covered hers in a searing kiss, and she knew she wanted impossibility of both. She wanted safety and yet, ecstasy. And she would never have both, because Niall, Lord Trevallyan, only offered danger and imminent heartache.

He pressed against her in the intimate way of men. Rolling her fully beneath him, he finally came to rest between the softness of her thighs.

Their gazes locked.

He lay on top of her, staring at her, his eyes glazed with the sheen of lust. Yet, she saw hesitance. Against her better judgment, she caressed the bandage on his arm, fighting the wild urge to kiss it and prove her contrition.

"Why do you look at me so?" she whispered, her gaze flickering shyly.

He kissed her breast. His tongue circled her nipple and dragged across the sensitive nub until she ached to cry out. But to stop or go further, she didn't know.

"I never thought I would want a woman like I want you . . ." His teeth grazed her smooth skin and nipped at the underside of one breast. "This feeling . . . 'tis eating me alive. . . ."

She closed her eyes, agreeing, but hating to think of separation. "Then . . . perhaps we shouldn't—"

"No." He kissed her, jamming his tongue into her mouth.

She shuddered with longing and surrender.

" 'Tis meant to be. You know it. I know it." He suddenly seemed to move like an animal after prey, intent on one thing only: capture. With a savagery, he pushed her knee up toward her hip; with anguish, he entered her, muffling her cries of surprise and incoherent protest with a kiss.

She went rigid. He thrust again and again, and she fought the sensation, causing herself even more agony. He watched her, and she knew he understood her plight. She was a virgin, but even willing as she was, it was still foreign to have a man inside her, particularly a man as eager and well-endowed as he. Without really even wanting to, she crushed her fists against him to make him stop.

But then he began to whisper in her ear.

"Touch me," he demanded, his voice hard and breathless.

She shook her head. Touching a man was as foreign to her as making love and she was clearly an amateur at both.

"Hold me," he whispered.

"Nay," she moaned, inexplicably anxious, but for what she didn't know.

He slowed to an excruciating pace. She cried out softly, her physical wants warring with her head.

"Touch me, or we'll end it right here." His voice was barely a groan above her.

Desperate to understand why she needed it so, she hesitated, then forced her hands to slide along his back. She found his skin smooth and the muscle pleasingly thick and well-toned. The years had been kind to him. His waist was still trim, and his chest that covered hers was still hard and firm, in erotic contrast to the lushness of her feminine bosom.

"That's right. . . ." he whispered when her wanton hands came to rest on his bare buttocks. Gripping them, savoring them, she found that she, too, was beginning to succumb to the ancient rhythm between them. And with every kiss, every strong thrust, she relented, more and more, until her body seemed to go liquid and the sensation he was giving her bloomed.

She released a sound deep in her throat and mindlessly threw back her head. Above her, she could hear him laugh in a deep, animal growl. He bent and took the tip of her breast in his mouth and she felt herself skirt a precipice.

The feeling intensified and she could see how wicked it was. It was so aching and powerful, she could understand those who fell into damnation to have it.

Trevallyan whispered once more in her ear. He told her naughty things, sweet things, that she shouldn't want but now craved. A man of fewer years might grunt over her like a pig and revel in the physical experience like a hog in slop. Not Trevallyan. The physical wasn't enough. He wanted all of her, and as he whispered, she realized he had won. The sensation building in her loins was sweet torture, and as he spoke more hotly, she knew she must either go with it, or die denying it. In agony, she cried out and gripped his back.

His words sent her over the edge.

The man was, indeed, a poet.

⊗

Trevallyan arose and left the sleeping girl behind in the large four-poster bed. Ravenna had fallen asleep sometime after midnight, but rest had eluded him. Seamus's death still weighed heavy upon him. Too, his consummation with Ravenna.

He touched his bandaged arm and cursed the soreness. It only reminded him of Seamus. Slipping into his trousers, he glanced at the black-haired beauty nestled beneath the heavy counterpane. She slept restlessly, and there was a tiny furrow above her tightly shut eyes as if her dreams did not soothe her. He could understand why. He, too, was unsettled by what they had just done. He really hadn't planned it. If he hadn't caught her with Malachi, things might have turned out differently. Perhaps he would have remained a gentleman forever.

He watched as she rolled to her stomach. Beneath her raised arm was the side of one breast, a generous, creamy half-moon of feminine charm. He stared at her, his jaw growing taut at the remembrance. Indeed, he might have remained a gentleman. But not forever. She had gotten into his blood. Her soul and body had tempted him past the point of no return. She was his now, and nothing short of a gun to the head was going to make him give her up.

He poured himself a whiskey and sat in his chair in the antechamber. As was his habit when he was pensive, he rubbed his jaw. Aggravated, he found it rough with beard.

Everything seemed to be unraveling. Seamus's death still numbed him. The man had been in his employ for as long as he could remember, and the fact that Seamus had been gunned down in a botched attempt to murder him left a cold feeling in the pit of his stomach. He'd almost believe in a *geis* now. Blight had arrived in Lir, and it was only a matter of time before whoever had killed Seamus would have another go at him.

He took a gulp from his glass, swallowing the burning liquid as if it were his anger. She shouldn't have been with Malachi. For all he knew, despite her denials, she might have been in on the plot to kill him, too. After all, did he really know her politics?

He stared at the cold hearth, unable to believe she would hurt him, yet cursed by the fact that she'd protected Malachi twice now from punishment. The lad meant something to her. There was no getting around it. And there was no telling what she might do for MacCumhal if the situation was dire enough.

Jealousy squeezed his heart like a thick green vine. At least Mac-Cumhal hadn't gotten to her first. She'd been a virgin, he knew that now. But did that change anything? Not much. He'd still found her with Malachi. Time and again, she was always with MacCumhal, protecting him, meeting him, comforting him. The boy was no fool. Malachi MacCumhal would have gotten her into his bed eventually. And then she would have been out of his hands forever.

" 'Tis late."

The whisper startled him. He turned around and found Ravenna standing in the doorway, wrapped in his dressing gown, her tousled hair falling across one shoulder in sensual disarray, her eyes heavy-lidded and weary. With a feeling of unease, he noted the reddish burn mark in the vulnerable hollow of her throat and realized he had made it.

He met her gaze. In the depths of her dark violet eyes, he saw worry and an emotion that lay somewhere between fear and hope. It was difficult to look at.

"You must tell me about my father now." Each word seemed to pain her as if she didn't want to talk to him. "The cottage . . . Grania—"

"Grania will know you're here." He took the generous portion of whiskey still in his glass in one blessed gulp.

"Tell me about my father." Her voice held pain. "I've earned it."

He grew silent, unsure how to talk to her. Their intimacy left a strange wall between them now he couldn't seem to scale. He didn't like the distrust in her eyes, yet he was sure it matched his own. "I'll take you to Antrim in the morning," he said. "You understand that you've no other way to get there without my help."

She looked away, barely hiding the anger in her eyes. He could tell she didn't want to be beholden to him, but now he wouldn't have it any other way. He wanted her gratitude as much as he despised the chill between them. It hadn't been nearly so cold in bed.

He gestured to the other chair, the one saved for Lady Trevallyan. "Come. Sit here. I'll tell you my agenda."

Slowly she crossed the room and lowered herself to the chair. She appeared stiff and uncomfortable, and he hated the look he saw in her eyes. It would haunt him for a long time.

"Just tell me where he is. I've never asked for your help. Not all these many years." She licked her lips, lips that were red and slightly swollen from kissing. They lured him and he had the urge to kiss them again, but he knew better than to test the shield of ice that surrounded her.

"I've done a lot for you and Grania. Doesn't that deserve some gratitude?"

The flare of rage in her eyes took his breath away. "You own me. You paid for my schooling, the cottage, Grania's upkeep. Does a slave feel grateful to her master?"

He shifted in his seat, unsettled by his own rising anger. He was losing control, and he could see no way to get it back. "You're not the one who's the slave, Ravenna," he whispered darkly.

She was silent, confused. Slowly, she said, " 'Tis not what Malachi would have me believe. He says we're all just slaves to the Ascendency and I'm even more so, now that I've . . ." She glanced at the bed in the background, and her beautiful eyes pooled with tears.

"Malachi is a fool." He fought the urge to touch her, to comfort her. "He's seduced you with his bad politics and 'tis only a matter of time before he'd stretch on the gallows and take you with him."

"Malachi treated me far better than you. He never used blackmail to have a go at me."

His anger rose. " 'Tis nothing like that," he snapped. "Our . . ." his own gaze drifted to the messed bed, "our union was nothing of that kind. I almost believe it was out of our control. As if it were meant to be."

"I'm ruined. Was that meant to be also?"

He wanted to close his ears to the anguish in her voice. His mouth dry, he said, "You're not ruined. No one need know of this. What occurred between us was quite natural. It happens to people all the time."

She refused to look at him, but she didn't hide the stain of color that rose to her cheeks. "Yes, I suppose it does. That accounts for all the bastards running around these Irish counties." In the smallest of whispers, she said, "Including me."

He crossed his arms over his bare chest, as if they were holding in his anger. "You can't help what you are. I don't sit in judgment of you."

The unshed tears glimmered in her eyes once more. "No. Of course you don't, magistrate. That's why you always open doors for me. Why you stand when I enter a room, why you make sure to greet me with the usual Trevallyan graciousness." She placed her fingers upon her trembling lips as if to still them. "Of course you don't sit in judgment of me, *milord*. That's why you've forced me to see tonight that I'm cursed with more of my mother than I would like to believe."

"I would fight to the death to defend what we've done here tonight." Anger squeezed his chest like steel bands, making it difficult to breathe. Her remorse and the accusing glimmer in her eyes left him furious. He wanted her on her back, crying out and holding him close to her heart, not staring at him with that anguished gaze. She didn't know it, but he felt as if he would do anything right now to take the look away. If he weren't careful, he just might go crazy and reveal the power she·wielded over him.

"Please. Just tell me about my father and let me go." Her face was drawn and pale. She looked as if she'd been given a severe emotional blow. His anger reached its boiling point.

"If the man I know of is your father, he was lord of Cinaeth Castle just north of Hensey." He stared at her, reveling in her need of him. It caused her no amount of torment, he could see that; still, he vowed to go to the grave before she would find her need for him gone. "The man's long dead, and that's all I really know. O'Rooney told me the story during one of his more lucid moments." A smirk lifted the corner of his lips. "I invite you to try to get more from him."

She said nothing, but he could see the machinations of her mind working. Working to be free of him.

"You can't get to Antrim on your own. You know that." He wanted to throw his head back and laugh. He'd caught her. He had her. And God damn his soul, he couldn't imagine ever wanting to let her go.

"I won't be beholden to you any longer." She lifted her proud head, her eyes blazing with anger.

The vision of her stopped his breath. "And how will you get there without me? Especially when I'm never going to let you leave this castle alone?"

Despair shadowed her visage like a falling veil. He could see she longed to lash out at him, to demand her freedom. He could also see she had the intelligence to know he wouldn't give it to her.

"I'll take you to Antrim in the morning," he announced quietly. "In the meanwhile, go back to bed and get some sleep. It's a long ride north."

"Is there nothing in my life you won't meddle with? I don't need your help. I don't want it. I only want to know about my father and then I want you to *stay out of my life.*" She wiped her silent tears with the back of her hand.

He stood and finally grabbed her as he'd been aching to do since she'd sat down. "You know I'm not going to let you walk out of this castle without a fare-thee-well. Accept it. Not after all the years and money I've wasted on you."

"I hate you."

Her words echoed in his ears like the gunshots of the previous day.

She clutched at the satin lapels of the dressing gown she wore as if desperate to hide her nudity. "Now if you will just let me go, I'll leave and you can be done with me."

"I can make you love me." He wanted to bite back the words. They were desperate, vulnerable. And he would never be that. Never.

"You cannot. You know you cannot."

He closed his eyes, fighting for control. "You underestimate me. There are a lot of things a man my age can do better than your young Malachi."

"Perhaps. But no man can do that."

The answer seized his heart. The gauntlet was thrown. His rage was like a blinding white light that obliterated every rational response. "Return to bed, Ravenna. We go to Antrim in the morning. Do not challenge me."

"I will challenge you."

"But you won't win. I'll orchestrate this trip to Antrim as I have everything else in your life." It took all his willpower not to shout. "And you'll obey me because you're in need of salvation and I'm the only man to save you."

Her fury seemed almost to match his. "You're not God. You can't play out my life like a move on a chessboard."

"And who will rescue you from me? That sniveling coward Malachi? A man who's running for his life? Or will Grania hobble over here and demand your return? The same old woman who's done her best to throw you at me."

He had driven her to tears once more. He'd shocked her with the news of Grania's loyalties, but the power of it felt sweet and necessary. He wanted her to know she was alone. There was only him now. And he vowed that was all there ever would be.

Her expression turned distant, angry and cold. "I'm not your prisoner," she said, her voice hoarse with despair.

"I beg to differ," he answered cruelly.

"How long can you think to get away with it?"

"Forever if I choose. I'm the magistrate, as you recall. Who will come to challenge me?"

"You're mad. What purpose will this serve?"

"I know of one," he said gravely. *I'll have you,* he reaffirmed to himself.

She twisted from his hold and stared at him as if he were anathema. He wondered, then, if he didn't hate her as well.

"I want you to know that all I ever wanted in this life was a woman to share it with and children to carry it on for me when I'm gone." Slowly, hesitantly, he made his confession. "A simple request for a man with my money, my power. But for twenty years that has eluded me. And in those twenty years, I've lost a wife—a woman I now know I did not love—and I lost a child—a child that I must claim publicly every day on the tombstone out there in the Trevallyan cemetery—a child that wasn't even mine. My mind brought me to the altar more times than I like to think about, but in the end my heart stopped me almost every time. I've ruled my life with intellect. I've sworn there's nothing stronger." He pointed at her as if she were merely a servant to do his bidding. "But I never felt about anything the way I feel about you."

If his words shocked her, she hid it well behind the beautiful mask of her face.

He gave a slight culminating nod. "You will never more go running around the countryside in your night rail, nor will you have clandestine meetings with men who would see me dead. I swear upon the graves of all the Trevallyans that if I see MacCumhal touching you again, I *will* kill him. I'll shoot him dead on the spot." He turned from her, dismissing her. Without even another glance her way, he poured himself a brandy and resumed his seat in his chair. "Now return to bed, Ravenna."

"I will not sleep in your bed."

"Sleep in the bed or on the cold stone floor for all I care. You're not leaving here. Know that." He dangled a large iron key in front of her. He wondered if she remembered him locking the doors to keep the servants out. He had done it right after the first time they made love. By the time he'd slipped between the sheets again, she'd been more than ready to go another round.

He pocketed the key in his trousers. She glared at him like a wet cat.

"Would you fight me for it?" he dared deliciously, the ghost of a smile touching his lips.

She released a short pent-up breath, the futility of the situation clearly pressing in on her. Giving him one last acid look, she intelligently ignored the dare and stomped to the bed.

"Go ahead, have your rebellion," he said as he watched her rip the heavy counterpane from the bed and head for the dressing room. "You'll still awake in my arms."

She paused at the door, her back furiously rigid. Giving him a lethal glance, she slammed the door closed as hard as she could, her anger a sight to behold.

He almost rather enjoyed it.

Chapter 20

THE TRIP to Antrim was luxurious and difficult. Luxurious because there was no better vehicle than the well-sprung English Barcroft brougham that Trevallyan used for long distances; difficult because the roads were as bad as the rolling landscape was green. And there was no companion more infuriating than Niall Trevallyan.

The day had come and gone in silence. Before they left, Trevallyan permitted her to pen a short note to Grania explaining her absence. He then sent it with Greeves to read it to the old woman, and together, having forced her into the carriage as if she were a prisoner, as indeed she was, they started out.

Though artfully balanced on thick leather straps, the carriage nonetheless made for a tiring ride. The constant shifting wore her out, and even the interior of the coach, plumply upholstered in the finest Moroccan leather, made her bottom sore from so much sitting. When they reached Cullencross, she longed for nothing more than a hot bath and the sound of a crackling fire. Anything was preferable to the silence inside the carriage and the company of the man who had sat opposite her.

The arrival of the fine coach at the inn sent everyone from the owner of the Hollow Crown to the stable boys scurrying to please them. Ravenna was taken in hand by a tall, gray-haired serving woman and shown upstairs to a bedroom richly draped in maroon velvet. A small meal was laid out for her, but when Ravenna professed her lack of appetite, the woman immediately saw to it that she was drawn a bath in an adjoining corner of the private room.

Ravenna marveled at the experience. The pedestrian-looking Hollow Crown was proving to be a far cry from the inns she had stayed in during her trip back and forth from London. Though the little inn seemed much like the ones she was used to: It had a main common room where men from the town plunked their pewter tankards down onto crude trestle tables without thought of damaging the decor—a decor that was only slightly more refined than the inside of a stable— and it boasted the usual surly barkeep and scruffy patrons. If she'd not been traveling with Trevallyan, she'd never have guessed that behind the four-to-a-bed philosophy of the common post inn there was a secret world of pampering and luxury seen only by the Ascendency.

She finished her bath, and because she had brought no other clothes to wear, she dressed once again in her blue woolen gown, leaving her corset laces a bit loosened for comfort. Trevallyan had stayed downstairs, and she was glad for it. She had no desire to see him until the carriage rolled in the morning.

At a little writing desk by the fire, she found paper and ink and fought the urge to start a diary. The circumstance—or rather, the company—of this trip was despicable, but it didn't stop her thoughts from becoming filled with idealized reveries of her long-dead father. It would be a pleasant diversion to write them down, so that one day, she could relive the anticipation and excitement she felt now at finally being on the verge of learning about the man who had fathered her. But she knew she would never become a diarist. She didn't want to have to write about her experience with Trevallyan. Nor could she afford the luxury. There were pages still to write on her faerie tale, and while work offered her a solid escape from the angry man downstairs, she would cling to it.

Stoically, she picked up the pen, twirled the glass tip in ink and began her nightly ritual.

"Is that horrible little troll always so wretched?" Grace asked after she'd devoured her second wheat cake and a chalice of warm wine. "How do you stand it? Can't you make him leave?"

"But then I would have no company at all," Skya answered, her perfect, smooth forehead a frown. She rose and filled her sister's chalice, adding another wheat cake to the wooden trencher in the middle of the table. "He's not so bad really. He can make me laugh at times."

"You've got to come home. End this self-exile, and return to Papa and the castle. I know they burn witches, but don't you see? The people will have forgotten what you are by now. Besides," Grace's frown matched her sister's, "there's the war now to make the kingdom forget. King Turoe falsely believes that we hold his son. Papa told me before I left that a thousand knights are coming from the north to seize the castle."

"A thousand knights?" Skya paled. Her beautiful woman's face seemed to turn to alabaster in seconds.

"Yes," Grace said somberly. "Even now they might be there, invading . . ." She grabbed her sister's hand. "Please, Skya, you've got to return home. We need you. Papa doesn't have King Turoe's son. Prince Aidan has fallen off the ends of the earth and no one can find him. The castle is under siege. Only your magic can save us from King Turoe's wrath."

Skya slowly pulled away, then wrapped her arms around herself as if she were suddenly chilled. Grace noted the elbows of Skya's linen kirtle were worn and frayed, and she felt shamed by her own ruby-encrusted girdle and the heavy brocade of her bliaud, with sleeves so long and rich they had to be knotted at the wrist just to keep them from dragging the ground. She felt sickened when she realized Skya was wearing the same childish kirtle that she'd worn when she'd left so many years ago.

"Oh, Skya, you must come home," she pleaded softly. "You can't stay here forever. Don't you want to marry? To have children? How can you hope to do that if you stay in these dark, terrible woods?"

"And have children like me?"

Grace's heart tightened at the expression on Skya's face. Even deepest despair had never seen such grief.

"Oh, Skya. . . ." Grace whispered, unable to bear her sister's pain. Skya's magic should have been such a blessing; it was a cruel and closed-minded world that had made it a curse.

As if well-schooled in hiding her hopelessness, Skya seemed to wipe her face clear of expression. She smiled brightly, perhaps a bit too brightly, and took Grace's arm in her own. "Come. The day grows old. You've got to return to the castle before nightfall."

"No, Skya. I've come to stay with you. To help you," Grace exclaimed.

"How can you help me? You're only mortal. You've no powers at all—"

"But I've the power to love. And I love you, Skya."

Skya's azure eyes darkened with woe, as if a cloud had covered the sun. "I love you, too, Grace. I'm surely mortal in that way."

"Then let me stay. . . ."

Skya shook her head and opened the cottage's crude batten door. "You have to return to Father. He can't lose two daughters. And he can't afford to come looking for you if there's to be an attack on the castle."

"But Grace—"

"No. Come. I'll lead you across the bridge so Troll won't bother you."

Skya led Grace down to the gnarly bridge. Grace couldn't even see the troll but with every step across, she wondered if he was directly below her, conjuring up awful mischief. Chills ran like rat's feet down her spine and she was relieved to see the other side.

"I can't leave you here in this place," Grace began, all the while glancing at the bridge and the dark, velvety shadows beneath it.

"You must." Skya faced her, her gaze intense as if she were trying to memorize her sister's face. As if she were afraid she might never see it again. "Just hug me once, for Godspeed," she whispered. "And tell Papa . . . tell Papa . . ." Her voice grew tight.

Grace threw her arms around her and wept.

Skya held her tight and finally, after a long, terrible moment, she whispered, "Be sure and tell Papa I'm looking out for him. Tell him that, will you, when he faces Turoe's knights?"

"Aye," Grace choked, unable to look at her.

"Then go, before the sun has time to set."

"I'll come back. I won't leave you here alone, Skya."

"Go. Before it gets dark." Skya dropped her arms.
Grace ran into the woods, weeping.

Ravenna looked up from her work and almost ached to be inside the pages she had written. In stories, there was a beginning and an end. The edges were clean; the lessons were clear. But real life was not so. Life was messy and too often left one feeling ambivalent. Like her feelings for Trevallyan.

She bit her lower lip and forced the emotions away. It had taken all her strength not to dwell on what had happened at the castle. All day in the carriage she had vowed not to think about it. Instead, she'd played games with her imagination, thinking up what she had just written.

But now, alone, in a strange inn on the way north to Antrim, the inevitable came creeping up on her. It took all her willpower not to break down and recall each terrible detail that had lead up to . . . the deed.

With a shaking hand, she put down the glass pen. It left a smear of ink across the white page. Suddenly, without wanting to make the comparison, she found herself thinking that if the ink were red, the page would look almost like Trevallyan's bedsheets.

She pushed back her chair, unnerved by the screech it made on the gleaming wood floor. It might take her months, but she was going to erase her memory of the night. She was still numb from the disbelief that it had even happened. In fact, she'd spent all day and most of last night denying it. There had been a moment of high tension between her and Trevallyan that had somehow metamorphosed into passion. When they were down in the staircase, Trevallyan had looked as if he wanted to beat her. The next thing she knew, he was kissing her and she . . . well, she . . . was kissing him back.

She closed her eyes, willing away the picture. She didn't love Trevallyan, in truth she hardly knew him. There was an attraction for him that she found difficult to explain, but she had never thought it would make her surrender her honor. And now, her pride. She couldn't believe all that had transpired. She still reeled from the shock that Trevallyan had been the one to oversee her care all these years and that it had been with Grania's knowledge and consent. The horror of her indebtedness was surpassed only by her horror of his manipulative powers. He'd even been able to persuade her dear grandmother, the one who loved her most in this world, to part with her and send her for years and years to that wretched English school. He'd doled out punishment with an iron hand. And hour by hour her shock was turning to anger. At times she berated herself and wondered why the revelation had even surprised her. It should have been obvious. Trevallyan's manipulation of her life explained so many things.

Yet it didn't explain last night.

She clutched the windowsill and watched a pair of young stable boys in the rear courtyard try to catch a hen that did not desire to be tomorrow's supper. The boys' antics amused her, but not enough to take away her dark thoughts. As much as she wanted to deny it, she couldn't. Not even a diabolical man could have made her do the things she had done last night. So why had she surrendered? Had it been loneliness? Frustration? Or was she just a weak woman and fair game for any brute who could overpower her?

She almost hoped the latter was true. As bad as it was, it at least took the power of choice out of her hands. Yet deep in her heart, a thread of titillating fear told her it wasn't so. She wasn't susceptible to just any man; she was only susceptible to one man: to Trevallyan. He could make her willing to do anything, it seemed. And it terrified her.

The thought made her stomach churn. But she wondered how to deny it. She was convinced that Malachi wouldn't have succeeded in bedding her. Trevallyan, on the other hand, seemed to have some strange kind of power over her.

She set her jaw. The only solution was to recognize that power and keep it from ever controlling her again. She could think clearly now, and she saw the pitfalls. There was no having a relationship with Trevallyan. He was too dangerous, but more than that, he was above her class. He was also crazed. The whole circumstance of this trip proved that. He thought to hold her prisoner; the very idea was frighteningly absurd. She could only conclude that it would be suicide to give her heart to such a manipulative, powerful man as he. He would twist it to his satisfaction, then trample it when his amusement was over. She knew better than to let him do that. Now that she had fallen, she was going to see to it that she never fell again.

A knock sounded at the door, startling her. She expected the serving girl, but she opened the door and, instead, came face to face with the devil who seemed to possess her.

"Yes?" she asked coolly, her hand grasping the doorknob in case it should prove prudent to close it quickly.

The corner of Trevallyan's mouth turned up in a weary, yet arrogant, smile. "You act as if I'm here for a visit."

"Aren't you?" She was proud of the way she controlled her voice. She wanted him to think she was as cold as stone.

"No." His hand caught the edge of the door, and he pushed.

Her heart beat a tattoo in her chest. She tried to close the door on him, but it was futile. He was inside her room before she could blink.

"You can't just storm in here. This is my room and I want to be alone in it," she snapped.

He unfastened his watch and fob and tossed them on the bureau. "Be alone, if you wish, but not in my room."

"Your room?"

He eyed her, his icy aqua gaze brazenly assessing. "Did you think this was your room? That this common little inn had a thousand rooms just like this one so that all and sundry might have their privacy?"

"I—" She clenched her teeth. "In truth, I hadn't given it much thought. You see, 'tis rare that one such as myself sees how the Ascendency lives."

He ignored her sarcasm and sat down on the edge of the bed. She watched him, noticing there was fatigue around his eyes; his mouth was a grim, troubled line. He had yet to remove his frock coat, and he rubbed his wounded arm as if it pained him.

A stab of guilt ran through her. Then one of anger. She had no responsibility for what had happened to him. She was not a rebel and had never been. Instead, she was an outcast, and if the Ascendency scorned her, the people of Lir did as well, for she was nobody to all of them; not Anglican, not Catholic, not even legitimate. Their troubles were not her troubles.

But somehow, as she watched him painfully try to ease out of his frock coat, she knew she was entwined in those troubles.

Frowning, she said quietly, "I don't hate the Ascendency. I didn't send that note to you. I wouldn't do such a thing. I would never hurt anyone."

In a deep, raw voice, he said, "Even if you had sent that note, it wouldn't change anything."

She looked at him, her eyes wide with surprise. "How can you say that? You were almost killed. Seamus *was* killed."

"It still wouldn't change my desire for you."

The words sent a strange tingle down her spine. Her gaze met his. He looked angry, as if he held her responsible for emotions he didn't want.

But possession was what really mattered to him, and at times such as these, she knew she'd do well to remember it.

"You mean it wouldn't change your lust for me, don't you?" she whispered.

"Lust, desire, love, what's the difference?"

She didn't answer. It was difficult to swallow her hurt. She thought about the vault where his dead wife and child—a child of betrayal—lay in eternal rest. The imagined faces of all his rejected fiancées passed across her eyes, and suddenly, just by his question, she understood why so many things had gone wrong.

He ignored her and began pulling off his boot. He cursed as he struggled without a bootjack.

"It seems you need your valet. Why didn't you bring him?" she asked, trying for an innocuous subject.

He looked up at her and smirked. "And where would I hide you in these small rooms? It wouldn't bode well for your reputation to have him see you here, don't you think?"

She might have been grateful that he had sought to protect her, but it was difficult to do so when he was so arrogant. Trying to head off a temper, she sat in a plush brown velvet chair by the fire and refused to even look at him. She was beginning to see just how difficult this journey was going to be.

Another knock sounded at her door, diverting her. Trevallyan answered it and opened the door to Gavan the innkeeper and his three boys. The stout man jovially set down the traveling trunks that each boy carried on his shoulders, accepted Trevallyan's coins with numerous ingratiating bows, then removed himself and his entourage, leaving the two alone once more.

The door clicked behind Gavan, and Ravenna returned her melancholy attention back to the fire. She made several ungracious mental remarks to herself about the master needing three trunks for his accoutrements when she, in her poverty—even if she'd been allowed to bring a bag, which she had not—would be hard-pressed to fill a carpetbag with all her worldly belongings. She was stewing in this idea when a sound made her look up.

It was almost like a small groan of pain. She turned her head and found Trevallyan still trying to remove his boots. On the bed next to him lay his frock coat, and he struggled with the boot in just his shirtsleeves. His left sleeve was ringed with blood.

A small gasp of shock passed her lips.

He gave her a censorious glance.

"Your wound . . ." she breathed softly.

He dismissed her with a flick of his cold eyes. " 'Tis nothing."

"But it's bled through your entire bandage." She couldn't stop the wave of concern that overtook her. As much as she might fear him, he was only mortal after all.

Against her better judgment, she rose from the chair and went to him. Silently, she grasped his boot and pulled. He watched her with a wariness in his eyes.

"You've done too much today," she admonished.

"I'm a grown man. I can decide what is too much."

"The wound may not be a bad one, but you were still shot." Heaving like a serving wench, she finally managed to pull off his other boot. "The blood on the bandage is fresh. It's not a good sign."

"T'ank you, Moother dere," he said in a lowly accent.

She wanted to hit him. "Where are some fresh bandages?"

"In my trunk."

She spun around. "You have three trunks."

"Mine is the wooden one. It belonged to my father."

She nodded and went to the old burl walnut trunk. "If this is your trunk, I should summon Gavan. He's brought us too many trunks."

"The others are for you."

On her knees, rummaging through his linen shirts, she looked up at him as if he'd lost his mind. "I have no trunks."

"I had Fiona pack some of my wife's things. Though the gowns are a little out of date, I think you'll find them satisfactory. I can assure you they were never worn. Helen's greed and caprice for new gowns was only surpassed, I came to find out, by her greed and caprice . . ." his jaw tightened, ". . . for men."

Ravenna stared at him, hating the way his hurt seemed to seep into her and mangle her emotions. She didn't want to feel it because if she did, she would end up in his bed again, without marriage or respectability.

"Here are the bandages," she said breezily. She walked over to him and placed the strips of boiled linen on the heavy velvet coverlet. He removed his bloodstained shirt and waited for her to begin.

Her nerves jumped from seeing him half-naked. Dark, tawny hair covered his chest, a chest that was still smooth and hard, and one that tempted her to run her fingers across it, damning her with the memory of how she had done just that the night before. Like a physician viewing a patient, she tried to mentally distance herself from Trevallyan's body, coldly attributing his youthful physique to the many years of hard riding to the hounds. Still, no matter how hard she tried to rationalize and extricate herself from her attraction to him, her emotions foiled her time and again. She drew close, and her shaking hands sloshed water from the basin she was holding. He rose to take it from her and the water spattered the wool rug. Becoming undone, she threw a towel to the ground and forced herself to concentrate on the bloody knots on his arm.

But as she feared, his proximity affected her. She couldn't stop herself from studying him. His silvery-blond hair was slicked back and brushed to his nape, a look well suited to him. The severity of it highlighted a classic profile and the cold beauty of his eyes. In his youth he'd probably been considered quite handsome, but now, having aged, his boyish prettiness had roughened, and matured, and secretly, she preferred him that way. He looked like a man. She inhaled and reluctantly relished the dark, sensual scent of him. He smelled like a man, too.

He groaned, and a muscle bunched at his jaw. She looked down and saw how careless she was being. The dried, bloody strips had nearly bonded to his skin, and she was pulling them away as if they were the slick peel from a grape.

She murmured an apology, then dipped the towel in the water and tried to dampen the stuck bandages. Mutely, he gave himself to her ministrations, and only after she'd wrapped the clean linen around his arm and tied the final knot did he seem to relax from the pain.

"That should feel much better now," she whispered, finding herself looking down at him, their faces only inches apart.

His gaze flickered downward to a glossy, raven-black curl that rested on her bosom. After her bath, she had neglected to pin her hair and now the heavy length of it hung loose and free. The headmistress of Weymouth-Hampstead had hated her hair, telling her time and again that the unruly mass was a sign of her sinful Irish ancestry. And Ravenna had been slapped too many times when the headmistress had found her tresses not properly pinned and tamed to rigid satisfaction to now not believe it.

But if it were true, Trevallyan's gaze refuted it. He touched the curl with something akin to worship in his eyes. Unable to even breathe, she stood still while his finger caressed it, his knuckles pressing into her breast, his thumb tracing the curve while a sensual tingle ran down her spine.

Then, without warning, he slipped his hand behind the dark curtain of hair at her nape and pressed her forward.

"Don't," she whimpered, their lips barely touching.

He searched her gaze for a long moment, pain lingering in his own.

"Don't," she pleaded again, terrified of losing her razor-thin hold on her self control with every brush of his hard lips.

He clearly wanted to ignore the protest. His hand tightened at her nape; another hand drew around her waist, pulling her between his knees.

"Don't . . . I beg of you. . . ." she wept, hating the melting sensation he gave her as much as she despised her wellspring of tears.

As if his limbs were made of wood, he slowly, awkwardly, reluctantly dropped his hold. But his eyes never wavered from hers. A silent communication passed between them. His desire for her was as obvious and eloquent as the knot in his cravat. The English gentleman within him had stopped himself upon her refusal, but the Celt in him, the warrior whose ancestors had claimed Ireland for their own, who had danced in pagan rhythms for their god, raged at the idea of being refused. By female instinct, she knew without a doubt that the bloodshed of this battle would ultimately be placed upon her brow.

He stood, and she stepped from the circle of his arms, wiping her damp cheeks, willing away her cowardice.

"Get some sleep. There's another long day ahead." He ground his teeth while he spoke, the muscles in his jawline creating a fascinating display of male anger.

"Fine," she said, her even tone belying her red eyes.

"I'll be downstairs if you should need me."

Thank God, she wanted to say, but stopped herself. It was too cruel. Even in her naïveté, she could see he took her rejection hard.

"Good night," he said stiffly.

"Good night," she whispered.

Then she was alone.

Later in the night, after restless dreams of joy and terror, Ravenna awoke in the large bed. Belowstairs she could hear the barkeeper barking orders to a servant. She surmised it was late, because she could no longer hear the jovial shouts and drunken singing from the patrons.

Then, like a convict who has glimpsed the face of his own damnation, she realized an arm was slung over her hip. A man's arm. Heavy and warm, in lax possession.

While she had slept, Trevallyan had entered the room and gotten into bed with her.

Slowly so as not to wake him, she reached beneath the covers. Her palm met warm, hard skin. A well-muscled torso. A line of smooth, crisp hair that arrowed downward to a place she was not brave enough to explore. She pulled her hand back, not surprised he slept in the nude. Once, at their last dinner at the castle, he'd told her he preferred to hear poetry to the hum and bustle of the city; preferred to see trees to even the most ornately painted walls; preferred to taste wine than waste his tongue with talk.

He'd told her his Celtic blood made him more a man of the senses than of propriety. And now, alone with her in this tiny inn, he'd convinced her of it.

"Go to sleep."

The voice rumbled from his side of the bed. She drew back to the edge of the mattress, but short of scrambling from the bed, she couldn't slide his arm from her hip.

"You shouldn't be here," she choked, unable to see him in the pitch black room.

"If I married you, if I gave you respectability, I could be here every night."

She stiffened at the implication. Her feminine guile told her this was what she should want. Maneuvering a rich and titled man into marriage was supposed to be the pinnacle of a woman's life purpose. So why did the temptation seem so hollow? So pointless?

If she loved him, wouldn't she throw herself into his arms?

If he loved her, would he hold her prisoner, manipulate her life as if he were marionetting a play, imply that she was somehow not worthy of respect until her name was permanently linked to his?

The answers stung her, confused her. But one thing she knew for certain: Marriage with Trevallyan would never work. Four women had come to that conclusion, three of them spared of the consequences. No doubt he would prove to be a tyrant. She would no longer be able to write; he would scoff at her dreams of publishing. The supercilious Lord Trevallyan would not permit her to be a person in her own right because the gulf between their social classes was unbridgeable. He would look down on her, patronize her, suck away all her will to fight. The only way a marriage would work would be for him to respect her. And he would never do that while she held so little power.

"I don't want to marry. I want to write."

Her answer left him silent. His arm grew heavier upon her thinly covered hip.

"I'll make you want this. I swear with all the blood on my Irish soul, I will do it."

The anger in his voice made her want to weep from the futility of it.

"I'll give you anything you want, Ravenna. Anything." He spoke the words like a curse.

"All I want is to see the home of my father." Her voice lowered to a whisper. "And to be left alone."

As she expected, he made no more vows.

Chapter 21

T HE NEXT day they drove into the Antrim mountains, keeping as far east as they could in order to avoid the muck and traffic of Belfast City. As the terrain grew more rough, Trevallyan grew more silent, more chivalrous, more distant.

But Ravenna's excitement swelled as they crossed each hill, as if she sensed a meeting with destiny. At one time the man who had fathered her had looked at these same green hills and dreamed, perhaps, the same dreams as she did.

"Your color is high this day," Niall commented, his gaze cool and faraway.

She turned her eyes from the open window. "When will we get there?"

"Not for another night. Cinaeth Castle is remote and difficult to reach. I fear tonight we may not even find ourselves an inn."

A blush stained her cheeks at the mention of the inn. The entire night had been spent in an unseemly fashion. Unable to summon the fight to make him leave, she had simply stayed in the bed, lying stiffly on her side, sure she would not sleep the rest of the night.

But slumber, if not propriety, eventually took over, and in the morning when she awoke, she was disturbed to find her limbs intimately entwined with his. She wore a night rail, one she had found in the trunks, but the thin, shell-pink silk was of little protection. Lying next to him, in the intimacy of one bed, she felt everything: the heat of his skin, the bunch of his muscles, the brush of crisp hair on his forearm as it lay across her chest, seemingly flung there in his sleep. She had tried to rise, but the long length of her hair was trapped beneath him.

Even in his sleep, Trevallyan held her captive.

Nothing was right. They were together at a strange inn, unmarried, and she, wearing the unworn undergarments fashioned for his deceased wife. Waking as she did should have been one of the worst moments of her life. But yet, the sun rose through the diamond panes of glass, laying a cheerful checkerboard of light over the bed. Swallows sang in the tree beneath the slightly open window. And though the hearth was cold, she was warm, wonderfully, wholly warm, and oddly well-rested, and enveloped by a foreign emotion that was very much like . . . rightness.

Even now in the carriage the feeling carried over. The sky overhead sparkled like a newly polished aquamarine, and the hills were quilted in Ireland's emerald green. Perhaps it was just the weather that had her feeling optimistic, but when she peeked at the handsome man sitting across from her in the carriage and remembered how he'd looked in slumber, the tension gone from his face, the hard lines softened until they almost disappeared, a boyish quirk to his lips that made her fight the strange urge to kiss him awake, to her dismay, the feeling of well-being deepened and bloomed. It was all unaccountable.

She gazed at Trevallyan while he looked out the window, a hard, pensive expression on his face. What an enigma he was to her. *Geis* or no, it didn't make sense that he should have helped Grania and her all these years. It didn't make sense that he'd treat her as callously as he had their last night at the castle, then leave Lir when Lir was troubled and needed his help, only to see that she was escorted to Antrim on the slim chance of finding some information about her father.

"You're staring at me, wench," he said, seeming almost omniscient, as he had not taken his gaze from the passing landscape.

Unnerved, she looked away.

He chuckled. And looked at her. "Do you find me curious?"

She returned her gaze. "You read my mind."

His mouth twisted in self-derision. "If only I could."

"I wonder about you. Sometimes you are so noble and yet . . ."

"And yet, sometimes I am so wicked, is that it?"

She nodded.

He stared out the window to the green Antrim hills. "I'm just looking for my place here on this land. As Malachi is. As you are."

"The *geis* tortures us with the belief that my place is with you."

He captured her gaze. His eyes held a darkness she had never seen before. "The *geis*, my lady, has thrown us together. It has no effect on whether we will stay together."

"What will determine that?"

"I will."

The look in his eyes stole her breath. It was lust, violence, and vulnerability combined into one. It tempted joy and ruin with the same dizzying passion. It was possession. Absolute. She found it difficult to look away.

"Whatever it takes . . ." he whispered.

Her heart hammered against her ribs, almost expectantly.

But he never spoke of love.

Numbly, she forced her gaze back out to the landscape. His powers of seduction wound more tightly around her with every moment she spent with him, and this knowledge sent a shiver of anxiety down her spine. His determination frightened her. She doubted her ability to fight it. He could make her feel passion in its full spectrum of good and bad, right and wrong, but she knew if she surrendered to his demands, he would devour her. He would own her, heart and soul, and she would become a mere foundling at his side, ever hopeful for attention or some kindness, all too heart-wrenchingly aware that she would never have his love. Because a man such as he could never give his love to someone he considered beneath him.

She thought of the man they had come to Antrim to find. Her father.

She wondered if he was really the knight she desperately wanted to believe he was. He might have been like Trevallyan. A nobleman who'd consumed a poor maiden in his path, then abandoned her while she was pregnant, unappreciative of the misplaced loyalty that had kept Brilliana's lover's name a secret to the grave.

A loud crack jolted her out of her depressing thoughts. The carriage heaved and she tumbled forward to the floor. If not for Trevallyan's steadying hand, she might have hit her head on the now gaping door jamb.

He brought her to her feet. Gathering herself as best she could, she stuttered, "Are we b-being attacked?"

His expression was lean and hard. "It seems like we've broken an axle. I'll check it."

She grabbed him so hard even he looked surprised by her passion. "No. I've a bad feeling about this. You might be ambushed again. Perhaps the boy-os are up to their tricks again."

"Do you think they would kill me here in this desolate spot, where there's no show of it?" Pensively, he ran his knuckles down her cheek. "I think not."

"I still can't shake this notion . . ."

Her words dwindled as he exited. Without pondering the consequences, she immediately followed, allowing the carriage driver to help her descend the now lopsided vehicle.

The two men knelt beside the vehicle and looked beneath it. Brushing a wisp of hair from her eyes, she leaned against the carriage and squinted into the surrounding woodland. All was quiet.

"The axle is splintered. No doubt about it," Trevallyan said, joining her. Walking up the road a bit, the carriage driver went to the next hill to see if another vehicle was in sight. She felt a strange fear as he turned to them and shook his head. No carriage was coming.

"Should we walk back to Hensey?" she asked.

Trevallyan said nothing. He kept his eyes on the carriage driver.

When the man returned, he stood next to them, scratching his russet-colored beard as if he were afraid to be the next one to speak.

"What do you think we should do, O'Malley?" Trevallyan watched the man with a gaze as sharp as a falcon's watching a field mouse.

"Can't say as I know, my lord." The chubby man crossed his hands over his large gut as if to appear he was thinking hard on the alternatives.

"Cinaeth Castle is farther than the last town, is it not?"

"Aye, my lord."

"Then we should all go to town."

"If you think it best, my lord."

"No. Perhaps we should head toward Cinaeth. Ravenna will rest better at the castle."

Ravenna's gaze whipped from one man to the other. She was astonished to see O'Malley begin to sweat.

"You could take her there, sir . . . but the town is much closer."

"Aye."

"And you canna be stayin' here. Not with a lady and and no way to defend yourself." O'Malley gave her a slightly uncomfortable glance, and Ravenna was suddenly struck by the notion that she knew the man behind the beard. His face was familiar; she agonized trying to recall who he was.

"Of course. You know this country best, O'Malley. Aren't your people from Antrim?"

"County Mayo, my lord. Teh name *O'Ma'ille* cums from the Gaelic word for chieftain."

Trevallyan leaned back against the carriage. Ravenna knew she would not want to be O'Malley beneath that terrible stare.

"Interesting. . . . Interesting. . . ." Trevallyan commented, his dispassionate tone incongruous with his piercing stare.

"Shall I get the bags, my lord?"

"Yes."

Trevallyan grabbed Ravenna's hand and began to walk arrogantly in the direction of town. "Just bring us a couple of valises. We'll meet you at the public house. From there you can procure us a new carriage."

"Very good, my lord." O'Malley gave Ravenna a last parting look; a worried look. "Take care, miss," he called to her. "The road ahead may be rough."

"Aye," Ravenna whispered before Trevallyan hurried her away.

Together, they trudged up the steep hill toward town. Unable to keep her thoughts to herself any longer, she hissed, "I don't think we should be going this way. 'Tis dangerous."

"Don't you trust Sean O'Malley?" he asked lightly.

"Sean O'Malley. . . ." The name definitely had a familiar ring to it. She picked up the dragging hem of the expensive purple wool cloak that she had retrieved from a trunk and repeated the name to herself a couple of times more. Then realization dawned.

"Sean O'Malley!" she said in a near-hysterical whisper. "I remember him now. He's changed so much—why, he used to be a tall, thin youth. He ran with Malachi and . . . well . . . and with . . ."

"You?" Trevallyan asked, raising a wickedly slanted eyebrow.

"Yes," she confessed, her answer hushed and frightened. "We were only children, but I would guess Sean is still running with Malachi, and if that's the case, then—"

"Then when we get to Hensey, I've got quite a surprise coming, haven't I?"

"We've got to turn back—"

His arm slipped around her waist and he said evenly, "Don't even think of turning back to O'Malley. He might shoot me right on the spot and not bother making an example of me."

"But then we've got to run into the woods. We can't go to Hensey."

"Did you help plan any of this?"

She stared at him in mute disbelief. He'd made love to her. How could he think she would intrigue to kill him?

He continued, overlooking her silence. "The carriage axle was sawed. Amateurish job, I would say, but who am I to criticize those who would see me dead? I can't fathom their purpose in this life any more than they can fathom mine."

"Please, I had nothing to do with this. I haven't seen Sean O'Malley in years. I didn't even recognize him, he's changed so much. Now we've got to hide from them. . . ." The hill loomed. The town of Hensey was a mile or more on the other side, but it was reckless to be walking in that direction when the most likely greeting would be in the form of a lead ball. At her back she could feel O'Malley's distant presence. They were trapped. If they didn't run now, Trevallyan—maybe both of them—would be killed.

"O'Malley's father worked for me. I thought when he offered to take Seamus's place he would be a loyal man." Trevallyan's mouth turned downward, as if the betrayal disturbed him deeply.

"The only thing older than the *ogham* in Ireland is a grudge. You cannot know why O'Malley turned against you. It probably has nothing to do with how fairly or unfairly you treated his father and more to do with who his friends are."

"You have the same friends," he said, with something akin to black amusement in his voice. "Are you leading me into the snare? Are you telling me to flee, only to lure me to where they really wait? It would be a brilliant plan because, of course, I would go with you."

She stared at him, shocked at his ideas, perplexed by his attitude. He had been shot before, his driver had even been killed. There was clearly a trap laid ahead, and yet he was calmly walking to Hensey, arm in arm with a woman whom he nonchalantly questioned as a conspirator. By the looks of things, he had every right to suspect her. In some ways, he would be a fool not to. But he wasn't angry; nor was he afraid. He seemed strangely accepting of the circumstances, whatever they might bring. He seemed to want the truth, even if it was ugly.

"I'm not the kind of woman to lure a man to the woods so that my friends can slaughter him," she said, the sentence bitter and foreign on her tongue.

They had reached the peak of the hill. Without commenting on her confession, he turned and nodded to O'Malley, who stood in the distance by the broken carriage. Sean had gotten the valises in hand and was just now beginning to follow them, many hundred safe paces behind.

"It wouldn't pleasure you to see me killed?" he asked, not looking at her, his profile fine and handsome in the afternoon sunlight. "I know at times I've seen something much like hatred in your eyes for me. You blame me for what happened between us at the castle. Too," his expression held a strange dark mirth, "let's not forget, I'm holding you prisoner."

She shook her head, her expression taut with fear and disbelief. "I wouldn't harm anyone like this. It's not my way."

He kissed her mouth, his lips warm and tender. She wondered if it weren't almost for O'Malley's benefit. "Then I'll run with you, away from this danger. On the other side of the hill, take me by the hand and leave the road."

"I—I will but—"

He looked down at her and began to lead her farther along the road. "But what, my love?"

"But how can you know to trust me? I could very well be luring you into a trap. You know I know both Malachi and Sean . . ." Her voice turned low and full of despair, "and at times, you know, I've taken their point of view."

"If you lead me to my death, then I would rather find it holding your hand than not."

She swallowed the lump of terror in her throat. It went against all reason to care for this man. He was difficult, arrogant, and sometimes, as now, she suspected he was just plain mad. But then, as now, he could touch her emotions as could no one else. For all he knew, she could promise to help him and lead him straight to a pistol. He was an intelligent man, and he'd been rough with her these past days. He knew full well the animosity she held for him, and he knew who her friends were. But he now placed his life into her small hands.

Fighting the urge to look back at O'Malley, she allowed Trevallyan to calmly lead her along the road, her arm in his, until they disappeared from O'Malley's view on the other side of the hill. As soon as they were out of sight, she ran with him down the hill and leapt across a rain-filled embankment. The woods were deep and thick on this side of the road, and they left no trail as they might have if they had fled through a dense field of rye.

"Has he seen us?" she cried, forcing herself to muffle her voice.

"Perhaps, but perhaps not. Just keep going."

She took his hand and pulled him deeper into the woods. The elms grew close and tangled, casting the forest floor into darkness. They ran until they broke into a field of scrub hazel. Finally, they came upon a stone wall that had turned green with moss and bracken.

"Is this where you've brought me? To a dead end?" With a strange light in his eyes, he grabbed her waist and pulled her to him.

"Where should we run?" she asked, panting from their flight, wildly looking about.

" 'Tis for you to say." He gazed to the west. The setting sun flooded the fields in liquid gold. A patch of blooming rapeseed was so yellow it hurt to look upon it. "But the day grows late," he added. "Wherever we go, we may need to tarry there overnight."

"There's a building in those woods to the north. Can you see the roof?" She pointed.

"Lead the way."

He looked down at her and her heart skipped a beat at the wariness in his eyes. She could be taking him to an ambush, and well he knew it. Even in the morning, he must have been struck by a premonition of things to come. She had noticed him placing a pistol into the interior of his frock coat. Now she wondered if he was glad he had it.

"Perhaps it's a strong-farm," she said, referring to the old medieval heirarchy of farms. "We may get some help there."

He said nothing. He only stared at her and held out his hand, waiting for her to take it.

They crossed through another copse of trees and quickly found the building they had seen in the meadow. To Ravenna's disappointment, it was not a strong-house, but an old abandoned barn that had not been used since the last century.

"Is this where your friends await, or is this where we may safely stay the night?" Trevallyan leaned against the moldering stone walls of the barn and crossed his arms.

She tossed him an irritated look.

He almost smiled. "Does this mean you want me to go in first?"

She nodded.

"Shall I see you again?"

An innocuous question, but she knew what he meant. He wanted to know if he was going to step inside an empty barn, or meet his Maker by the barrel of a rebel's gun. Watching him, she decided he was either a terrible fool or a very brave man. Or perhaps both.

"I'll be right behind you," she whispered.

He gave neither approval nor condemnation. He merely nodded and accepted her words. Taking her hand in his sure, hard grasp, he kicked open the batten door that was almost off its hinge.

Though she knew there was no trap, a tingle of fear crawled down her spine. It was possible that Sean O'Malley could have somehow followed. He and his cronies, perhaps even Malachi, could be waiting in the dark corners. . . .

Trevallyan walked inside.

There was nothing. Merely a tall pile of dried straw and ramshackle farm tools, broken and left behind. Above, the thatched roof had given partway. Half the barn was protected, the other half open to the velvet evening sky.

Niall turned to her. She couldn't stop herself from releasing a giggle of relief.

"I told you I wasn't with them." She squeezed his hand.

All at once he picked her up off the ground. She gasped in surprise at his laughter while he spun her around. Finally, he let her slip to the ground, her chest crushed against his, her waist locked within his arms.

He stared at her; she couldn't have looked away if her life depended upon it. He entranced her. Smiling, he appeared young and handsome, so much so, she hardly recognized him. He seemed another man altogether—a youth really—a youth she could see herself falling in love with.

"My beautiful girl, don't ever disappoint me," he whispered.

"You speak as if it's my duty to please you." There was playfulness in her voice, but disillusionment too. She'd yet to know where she stood with him. Did he view her as an equal, or as a whore? As a companion, or as chattel? It hurt to ponder it.

"No, it's my duty to please you. But my curse is that I have yet to figure out what will please you." His eyes darkened. She was trapped by the intensity of the emotion hidden there. "So what will please you, Ravenna? What can I do to win you?"

"I don't know." She believed he hated her answer more than she did, but she had to utter it, for it was the truth. She didn't know how he could win her. He couldn't force her feelings. They either bloomed or they perished on their own.

"Perhaps that's the wrong course to take with you." A smile graced his hard lips. Deviltry sparked in his eyes. "Perhaps I shouldn't ask what will please you. Rather, I should ask what displeases you. For example . . ." He bent low toward her face. His breath was warm upon her cheek. "Does this displease you?" His lips caressed hers in a feather-light kiss.

He straightened and studied her.

Blushing, she shook her head.

"Are you telling me to stop, or are you telling me that my kiss does not displease you?" He caressed her lips with his thumb.

"It does not displease me." She could feel her cheeks turn to fire. The evening darkness was quickly becoming a blessing.

"And this?" He bent his head and kissed the hollow of her throat.

Her pulse quickened. His moist, hot tongue burned along her vulnerable skin. She ached for him to continue, but all too soon he broke away.

He whispered, "Tell me truly. Does it displease you?" He waited for her answer with all the patience of Job.

Slowly, she shook her head, unable to lie.

His hands slipped beneath the wool cloak and found the bodice of her borrowed dress, a heavy silk woven with gaudy Dutch irises. He found the hooks at the back as if he were well versed in removing women's clothing. He'd sworn that his wife had never worn the clothes in the trunk he'd brought, but the experienced manner in which he released each hook made her wonder if he had lied.

"No—please—you must stop—" She grabbed his forearms. Her fingers dug into his flesh.

"Does our lovemaking displease you?"

His question was pointed, but yet much too simple to answer. She struggled with it, but it was like trying to wrench a rope off a whale.

"No. . . ." she moaned. She shuddered, more from vulnerability than the cold. "But the answer is 'yes,' as well."

He stepped behind her, resting his hands upon her shoulders. Slowly he bent his head to her nape. His lips trailed down her sensitive skin. She shivered while he warmed her ear with his quickened breath. "Which is it? Yes or no? It cannot be both."

"It does not displease me." Her voice came out low and husky. Afraid.

He turned her around. Slowly his hand lifted her jaw. "Then let me please you as a man pleases a woman."

She did nothing, and again inaction became her affliction. He released a low, animal groan and bent to kiss her. All she had to do was tilt her head away and she knew he would have stopped. Instead, to her shock and dismay, she rose to meet him. His lips crushed against her all-too-eager ones and the conquest was complete.

The last time she had made love to him in a daze of sensation, but this time she felt everything with razor keenness. His scent rubbed against her mouth until it became more a taste than a smell. The soft purple wool of her cloak scratched at her back as he lay her down in a bed of straw. Her silk gown rustled like falling autumn leaves as he unhooked her; the pale pink undergarments fell away like rose petals.

She told herself she wanted to stop. Good sense lectured her that she was weak and wanton. But it didn't make her quit. Lord Niall Trevallyan wove a spell around her that was as tight as any warlock's, and soon she found him atop her, naked, warm, hard; kissing her with all the matching fervor in her own wicked soul. His mouth covered her nipples, her belly, the dark mound of her womanliness. Nothing shamed him; and therefore, nothing shamed her.

He laid her back by twisting his hands worshipfully in her hair, reveling in her raven-black tresses. He licked her skin as if it were warm cream and he a starving man. He wanted her. Desperately. She could see it in the tautness of his expression. In the fire in his eyes.

Without a protest, she let him part her thighs.

"When you think of me, think of this moment." He stared down at her, his emotions roiling in his darkened aqua gaze. Slowly he took her hand. He laid a burning kiss deep into her palm, then ran it across the ruddy alabaster of his Celtic fair complexion. "Think of the man you hold in your small hands, Ravenna. And I beg you, have mercy on him."

He entered her with one greedy push. She tossed her head back in the straw, sensation rendering her incapable of comprehending his words. In pagan rhythm, he made his magic. The stars above the fallen thatch roof began to dance and shoot across the sky. Pressure built within her loins with every rock of his body.

Only once did she dare look at him and acknowledge her surrender. It was a fatal mistake. The need in his soul gripped her as tightly as her legs gripped him. She couldn't look away, until he forced the stars above to shower down upon her. With sweet damnation, he gave her release.

∞

The stars took some time to return to normal. But finally, when at last Ravenna's breath came slow and satisfied, she looked overhead and saw the heavens as she knew them; the stars placidly twinkling like crystals from a shattered vase.

Without a word, Niall rose and gathered his trousers and shirt. She hated the cold that rushed over her. If his warmth was sin, she wanted sin, not the cold hell of his abandonment.

Wrapped in her cloak, she watched him pull on his boots, his expression unreadable.

Harshly, he announced, "The evening grows cold. We'll stay here for the night and walk to Cinaeth Castle in the morning. I'll build a fire."

She nodded, not even bothering to fumble with her dress that lay next to her. It was only her second experience, and yet she already wondered how a man and a woman could be in the throes of wild intimacy one minute, only to grope through the perdition of awkwardness the next.

Unable to think of a way to cast aside the sudden chill between them, she mutely watched him work, confounded by her own tangled emotions.

Soon he had built a small blaze at one end of the barn. The smoke trailed up thirty feet to the roofline, sucked into the open sky where the thatch had fallen through.

In the firelight, she watched him. The flames licked up between them, casting his features into evil relief. His slanted eyebrows, his piercing gaze made her think of druids, Celtic warriors, and kings long dead. Men of myth. Men who weren't supposed to be found in this modern age, especially building fires in barns, and wearing black leather boots and trousers of bottle-green corduroy.

"If I had a pot I could at least make us some nettle soup for our dinner. We've enough of those," she commented, desperately hoping that he would talk.

He looked up at her. Ruefully, she lowered her gaze to the nettles caught in her cloak's hemline.

"Nettle soup? Is that something witches eat?" The expression in his eyes lightened. He quirked his mouth in a way that made her want to smile.

"Nay, we only eat *bairi'n breac,*" she said, mischief dancing in her eyes as she referred to the bread eaten on Hallowe'en, ". . . and little children, of course."

"Of course." He nodded his head as if they were merely two old acquaintances conversing over tea.

"We find noblemen quite indigestible."

"A pity." He watched her through heavy-lidded eyes. "I always fancied being eaten by a witch."

An odd excitement trilled in her belly. His naughtiness never failed to disconcert her.

"Come, sit by the fire with me." He held out his hand.

Slowly she rose, wrapping the cloak around her nudity. Her hair was in knots; her legs wobbly and unsure. It was a relief to feel his hands on her hips, sliding her between his legs near to the fire.

They stared into the flames, a restless silence between them.

Finally, he lifted the hair at her nape and kissed the soft jet curls at her hairline. "You smell . . . mmmm . . . how to describe it. Mystic. Like crushed orchids."

"What is an orchid?"

" 'Tis a flower. From the darkest jungle. They're very fragile. I've come across their fragrance many a time in the queen's botanical gardens at Windsor."

"You mean—the actual queen?" Her heart sped at the thought. She couldn't imagine being in the presence of the queen. The pomp and circumstance was just too awe-inspiring.

"I've been to Windsor many a time. Albert likes a good hunt as much as any man."

She shut her eyes, hating the jolt of despair that shot through her. He consorted with the queen and her royal prince, while she scratched out her miserable fairy tales and dreamed of one day clerking in Dublin. The gulf between herself and Trevallyan was too large to bridge. They were worlds apart, and his talk of Windsor had brought the reality right to her doorstep.

"Why so quiet?" he whispered, nibbling on her ear.

"Am I?" she asked distantly.

"Yes." There was a playfulness in his tone. "Does my talk of the queen annoy your rebel Irish nature?"

"No . . ." She stiffened.

He ceased kissing her.

"What is it?" he whispered against her neck.

Her mouth grew dry as she forced out the words. "You—you say you want my love . . ."

"Yes?"

". . . and yet, you've never spoken about your love."

His hands tightened on her shoulders. There was a long, painful silence. "Once, long ago when I was just a lad, I thought I gave my love to Helen, my wife."

"Did you?" The words were so low as to be inaudible.

"She cuckolded me. She led me down a fool's path." His voice was harsh and yet dispassionate, as if he were speaking of wounds now healed. "I now realize what I felt was never love. It was rebellion, a need to ease my loneliness."

"And—how—do you feel about me?" She braced herself for the answer.

"I *never* wanted her like I want you."

"And the others?" she gasped, thinking of his chorus of fiancées.

"I desired a wife and children. You must understand. You were just a child, Ravenna. With every year, with every woman I knew I could not lie to, I saw my dreams slip through my hands."

"And so . . . you love me?"

His struggle was almost palpable. She could feel it in the grip of his hands, in the wooden manner in which he held himself. "I don't know," he finally confessed. "I see now I know nothing about it. I've never felt it before." He cupped her chin and turned her head so that she would be forced to look at him. She did, with eyes glittering with tears. "I only know that I want you. Desperately. So desperately that my need for you eclipses everything else in my life. I want you so much it frightens me. I fear it may destroy me, and I cannot stop it."

Possession. It ran through his veins like blood. She would not destroy him. He would destroy himself.

"I've told you before," her voice was a choked whisper, "I don't want to be owned. I'm already too indebted to you." She looked away, hopelessness dulling the sparkle in her eyes. "I should have run from you back at the castle. Now I'll owe you for finding my father."

"You owe me for nothing. I've given you these things, free and clear. When Grania told me about your need for silverware at that infernal school of yours, did I send it with a bill? I did not."

She looked at him, grim-faced, reminded how he'd even provided the silverware and had her initial engraved on each piece. His manipulations had been deep; they knew no boundaries at all.

"I'll pay you for the silver promptly when we return to Lir," she told him.

He ran his hand down his face, then rubbed his lightly bearded jaw in frustration. "I don't want the money. Don't you see? I only want to make you happy. Whatever you want, I'll get for you. You want those silly tales of yours published—well, I've a friend in Dublin who publishes books. He'll publish them for you. I will do all that, to make you happy."

She recoiled as if he'd burned her. He didn't understand anything that she wanted. "You can't do that. I shall publish on my own, or give up the endeavor. I won't humiliate myself by using your powers to see my words in print."

"Why are you so pigheaded? You won't get them published any other way."

"I'll do it by my talent, or I won't do it at all."

He heaved a sigh and studied her as if she were some sort of alien creature. "Fine. Do it the hard way. Accept your failure. I don't care. As long as you stay away from Malachi and his ilk, and behave like a lady, then you may do as you please."

" 'Behave like a lady.' And how may I do that when you've seen to it twice that I'm no lady at all?" She couldn't cloak the venom in her tongue. The truth was too raw.

His anger frightened her. He shook her until her teeth rattled. "Don't you ever say such words to me again. What's between us is good and fine. Don't ever imply otherwise."

She almost wept her impassioned rebuttal. "Grania told me about pleasures of the flesh when I asked about my mother. She never put constraints upon me. She made me believe the union between a man and woman was beautiful and creative, and because I was not Catholic, and raised outside of society, I believed her." She wiped the tears spilling down her cheeks. "But then a man sent me to an English school. There they drilled into me exactly the kind of woman my mother had been. You say I'm to be a lady. Well, the headmistress of Weymouth-Hampstead would have another word for me—"

"Bother that! They were not responsible for molding you. I saw to that. Your upbringing was, and is, mine to control, and I tell you, the headmistress of that bloody English gaol I sent you to was wrong in this regard. The world is made of many rules. You play by all of them and you are miserable."

"You play by none of them . . . and you die alone." She stared at him. She watched the anger pass across his features.

"I flaunted the *geis* and found nothing but misfortune. Now I'm willing to embrace it, but it's not working. Both paths seemed doomed. So which do I take? Which do I take?" He spoke the question like a monk's chant.

"You follow your heart."

"Yes."

She looked up at him and for one brief second, she saw a want on his face that she had seen in no man. The emotion was loneliness and despair combined, further tortured by an acute intelligence that couldn't be comforted by delusions. The emotion was raw, and so vivid that she felt it pass through her very soul like a wind off the Irish Sea.

But quickly, artfully, he shuttered it away behind the terrible facade of the brooding Lord Niall Trevallyan, and it vanished like a wraith, leaving her to wonder if it were not something she had imagined.

Yet it had been real. For if it hadn't been real, then she would be able to erase the bittersweet ache it had left in her heart.

"I won't let you go, Ravenna," he said softly.

She hardened her heart, forcing herself to fight when all she wanted was to surrender. "You can't keep me if I don't love you."

He held her against his chest, his eyes alive with the reflection of the flames of the fire.

"Watch me," he whispered ominously. "Just watch me."

Chapter 22

D AWN WAS still a gray ghost on the horizon when Ravenna woke within Niall's embrace. The straw was warm where they lay beneath her cloak; it was difficult to think of leaving, but she wanted to be gone. She knew she must leave him while she still had the strength of will to do it. Now, just paces from Cinaeth Castle and the truth about her father, she knew she must break free and do this by herself or suffer the consequences of Trevallyan's all-consuming manipulations.

She looked down at Trevallyan. He slept well. She hated to even think of the reasons why. The soreness between her thighs spoke eloquently of the activity the night before. Furious with him, she had meant to sleep alone, wrapped in the false security of the purple wool and velvet cloak, but then he had lain down next to her. She tried to remain stiff and unapproachable, but he ignored her mood, and pulled her within his arms. He held her so close, she swore she could feel the strong beat of his heart, and, not wanting to, she had nevertheless turned to him.

He kissed her. His hand familiarly cupped her breast. She had hated herself then, as she did now, because instead of pushing him away, she had kissed him. He took her hard and swiftly, as if binding her soul to his, and she had let him, only because her plans for today had solidified. She was going to leave him, even though she thought she might be in love with him after all.

Pulling on her dress, contorting herself to reach the hooks at the back, she stepped away from the pile of straw that had been their bed. The sky overhead through the thatch was graying to the color of doves. It would be light soon. She had to find the road, and there were miles perhaps to walk to Cinaeth Castle. He would follow her there, she knew it, but at least she would have an hour or two alone with those who might have known her father. She would fight for that much. It wouldn't do to linger.

Silently, she swept the cloak over her cold shoulders. She looked at Niall one last time and wondered about when they would meet again. She knew it would be in anger, but she still hoped not. He had given her no choice. It was either begin to break away, or fall in love with him and entwine herself. He would force more and more dependence on him until she would be obligated forever. And he was too powerful and vindictive a man to become indebted to. She would be nothing but a slave to him, an Irish peasant to do his bidding because he had shown charity to her. Because he had lusted after her. She was not his possession. She was no man's possession. She would no longer accept his good works, including the one he attempted now in leading her to her father's ancestral home.

She tore her gaze from his sleeping, half-nude form that was partially hidden in the mounds of straw. The urge to kiss him farewell was strong, but she swallowed it like bile. If she kissed him, he might awaken. He might kiss her back, and then she'd fall again beneath his warlock's spell and take the wanton pleasures he offered.

Without another look back, she tiptoed from the barn and ran into the thick elms.

Cinaeth Castle was a breathtaking sight to a girl who had been born in an Irish hovel. Ravenna climbed the small rise in the road, squinting in the early afternoon sun. She didn't need to look hard. In the distant forests, it spired up from the treetops like a sentinel guarding the hills. Delicate, and relatively modern in comparison to the dark, brooding, millennium-old Trevallyan home, the sandstone castle was a princess's dream. It was the color of wheat, the turrets patinated to a fine copper-green. Ravenna felt she had stepped right into one of her faerie tales. It was all she could do to keep herself from running along the white-pebbled drive and throwing herself at the gilded front doors.

As she passed through the iron and gold gates mounted with English neoclassical gryphons, she wished fervently that she could make herself more presentable. Her hairpins had been lost in the straw, and her hair, though tied with a silk ribbon, hung loose down her back, mercifully covered by the wool cloak. There were nettles still woven in her hemline, and her silk dress, yesterday fresh and pretty, was now a rumpled, embarrassing rag.

Other worries assaulted her. How would she present herself? How would she ask about her father? She had tried to think of these things during the trip, but Trevallyan had presented so many distractions, she hadn't had time to properly think. Now she wished she had given it all more thought. As she walked to the French, gilt-encrusted doors, she remembered the old saying, "Fools rush in . . ."

"Who are you?"

Before she had even time to knock, the door opened, and a butler peered down at her, a man quite the opposite of Greeves. With his missing arm and Irish-English accent, Greeves was only too human. But this man, this cold, aristocratic paragon of pomposity, seemed in no way touched by human feeling. He looked down upon her as if she were the girl who emptied the chamber pots. One who now dared to enter the front of the castle as if she were a peeress.

"I've come to see . . ." Her words died on her lips. Who had she come to see, after all? She was certain the man who had been her father was dead. So who would tell her about him?

"Lord or Lady Cinaeth, please," she announced, hating the fact that the butler's stare made her want to cower.

"What is your concern?" The butler flicked his gaze to her wrinkled cloak and dusty hem, as if he were doubtful of her upbringing.

Bitterly, she couldn't in all good conscience deny what he thought. All she could do was fight. And fight she would.

"Show me to Lady Cinaeth or it'll be the worse for you." She despised the way her accent came out when she was angry. The last thing she wanted was to look hopelessly Irish to these people.

"The viscountess, Lady Cinaeth, is trimming the roses in the greenhouse. She cannot be disturbed."

Showing more cheek than she thought she possessed, she walked past him into a beautiful hall lined with windows and pastoral Watteau-inspired tapestries. She pointed her finger toward a door and said, with a haughtiness learned by example, "Take me to the morning room and bring me a cup of tea. I'll wait for your mistress there."

The butler stood mutely by the door. She turned her back so that he could remove her cloak.

A long moment passed while he obviously thought about the consequences should he turn her away. With a small feeling of triumph, she felt him reluctantly slip the cloak from her shoulders.

"Follow me, miss. I'll tell Lady Cinaeth you are here." He led her through an archway that hid a pair of glass French doors. Throwing them open, he ushered her into a small drawing room. Light poured in from a breathtaking twenty-foot window, framed in an astounding amount of plum-colored velvet.

"Your name, miss?" The butler watched her seat herself on a green and gold settee.

"Ravenna." She gave him her best witchy stare. If that wouldn't ward off his questions concerning her lack of a last name, nothing would.

"Thank you. Tea will be here shortly." He gave her a supercilious, dubious look, then bowed and left to fetch his mistress.

With a shaking hand, Ravenna gripped the serpentine arm of the settee. She had made it this far, but terror struck at her heart at the thought of broaching the subject of her father to Lady Cinaeth. She knew nothing about Lady Cinaeth. The woman could be her grandmother or her aunt, even her cousin. Certainly, it was possible that the old woman would kick her out the door the minute she brought up the subject of her father. Lady Cinaeth could be a dragon.

Ravenna gazed at the clouds painted on the gilt ceiling above, the view reminiscent of princesses and spellbound castles. An ogre couldn't be living in such exquisite surroundings. She suddenly grew more optimistic. Perhaps the woman would embrace her as a long-lost relative. The granddaughter she had never had. They would be friends, and Ravenna would finally have a family other than Grania.

"Who are you to take me from my roses?"

Ravenna's gaze riveted to the door. There stood a beautiful brunette woman, perhaps fifteen years older than herself, dressed in a gown of Paris green satin. On her intricately coifed head she wore a chip bonnet laced with lavender ribbon and sprigs of costly artificial violets. Her mouth, though nicely curved, formed a horizontal line as she peered at Ravenna disapprovingly.

"Who are you?" the viscountess asked, giving her a hazel-eyed, imperious stare.

"My name is Ravenna. I've come from County Lir." With cheeks pale with fear, Ravenna rose to her feet and faced the beauty.

"What is your business with me?" The viscountess impatiently slapped her palm with a pair of pruning shears. She wore cheese-colored goatskin gloves that covered her to the elbows, protecting her from thorns. When Ravenna didn't answer, she threw the shears and gloves onto a Louis XVI commode and stepped into the room.

"Are you a Gypsy? Hebblethwaite, my butler, thinks you are. He thinks you mean to rob us." With distaste, Lady Cinaeth took in her loosely bound hair and her soiled hemline.

Helplessly, Ravenna could do nothing but whisper, "I'm not a Gypsy," while the woman condemned her with her stare. She couldn't even blame Lady Cinaeth for her derogatory thoughts. A night spent in a barn had made her look less than presentable, and Ravenna knew she'd always looked a bit wild, a trait Weymouth-Hampstead had valiantly tried to whip out of her. Looking at herself through the eyes of the titled beauty before her, she almost wanted to die. Too late, she could finally understand the merits of Weymouth-Hampstead's teachings.

"So what is your business?" Lady Cinaeth raised her hand when Ravenna made to speak. Continuing, she said, "I'll have you know right now if you try to sell me charms or tell my fortune, I'll have you arrested. We don't countenance Gypsies here. The Irish are bad enough, little potato-eating drudges. . . ."

The viscountess lowered her hand and waited for the expected denials.

Ravenna remained silent, her stare fixed on Lady Cinaeth's hand. Not a scratch marred its creamy length. Each nail was buffed to pink perfection. It was clean and soft. A lady's hand.

Then Ravenna thought of Grania's hands. Her grandmother's hands had always seemed ancient and work-worn, wrinkled and gnarled with disease. But they had always touched her with gentleness and love. They were never unkind. As these hands could surely be unkind.

"I'm on a quest to find my father," Ravenna said, her anger and pride beginning to surface. She was no potato-eating drudge, and if some of the Irish could be described that way, it was only because they were made poor by the English dogs that had raped them of their wealth.

"Why would I know your father?" The viscountess looked truly irritated.

"I have reason to believe he hailed from Cinaeth Castle. I know he was a nobleman. . . ." Ravenna had difficulty finishing. The journey north to Antrim seemed so pointless now. This Lady Cinaeth with her beautiful, cold, hard face was never going to help her. She had come far, and at great cost, for nothing. Clinging to one last hope, Ravenna stared deep into the desert of the woman's eyes and sought compassion.

She found no oasis.

Lady Cinaeth's beautiful mouth quirked in disdain. "If your father were a nobleman, surely you would know who he was? I do believe propriety dictates one recognize one's legitimate children."

Ravenna felt each word like a knife slicing through her heart. She knew she was a bastard, but hearing the implication from this wealthy, privileged beauty—a woman who was perhaps even one of her own blood relations—cut her to the bone. With a dark, wounded gaze, she whispered, "He loved my mother. I know that. I *know* it."

"Then he ought to have married her."

"Lady Cinaeth, are you his sister? My aunt?"

Ridiculing laughter echoed along the bank of windows. "Don't be ridiculous. Me, an aunt to you? If the previous Lord Cinaeth spawned a bastard daughter before he died, 'tis my husband's concern. He was his · brother, not mine."

"And your husband is Lord Cinaeth? My father's younger brother?" Ravenna thirsted for the truth. She ached to know anything. Even if it hurt her. Even if it was misery.

"My husband is Lord Cinaeth, indeed. Now," she raised an artful eyebrow and glanced at the door, "be off with you. I haven't the time to talk with misbegotten Gypsies."

"Please," Ravenna begged, her eyes filling with tears of rage and hopelessness. "I must just know his name. Just tell me my father's name. What was the name of Lord Cinaeth's brother?"

"Don't be ridiculous. I'll tell you nothing. Either you leave at once or I'll have Hebblethwaite throw you out." Lady Cinaeth calmly took the garden gloves and the shears from the marquetried top of the commode.

"Please. I've come very far—"

"Get out. And pray my husband doesn't find out about this. Why, he would probably put you in gaol for your presumptions."

"I will go to gaol then," Ravenna gasped, desperation pounding through her veins like blood. "Just tell me his name. Give me that much."

"Oh, you Irish are all alike. We give you a little charity and soon you expect to have our homes and land, too."

"Just tell me his name," Ravenna pleaded, fighting the tears that sprang to her eyes. Despair threatened to engulf her like floodwaters. She had come so far. Her hopes had been so high. Now her despair was crashing down on her like a wave she had no power to withstand.

"My lady."

Ravenna looked toward the morning-room doorway. Terrified, she found the butler stood there, clearly readying himself to expel her from the castle.

"Hebble, take this—this—" Lady Cinaeth flicked a dismissive glance down Ravenna's figure. "Take this *creature* and deposit her outside Cinaeth's gates."

"No. . . ." Ravenna choked.

"Lady Cinaeth, there is another visitor at the door." The butler shifted uncomfortably. " 'Tis Lord Trevallyan from Lir."

Ravenna stiffened. The inevitable had finally arrived to once more snatch away her independence.

Lady Cinaeth rolled her eyes. "Oh, the travails of this day." She looked down at her pristine satin gown. "And I'm a mess. I can't very well greet one of the most highly regarded earls this side of the Irish Sea in my gardening frock." She nodded her bonneted head toward Ravenna. "Throw the chit out, Hebble, and tell Lord Trevallyan I'll meet him in the drawing room in ten minutes."

Hebblethwaite looked decidedly torn.

"What is it now, Hebblethwaite?" Lady Cinaeth snapped. "Haven't I enough to do without guessing what's on your mind? Throw the girl out and bring Lord Trevallyan a drink."

"Lord Trevallyan . . ." Hebblethwaite paused and glanced at Ravenna. Ravenna's heart rushed in anticipation of what he was going to say. Clearly Trevallyan had come to help her. She hadn't wanted his help, but now she could see that she must either take it or never know about her father. Ruefully, she comforted herself with the fact that she had at least paid well for the service beforehand.

"Lord Trevallyan has come looking for his wife." Hebble glanced at his mistress with the eyes of a chastised puppy. "It seems Lady Ravenna is his wife."

Lady Cinaeth's face drained of all color. Ravenna suffered a bit of shock herself but schooled herself not to show it. Trevallyan had gall, there was no doubt about it. Usually it made her rebel, but this time, even though it made her extremely uncomfortable to be thought of as his wife, she was grateful for his tactics.

Lady Cinaeth's gaze darted to Ravenna. The woman murmured an undecipherable apology and quickly exited the room, mumbling something about finding Ravenna's husband.

A minute later, Ravenna heard a familiar voice.

"Ah, there you are, darling. Thank God you're safe."

She gazed at Trevallyan standing in the door, still in his corduroys and black boots. He strode toward her and kissed her forehead like the adoring husband, but his eyes were steely with dormant anger that she knew would awaken the moment they had a chance to be alone.

"My lord husband . . ." Ravenna greeted, her gaze flickering in her embarrassment. For some inexplicable reason, as all his reasons were inexplicable, he had chosen to avoid embarrassing her. But she would pay for his mercies. She knew it.

"When you were lost to me in the woods after our carriage breakdown, I despaired." Trevallyan looked down at her, the emotion in his aqua eyes ominous. "Now that I've found you again, I see I must never let you out of my sight."

Ravenna swallowed, her mouth strangely dry. "My lord, I am well. I can, when needed, take care of myself."

He lowered his voice for her ears only. "Yes, and how I despise it." He straightened and cleared his throat. Taking Ravenna's hand in his own, he said, "Lady Cinaeth, my wife is here on rather a delicate mission. I don't know how much she's told you—"

"Oh! I understand everything, Lord Trevallyan, everything. This situation must be handled with the utmost care." Lady Cinaeth nodded her head too enthusiastically. "But tell me, my lord, when we last met in London, you were not married and I heard of no wedding—"

"We were wed quietly, my lady." The corner of Trevallyan's mouth lifted in a wicked smile. "My wife's situation is much like your own, Lady Cinaeth. When Lord Cinaeth chose to marry a cobbler's daughter, it was prudent to downplay the marital festivities."

The woman colored three shades of red. Ravenna was almost heartened to see this grand beauty cut down to size. "Of course, my lord. It was quite prudent," she mumbled.

She pressed Ravenna's hand. Whispering, she said, "You must forgive my earlier behavior." More loudly, she announced, "I must get Edward. I know he would like to see you—" Her nervous gaze flickered between them. "*Both*," she finished, then departed.

"Allow me to bring refreshment." Hebblethwaite bowed and then he, too, departed.

Alone, Ravenna had a difficult time meeting Trevallyan's gaze. She wandered to the settee and lowered her tired body onto it. "I must thank you for intervening. You arrived just as she was throwing me out the door."

"I could have told you that was the kind of reception you could expect." He stepped to her. His hand gripped her jaw, forcing her head up and her gaze to lock with his. "Why do you do such foolish things? You run away from me, you refuse my offers. What do you hope to get out of this life that is more than what I can provide for you?"

"Independence," she whispered.

His eyes glittered with new anger. "And is it worth dying for? You could have been killed, wandering around in unfamiliar woods, alone and unprotected."

"Does Malachi think it's worth dying for?"

"It's not the same thing."

Quietly she said, "I don't fight for a country, but rather, for myself. I'm not Catholic, I'm not Protestant. The people of Lir heartily distance themselves from my kind. To them, I'm an outcast, a misfit. Still, I've been victim to the hellish treatment the English dole out upon the Irish. I am nothing, I *have* nothing, but myself. And I will not let you have that to do with as you wish."

Her words seemed to move him. She knew he understood; she knew, too, that his understanding could only bring more anger, more frustration. "Why must you be so bloody articulate?" he cursed softly.

"You're the one who sent me to school. I'm your creation."

"And now you've turned on me."

"No. Not turned on you. You were never my master for me to do such a thing."

"I hear footsteps." He heaved a burdened sigh and his grip on her jaw turned to caress. "We'll discuss more of this in our bedroom."

She wanted to protest but suddenly saw the trap he had shut on her. She could either respectably pose as his wife, including sharing a room with him, or announce the ploy and leave in disgrace, her dreams gone of finding her father.

"You see, I still vow to keep you," he taunted as the hurried footsteps drew closer.

"But you'll never hold me." She gave him a challenging glance. "I'm an outcast, remember? And when you cannot turn outward, you turn inward. My love is so buried, I fear not even a man of your genius could find it."

A muscle tensed in his jaw. "I *will* find it. Just keep in mind who it is you're denying. And never forget, if the *geis* is true, you throw misfortune on all of Lir when you say such things."

"The *geis* is frippery and nonsense. But if it isn't, the failure lies with you, not with me."

"Bitch," he said calmly, unwilling to raise his voice with the approaching visitors. "You'd never know all the fire in your eyes hides a heart of ice."

The words stung her, but the tone wrenched her soul. She looked at him and could almost believe he was in love with her. But he didn't love her. To him, she was not much better than the shepherdess who watched his cows in the pastures, or the seamstress who stitched his fine wool from his flocks of sheep that grazed on the Sorra Hills. She was just another kind of servant to him. One whom he saw merit in courting. One with whom he seemed to find his particular pleasure.

No, she wanted more than he offered. Even if she found herself falling in love with him—a precipice she wasn't sure she had avoided —she still must have his love in return. And he would never give that, for he had yet to bow his head and humbly ask anything of her; instead he only demanded and expected her to obey. Asking was not in his nature, not in the social structure to which they were all confined. Somehow, if they were to find love, she must make him see that she was his equal, but that seemed an impossibility because she knew that he, one of the Ascendency, could never admit to such a thing.

The door burst open with Lord and Lady Cinaeth. Unnerved, Ravenna jumped to her feet and stood mute before the man who might be her uncle.

"Trevallyan, good to see you." The viscount heartily shook Niall's hand. Ravenna watched on the side, analyzing him.

Lord Cinaeth was a tall, handsome man of almost fifty years of age. Barrel-chested, with a wide, quick smile, he exuded congeniality. Though his hair had gone silver, Ravenna suspected by his coloring it had once been a dark brown or black, and he had astonishing blue, almost violet, eyes, the color of periwinkles.

"My wife has told me something rather incredible, Trevallyan," Lord Cinaeth said as his gaze rested on Ravenna.

"I fear Lady Ravenna chafes at the bit, my lord." Trevallyan squeezed her arm. "She's much too headstrong for her own good. Our carriage broke down and we were forced to tarry overnight in a barn. In her haste to arrive here, Ravenna got away from me and now I find she's burst in on you. Please allow me to apologize and correct the damage."

Lord Cinaeth laughed. "No apology necessary, my good man. 'Though when Lady Cinaeth came in with this story, I must say it shocked me."

The hand on Ravenna's arm turned to lead. Trevallyan laughed, too, a little mirthlessly. "Of course, a story such as that would. You must forgive my wife her youth and impetuosity."

"Yes, yes." The viscount motioned to the settee. "Would you care for refreshment?"

Trevallyan paused. He looked down at Ravenna and thumbed the lavender shadows beneath her eyes that revealed her weariness. "If you would, Cinaeth, my wife has been through a lot to get here. As I said, our carriage broke down—"

"How stupid of me," Lady Cinaeth sputtered. She immediately nodded to Hebble and said, "Please show Lady Trevallyan to a room so she may rest. Tea and cakes and whatever she likes must be sent up immediately."

"You read my mind, Lady Cinaeth." Trevallyan smiled.

Lady Cinaeth regained some of her poise. "My lord, how gracious of you to be so patient with us."

"I must tell you, Trevallyan," Lord Cinaeth broke in, "you know not how fortunate you and your lovely wife are. Have you heard of the murder in Hensey?"

Ravenna felt Trevallyan stiffen. A tingle of icy fear ran down her spine.

"Murder, did you say?" Trevallyan asked calmly.

"Yes." Cinaeth nodded. "I don't want to alarm your wife, but it would be prudent for you both to stay here as long as necessary until

your carriage can be fixed. Yesterday in Hensey, a man was shot dead
just as he walked into town. The blokes who killed him ran into the
hills, cowards that they are. They haven't caught them yet. The dead
man wore a jacket he'd bought from his master only last month, and if
old Jack Kilarney weren't an Irisher, I'd think he in his fine new jacket
was mistaken for an Englishman, and that the boy-os were the ones
that did the shooting. Otherwise, it just doesn't make sense."

"No, it doesn't make sense," Trevallyan murmured.

Ravenna looked up at him, unable to hide the fear in her eyes. Jack
Kilarney no doubt had been mistaken for Trevallyan. The man had
been ambushed, and if not for Niall's presence of mind yesterday, he
might have been the one killed. In fact, this time they both might have
been murdered. She couldn't shake the horror that now gripped her.

"Go, my love, and get some rest," Niall said, his gaze locking with
hers. "I'll join you shortly."

"But—" The concern in his eyes killed her protest.

"There'll be another time to speak of the matter we've come about,"
he whispered.

She wanted to refuse, but she knew he was right. There would be a
better time, an easier time, to bring up the issue of her father. She
acquiesced, nodding to Lord and Lady Cinaeth. "I suppose I am tired.
Thank you so much for your hospitality."

"We're glad to have you, Lady Ravenna." Lord Cinaeth's voice held a
curious note. Before following Hebble, she looked back at him and was
struck by the notion that he seemed as unsettled as she to confront a
pair of eyes so much like his own.

☘

"We've come here to find Ravenna's father." Trevallyan took a long
pull of his brandy and stared at the viscount. Lady Cinaeth had gone to
see about dinner, and now the two men were ensconced in the library,
drinking by a roaring fire.

"There was an account by an old storyteller," Niall continued slowly,
"that Lady Ravenna's father hailed from here. I know it sounds lunatic,
but we believe he was your brother."

"My brother, Finn Byrne, Lord Cinaeth, is dead."

"We knew that."

Lord Cinaeth looked at Trevallyan with a quizzical expression in his eyes. "And how did you know that?"

Trevallyan released a sardonic laugh. "Ravenna's grandmother told her her father was dead. The old woman just . . . knew."

The viscount raised his eyebrow.

Niall grinned. "There are some in Lir who take Ravenna's grand-mother for a witch."

Lord Cinaeth burst out laughing. "Fascinating. Quite fascinating. I must meet Ravenna's grandmother sometime."

"I think Ravenna is your niece, Cinaeth."

The men stared at each other and suddenly turned sober.

"Finn Byrne died unexpectedly twenty years ago," Lord Cinaeth said. "That's when I inherited the viscountcy."

"We don't know how he died." Niall waited expectantly.

" 'Twas a terrible tragedy." The look in Lord Cinaeth's eyes grew distant as if he were thinking of something that still hurt. "Finn Byrne was five years older than I and next in line to become viscount. Before Father died, I got a commission in the Royal Navy. I was twenty-eight at the time when Finn came to London to see me. In his note he implied he had something important to announce. We were very close. He said I was to be the first to know . . . but know what, we never found out."

"What happened to him?"

"Finn was to meet me at the old armory, our usual place to meet when he came to London, for he was not allowed inside the barracks. I had no idea it was being worked on. Scaffolding covered the entire front of the building on the street side. Between the pedestrians and the workmen, we had difficulty finding each other. Later I was told the medieval structure was unsound, hence the reason for the repairs." His voice grew hoarse. "Little good it did for Finn."

He took a deep breath. He continued, grim-faced and tight-lipped. "We had a jolly meeting when we finally spied each other. I remember how glad I was to see him. He looked fit and happy, so unusually happy, I couldn't wait to hear his news. We were off to the Rod and

Staff, an old pub we liked to frequent, when we heard the screams of a woman.

"Even now it plays out in my mind again and again like a nightmare I can't escape. We rushed to the poor woman's side and she pointed heavenward. A little boy—perhaps five years old—was way up on the scaffolding, so high his mother had no hopes of climbing up and retrieving him. Somehow he must have escaped the woman's notice while she had paused to speak with some old friends she had met on the street below, and we could only watch in horror as time and time again, the boy slipped and regained his balance, only to climb higher, for he had become too frightened to climb his way down.

"Finally, Finn could take no more. Here I was the commissioned officer, a beribboned hero of King George IV, and I stood frozen to the ground while Finn acted.

"He climbed onto the scaffolding and made his way up perhaps thirty feet. We held our breath while he managed to locate the boy. Above him, the poor child was wailing for his mother; below, the mother wept quite as fiercely. The effect on the nerves was indescribable. Every step was costly to watch, for fear that Finn or the child would tumble.

"Finn reached the little man and flung him onto his shoulders. Down and down he came, another assault to our nerves as now we watched both of them skirt the precipice of a sure and sudden death. He was but ten feet from the ground when the boy broke from his back and made his way on his own down to his mother. Then it happened.

"A spire broke from the stone tower. It came like a javelin, gaining speed as it fell. I only remember seeing the scaffolding fall. By this time, the boy was safe in his mother's arms, but Finn had yet to come down from the scaffold. When we found him in the rubble, he was beyond help. The spire had skewered itself into his chest." Lord Cinaeth grew quiet, as if he could not speak. At last, he said softly, "He was impaled."

The blood seemed to drain from Trevallyan's face. He turned grim, as if thinking of the geis, of the consequences of defying fate. "You never found out what he wanted to tell you?" he asked.

The viscount shook his head mournfully. "There were few clues. We did all we could. When I got to Finn, I held him in my arms as he died.

He said only these words, 'I want—I want . . .' and then he called out the name of a woman."

"And what was this woman's name?"

Lord Cinaeth looked at Trevallyan. He said slowly, "I see the resemblance between Ravenna and Finn. The eyes, the mouth, they are the same. In her, I believe God has blessed me with the return of my beloved brother. More than anything I want this to be true. I want Finn Byrne's child. So tell me, was Ravenna's mother named Mary?"

Trevallyan stared at the viscount in disbelief. After a long, numb moment, he squeezed his eyes shut and took a draught of his Old Pale. "Surely, there might be some kind of mistake," he offered, his face unusually stern. "The man was dying. Could you have heard him wrong?"

Lord Cinaeth looked bitterly disappointed. "There is no mistake. Mary was most definitely the name he spoke."

"Ravenna's mother was not Mary. I'm afraid Finn Byrne was in love with another."

"Ravenna could still be his daughter."

Trevallyan nodded his head. "Agreed, but how to prove it." He stared into the fire that roared beneath a black marble mantel. "Perhaps 'tis best."

"Finn was cursed, Trevallyan. That girl is his daughter. I'm sure of it."

"Perhaps the name was garbled. He must have been in great pain," Niall suggested. "Are you sure there could be no mistake?"

Lord Cinaeth shook his head in despair. "I heard the name clearly. Even now it haunts me. Ravenna is Finn Byrne's daughter, but how can I recognize the girl in any capacity if I can find no connection to her?"

"You can't." Trevallyan raked a hand through his hair in a gesture of frustration. "Ravenna will just have to accept her bastardy."

"But Finn was no rake, Trevallyan." Lord Cinaeth softened and his eyes grew dim with memory. "I wished you'd known him. He was as honorable a man as they come." He slammed his fist on the cushion of the settee. "My brother just wasn't the type to drop bastards and abandon them!"

"Everyone has a fall from grace at some point."

But Lord Cinaeth stood his ground. "Think about it. It doesn't make sense any other way. Ravenna is about the right age for Finn to have been courting her mother when she was conceived. He was on his way to London to tell me about a woman, I'm sure of it. It had to be Ravenna's mother."

"What did Finn Byrne say again, when he was dying?" Trevallyan watched him with a dark, piercing gaze.

Lord Cinaeth ground his teeth in obvious hopelessness. "Even now, thinking of it makes me ache. The name was quite clear. We looked everywhere for the woman, but she was untraceable."

"What *exactly* did he say?" Niall's dark gold eyebrows slanted in a frown.

"He said, 'I want—I want . . . Mary Brilliant.' We looked everywhere for her. The only Mary Brilliant we found was some kind of an opera singer in London. The woman was fifty if she was a day. She was not the woman to win the love of my brother."

While Lord Cinaeth jabbered on, Trevallyan stood fixed to his place by the mantel. A glint flared in his eyes. Lord Cinaeth was still expounding on his frustration and loss when Niall excused himself to join his wife.

⚭

Trevallyan entered the apartment that Hebblethwaite had directed him to on the third floor of the castle. Ravenna stood near lushly fringed gold drapes and stared out the window. Her face was pale. Her eyes haunted with despair. He ached to see her laugh.

"Ravenna," he whispered as he pulled her stiff, reluctant form into the circle of his arms. "All is not lost."

"When may I speak with Lord Cinaeth about my father?" she whispered, not looking at him.

"I've already talked to him." He looked down at her, wishing she would meet his eye.

"And what did he say?"

"He said his brother, Finn Byrne, was indeed dead. He died twenty years ago."

"Finn Byrne," she whispered as if savoring the name. "Was there anything else? Did you find out if he—if he—" She couldn't seem to form the words.

"The viscount could find no connection between you and his brother." Niall stared down at her, savoring the anticipation of the moment when he would make her dream come true and explain the heart-wrenching mistake Lord Cinaeth had made. The power of it made him almost heady. He found it difficult to let it go.

"It's settled then," she said in a small, controlled voice that barely hid tears. "If there was evidence Finn Byrne had loved my mother I suppose I might try to presume a relationship. But since he did not, I won't take any more of your time, nor the viscount's. At first opportunity, we must leave." She stood woodenly in his embrace, neither fighting it nor accepting it. It was almost as if she didn't even notice he held her.

He touched her cheek and smiled. "We'll depart as soon as the carriage is fixed and brought from Hensey."

She nodded, appearing confident that her emotions were under control. But then, almost against her will, she whispered, "What was wrong with my mother that he could not love her?"

The question shook him. The honesty of her emotion was more than he bargained for. "He loved her, Ravenna. I saw your mother only once, but I have it by the best account that she was as beautiful inside as out. I know he loved her," he added meaningfully.

"Then why . . . ?" Her voice cracked. She didn't finish.

He held her close against his chest. Strands of black hair, as usual, had fallen across her eyes. Lovingly, he brushed them aside, and swallowed the desire to kiss her. Now was definitely not the time. Not when a question was suddenly pressing in on him, a question that he feared to ask.

"Let me ask you, Ravenna," he said slowly. "If we had come here and you had found out that Finn Byrne had indeed loved your mother, had even wanted to marry her, what would you do? Would that be all your heart desires?"

She looked up at him, a strange kind of surprise in her eyes as if she had just awakened and found herself in his embrace. "Would that be my heart's desire? Why, of course it would be. Everything would be changed then." Her full, pink mouth trembled. "Lord Cinaeth—he's a kind soul. If I could prove my relation to him I know he'd give me some recognition . . ." Her gaze flickered to his face almost guiltily. "And if I were recognized by a viscount, you would have no more hold on me. My uncle would set me free. He would not permit you to treat his niece this way."

Trevallyan felt as if a fist had just slammed into his gut. This was not the reaction he'd been hoping for. He'd rushed upstairs, taking the treads two at a time with that supercilious butler panting to keep up, so that he could break the news to Ravenna that Finn Byrne had indeed loved Brilliana. Now he faced the ugly choice of telling her and watching her flee from his clutches using Lord Cinaeth's protection, or not telling her. Of keeping her from the news that he knew would make her happy. But he had hoped the happiness would bring them closer. Foolishly, he had visions of her throwing her arms around him and hugging him, of her laughing through her tears, and placing a kiss of gratitude upon his lips. Lips that despaired for it now.

"You have no obligation to me," he said a bit too forcefully.

She looked up at him, her eyes wary. "You hold me prisoner. You bend my will to yours at every turn. Do you think if I were not in your power you could do such things to me?"

"If you were not, what would you do?" His hands tightened on her arms. Anger rode through him like wild horses. He had to force himself not to shake her.

"If Lord Cinaeth recognized me . . ." her eyes grew dreamy as she thought upon it, "I suppose I would travel. I would see the world. I would live a life completely different than my own."

"I can give you that."

She looked down at his grip on her arms. Her brow furrowed prettily. "Not like this. Never like this." She looked at him.

He closed his eyes. He hated himself. He loathed and despised what he was about to do, but like a wild Connemara pony that had its head, he could not stop it. If he gave her the knowledge to let her loose, she would never choose to be at his side again. And why would she? She was young and beautiful, and with Cinaeth's money and station, she would be free. She'd have proposals from the highest realms of the peerage. She could pick and choose. And what could he offer her that would be better than the rest? Only his heart and soul, and he could already see that beautiful mouth laughing at him, mocking his pledge of love when she had so many others; that beautiful mouth that he had wicked fantasies about too numerous to count. That beautiful mouth that he knew he would die for.

"Let Finn's betrayal be a lesson to you," he said, caressing her face with all the command he could muster. "Brilliana was like you. She was vulnerable; not of a class that elicited protection from men such as Byrne. That's why he left her." The lie choked him. But telling the truth was worse. Infinitely worse.

"You know he left her?" The news seemed to shock her. Her face grew pale and her eyes wide.

He felt a rush of power that was as sweet as it was cruel. "Cinaeth told me the name on his lips as he lay dying was Mary. Mary. I have no doubt you're his bastard, Ravenna, but Cinaeth said the name of his love was Mary."

She looked frozen, as if there were a knot of tears stuck in her chest that she could not shed.

"You should be more grateful to me." He felt diabolical, and the feeling was not altogether unpleasant. He looked down at her and gave her a patronizing nod. "I'm promising to treat you differently than Finn Byrne treated your mother. I don't want you to end up like Brilliana—poor and abandoned."

"I won't," she said coldly, turning from him to look out the window.

He stepped next to her and watched as her eyes filled with hate. They stood there for a moment and listened to the wind softly playing through the giant elms that lined the path to the castle, and he wondered if she hated the castle now because she might have once loved it. The thought made him cringe.

"Then it's settled. You'll stay willingly with me," he said roughly.

"I won't be your prisoner."

"I want you to be my wife."

Clearly surprised, she looked up at him and captured his gaze.

Her magic was potent. When he looked in her eyes, he knew he would do anything for her. Anything but let her go.

"You're proposing to me," she said softly.

"Yes," he whispered.

"You intend to make me your wife."

"Yes," he answered adamantly.

"But all I'll really be is your pawn to do with what you like."

"No," he said, his denial fierce and hot. "You'll be my wife."

"In name but not in deed." There was hopelessness in her voice. "You want me, as Finn Byrne wanted my mother. You might offer me marriage, but only because the *geis* has got you scared. You think with all the bad luck that it might be true after all. You want a wife, and why not me?" Unshed tears made her eyes glitter like amethysts. "If I marry you, you can order me about forever because I am not your equal and never will be. You don't need me. If you did, you'd beg for my every favor, stand when I entered the room, treat me as you treated Lady Cinaeth. Instead, all you've ever seen fit to do is pull these strings that make me your puppet."

He didn't deny what she said, and he knew his unwavering stare was more than an affirmation of the truth. He had no doubts that she hated him almost as much as she hated Finn Byrne at that moment.

"I won't be anybody's puppet," she whispered, turning away.

He shook her. His insides screamed in agony. He was losing her anyway. And he knew the more he held her close, the more she slipped away. But what choice did he have? He was desperate. There seemed no alternative but capture.

"You're going about this all wrong," he ground out. "It's a mistake. You underestimate the power of my feeling."

"No." She glanced away, anger snapping in her own eyes. "Every time you've touched me, I've seen the power of your feeling. But what good does it do when you still see me as that raggedy child who once sneaked into your room to steal a bit of hair? You're Ascendency, my lord. Just like my father was. Brilliana was never Finn Byrne's equal, nor will I ever be yours. After all, what does a lord need with a peasant?" Her voice began to tremble. "Not much, as Finn Byrne showed me."

He opened his mouth to refute what she had to say, but then closed it, realizing the trap he had set for himself. His damnation wove around him like a spider's web.

" 'Tis an unfair standard by which you judge me," he finally said, despising the weakness of his statement when there were stronger arguments that he now dared not put forth.

The tears she could not shed a minute ago now slipped down her face. She looked at him, hopelessness like a veil drawn over her beautiful features. He could see that finding Finn Byrne put to death the culmination of all her dreams, but he did nothing to stop it. Niall Trevallyan then realized he was a selfish, hedonistic man. He could not watch his own dreams executed in order to save hers.

"Can't you see that you cannot force me to love you? This *geis* was more wise than we give it credit for being," she said, her hands outstretched, pleading. "It speaks the truth."

"What will win your love? Tell me, and I'll do it for you." The bitterness of his whisper burned in his throat.

"Physical desire is not all I want out of life—"

"I know that," he interrupted, hating the desperation in his voice.

"I would choose Malachi if that were so. He lusted for me, but I knew that was all I would ever get from him . . . and I want more."

"Tell me what you want."

"I want love and equality. Without them, I'll be but another servant to see to your needs."

"Don't you ever get lonely?" The question shocked even him. He hadn't meant to say it, but there it was, like a gremlin between them, ready to be friend or foe, at whim.

She stepped from him and presented her back to him as if she didn't want him to see the emotion on her face. "My lord, I am the loneliest soul on this earth. I've never belonged to anything or anyone but Grania. I love to write but even my love is lonely. Writing is as lonely as all the barren, friendless years behind me."

"Then come be with me."

"And how do you propose we meet on equal ground?"

He couldn't answer. Her tears came in an uncontrollable wave. She dropped her face in her hands and wept, every tear twisting a noose around his neck.

"Please, my love. Don't," he whispered against her hair as he took her again in his arms.

"I know he loved her." Her teary gaze found the window and the rolled green lawns of Cinaeth. She looked as if she never wanted to see them again. "Grania told me he did, and I'll believe it till the day I die."

"Believe it then. Believe it," he whispered, willing away the lies that threatened to hang him.

Chapter 23

I N THE carriage home, Ravenna kept thinking of Lord Cinaeth's eyes. Dinner the night before had been an awkward affair, with conversation strained and tense. Lord Cinaeth seemed almost mournful; his wife relieved. There were moments when Ravenna wanted to grab the viscount by the lapels and demand that he deny what Trevallyan had told her only hours earlier, but she knew it would do no good. She could tell the viscount had told the truth. She could tell by the sad expression in his eyes. Eyes that were hauntingly like her own.

Ravenna did the best she could to accept the situation. She swallowed her tears along with her outrage. The man Finn Byrne, viscount of Cinaeth, had loved another more than her mother. He had used Brilliana for the carnal pleasures she had given him, then he'd abandoned her with child, deserted her with her foundering hope that he'd loved her and would come back for her. Brilliana had died with his name on her lips; the viscount had died whispering the name of another.

Ravenna wished she felt tears etch like acid down her cheeks.

She longed to scream in rage and revile the god who had allowed this injustice to occur. But release wouldn't come. With the utterance of one name, her innocence, the childish part of her that longed to believe in love and faerie tales, died a swift death, and there was no remedy for it. What the viscount had done to her mother was a cruel, all-too-common practice. Now Ravenna could fully understand the hatred for the Ascendency.

❧

" 'Tis a beautiful day." Trevallyan looked at Ravenna from across the carriage. They had been traveling for two days. In his haste to have Ravenna gone from Cinaeth Castle and Lord Cinaeth's dangerous tongue, he had instructed the carriage leave at daybreak. That was the day before; County Lir was now only miles away.

"Indeed."

Trevallyan could feel the chill even from his side of the carriage. He was desperate to warm the interior. Ravenna had fallen into a depression. She looked as if nothing would ever cheer her again.

"It was kind of Lord Cinaeth to give you Finn Byrne's ring," he said uneasily.

"Yes."

He watched her look down at the large gold ring on her thumb emblazoned with the Cinaeth arms. By her darkened eyes, he believed she could toss it right out the carriage window for all she seemed to care about it. Finn Byrne was her father; he could see even she knew it in her heart. She had found her father and learned to hate him in one short moment. All because of him.

A stab of guilt sliced his insides but he fought it. Relaxing, he leaned back against the upholstered seat and studied her. She was cold and distant, decidedly preoccupied. She sat opposite him, wrapped in the purple wool and velvet cloak, her thick black hair tied with a ribbon that sometimes appeared blue, sometimes violet, depending on the light.

She was slipping from his grasp like a ghost.

The thought left a knot in his stomach the size of a cannonball. He had tasted defeat before, but this one was becoming more than he could bear. He loved her. He knew he loved her. With every kiss, every touch, every moment spent by her side, he fell more and more deeply in love. No one had ever made him feel like this. Even in the throes of his stupid youth, even with Helen, he had he never felt an emotion so intense. His desire for Ravenna was a creature unto itself, growing with every glance into her hauntingly beautiful eyes. He was starved for any small attention. When her sweetly curved lips spoke to him, he felt a thrill he had never before experienced. He was an old man in her presence, and yet his love for her made him a child, awkward and afraid, terrorized that any wrong move would leave him abandoned.

He hated to admit it, but the geis was true. Not literally, of course, for the situation would have to become pretty bad before he found himself believing in old Celtic curses. But the damage was done, none-theless. The geis had entwined his fate with Ravenna's just by the sheer fact that the geis existed and the old men believed that Ravenna was the one for him. If he had never met her, she would not be torturing him now with her distance. Yes, indeed, the geis was true. There was no greater torment than to love and not be loved in return. If the Celts had wanted their revenge on the Trevallyans, they could not have picked a more perfect one.

"When we get to the castle, you must remind me to have Fiona pour you some chocolate. You look chilled." His gaze flickered to the carriage windows. The sun was warm and shining, but it lied. Frost had covered the ground until late in the morning. It was unseasonably cold. Inside the carriage and out, he thought bitterly.

"I've been thinking of your offer of marriage."

Slowly he turned his eyes to hers. He said nothing.

She bit her lower lip. Her eyes held confusion and hurt. "Perhaps I've been too cavalier in rejecting the idea outright. I see now I should at least consider it. My mother . . . she would have given anything to have married Finn Byrne."

"Your mother loved him," he said, uncomfortable with the subject.

The hurt in her eyes grew deeper; the confusion, more tangled. "Yes, she did love him." She looked out to the fields that rolled across the landscape like a many-hued carpet. "Perhaps, given time, I will feel that kind of love, too, and be able to accept your offer."

Her words seemed to take hold of his heart and squeeze it. He understood her overwrought emotions right now. Their visit to Cinaeth had been a disaster. She was given too many debauched examples of the Ascendency to believe he could be different. But he was different.

A repressed anger simmered inside him. He *was* different. He was no wastrel, no drunkard, no rakehell. He was an intelligent, honorable man whose patience was being tested to the breaking point. The girl didn't understand how rare he was. Men of his position didn't beg women of hers to marry them. They didn't ask for their love; they took it, and rarely paid any consequences. By all that was holy, he longed to quit playing the gentleman and take away her choices.

"I'm not a dog to beg for my mistress's attention." His voice was low and a bit mean.

Her gaze locked with his. His words had clearly reached their mark.

"I'm not asking you to make me love you. You already know you can't. But perhaps in time—"

"Perhaps in time," he spat. "You in your youth—no doubt you think it's endless. How many eons do you propose it will take for you to finally make up your mind?"

"I've told you I can't marry a man I don't love. I can't. I just can't."

"Why can't you?" His jaw hurt from gritting his teeth. He was slowly losing control.

"I don't know why. I don't know what you can do. I only know that as a woman I'd rather be like my mother. With all her pain and anguish, I'd rather bear the bastard of a man I did love, than to never love at all." Tears of frustration filled her large eyes and she shifted her gaze away from his face to a spot just behind him.

He stared at her, wanting to release all the rage in his soul and make her see what a fool she was. But the lies he had spun were his. And he knew his fury would only harden her against him. With Herculean effort, he reined himself in, just barely finding the strength to say calmly, "There has been many a successful marriage that was begun without love."

"Let me think on it. I promise to weigh everything." Wearily she rested her head against the leather seat-back and closed her eyes. "Just give me some time. I want to do what's best."

"You've never done what's best for you yet."

She glanced at him, anger sparking in her half-closed eyes. But she said nothing.

❦

Ravenna had dreams rattled by carriage wheels and the ever-present gloom of the man who sat opposite her. Lir seemed to be just around the next bend in the road, just on the other side of the next hill, but the miles stretched on with no sight yet of home. Slumber was her only escape from the troubles that bedeviled her. In her dream, she told a story to a group of young children seated on the thick green lawn of Cinaeth Castle. All the little girls and boys had the same unusual blue-violet eyes as herself, and they listened to the tale of Skya and Aidan with rapt attention.

Skya watched Grace depart, her own eyes stinging with tears she could not afford to let loose. She knew if she should begin to weep, even the large brook that tumbled and splashed by the cottage wouldn't be able to hold all the grief she had kept locked in her soul these many long years.

"She's gone and good riddance! You have no right to visitors. This is my bridge and my water. Your people have no business trespassing!" The troll's voice was a distinct squeaky whine that emanated from the shadows beneath the bridge.

Skya stepped upon the first tread, not bothering to even answer him. Her sorrow was too great.

"No more, I tell you! This is my bridge and my water. I will not share! I will not share."

Without even thinking about it, she lifted her finger and gave the darkness beneath the bridge a small zap right in what she believed was the direction of the troll's behind. She almost smiled when she heard him give out a loud, "Yipe!"

"That should teach you," she said softly.

She crossed the bridge and closed the door to her cottage, but it was lonely inside, lonelier now that she'd had some company and it was gone. She poured herself a trickle of mead and sat on a bench near the fire, but even that failed to chase away her melancholy. Thoughts of home, her mother and father, Grace, all flooded her mind, making her ache for want of them.

A small furrow marred her smooth brow. She tossed back a long hank of blond hair and turned around. Lost in her sad thoughts she had failed to hear the cranking sound right outside her back door. He was doing it again. After all the trouble they'd had the last time, he'd dared to be so obnoxious. When would he learn his lesson? She shook her head in despair.

She stood and crept out the front door. Clinging to the packed mud of the outside walls, she turned the corner toward the back and let her eyes adjust to the darkness. The troll was there, just as she'd thought, his short, squat form highlighted in moonlight that thinly filtered through the canopy of oaks. He had a small spinning wheel in his hand, but instead of spinning wool, he was spinning snakes. They were everywhere, draped over limbs, writhing on the ground. All he had to do was to crack open her back door, and her cottage would be filled with them.

"How dare you try this again? You know I don't like snakes." She stepped from behind her house into the wavering moonlight.

The troll gasped and turned around. He stamped up and down in his frustration.

"Yes, I've caught you, as I always catch you." She folded her arms across her bosom. "So take your punishment." She waved a finger. The snakes turned into inert skeins of wool. "Weave me a fine kirtle out of that. I may forgive you if it pleases me."

"I won't! I won't!" he cried, jumping up and down in a frenzy. "You always win! But I won't let you win now!"

"And what are you going to do about it?" Skya resumed her bored expression.

The troll could not contain his rage. He spat, "This is what I'm going to do about it!" He charged her, running at her with nails bared, his little stumpy feet moving as fast as they could.

Skya opened her eyes wide. She only had to step aside to avoid him, but instead, her instincts took over. She was being attacked. She would defend herself.

She raised her hand. The troll sailed backward in the air. His solid little form met with her battened door. He crashed through it and landed uncon-scious in the corner of her cottage.

"Oh, dear, oh dear. . . ." she whispered as she picked through the wreckage to go to him. She hadn't meant to hurt him. He was, after all, her pet, her only company. His magic had been given to him by her, and sometimes she was forgetful of that. He was no threat to her, only a source of amusement. But she never thought he'd truly attack her. It just surprised her. That was it. And she had reacted before she thought.

"Wake up. Oh, please wake up." She lowered her voice and caressed his sad, horrible features. "I'm sorry. I never meant to hurt you. You know I'd never hurt you."

He was out cold. Not even a muscle twitched.

Racked by guilt, she straightened and looked down at him. His mouth was open and a string of drool was just beginning to drop over his chin. She wrinkled her nose in ladylike disgust.

"Should I?" she whispered to herself, biting her lower lip. She rarely got the chance to peek at him. The troll was so unpleasant that she usually avoided him.

Except for that one terrible rainy night. She shivered just thinking about it. She'd been so lonely she thought she might snap if she had no one to talk to. It had been wrong to summon the troll. She should have left him be. Left him as her magic had made him.

She shouldn't have turned him back into himself that rainy night. But he had eased the howl inside her, if for only a few days.

And then he had cursed her for making her crazed with want to do such a bad thing again.

"I mustn't." Her eyes filled with an equal mix of dread and curiosity. It had been so long since she'd released the spell and gotten a good look at his real face.

The troll let out a small moan and she knew she had to make her decision. He was waking up. She didn't think she could control him if she changed him and he awoke.

The tips of her fingers ran down his homely brow. In the blink of an eye, her magic took away the troll's visage and revealed instead the face of a handsome, black-haired man. The troll's stumpy body disappeared too, but his clothes remained, now nothing more than tight rags on a large man's form. Instead of a dwarf slumped against the corner of the wall, Skya's touch had removed the magic that had kept the troll a prisoner. In his place, there was a lean, hard man, his head tipped forward in an unconscious state, his real legs, long and well-muscled by the many years of gripping a destrier, outstretched before him.

"My prince," Skya whispered, unable to take her eyes off him. His handsomeness, as always, stole her breath away. Aidan's brow was fair, his nose straight and fine, his lips hard and . . . and . . . lying.

Her expression grew thunderous and she forced herself to be rational. She had to use caution. She mustn't get too close. Her little pet was dangerous. Even more so when her magic did not keep him contained as a troll. A year ago, Prince Aidan had come riding through her woods to make war on her poor father. She'd had no choice but to detain him. And what better way to do it than to turn the prince into a troll? She rarely changed him back. The troll was never vulnerable enough for her to do it. And she was afraid of Aidan. The prince hated her.

Though there had been that one rainy night. . . .

Unable to ignore her desire to be near him, she seized the moment, discarded her prudence, and bent down to him, her hand this time caressing a beautiful male face. Unconscious, he looked almost boyish, impossibly handsome and rugged. A black curl fell across his forehead and she longed to tweak it. It would be wonderful to watch him laugh and look at her with warmth in his blue eyes. And not worry about losing her life.

He was the lion tamed, but even when her spell had kept him as a troll, she knew she couldn't tame him forever. Now she had other worries. Her head pounded with the agony of her sister's news. The king was looking for his son. There would be war now surely if this unconscious man before her was not found.

She'd always known one day she would have to let him go. Now the day was fast approaching. But how could she let him go? How could she watch him run from her as if she were some terrible freak of nature, never to see him again in these dark, lonely woods? He was her only company. Unwilling company, sometimes even hateful company, but he was the companion she'd desperately needed. No, she couldn't let him go. She couldn't forget about him and that one long, rainy night. . . .

A large, steely hand reached out and clamped over her slender wrist. Her breath caught in her throat. She looked down and terror seized her.
Prince Aidan was awake.

Ravenna's eyes popped open, the dreamed incident startling her awake. Her hands itched to jot it down, but no pen was available. In the carriage interior, her gaze found Trevallyan and she thought of the children in her dream whom she had been recounting the tale to.

She hadn't known who the children were, and now their identity haunted her. She wondered if they were their children. Hers and Trevallyan's. The idea caused her no small anguish.

"We're in County Lir," Trevallyan said, his face strangely pallid. "Have a look. See what your reluctance has wrought."

Her palms grew sweaty and her mouth dry. She rolled up the oiled linen window flap and gazed out at a place she didn't know.

The miles of green potato fields were blotched with sickly yellow. Men and women in raggedy clothes lined the roadside, desperately digging what crop had not yet been tainted by blight. But the crop was clearly ruined anyway. Those potatoes mature enough now wouldn't keep through winter. Blight was that thorough.

A few of the men nodded to the passing carriage, their faces white and afraid. Ravenna found she couldn't look them in the eyes. The emotion there was like a barren, wind-mangled landscape made even more pitiful because of the abundance that had gone before it.

"Dear God, it's worse than we thought it would be," she whispered, her throat thick with pity. Her beloved Lir, so green, so fertile, now seemed as hostile as a witch's womb.

"I'm bringing in cattle and perhaps corn and we'll see if it will fare better." He spoke in a painfully controlled monotone.

"Yes," she answered, hardly looking at him while the land rolled by, scarred by this terrible disease.

"But I cannot cure Lir if you are the cause."

Her gaze riveted to him. She could hardly believe what he'd said. She choked, "Surely you don't think—"

"I believe it more and more now." His face was unnaturally pale. He looked angry. She was suddenly, irrationally afraid.

"But you can't. The *geis* is nothing more than superstition."

"Is this blight from our imaginations?" His fine lips curled in contempt. "It looks all too real to me."

"Blight is all over Ireland. We've avoided it; now it's our turn." She hated the way her voice shook, but she had never seen Trevallyan so. He sat in a dark corner of the carriage, dressed in his usual black, his eyes glittering with an almost unnatural gleam. She could do nothing but tremble under his gaze.

"And were the attempts on my life just another occurrence in a reign of bad luck?"

She swallowed, unsure how to proceed. "Your thinking has turned in this direction because it's to your benefit to believe in the *geis*. It gives a reason for all the troubles—you can blame them on me, then get me to do your bidding. But I won't, I tell you. I won't." She jutted out her chin and gave him a look of defiance. It rankled that he would try to dump all the troubles on her. It offended her and burdened her with an unwarranted sense of guilt as well.

"I am a rational man. A well-educated man." His hand reached across the carriage and touched her cheek. "But I can't explain what's happened here. I can explain this blight and the mischief of these hooligans. But I can't figure out my unholy desire for you, and if the *geis* will explain it, then I fear I am compelled to believe it."

She closed her eyes and took a deep breath. Thank God they were home. She just wanted to get away from him. She wanted to think without him making demands upon her that she found herself succumbing to and regretting.

She stared out the window. They had passed the *ogham* stone now and were just about to cross the dusty road that led to Grania's cottage. Taking the situation in hand, she reached forward to the trapdoor right behind the driver's legs. Before Trevallyan could block her, she said to the driver. "Please, stop the carriage here. I'll be getting off."

The trap was slammed shut by Trevallyan's hand. She'd suspected he'd be angered by her dictates to the driver, but she didn't care. She was going home to think, and he would let her do it or forever lose his chance for her love.

The carriage rolled to a halt. She had her hand on the gold door handle before he could stop her.

But all at once, she was pulled back. His arms circled her waist and he held her captive on his lap.

"You will not do this," he said, his voice a mere rasp.

"You must let me go. I am not your prisoner, and you cannot continue to make me one." She pulled on his locked fingers. They didn't budge.

"Driver, drive on!" he shouted, unwilling to free his hands and make use of the trapdoor.

There was a pause of indecision. The horses jangled their harnesses and stamped their feet, anxious to get to their hay at the end of the ride.

"No! Wait! You must let me out of here!" she screamed, pulling and struggling with Trevallyan's iron hands.

"Drive on, I said! Or you'll be out there in the blighted fields by morning with no employment!"

She moaned and made one last attempt to be free. But the carriage began to roll, throwing her hard against his chest.

"What are you doing? Have you gone mad? I'm not going back to the castle with you. I'm not!" she said through clenched teeth.

"I won't let you go. I'll never get you back if I do." The words were steely, yet mournful. If they hadn't sealed her fate, she might have almost felt pity for him.

"Don't make me hate you," she moaned, throwing her head back against the seat, his hands like a vise around her waist.

"If you can't love me, then hate me. Hate me, I tell you, for 'tis the next closest thing." He loomed over her.

To her agony, his hands gripped both her cheeks and forced her head to be still. Then he crushed his mouth on hers. And sentenced her with a kiss.

Chapter 24

SHE WAS his prisoner.

Ravenna had been locked in the keep room for a day. Not once did she see Trevallyan. Maids brought her pen and paper, meals and baths, but no word of the man who ruled the castle, no assurances that his madness was soon to end. She paced and stared at the doomed yellow fields that ringed the *ogham* stone. At night, she had tried to scratch out more pages of her novel, but the candlelight made her sleepy. Finally she had crawled into the huge four-poster bed—which was, after so much time spent in it, her intimate friend—and tried to slumber, but she was tortured with wakefulness, her thoughts churning with anger and ill-fated plans.

She was caught in a maze of no escape. Locked in the tower, there was no leaving it except through the servants' door or the formal doors, and both were tightly fastened. And she was sickened by the thought of how Grania must be worrying about her. She knew to expect Ravenna back by now. Had Trevallyan sent word? What would he say? *I've taken your granddaughter captive. I don't know when she'll be returned.* It was ridiculous. The entire situation. She had never seen Niall in such a black mood as when he brought her kicking and screaming to the tower bedroom. He looked as if he hated her every bit as much as she hated him. He would not listen to reason. He would not free her. Even when she refused to allow his valet entrance to his dressing room so that the master might have a fresh change of clothes, no word had come from Trevallyan. There was no anger, no disapproval, no note. Simply a silence. And when she saw the tailor arrive from Belfast this morning, she knew he had chosen to send for new clothes to be made rather than continue to challenge her.

The wall of silence was beginning to wear on her. She thought at least she would get to vent her emotions when he came to her for the night. But he had not come. He ignored her. She was his invisible prisoner. Even the pleasure she gave him was not enough to lure him into her lair. And if she could not even come face-to-face with her captor, she despaired of ever gaining her freedom.

With every passing hour, her nerves grew more and more frayed, her luxurious jail more and more stifling.

She rose from the bed and turned up the lamp. The pen and paper were ready for her on Trevallyan's overly-carved mahogany desk. She should be writing, using the time to finish her novel, but Skya and Aidan seemed ethereal, as if she'd dreamed them and had now awakened without being able to recall all the details. Her mind was too full of anxiety and dread to surrender to imagination.

Trevallyan had finally managed to take that away from her as well. The thought sent a shroud of despondency over her. Nothing seemed worthwhile in this cage. She would never get her novel published. Trevallyan had been right. It was the silly dream of a stupid Irish girl who was deluded by an education she could never use.

She sat at the desk, staring at the mockingly white sheets of paper until dawn, when Katey brought in her hot water and breakfast. With a slight frown on her face, the woman asked her if there was anything else she needed. Ravenna shook her head and glared. Hours of pleading had yet to move Katey to let her go. Now she no longer felt like fighting.

Katey left. Ravenna pushed aside her tray, for the second day in a row refusing to eat.

※

Lord Chesham jumped from his mighty black steed and threw the reins to the stable boy.

"It's a mighty fine gallop today, lad! 'Tis just what I've come from London for!" he called to the stable master, an Irishman old enough to be his father.

"Lord Trevallyan awaits you in the library, my lord," the man said as the stable boy took the Thoroughbred away to walk him in the yard.

"Library? Fine, fine," Chesham grunted, pulling off his gloves. In the hall, he threw them and his top hat to Greeves. He entered the library, emitted a low whistle and said, "Cousin, you look terrible. Not the gout, I hope."

"*Gout.* Christ almighty, I'm not that old." Trevallyan looked up from his desk and the pile of papers stacked upon it. He gave Chesham a rather disapproving once-over and said, "I've been told you've been here for days. Ever since I left for Antrim. London didn't suit you?"

"No, indeed. If the castle weren't so damned big, cousin, you'd have seen me last night."

"Well, I didn't." He shoved aside the bills and stood. "Greeves just informed me you plan to have a ball here in less than a week."

"Nothing more than the usual. Perhaps two hundred."

Trevallyan crossed his arms over his chest. "Cancel it. This is not time for a ball. The people of Lir are terrified. I won't have them seeing us dancing while they weep."

"Invite them then."

"Why not tell them to eat cake instead?"

Chesham donned a bored demeanor and threw himself into a leather wing chair. "Don't be such a pill, cousin. Perhaps they could use some cheer. Besides, you'll get them all out of this blight thing. I know it."

"It won't come without a price. I've got cattle to buy and corn to haul way over here. If I'm to pay for their salvation, I can't afford balls, too."

"Bloody hell you can, and you know it. You'll buy them all a flock of sheep and triple the profits before a body can blink." Chesham studied his nails, rubbing them on the velvet collar of his pink huntmaster's jacket.

Trevallyan merely ground his teeth. "Still, this is *not* a good time for a ball—"

"No, it's the best time for a ball." Chesham looked at him. "I haven't seen Ravenna in a while. There's rumors she's been seen here at the castle in my absence. You aren't chasing after her, are you? I had hopes of wooing her myself, you know."

Niall's expression grew taut as if he were utterly displeased. "Do you think a ball would change her mind toward you?"

"Ah, but think of it. Music, champagne, waltzes in the garden. I can do a lot with those things."

"Do what? You just want to get a leg over and you know it."

"Certainly. What man wouldn't—" Before Chesham could finish the sentence, Trevallyan was standing over him with a grip nearly tearing his velvet lapels. "Wh-what is it?" he stuttered, bewildered by Niall's anger.

"I want you to leave the castle. Accept it. You're not going to have Ravenna. Not now. Not ever."

"I'm not going to have Ravenna. Not now. Not ever," Chesham repeated stupidly. "Now will you please let me go?"

Trevallyan abruptly released his jacket.

Chesham slumped back in the chair. "What was that all about? Have you taken a liking to her, then?"

When Trevallyan didn't deny it, Chesham quirked his lips in a wry smile. "So is she to become your mistress?"

"I've asked her to become my wife."

Chesham looked as if he'd just been knocked clean off a steeplechaser. "Are you telling me the truth?"

"What do you think?" Trevallyan snapped.

Chesham gulped. "I'll admit, I've a fancy for the girl. She's beautiful, but—but—she's a commoner. Worse than that, she's Irish. Dear lord, Niall, you'll tire of her and then . . . aaarrgh, I can't even think of it. It's too awful. *Lady* Trevallyan . . ." he muttered to himself, as if he were putting the name on a Dublin doxy.

"You forget yourself, *cousin*." Trevallyan's baleful stare could have pierced granite. "You forget that my mother was Irish, my people are Irish, *I'm* Irish."

Chesham's jaw bunched with annoyance. "She's not your kind of Irish, and you know it. You're bloody having me on, aren't you? We'll all be laughing at this at dinner."

Trevallyan clasped his hands behind his back and looked out the window to the ravaged fields. "No, it's true. I'm in love with her. I've asked her to be my wife, and she has thus far," he paused as if he felt a pain to his gut, "declined."

Chesham rose to his feet, appearing as if he were doing his best to absorb the shock of the news. He looked as if he wanted to make light of the situation, but as if he'd recalled Trevallyan's violent temper, he seemed to most definitely think better of it.

"How could she decline an offer of marriage to a wealthy, powerful earl, one of the most important men of the county, perhaps of Ireland as well?" Chesham's confusion wove through his voice.

" 'Tis a long and painful story." Trevallyan sighed. His aqua eyes searched the fields for hope. He seemed to find none. "One which I'm not inclined to explain. Just suffice it to say I'm in no mood for a ball."

"Perhaps that's your problem. Perhaps she wants to be courted. A ball's just the thing for that."

Trevallyan spun around to face him so quickly, Chesham startled.

"From the mouths of babes . . ."

"What was it I said?" Chesham shrilled.

"Perhaps 'tis the thing to do after all." Niall's brow furrowed as if he were deep in thought. "A ball. A grand county-wide celebration. We'll let the people of this county thumb their noses at the blight for one magical evening, and there I'll announce my plans for a new economy for Lir—of cattle and sheep and corn. Then Ravenna will see that I'm not . . ." His voice lowered to a hush. ". . . not . . ."

"Not what?" Chesham piped in.

Trevallyan looked at him as if he had just now noticed him. He didn't answer.

Chesham shook his head in despair. "If the situation's as bleak as your face, coz, I recommend you try anything and everything."

"Perhaps I shall," Trevallyan answered absentmindedly, already ringing for Greeves.

⧖

Ravenna knew when Trevallyan had entered the apartment. It wasn't that she heard him, exactly; rather, she felt him. As Grania felt spirits by the imprint of emotions they left behind on the mortal earth, she felt the anger enter the room like a specter who had taken up haunting.

She said nothing. Looking up from the desk where her writing had soured on the page like the blotch she had left with her pen, she mutely met his gaze, took the inkwell in her grasp, and hurled it at his head.

He stepped neatly aside. It crashed against the wall, leaving behind a weeping stain of indigo.

"Is that how this is to be?" he asked grimly.

"How else would you have it? I told you a slave has no love for his master." She grasped a small Staffordshire figurine of Isis and threatened with it as well. "Unless you plan to free me, get out."

"I came to invite you to Chesham's ball." His gaze wandered to the direction of his dressing room. "And to get a change of clothes. Even my tailor can't work miracles overnight."

"Oh no you won't." She skittered toward the dressing-room doorway. Holding the Staffordshire goddess as a weapon, she blocked his entrance. "Get out. Your clothing is my hostage here. You want fresh linen, then you'll free me first."

He stepped toward her. She lifted the figurine higher.

He ducked just as the piece sailed over his head and shattered against the carved doorway in the antechamber, scarring it.

"Are you through with this temper tantrum?" he asked quietly.

Her eyes filled with tears of frustration. "You call yourself a modern thinker, yet you hold me captive here as if you were as backward as your American slaveholding friends."

"What choice do I have? If I set you running, you'll run so far I'll never catch you."

"You've gotten that right," she spat as he lifted her aside and walked into his dressing room.

He chose a few necessary articles from the wardrobe drawers and faced her once more. "No opinion on my ball?"

"You must be mad if you think I would attend a ball as your prisoner." Her eyes blazed with fury.

"Even if I were to invite the whole county? Even if your grandmother were to attend and it would worry her sick if she were to believe you a prisoner here?"

Ravenna stared at him, despising his blackmail. "You know I'll escape if you let me down from here to attend a ball."

"You'll never leave my side."

"Impossible. You can't keep me with you all night."

"Try me."

They stared at each other, locked in a battle of wills.

Finally she said, "Go on, have your ball. I'll be gone from here by then. Even if I have to summon Malachi to come help me."

He twisted his lips in a terrible smile. "If Malachi shows here, I'll kill him and well you know it. Is his death worth a little freedom?"

"I hate you," she whispered.

He stepped toward her and looked down at her, almost nose to nose. "Savor it."

He quirked his lips in farewell and locked the door behind him.

⊗

The afternoon brought a flurry of activity for the usually quiet keep. Katey came with servants bringing the copper bathtub, but she left as soon as Ravenna sank into the fragrantly scented water.

And she took with her Ravenna's only dress, the blue woolen.

Stumped, Ravenna soaked, and wondered what Katey was up to. It only took a few minutes before the servant returned, dress in hand, and then Ravenna didn't need to question her. By the brigade of maids trailing in from the dressing room, all bearing bolts of silks and satins in their small arms, Ravenna knew trickery was at hand.

"Tell Lord Trevallyan that I don't want any gowns made," she said as soon as she had risen from the tub and wrapped a linen towel around her wet body.

"You cannot be wearing this old gown forever, miss. And what about the ball? It's in two days." Katey laid the tired blue wool gown across a chair, readying it for her mistress to don once more.

Angered, Ravenna pulled her old, rather snug, chemise down over her bosom so quickly, she actually ripped it. "Bloody hell," she murmured, poking her finger through the seam beneath her arm.

"What did you say, miss?"

"One of Himself's favorite expressions." Ravenna grabbed her corset and began to lace it. All the while she fumed. Katey certainly had cheek, there was no doubt about it. The servant had never quite approved of Ravenna's illegitimacy. The woman seemed the last sort to go along with this kidnapping, but here she was, the devil's handmaid, assisting Trevallyan with every task.

Ravenna glanced at her. Sadly, she knew all too well why Katey went along with it. The rules were different for Ascendency. And they were different for outcasts. A decent sort could look the other way for one but not the other.

"I'm not going to Chesham's fool ball, and that's it." Ravenna wriggled into the bodice of her gown and shook out the skirt. The gown was no better than a rag, even compared to Katey's plain black linen dress.

"You've got to go to the ball, miss. Everyone's invited. The entire county. Besides," Katey's voice lowered, "I hate to think what Himself'd do if you failed to show." She ignored Ravenna's attempted retort. Stepping to the bed, she dismissed the maidservants and held up each bolt of exquisite fabric. "Which do you like the best? The master wants you to pick out five."

Ravenna flicked her gaze at the costly mound on the bed. There was a moire the color of bordeaux, a heavy purple satin stripe, even a plaid taffeta in subtle shades of rose, black, and green. All of them were gorgeous. Costly. Downright heavenly. In any other circumstance she might have gloried in having a gown made of any one of them. But not as a gift from Trevallyan. She wasn't his mistress, nor his slave. She could clothe herself.

"Take these away. I won't choose any of them." She turned her back to the bed and hooked the front of her blue gown.

"But, miss—" Katey closed her mouth upon seeing Ravenna's dark frown. "All right. I'll take them away," she said uneasily. "But don't be surprised if Himself makes *me* chose the silks for you. He was the one who told me to get your measurements from that dress you're wearing now."

"Just take them away. I don't want any dresses." Ravenna turned to her. "You'll tell him, won't you?"

Katey nodded her neatly pinned gray head. "I will, miss. You can be sure of it."

Katey left the room, locking the servants' jib door behind her. Ravenna squelched the urge to throw something at it as well.

Dinner came and went without Katey mentioning the dresses. Ravenna couldn't have cared less if they had sent the silks back to France, or Spitalfields, or wherever they came from. She didn't want to think of them anymore.

But then evening came, the long stretch of darkness before bed, with nothing to do but huddle by the fire, squint at a book in the candlelight. Depression fell over her as she despondently stared at the flickering hearth. She wanted to go home, not just because she missed Grania, but because she wanted the company, too. All these days in the tower with no one but Katey to speak to were beginning to wear on her.

She tried not to think about Trevallyan, but her thoughts wandered to him against her will. She wondered what he was doing now. Greeves had probably served him dinner in the small tapestry room. No doubt, he had had company in to dine. Chesham was at the castle. The two men were probably right now laughing over some bawdy tale in the library. Trevallyan probably hadn't thought of her all day.

She shifted in her chair, forlornly playing with a thread that had come loose on her sleeve. Trevallyan was not to enter her thoughts, she commanded herself; still, the image of him smiling, laughing, brooding seeped into her mind. Too, came the picture of herself that afternoon, bored and restless. The thought of it made her cringe. She had had nothing to do so she'd entered the dressing room and decided to explore its contents in hopes of finding perhaps something that might help her leave the keep. She'd found nothing, except another disturbing revelation.

Upon opening the wardrobe where he kept his shirts and frock coats neatly hung on gold hooks, she'd been struck by a scent. It was Trevallyan's smell. It lingered inside his clothing and permeated the mahogany interior of the case, and gave her a distinctly strange feeling deep inside her belly, as if her body were reacting to the scent, even if her mind would not. She hadn't wanted to, but she had closed her eyes and tried to imagine his face. She'd succeeded with aching clarity, just as she was succeeding now. And her punishment for such folly was to feel even lonelier than she had before.

She pulled the thread and rent her sleeve. Feeling tears of frustration come to her eyes, she stood and headed for the bookshelves. She was not going to think of Trevallyan. She was *not*.

But she did think of Trevallyan. And as if her thoughts had conjured up the reality, she looked to the door and there he stood, watching her from the shadowy threshold, his eyes needful, yet angry.

"Have you come to let me out, or would you have another figurine hurled at your head?" She raised one eyebrow, mocking his own mannerism. Coolly, she turned her attention back to the tomes on the shelf, hoping she well hid the fact that her hands were shaking and the room had suddenly turned warm. A little too warm.

"Katey tells me you haven't been eating or writing." He pulled the doors closed behind him and stepped inside the circle of light.

Ravenna wanted to growl. So that was why every chance she got, Katey shuffled through the papers on Trevallyan's desk. "I hope you pay Katey well. Spying should not come cheap."

"She's loyal." He eased himself down in the chair opposite hers, the worn one.

"Too loyal," she muttered.

"I can understand your lack of appetite, but why haven't you been writing?"

She turned around, her fury a magnificent sight to see. "How could you possibly think I could do anything here?"

"I want you to write." His gaze never wavered from her face. "You need to write."

Filled with doubt, her eyes were unable to lie. In a low, defeated tone, she said, "I've decided not to write anymore. It's a waste of time. I believe you now when you say I'd never have gotten it published."

"Ridiculous. Your writing was excellent. I want to hear more of the tale. Tell it to me."

She couldn't believe it. He was now commanding her to write. The man had no end to his gall. "I'm not about to spend the evening with my captor, entertaining him with faerie tales."

He kicked her chair a few inches nearer to her. In his usual arrogant manner, he said, "Sit down and spin me a tale. Tell me more about this little heroine of yours. And then tomorrow, you'll have something to write."

"I won't." She furrowed her brow and studied the books on the shelf. The subjects were about as titillating as watching Father Nolan eat cabbage soup.

"Come. Read to me a tale that's yet been written."

She squeezed her eyes shut. She didn't want to do this. Any time spent with him was spent as a traitor to her own self-worth.

Slowly she turned to face him. Hating herself, yet oddly grateful for the company, she lowered herself upon the seat opposite him.

"What's her name?"

She knew what he meant. "Skya," she whispered.

"And him?" He stared at her in the firelight, his face stern and unnatural in the shadows. She felt as if summoned to perform by Cuchulain.

"Aidan," she whispered.

"And where did you last leave them?"

Ravenna touched her flushed cheeks. Her gaze was held in bondage to his. "Must I tell you?"

"You want to tell me, my love," he said, his voice a rough whisper. "You're a bard. You're a bard, though you might not know it yet."

She wet her lips. Hesitant and uneasy, she began to speak.

Skya twisted her arm, but the grip was like an iron band that grew tighter the more she struggled. Moaning, she slumped against the mud wall and felt fear trickle like cold rainwater down her spine.

"Let go of my arm," she whispered, frightened of his angry blue eyes.

"It's my turn to take you captive." His handsome features grew taut with supressed rage. "Do you know what it's like living under that bridge, in the dampness? Upon my grave, I'll never do it again."

"You know you can come stay in the cottage with me. But you don't behave." She tugged on her arm.

He held fast, yet admirably refrained from hurting her. "Behave. 'Tis laughable. One day I'll be king of all Clancullen. I'm a prince, not your little puppy."

"I—I don't want you to be my puppy." She lowered her eyes. Her cheeks flamed. "I just want you to be kind. To like me . . ."

He rolled his eyes. "Like you? You cast a spell on me, turn me into a hideous troll, throw me beneath that bridge, and you want me to like you? No mortal could ever like a witch such as you."

"But there was that one night."

Her answer seemed to make him pause, as if he, too, were remembering. The expression in his eyes grew dark and distant. His jaw flexed as if he were grinding his teeth. "It was storming that night. Sometimes I don't believe it even happened."

"It did," she whispered, wishing she could again put her arms around his hard, bulky chest and lie with him on her pallet of straw.

"Then you put a spell on me and made me do it," he said crossly.

"But you know I didn't." She put her hand out in supplication.

"Witch," he muttered as if it were the most terrible name he could call her.

"I didn't want to be a witch. Does that make a difference?"

"No. You're a witch, and the fact that you don't have straggly gray hair and warts all over your nose makes me think that you hold a spell over your appearance." He grabbed a heavy hank of gold hair and pulled her gently down to him. "You see my true self. Now show me yours."

"You see it," she confessed in low tones.

"I don't believe you." He let go of her hair and ran his fingertips across

her cheek, down her slim nose. "You're too beautiful. No ugly, vile, wart-
nosed witch could look like you."

"If you talk that way to me again, I'll turn you back into a troll." She
twisted her arm to be free once more, but he held her in a vise. Meeting his
gaze, she wondered if he ever knew how much he hurt her. His sarcasm
wounded like Toledo swords.

"If you ever turn me back into a troll, so help me God, there's not a man
in the kingdom who would blame me if I killed you."

She gave him a hurt-filled glance. "Why must you say such things?"

"Why must you hold me here? Why must you keep me as a troll?"

He leaned toward her like a stalker.

She leaned back, terrified.

"If you ever turn me again into that beast, I'll—"

He never finished. The prince was gone.

"I'll kill you! I'll kill you! I swear I will!" The troll squealed, jumping up
and down in the corner.

Skya stood and rubbed her sore arm. She hadn't wanted the troll to
return, but the prince had frightened her with his black, angry looks. Instinct
just drove her sometimes, as it had done with the dragon. She wished Aidan
could understand that and quit frightening her.

Her gaze settled on the troll. The prince made a better sight than the ugly
little ogre, but Aidan's strength was far more fearful than his.

"Begone, then. Back to your bridge."

"I won't! I won't!" The troll bunched his little fists and waved them
impotently at her.

She hurled the worst kind of insult. She laughed. "Begone. Go back to
your damp, dark bridge."

The troll quit jumping. He stood staring at her with sad, dumb eyes.

"So you don't like that bridge, do you? You'd like to stay here, by the fire."
She walked to her hearth and stirred something in a black cauldron. "I've
mead—and honeycakes. My friend the old owl from the hazel tree even
brought me a rabbit for my supper." She glanced at him from the corner of
her eye. "Prince Aidan, you're welcome to return, if you behave."

The troll clasped his hands in front of him and bowed his head. The
picture of contrition.

She laughed again. Another evening with him was exactly her heart's desire. When she had brought him from the bridge that terrible rainy night, Aidan had spoken of his father, and war, and kingdoms. Gently, he had held her because, she suspected, the darkness under the bridge was just as lonely as the comfort of the cottage. In the rain, there was nowhere to flee. She offered him mead and honeycakes then, and he'd eaten enough for a battalion. And then, chilled from the rain and so far from civilization she supposed he'd half–given up on ever seeing another human again, he'd pulled her to the pallet, and made ferocious love to her until they were both sticky and satiated. They fell asleep in the dying firelight.

She awoke alone.

It had taken her all day to find him. Magic towed him back to the cottage; betrayal put him back underneath the bridge. But nothing had repaired her broken heart. There was no ocean great enough to hold all the tears she had cried. In the throes of passion, she had told him she loved him. And he had run from her as if she were—as if she were—a witch.

Her eyes grew sad. She looked at the troll and bit her soft lower lip. "Perhaps I better not be so foolish. Perhaps you'd better go back to the bridge."

As if the creature were a child, he grabbed a small three-legged stool and sat in the corner, head bowed, hands folded. He was so homely and pitiful, she could almost forget he was an ogre of her own creation, not of God's.

"All right. I'll let Prince Aidan come back." She picked up the skirts of her linen kirtle and squatted before him. "But you must behave."

He nodded.

She snapped her fingers again.

The prince returned with all the fury of a cyclone.

He lunged for her.

She snapped her fingers.

The troll returned, even more furious than before.

She smiled in relief. If not for the tiny three-legged stool tripping Prince Aidan, she might be the one stamping her feet in fury.

"Why can't you behave? Do you hate me that much?" She wasn't sure she really wanted the answer.

The troll righted the three-legged stool and resumed his penitent posture. She chose to ignore him for the moment and instead, she walked to the board and picked up a honeycake.

Torturing him, she ate every sweet crumb right in front of him.

"There." She rubbed her belly. "Delicious. And look, I've so many left, I don't know how I'll eat them all." Her lids lowered mischievously. "And what do trolls eat for their supper? Cold toads? A poisonous mushroom or two?"

The troll's face twisted in disgust. When she pointed to the door, urging him to exit, his face twisted in horror.

"So you want to stay and have all my mead and honeycakes, do you?"

He nodded.

"I'll give you one more chance. Be a good little prince, or there'll be the devil to pay."

She snapped her fingers. The prince looked up.

"How quaint you look," she said to him.

Aidan's mouth curved in derision as he found he was seated on the tiny little stool.

"How beautiful you look." He stood but came no farther.

She blushed. He didn't know it, but when he was kind, the spell he wove around her was far stronger than all her magic.

"Come. I'll pour you some mead." She smiled sweetly and dipped a cup in the cauldron. She placed it on the board within his reach.

"You may sit if you like."

Cautiously, he made his way around the board and took a seat on the bench near the hearth.

He drank his hot mead and didn't take his eyes from her. He watched her like a knight watches his enemy.

"You have to release me, you know," he said in the deep-timbred voice of her dreams.

"Why?" she whispered.

"I eavesdropped on you and your sister. My father is going to storm your father's castle. King Turoe will murder everyone. I'm his only son."

"It was to keep you from murdering them that I've kept you here."

He scowled. A breathtaking sight, she thought, in one so handsome. "I came through these woods because I was lost. Indeed, my journey was to investigate your father's artillery, but I never quite had the chance, now, did I?"

She smiled a little sheepishly, but the news pressing on her made her quickly grow glum. "King Turoe will be defeated."

"His army is stronger than yours. You know it."

She stared into the flickering fire. "If I let you go, you'll join your father and take the castle anyway. It's just an excuse. All from Clancullen are warmongers."

" 'Tis our right to gain land if we have the strength to do it."

She glanced at him. He was so strong, and his convictions so simple and pure. She had no doubts he could take her father's castle even without King Turoe's help. "But we are a peaceful people. We don't want war."

He slowly reached out a hand and covered her right one, the one that made magic. "Witches do not aid the peace. They only stir up hatred and loathing and fear."

"I don't want to be a witch." She cursed the tears that wet her eyes. It was time to be brave, not weep like a child. "I've exiled myself here in order to keep peace. I can't let you or your father spoil it."

"But the peace is spoiled. Right now, my father might be taking his broadsword and—"

"No!" she cried out, jumping to her feet. Her mead sloshed onto the hard-packed earthen floor. "Don't even think such things."

"Do you love your family? Then save them," he commanded.

"But how? Which is the right path? I can't let you go only to find you've made war on them."

He grabbed her, one muscular arm sliding around her narrow waist, one hand interlocking fingers with her right hand. The hand that made magic.

A panic seized her. She couldn't protect herself if he held her hand that way. She tried to pull free but it was useless. He was too strong. Even if he did relinquish the arm around her waist, if he held on to her hand, she'd be as weak as a mortal.

She stared up at him, a sickening feeling settling in the pit of her stomach. Without the ability to use her right hand, she was powerless. By his smile, well he knew it.

He looked down at her, his mouth handsomely curved in a wicked grin. "Now you're my prisoner, aren't you?"

She licked her lips, her gaze captured by his. "I'm your prisoner until you let go of my hand, which you must do eventually."

"Yes, but in the meantime, I can torture you as you tortured me."

"But how did I—?"

"That rainy night—you think I wanted to come here and make love to a witch?"

Her azure eyes glittered with tears. Depression seemed to weigh upon her body until it slumped like an old woman's. "I did not think the night so terrible," she whispered, holding back a sob.

"It was exquisite."

His face hardened with some strange emotion she could not quite identify.

"You seduced me," he whispered. "I didn't want to make love to you, and after you took me, you cursed me with it. You were all I could think about underneath that slimy dark bridge. But I was a little impotent troll. I could never have you again unless you took pity on me and changed me back." His lips trailed hotly along her ear. "But you've turned me into myself again, and here you are, mine for the taking."

"Yes, but as you said my beauty could be just a facade. . . ." she panted, his mouth leaving her breathless.

"Show me your old ugly self, if you have one, and perhaps I'll leave you alone. It's your only salvation."

She tilted her face toward his and studied him. She could, of course, change her appearance at will, but she was herself now, as he was himself. Her eyes darkened. Also, she wanted him. There was a naughty little voice deep inside that cajoled her into going along.

He whispered against her hair. "So where is she, the old wart-nosed hag?"

"She doesn't exist," she answered, dooming herself.

"Good. Good," he rasped, covering her mouth with his.

Her free hand instinctively tried to stop him. It rode up his hard, hairy chest, all of him that was exposed by the ripped rags that were once the troll's clothes. She pushed on him, but it was like pushing on a wall; he didn't give. He just kept kissing her, his large hand running up and down the back of her linen kirtle until he sent a shower of delight through her belly.

"I knew you were a witch the minute I kissed you," he groaned, burying his face in her golden hair.

"But how does a witch kiss?" she asked artlessly.

He chuckled. The sound made his chest tremble beneath her hand. "I *suppose it must be all the practice you've had holding men captive and taking from them their sanity."*

"Oh no. . . ." Her eyes widened in amazement. "There are no others. There's only been you. I love only you."

He seemed stunned by her confession, and she wondered briefly how he would use it against her. She prayed he would not.

"What spells you weave," he murmured before taking her chin in hand and lifting her for another kiss. When he was through, he stared at their clasped hands and said, "Let's find your pallet."

"And tomorrow?" she asked in a scared, hushed voice.

"Tomorrow I'll be gone, and this time I'll make sure you don't follow me. It'll be your turn to want what you cannot have."

"But you must never let go of my hand. Promise me, you'll never let go of my hand," she pleaded softly.

With a searing kiss, he took all thoughts from her mind. And left the promise unspoken.

Ravenna looked up at Trevallyan as if just remembering he was still in the room. He stared at her, seated in his chair, his eyes piercing, yet brilliantly cloaking whatever genuine emotion he felt at that moment.

Unable to stop herself, she flushed, hating the way her cheeks revealed all her insecurities. "I've gone on too long."

He said nothing. There was simply that piercing aqua stare, bathed golden in the firelight.

"I think perhaps the story isn't working. After all, who would believe it? A woman holding a prince captive—"

"You must finish it."

The conviction in his voice surprised her.

"For what purpose? To see it rot in a bureau with my hair ribbons?"

"No, to see it published and in the homes of all who would admire it." He shifted his gaze to his desk and all the unused paper and ink. "Tomorrow you're to write all this down."

"I'm to write by your decree?"

"Not by my decree, but because you love to do it. And because . . ." He stared at her through half-closed lids. "because you *can* do it, as others cannot."

"If I publish, I shall move to Dublin," she said convincingly.

"No, by that time you'll be my wife. What a shock to tell the peerage that Lady Trevallyan is actually a writer." He smiled and lowered his gaze to his clasped hands. "In fact I can hardly wait."

"You're so sure of everything."

He stared at her, clearly not having missed the acid in her voice. The old anger in his eyes was back. "I'm not sure of you. You're so difficult, you make everything else seem easy."

She said nothing.

He rose from his chair and stepped to her. "Good night." He caressed her cheek. "If you get lonely, summon me."

She turned her head away. How could he think she was not lonely in this tower, far from anyone who cared for her?

She watched him leave. He cared for her in his perverse, needful way. If only he would take his love further and let her go.

Because then she just might come back.

Chapter 25

RAVENNA WAS ready for the ball. As threatened, Katey chose the fabrics for her, and five gowns were ordered. Now, though Ravenna had fought it, she was dressed, and she stood in front of an oak cheval mirror and studied her reflection.

Katey had coiled her hair into smooth heavy loops and pinned them to her nape, but even under a violet-scented pomade, downy curls sprung along her hairline, giving her more of a Renaissance look than a modern one. Her gown was a royal purple satin with black hand-painted scrolls along the flounces of the skirt. The pièce de résistance of her attire, however, was not actually the dress, but the exquisite black-purple posy of velvet violets that was artfully pinned to her décolletage.

Ravenna hardly knew herself. Gone was the street urchin of old. Gone, too, was the studious young woman who had returned from Weymouth-Hampstead. In her place stood an aristocratic lady. All self-doubts and insecurities were hidden behind the gown's artful drape and flounces; physical flaws were rendered invisible. She was awestruck by the transformation;

flattered by the adornment. The new gown made her feel beautiful, and she liked the feeling. It was kissed with power.

Still she was *not* going to attend this ball, no matter how much she adored the ballgown.

"You'll be visiting with your grandmother tonight—won't you be liking that?" Katey mused as she straightened Ravenna's skirt and hooked the last hook on the back of her bodice.

"I'll like it fine. I'll tell her that Trevallyan's been holding me prisoner," she retorted, sneaking another peek at the stranger in the mirror.

"Hush now. None of that talk. You know it would only upset your grandmother for you to say such things. She thinks it's grand Himself has taken you under his wing." Katey clipped a thread from the heavily boned satin bodice and popped the tiny scissors into a drawstring purse adorned with a huge silver tassel.

"Why is everyone so uncaring of me?" Ravenna couldn't look at Katey. She didn't want the servant to see the fury in her eyes. "You treat Lord Trevallyan as if he were a god and me but a rebellious servant who doesn't know her place."

"But it's not true! We love Himself, aye, 'tis so, but we care about you, too, miss. If not for you, how would we all get along? The county would go to rack and ruin."

Ravenna spun to face her. Surprise sparked in her eyes. "So you know about the *geis,* too? Why—has everyone here known about it—even all the years I was kept ignorant?"

" 'Tis only that my sister once cleaned for Reverend Drummond. Word spreads, miss. There isn't much to talk about 'round here—or they wouldn't call the obituaries Irish entertainment, now would they?"

Ravenna smirked. She crossed her arms over her chest, careful not to crush the costly violets. "Who else knows?"

"Well, I know for certain that Greeves does. He must. He used to hoist a jar with Peter Maguire, the old mayor."

Pulling away from Katey, Ravenna flung herself onto a black needlepoint bench. "I will not be forced to marry Trevallyan."

"No," Katey answered smoothly.

"So why not let me go? You can't keep me here forever."

"You'll love him one day, miss."

"How can you know that when I don't know that?"

"Because all good men are loved in time."

Ravenna glanced at her reflection. The expression on her face certainly contrasted with the festivity of her gown. "I would think better of him if he let me go."

"Can you run so far from your destiny, Miss Ravenna?"

Ravenna watched Katey in the mirror. "I would like to try. That's all I want, just the chance to try to run free. I've got to have it."

"Then God go with you, miss. Remember: Regret is a wound that seldom heals." Katey gave her a troubled smile. She studied Ravenna's appearance, then, as if patting herself on the back for so fine a creation, she curtsied, and left the tower.

The clock in the antechamber chimed eight times at exactly the moment Trevallyan entered the tower room.

Ravenna stood at the window, watching the stream of carriages pull inside the bailey and release their passengers. Lanterns lit the broad grass lawn that swept toward the looming shadows of Briney Cliffs. Already half of Lir seemed flocked on the lawn, laughing and drinking. Somewhere a fiddler played "The Piper's Chair."

"I see Katey got you ready despite your protests."

Ravenna glanced at her visitor. Niall looked devastating. Dressed in black with a gold satin waistcoat, he was as refined and handsome as a prince from a maiden's fairy tale. Any woman would be proud to hang on his arm. Though he was not the tallest gent, nor did he possess Fabuloso's overly muscular physique, no other man could attain Trevallyan's aura of power. Even in a crowd—as Ravenna had seen time and again—all eyes were helplessly drawn to him. Lord Trevallyan didn't just enter a room, he took command of it.

As he commanded it now.

"I'm not going." She stared at him, defiantly standing her ground while his gaze raked over her attire. He clearly didn't like her rebelliousness; still, it seemed his eyes held only admiration for her appearance.

"Did you hear me? I'm not going," she announced.

"Yes, you are." His statement brooked no argument.

"What are you planning on telling people? That we're engaged despite my refusals?" She petulantly thrust out her small, pointed chin. She didn't want to act like a child, but he drove her to it. This insanity of holding her in the tower was making them both into fools.

"I don't plan on telling them anything. . . . Do you?" The corner of his mouth lifted in a wry grin. He casually walked through the antechamber, then leaned on one of the bedposts.

She snatched up her skirts and stomped past him. "They'll know I'm staying here when I appear with you. Do you really want to marry me then, with all the county believing I'm your mistress?"

"I don't care what they believe. Besides, they won't think a thing of it. Grania and Father Nolan came early. When you appear at my side, everyone will think you came with them."

"You think of everything, don't you?" she said bitterly.

"Yes."

He caught her hand and put his arms around her. A tingle went down her spine the way his hands rubbed the slick, boned satin at her waist.

Her gaze locked with his. He whispered, "And yet I haven't thought to tell you how beautiful you are tonight." His words seemed to come as an unwilling confession. "Ravenna, you take my breath away."

She closed her eyes. His hands rode well at her hips. All she had to do was tilt her head and she knew he would kiss her. His seduction once again proved to be an intoxicating elixir.

She felt cold metal slip around her neck. Her eyes popped open. In the far pier mirror she could see he'd slipped a fortune in emeralds around her neck.

"They were my mother's. The Trevallyan emeralds." He also stared in the mirror. "I thought they'd look betwitching on you . . . and they do."

Her expression clouded. "Not even jewels will make me go to this ball. I tell you, I won't go."

His fingers played upon her tightly corseted ribs. His breath tickled her bare shoulder. "But you don't want to disappoint Chesham. It's his ball, remember that. Besides, I believe the only reason he did it was in the small hope of seeing you tonight."

She arched one black eyebrow. He had finally driven her to pettiness. "Lord Chesham? Of course, it's *his* ball, isn't it? So you may tell him he may escort me downstairs. He's such a dashing young man, isn't he?"

"A true gentleman," he answered, playfully chastising her with a bite on the neck, "as you will recall when he so rudely interrupted your bath."

"But he's young and handsome, nonetheless. And he courts ever so well."

"Yes. Give him a leg over and he'll be all yours."

She broke away, irritated. Trevallyan always had the upper hand. "Have you given enough thought to the fact that I might actually win a proposal from Chesham?"

"Yes," he answered, his expression grave as he watched her walk away. "Tonight, with you in that gown, I believe any man might propose to you."

"And without this gown? Without these jewels? Am I nothing then?" She couldn't hide her wounded feelings.

He stepped behind her and wrapped his arms around her once more. His knuckles gently grazed the plump top of her breast that was barely covered by the low neckline. "If you were to go without a gown, a man might kill himself over you. So don't even think about it."

She glanced up at him. Possession lit his beautiful eyes.

He kissed her neck and murmured, "You forget, my love, I've seen you dressed and undressed. I most definitely prefer you undressed."

She wished Katey had not slipped her fan inside the silver-tasseled purse for she could have used it now. She ached to rap him on the head. Besides, she didn't know why but the normally cool tower room had become unbearably hot.

"I wish it weren't time to go. Are you going with me, or shall I send Greeves a message that I'll be detained up here for the night?"

He gave her no choice. Either go to the ball and try to escape, or fight him off the entire night. And the devil of it was her fighting skills where he was concerned were always too weak to win.

"I'll go to this bloody ball, damn you," she moaned, pulling herself from his kiss.

He brought her close again, clearly relishing the struggle. "You don't have to. I've always enjoyed our cat-and-mouse."

"Too much," she spat. "Now take me to Chesham's infernal ball."

"Did you write your pages today?"

"Yes." She bit back her fury.

"You must make sure to tell me the end of your story."

"The end is still unwritten."

He stared down at her, the expression in his aqua eyes amused and yet hesitant. "But you must let me know: Does Skya win Aidan's love?"

A strange kind of pain tugged at her heart. It caught her off-guard. Her anger melted like the mists on Sorra on a sunny day.

She shrugged, and forced herself to walk away from the warmth of his embrace. Mournfully, all she said was, " 'Tis yet unknown."

Instead of making a grand entrance to the ball, Trevallyan took Ravenna along the servants' corridor and brought her to the library. There they emerged into the great hall, quickly mingling with guests— friends of Trevallyan's—so that no one was the wiser about Ravenna's lodging.

Determined to bedevil her captor, Ravenna took every chance she could get to wander from Trevallyan's side.

But it was no use. When the Earl and Lady Devon rushed to greet Niall, Ravenna's hand was locked on Trevallyan's arm. When they sauntered through the hall, packed with hundreds of revelers, Trevallyan kept his hand squarely on her back. One questionable move, and she had no doubt he would sweep her off her feet and rush her to the tower, and bother the gossips' wagging tongues.

"There's someone I want you to meet," Trevallyan whispered in her ear. He then nodded to an older gent. The gray-haired man turned, and Ravenna was shocked to see it was Lord Quinn.

"Quinn, how's the new barn coming up?" Trevallyan asked, pulling Ravenna forward.

The man's devilish blue eyes immediately lit upon Ravenna. By the way he swayed, he was clearly drunk. "Fine, fine, Trevallyan. And who is this fetching morsel? How nicely she fills in that dress . . ."

Ravenna drew back in disgust. Lord Quinn was old enough to be her father. Indeed, he had a daughter her exact age. Her image of him as stately lord and protector was now hopelessly tarnished.

Trevallyan ignored the man's remark. To Ravenna's shock, he turned to an older woman who stood next to Quinn and bowed. "Lady Quinn, how are you this fine evening? Ravenna, may I present to you Lady Quinn."

Ravenna's innocence about the Ascendency was quickly diminishing. She couldn't believe Lord Quinn had said such a thing with his wife at his elbow, nor could she believe that the drunken, ravaged, gray-haired beauty who stood next to him was Lady Quinn.

"My pleasure to meet you, Lady Quinn," Ravenna choked out, unable to reconcile that this woman who watched her with bleary, reddened eyes was the same woman she had seen years ago primly riding in her carriage. To Ravenna's dismay, she realized she had not known anything about the Quinns at all.

"Was Lady Kathleen able to attend?" Trevallyan asked, clearly jaded to Lord and Lady Quinn's appearance.

"Yes, she's here, Lord Trevallyan." Behind him, Quinn pulled a blond-haired girl from the throng of guests.

Ravenna was finally in the presence of the queen who had ruled her childhood. All her life she had admired Kathleen Quinn, perhaps even hated her at times for her privilege and wealth, but now she saw that the queen had been downtrodden by her elders. The pale, shy beauty who curtsied to her and Trevallyan was nothing Ravenna had expected her to be. The haughty Kathleen Quinn existed only in her imagination.

Far from envying her now, Ravenna felt a wave of pity as Lady Quinn pushed her daughter toward Trevallyan and said, "Kathleen, my child, say something. You shame us with your lack of wit. Can't you find something fetching to say to the most eligible bachelor in Ireland?"

Kathleen turned beet-red. Her lovely azure eyes filled with tears. Ravenna was grateful to Trevallyan, who smiled kindly at the girl and ignored her mother's cruel remark.

"Lady Kathleen," he said gently, "I'd like to introduce Ravenna to you. You've much in common. I predict you two may be great friends one day."

Lady Kathleen nodded her head. Ravenna was terrified the poor young woman was going to burst into tears.

"How nice to meet you—you cannot know how long I've admired you," Ravenna burst out, desperate to console her.

"It's wonderful to meet you, too," Kathleen said, averting her eyes in her embarrassment.

There was a terrible pause as Ravenna groped for something else to say. In despair, her gaze met Lord Quinn's. His eyes were decidedly fixed on the handmade violets pinned to her bosom, or at least on the flesh that pushed up above them.

Feeling her cheeks flame, she turned to Trevallyan for assistance. He nodded and murmured something about seeing Ravenna's grandmother. He took her by the arm and led her away. Ravenna gave one last glance at Kathleen. The girl was being soundly berated by her drunken mother.

"I had no idea . . ." Ravenna whispered, mostly to herself.

Trevallyan looked back at Lord and Lady Quinn before they were engulfed in the crowd. "He philanders and she drinks, and the brunt of it all falls on Kathleen." His mouth turned down in disgust.

"I feel so sorry for her. She seems trapped." Ravenna met Trevallyan's gaze.

He gave her an appreciative smile. "I believe what I said is true. I predict you and Kathleen will become great friends one day. You both have a lot in common. Your strengths are different, but you've both had to rely on them."

"I thought I admired her a great deal once." Ravenna's gaze grew distant. "But I think perhaps I admire her more now."

"She's had money but not much else. She's terribly lonely."

"And terribly beautiful." Ravenna felt a knot in her throat, something akin to jealousy. Trying to remain nonchalant and yet unable to, she asked, "Why have you not courted her?"

He locked gazes with her. Slowly his thumb stroked her cheek. "Because my heart was captured by another."

She looked into his eyes and saw things he seemed unable to put into words. In there, too, was the possession she had grown to hate. The possession she feared he misinterpreted as love.

"Ma chère," a familiar voice cut into her thoughts.

Ravenna looked behind her. Trevallyan was already scowling.

"Ah, Monsieur de la Connive, how nice to see you again." Distractedly Ravenna put out her hand. Guy bent straight at the waist like a wooden soldier and kissed it.

"You must give me this waltz. I cannot go on living without one." He posed for her, giving her *the stare*. His black, brooding look was so hopelessly contrived she felt a giggle swell in her throat.

" 'Twould be my pleasure, *monsieur*." She glanced at Trevallyan. He gave Guy a stare also. A terrifying stare. One that was definitely *not* contrived.

His face taut with displeasure, Niall said, "Ravenna cannot—"

"Cousin! Finally you've deigned to arrive. And look what we find on your arm. Don't think you can have all of her. She's here, and by God, we want to dance with her. How are you, my darling?" Lord Chesham appeared in front of her. He bowed and kissed her hand also. "Have you met my new acquaintance, Stavros?"

A Greek youth with long, dark, affected curls stepped from the crowd. With his billowing poet's shirt and much-too-pretty face, he could only be described as a rather effeminate Lord Byron.

"How nice to meet you," she said, uneasy in the crush of preening men.

Niall whispered in her ear, bedeviling her with thoughts she would never speak aloud. "If they weren't so taken with themselves, I'd believe they were taken with each other. Think about it, my love."

"You wicked man," she whispered behind her fan, wanting to laugh and rap him on the head at the same moment.

"Dance with me," Guy prompted.

"And then with me," Lord Chesham said, his lips pressed against the back of her hand.

"Of course." Ravenna placed her hand on Guy's brawny arm, hardly daring to peek at Trevallyan. She already could picture him, staring at Guy as if he wanted to cut out his liver and eat it. But what could he do, she asked herself, amused. He had to let her dance or make a public spectacle.

"A lovely night for a ball, almost as lovely as you, sweet lady." Guy swept her around the pandemonium, expertly guiding her in and out of the jumbled crowd. He waltzed as handsomely as he looked, but his conversation made her wish to flee. It was cloying, like the smell of rancid honey.

"And what exactly is the color of your eyes, Ravenna?" he asked, again giving her the stare.

She half-felt like swooning just to make fun of him.

"Dear sweet God in heaven, they leave me speechless with their beauty . . ." he prattled. "By God, they are as purple as the heather that grows on the mount when the violent sea turns to spurning the shore—"

Speechless! she thought incredulously.

"My turn, *monsieur.*"

Ravenna was almost grateful that Chesham cut in. Trevallyan might at times annoy her with his disposition, but at least he didn't insult her intelligence with disingenuous compliments.

"I really think I must rest. Would you mind if I sit out this dance?" She peeked up at the handsome lord, then let her eyes scan the crowd for Trevallyan.

She found him at the edge of the dance floor. For one brief moment, their gazes met and a shock ran down her spine. They were far apart and yet she could feel his anger and frustration as if it were he who held her and he who turned her about the room. Their connection disturbed her. She was glad when the crowd moved in and she could see him no more.

"You do look pale, my beauty." Chesham gave her a wolfish grin. "Shall we retire to the lawn? I know a private little bench right near some hedges."

She glanced at him, taken aback. She wanted to leave the ball and Trevallyan's influence as badly as she wanted to return to Grania and home. But on Chesham's arm, in the dark, she knew she had to decline.

"My turn for dance. Long, long time I pay my due."

Chesham stopped dancing as if he'd run headfirst into a plow horse. Ravenna caught her breath and looked up. Count Fabuloso had his hand on Chesham's shoulder, effectively stopping them dead. Resplendent in a black frock coat and beaver hat that the clod hadn't the grace to remove, the count was still by far the most ravishingly handsome man she'd ever seen.

"Listen here, I've just begun this dance," Chesham complained.

Just like you to be a sore loser, Ravenna thought before she allowed the count to remove her from Chesham's arms and hold her in his own.

It was the chance she'd been waiting for. It wasn't likely she'd have been able to escape Guy or Lord Chesham, but the dolt who danced with her now was like a lump of clay, ready to be molded by her small little hands.

"Oh, dear," she said, after they had begun to dance. Touching her temple, she covertly glanced at the count. "I've got the worst headache. May I continue this dance in a moment? I'd like to step outside and get a breath of fresh air."

The count nodded, his handsome eyes blank.

She quickly slipped past him. Once outside, she covered her smile with her black-mitted hand. She wouldn't be surprised to find him still waiting on the dance floor two nights from now. She could already imagine what he'd say.

Long, long time I wait for girl.

She burst into a giggle and ran down the crowded lawn, her heart light and free. She could finally seek out Grania. She could finally go home. No more prisoner of Trevallyan Castle.

"There you are, you delicious creature." Lord Quinn stepped from behind a topiary and made to grab her. Shocked, Ravenna artfully stepped out of his reach and stared at him with wide eyes.

"My Lord Quinn, no doubt your wife is seeking you just this minute," she couldn't stop herself from saying.

"Not possible, my dear. I left her asleep on a settee in the ballroom."

"Then perhaps 'tis time to take her home."

"But why? Now I've a moment for more pleasurable pursuits." He grabbed at her again. She dodged it, tripping down the velvety lawn.

"My lord, if you'll excuse me, I believe I heard Lord Trevallyan calling my name." She was pleased when that seemed to make him pause. He lifted his head and tried to listen.

"I must go. As you know, Lord Trevallyan has a foul temper."

"Yes. Yes," Lord Quinn agreed. "Perhaps another time."

"Perhaps not," she said, hoping it soundly chastised the old lech. Without looking back, she lifted her skirts and ran down the lawn, past the crowd.

The night was almost magical out on the castle lawn. Candlelight from the many windows left a checkerboard pattern on the grass, and laughter from the guests trickled through the thick copse of trees. Ravenna almost hated to leave it, but she was desperate to go home. More than anything, she wanted to go home.

"*Á mhúirnín,*" someone whispered behind her.

Ravenna turned around. Standing in the grove of ancient yews and hazel trees that stood sentinel around the Trevallyan graveyard, she had thought she was alone.

"*Á mhúirnín,*" the whisper came again.

"Who is it?" she asked, stepping around a large tree.

"Ravenna." A hand reached out and grabbed her by the waist. She was shoved into a man's chest, his large grubby hand covering her mouth.

"Don't you be saying a word, all right?"

Her eyes widened. She finally recognized the voice of the one who had grabbed her.

Slowly she nodded her head.

He released his hand.

"Malachi, what are you doing here? Trevallyan will see you hanging by your neck if he finds you," she whispered.

"It's him who'll be swinging. I've come to warn you. They'll be burning the castle down tonight."

His words sunk in as slowly as water into sand. Sickened she looked up the lawn to the ancient pile of stone that was Trevallyan Castle. In the light of the festivities, it shone like a beacon of human endurance. A monument to a fragile, vulnerable truce.

"You've got to tell them to leave him be, Malachi." She grabbed his shirt and pulled him to her though he weighed several stone more than she did. "Can't you see? He's not the evildoer that you make him out to be. He's the only hope of Lir overcoming the blight. He's bringing in sheep and cattle and corn to get us through this terrible time. Trevallyan and only Trevallyan will help Lir. If you succeed in killing him, what will be left?"

In the darkness, he looked down at her, and she could see his eyes missed nothing, not the costly gown, and especially not the glittering emeralds strung on her neck like a priceless noose. "Sean O'Malley told me you went with him to Antrim," he whispered, his expression thunderous with frustration. "He told me he thinks you been lyin' with him. Does Trevallyan's money make you moan louder when he's on you?"

She slapped him before she had even realized what she had done. Shocked, she stared at him, hardly able to see him in the shadows. He didn't move; he didn't even rub his scruffy jaw. Gradually she began to realize that her hand now hurt almost as much as her heart.

"Do you love him, Ravenna?"

The question hung in the air like an accusation. She wanted to deny it, but she couldn't. She went limp against the ancient, gnarled trunk of the hazel tree and held on to it as if it were the only thing holding her up. Her thoughts were so overwhelmed and tangled, she could hardly make sense of them.

Watching her, gauging her, Malachi finally said, "You've good and had him then. So be it. You'll have him no more."

"No," she whispered, her voice raw. "You've got to tell Sean and the rest of them to leave him alone. If they burn the castle tonight they might be hurting many of their own." A new surge of fear coursed through her. "Grania's in the castle and Father Nolan, too. Will you be killing them just to get to Trevallyan?"

"I don't want to kill anybody." Malachi shook her, clearly exasperated. "But don't you see? The boy-os need an example. Tonight with the ball, 'tis the perfect night—"

"I thought you were leaving them! I thought you were going to Galway!" Her words were full of despair. "You've got to tell them to leave Niall alone."

"They don't listen to me, *á mhúirnín*. It's out of my hands. I just wanted to see you tonight. To make sure you weren't in the castle—"

"I will be in the castle. So stop them, stop them!"

She struggled out of his arms and began to run up the lawn. He went after her, grabbing her back as if she weighed nothing.

"You can't save him!"

A small animal cry rose up in her throat. Acting on instinct, she bit his forearm and, freed, began running again.

"Ravenna!" he called, unable to follow her in the crowd.

"Stop them! Or I'll be in the castle, too, Malachi!" she cried, picking up her heavy satin skirts and running up the crowded lawn.

She didn't look back to see him scoop up the delicate posy of violets that had fallen from her bosom.

Chapter 26

KATHLEEN QUINN wandered out onto the darkened terrace. Behind her, the sounds of merrymaking emanated from within the castle, but she seemed not to notice.

She stepped to the edge of the terrace. Embracing the shadows, she found a halfpence in her purse and dropped it off the edge. It rolled and bounced off jagged rock that dropped for one hundred feet until it ended in the Sorra River that emptied into the sea.

She placed her hands on the terrace wall. A cloud drifted away from the moon, revealing the diamond glitter of tears on her cheeks. She was making up her mind. About what, no observer could know. The only thing obvious was that determination cast hollows in her face. She slowly opened her eyes. Even more slowly, she lifted her skirts and stepped onto the top of the terrace wall.

Then a shadow moved alongside her.

It startled her so, she actually turned around to see what it was. It had come in from the night, where the terrace met with

woodland and the cemetery beyond. If she believed in ghosts and
shades, she might have thought she had seen one.

"Who's there?" she called out to the figure that loomed by the iron
French doors from whence she had come.

The ghost did not speak, but its head turned in her direction. It
spied her form, and like a wind she could not hold back, it rushed to
her and grabbed her down from her perch on the wall.

"Who the bloody hell are you?" the ghost said, yet it was no ghost,
but a man of warm flesh and a biting hold.

"You're hurting me," she gasped, not even bothering to struggle with
him.

"Who are you and what are you doin' here?"

"I should be asking the questions of you. I can tell by your voice and
your bad manners that you're not one of the Ascendency." She didn't
mean to sound haughty; she was only recounting fact.

The clouds cleared the moon. She looked up at the man who held
her. To her shock, he seemed taken aback by her appearance. She had
no recognition of him; that was clearly not the case with him.

"Who are you?" she whispered.

He just stared at her, as if unable to believe what he was seeing.

"Do I know you?" she blurted out, unnerved by his stare even in the
thin light of the moon.

"No," he said, a strange look on his face. His hand went to her
cheek, and he touched the tears still not yet dried. "You've been weeping. Why so?"

" 'Tis none of your business."

"What were you doin' over there on the terrace wall? 'Tis a long step
down to the river."

She turned her eyes away from him. She said nothing.

"Are you snuffin' yourself for a man? Do you fancy yourself in love?"
He seemed to mock her. "I didn't think the Ascendency did such
things. I thought your hearts were too hard."

"Do people actually die for love?" She wiped her cheeks and gave
him a haunting wry smile. "I thought they only died for lack of it."

"You're thinkin' no one loves you?"

Fresh tears coursed down her cheeks. Again she didn't answer.

" 'Tis unnatural for a woman to weep so silently," he said almost as if cursing.

"Tears turn silent when there's never anyone to hear them."

A strange emotion crossed his face. She moved him, and he clearly did not want her to.

"Begone with you. This is no place for you to be," he snapped.

"Are you causing mischief? Are you one of the ones that burned down our barn and killed my dear Windsweep?"

"I lit no such fire." His confession was mixed with equal parts defiance and self-loathing.

"What's your name?" she asked softly.

"I'm no fool to tell you that." His hands tightened on her arms. "But I know who you are, Kathleen Quinn. You're the girl with the pretty dresses . . ." his voice turned low, ". . . and the pretty face."

"Who are you? Just give me one name."

"And find myself lynched in the morning? No thank you."

"But I know what you look like. I see in the moonlight that your hair is red. And your face is rough . . . but I think I see kindness in it."

He pushed her away. She backed into the terrace wall.

"Let me give you some advice, pretty Kathleen Quinn: Leave the castle right now and don't you be comin' back. There's trouble to be had tonight. You'd best stay out of it."

"You have the temerity to give me advice? Why, you're one of the men they speak of. Those lads who go out on the glen at night."

"I saved your life," he cursed, shoving her away from the wall. "You're just one of the Ascendency. You may not know anything of gratitude, but you should be doin' the same for me. Now off with you. Stay away from the castle."

She crept away from the terrace wall, silent as an elf. But before he disappeared into the grove of gnarled woods, she asked, "Have you ever felt love, rebel?"

"Aye, but she does not love me."

"Don't be hurting others to spite her."

His profile hardened. "This has little to do with her."

"I see."

"Begone from here, Kathleen Quinn, and keep your pretty face," he growled.

"You know I'll warn them once I'm away."

"Yes, but go anyway."

"Why have you spared me?" she whispered.

"Because my weakness is lassies with pretty faces—even if they are Ascendency."

"Pray we get what we're after, rebel. I think we seek the same thing."

"Aye," he whispered, unable to take his gaze from her vanishing form.

❧

Ravenna ran through the crowd on the lawn until her chest clawed for air. Her side ached, her dress was torn, but all she could think about was finding Trevallyan. She had to warn him. She had to save him.

"Child, child, why be you in such a rush?"

She spun around and found Father Nolan calling to her from the crowd. She couldn't stop to tell him of the coming tragedy, for she had to find Niall, but suddenly, she saw Grania sitting on a bench behind him. Her heart leapt to her throat and she ran to her.

"Grania! Grania!" she cried. She stumbled toward her grandmother and fell at her feet. "Grania! I just saw Malachi! You've got to leave here! He told me they're to burn the castle tonight!" She swept the tears from her face. "Tell me, is this so? Have you had any visions?"

Grania stroked her granddaughter's hair. Ravenna looked up at her, noticing for the first time how incredibly old Grania appeared. She hadn't seen her in days, and yet it seemed years.

"Ravenna, my dear sweet Ravenna. I've wondered about you so. I've had no visions, child."

Ravenna clung to Grania's skirts and forced herself to be brave. Niall needed her now. She had to go warn him.

"I must find him, Grania. They want to kill him," she sobbed, terrified. Panic gripped her as she realized she might now lose what she had never known she had.

"You finally love him, don't you, child?" Grania looked down at her with white, sightless eyes. The flicker from the torches on the lawn made her look like a witch, old and ugly, with warts on her nose, just as Aidan had imagined. But witches were not loved as Ravenna loved her grandmother. Impulsively, she hugged her and wept into her bosom.

"I think I must love him, Grania, for he gives me a fair wondrous feeling at times, and now . . . I fear for his life, and I believe I would rather they take mine than his."

"Then go to him, and give him your love."

"Yes, yes," Ravenna cried, scrambling to her feet. She looked at Father Nolan and said, "There's going to be trouble here. Take Grania home." She clasped her grandmother's hand. "I'll be at the cottage soon, I promise. He won't keep me prisoner when he knows I love him."

"Tell him, my child. Give him all of your heart, and I have seen he will give all of his."

Father Nolan helped Grania rise. To Ravenna, he vowed to watch over her grandmother. With that, Ravenna fled to the castle.

⚛

"My lord, there's smoke in the servants' passage. Lady Kathleen Quinn has just informed me that she came upon a rebel trying to break into the castle." Greeves's face was a grim mask of concern as he looked upon his master.

Trevallyan crossed his arms over his chest. Reverend Drummond, with whom he had been in conversation, looked as pale as a wizened ghost.

"Clear the rooms. See that everyone is out and accounted for." Trevallyan pulled the butler aside. Quietly, he said, "Find Ravenna. I think she's gone back to her grandmother's, but see that it's so. I must know she's safe."

"Aye, my lord."

Drummond called to a group of revelers just now entering the drawing room, "Send to the barn for the stable master! We must organize a bucket brigade! There's a fire!"

Niall strode across the drawing room toward the servants' passage. Already smoke wafted beneath the jib like blue mist.

He stepped back, then kicked open the door. Smoke billowed in, curtaining the room.

"Damned boy-os!" A reveler bellowed behind him.

Trevallyan ignored him and tried to enter the passage. After a moment, the smoke thinned, and he took a step inside.

"What's this, Trevallyan?"

Behind him, the man drunkenly stooped down and picked up an article from the passage floor. He left the passage and placed the article on a table in the drawing room where everyone could see it.

Niall had no choice but to turn back.

"What is it? What does it mean?" several partygoers murmured.

Niall felt his blood run cold as he looked at the object on the table. It was a crumpled posy of velvet violets.

"Didn't I see this pinned to that young woman's dress?" A lord accused.

"I saw those flowers on Ravenna's gown," a reveler in the crowd piped in.

"But she was at the ball. What would she be doing in the servants' quarters?" another chimed in.

"Don't forget, the chit's long been friendly with that wretch MacCumhal. Everyone knows his father was out with the White Boys."

"Enough," Niall told them, silencing them with a glance.

"She's taken after that rogue MacCumhal," another reveler offered. Niall looked up, and Lord Quinn swayed into the room. "Tha's right, Trevallyan. I just saw your 'amour' down near the cemetery, hugging on MacCumhal, not fifteen minutes past."

Trevallyan was quiet. The accusation left no room for defense. The crowd began to murmur and men shook their heads. They watched him as he stood like a statue in the beautiful smoke-filled Adam drawing room, his gaze helplessly pinned to the bouquet of crushed violets.

"Come along, men. We'll get the harlot who helped do this to you, Trevallyan," Quinn announced.

"Clear the room," Trevallyan whispered.

"Eh?" asked Reverend Drummond, his hearing not what it used to be.

"I said everyone clear the room. The fire may be here soon. I don't want anyone hurt. You'll just get in the way of the bucket brigade." Trevallyan stood numbly at the table, still staring at the violets.

"Aye, aye," Drummond agreed, his expression troubled and far away. He headed for the door, his old bones, for once, cooperating.

"I'll look for her in the crowd, Trevallyan. The lass should be hanged for this. We'll have no more mischief." With that proclamation, Lord Quinn and the rest of the ballgoers left the drawing room.

Trevallyan remained behind, staring in disbelief at the violets, his expression disconsolate.

Minutes ticked by. The stable master arrived with a line of strong young men. Together they passed leather buckets filled with water down into the bowels of the passage.

But the fire raged, fed on ancient dried-out timbers and heavy velvet drapery. Before the fire was put out, it was reported to Trevallyan that the entire east wing of the castle had been consumed. He took the news well. In fact he seemed not to care. When the raucous noise of firefighting had become too much, he'd scooped up the posy of artificial violets and left for the keep.

It was there that Ravenna finally found him. He sat in his leather chair in the antechamber, staring at something in his hand. Her dress torn, her face blackened with soot, she knew she must follow the impulse of her heart. She ran to him and fell to his feet.

"I've been so worried," she whispered, pressing her cheek against his knee. She hugged his leg, her soul immeasurably soothed by finding him alive and all right. "I tried to warn you, but I couldn't find you . . ." She looked up at him. It took a moment for her to realize he did not return her touch. There was no gentle hand on her head, no tender caress of her hair. There was, in fact, nothing.

She shivered from a sudden chill. "What are you doing up here in the tower, my lord, while your castle burned?" Her eyes filled with worry and dread.

He stared down at her. Without even looking at them, he held up the crushed posy of violets that had fallen from her gown. "Lord Quinn found these in the passage. He said he saw you hugging MacCumhal near the cemetery just minutes before the fire started. Is this true?"

"Don't be going after Malachi—I beg—"

"Is this true?" he bellowed.

"Yes," she gasped, "but it wasn't a planned meeting. He just found me there and he wanted to warn me of the fire. I think he even wanted to warn you."

"Quinn told everyone about seeing you with MacCumhal. Everyone. Now they think you started the fire. . . . Or at least helped those who did."

She took the posy from his hand. Trembling, she said, "I had nothing to do with it. I came to warn you."

"Lady Kathleen was the one to warn me, not you."

"But I was nowhere near the servants' passage. The violets fell off my gown when—" She closed her mouth. Anguish furrowed her brow.

"Malachi put this in the passage, didn't he?" He spoke slowly. "He wanted to make sure I knew you were with him. It was his message to me."

"Our meeting meant nothing," she whispered.

"Yes, nothing." He couldn't seem to hide the bitterness in his voice. "He was only near enough to you to unpin this posy from your bosom."

Guilt darkened her eyes. She'd done nothing wrong, but she had no way to explain it without condemning herself further.

"You were running from me when you met him, weren't you? You couldn't wait to get away. You ran from me, only to go to him."

Again, she just stared at him, forced to condemn herself with silence.

He wrapped his hand in her hair and gently pulled her up to him.

"I'm the magistrate. Quinn and the rest of the Ascendency that were here tonight want an example made. They blame you."

"But you don't blame me. Surely you don't," she said, her eyes filling with tears.

"I love you. My curse is that I love you."

She hugged him, weeping softly against his satin waistcoat. "I wouldn't hurt you. Haven't I already proved that? I came to warn you—"

"Your warning came too late."

She rose from his lap and stared at him with a tearstained face. "But I tried to find you. This castle is so wretchedly big, I just couldn't."

"You couldn't wait to flee from me. You took your first chance and you were gone."

"Don't look at me so," she cried out, hating the way his gaze tortured her soul with accusation. "I've done nothing wrong. I came back to warn you."

"You came back to save yourself. You don't want to face the gallows like these rebels surely will when I catch them."

"No, I came back because—"

"Admit it. You'd love to have revenge on me for holding you all these weeks. Your reasons aren't political, they're personal."

"My path has crossed with Malachi. You know that. But you also know I've had nothing to do with any mischief—"

"First there was the note that sent Seamus to his grave, then your old mate Sean O'Malley who tried to lure me to Hensey." He seemed to be battling tears of his own. In a hoarse whisper, he spat, "Everytime I turn around, there you are in the midst of this mess. And here I was beginning to fear this infernal *geis* when all along I should have feared you. You and my bloody heart that you've taken prisoner."

"But you should fear the *geis,*" she begged, tugging on his lapels, "for 'tis true. Don't you see it now? The *geis* is true. I finally believe it. Things will get better."

"Why?" he accused.

"Because I—"

She wiped her cheeks and stared at him, gaining the courage she needed to hand him her heart and soul.

"Because I love you," she whispered in wonderment of the emotion that ravaged his face. "Don't you see that now? I finally know I love you."

The anger left this face, replaced instead by hardened acceptance. He took her face in his hands and studied her as if she were a confessor and he the executioner. A minute ticked by, each second agony as she waited.

Coldly, he whispered, "How convenient."

"No. . . ." she moaned, unable to accept what he was thinking. But before she could say more, he brought her mouth to his own and kissed her, tasting her thoroughly with his tongue. She tried to release herself; to defend herself, but he wouldn't let her go. With her every struggle, his kiss grew only deeper, more demanding, more accusing, and she hadn't the strength to fight it.

"Sweet lying bitch," he whispered, his voice filled with bitterness and fury.

Weak from fear and want, she shuddered against him, unable to summon the impossible words that might acquit her. In the end, her submission only damned her further. His mouth took hers in a punishing kiss, almost daring her to deny what he thought of her, and, in the end, she couldn't. All she could do was hold back her tears and relinquish her body to his all-too-capable hands.

"Believe me, please believe me," she whimpered uselessly while his lips claimed hers time and again. She moaned as he clawed at the hooks to her bodice. Her instincts told her to pull back, to beat some sense into him, but with every kiss, every heated caress, her logic informed her she was trapped. She loved him. Even in anger, she wanted to be with him. But though her heart was full of the soaring need to give him her love, it despaired at the guilt he'd resurrected around her. He was convinced she was the enemy. She rebelled at making love to him while he was so furious, but she knew it was meant to be. In order to convince him of her innocence, she knew she had to first convince him of her love.

So his eyes accused, his hands seduced, her body surrendered.

His lovemaking was as white-frothed and angry as the waves that crashed upon Briney Cliffs. He treated her little better than a whore. He bared her breasts and shamelessly cupped them with both hands while she stared at him with tears shining in her eyes. When she was finally nude and lying beneath him on the bed, her heart shattered with his roughness, but her soul still delighted in the union.

She loved him, and with every thrust, she told him so, until, spent and groaning, he covered her mouth with his own.

As if he were unable to hear the lie anymore.

PART FOUR

Na Sé Seachtaine Dona

(THE BITTER SIX WEEKS)

April is in my mistress' face,
And July in her eyes hath place,
Within her bosom is September,
But in her heart a cold December.

Thomas Morley
1594

Chapter 27

S HE WEPT until she hadn't any tears left.

Sore and despondent, Ravenna rose from the bed and began to dress. Trevallyan stood at the window wearing only unbuttoned trousers, his stare fixated on the moonlit silhouette of charred ruins that had once been the wing farthermost from the keep. He said not a word. Even when the sounds of her weeping had reached him like the moan of the wind, he made no move to comfort her. His expression was as static as if hewn from marble. No emotion showed save for the wretched bitterness in his eyes.

Her numb fingers clumsily relaced her corset. The purple satin dress was ruined but it was all that was within her reach. She pulled the soot-stained skirts over her head and fastened what hooks she could, leaving the rest undone down her back. The shoulder of the gown dropped down one arm, but she couldn't be bothered with it. She didn't care how she looked. Strangely, she didn't seem to care about anything at that moment.

She stared at his back, her heart breaking. Reason seemed no longer able to penetrate his mind. He seemed immobilized by his grief over his castle and his grief over her. The man ruled by intellect seemed to have fled. Now there stood only one in the grip of anger and obsession.

"My lord," she whispered, unsure of what she could say next.

He didn't turn to her. Instead his gaze fell on the doorway. "What do you want?" he snapped at the person standing there.

She turned her head. Greeves slowly entered the room. His face was pale, his lips thinned to a grim, nearly invisible line. "Lord Trevallyan, I've come to tell you that we've assessed the damage. The east wing is lost, and there is smoke damage to a number of the castle's antiquities."

Trevallyan nodded a dismissal as if it were nothing he hadn't already guessed.

"There's more, my lord. They've caught one of the rebels."

Ravenna could feel her fists tighten around the counterpane. Was she to see Malachi hanged after all? The thought sickened her.

"Who is it?" Niall asked, his gaze turned to her.

"Sean O'Malley," Greeves said.

Ravenna felt herself go limp. She didn't want to see Sean O'Malley hanged either, but she suspected he was one of the ringleaders of the rebellion. Without him, perhaps Malachi would find a truer path.

"Thank you, Greeves, that will be all," Trevallyan said, his gaze still fixed on her.

"I've had the boys stow him in the old dungeon for now, sir."

"Yes. Thank you. I'll deal with it in the morning."

Greeves still hesitated.

Finally Trevallyan snapped, "There's more?"

"Aye, my lord." Greeves' gaze flickered guiltily toward Ravenna who knelt on the bed. "There are six men downstairs in the library, my lord —all peers, Lord Quinn and Lord Devon among them. They want Ravenna put in the dungeon with O'Malley. They've sent a party to search for her. A servant told them they saw her wander up here."

Ravenna's heart pounded in terror like the war drumbeat of a Celtic *bodhrán*. She looked at Niall. He had shut his eyes as if he were in great pain. Shaking his head, he muttered, "God save us all."

"They want the rebels caught and punished," Greeves continued.

"They demand that you as magistrate do something before the rebellion spreads and they find their homes aflame."

Niall's fist slammed down on his desk. But he said nothing.

"What shall I tell them, my lord? That I could not find her?"

Trevallyan stood still for a long moment, then he lifted his head. "Bring two men up here and have them take Ravenna down to the dungeon."

"No," Ravenna gasped, too shocked to believe her ears. Greeves sent her a pitying glance, then he spun on his heels and retreated.

"You cannot do this! You know I had nothing to do with the fire! I beg of you!" She swallowed a sob, then lowered her head in defeat. "I love you. *Don't* do this," she whispered.

"You ran from me. You *left* me. Only to go to him," he said, his voice cleansed of inflection.

"Don't make me hate you," she choked.

"Why not? You never loved me." He stepped to the bed and dragged her from it. In low, husky tones, he said, "At least you'll never be his. If it means keeping you in my dungeon, I swear you'll never flee me again."

"You don't have to own me to have my love," she cried. "Don't you see that? You already have my love."

The corner of his mouth lifted in a dark, cynical smirk. "Save me from your love, Ravenna, if it comes like this."

Vengefully, she couldn't stop herself from crying out, "And save me from your love, my lord. That is, if you have any in that cold heart to give."

An ominous silence passed. He appeared as if he wanted to say something, to refute her words, but he didn't seem capable of it. He stepped from her and looked at his reflection in his shaving mirror. Then his hand reached out and in one violent sweep, he shoved it off the top of his bureau.

She started at the crash. Shards of glass scattered everywhere, threatening her bare feet, but she didn't care. She was too numb to care. No matter where she looked, there seemed no way to convince him of her innocence, her love, the truth.

"Why? Why did you leave me? Why must you always run from me?"

She couldn't answer him. All she could do was shake her head and wrap her arms around herself to keep from trembling.

"Just tell me why?" he said tightly.

She didn't answer, and a dam seemed to break within him. He reached down onto the stone floor and picked up his straight razor where it had tumbled in the crash.

Angrily, he grabbed her and held it to her gaze. "If you and that *geis* wanted to ruin my life," his face drew closer to her own, "why didn't you just take this and cut my throat one night while I lay sleeping in your arms?"

"Stop it," she moaned, unwilling to play along.

He took her hand and wrapped it around the mahogany handle of the razor. Pressing it against his chest, he groaned, "Or even better, why didn't you just cut out my heart, as you're doing right now?"

She struggled to release her hand, but it seemed cinched to his chest with an iron band. "Please." The word was a bare whisper.

He had no time to answer. Someone pounded at the door, and he bade them enter. Two burly groomsmen came into the chamber with Greeves, ready to take her away.

She stared at Trevallyan, clinging to the hope that somehow he would put an end to this madness. When he said nothing, her mouth could no longer form any pleas, but her eyes still begged him to accept the truth: she loved him.

"Miss Ravenna?" Greeves motioned politely toward the door.

She felt like Anne Boleyn on the way to the chopping block.

"Wait." Niall put a hand on her elbow. Slowly, as if it hurt him, he lowered himself to one knee and lifted her gown. He took her bare foot in his hand and painstakingly buckled her slipper onto it so that she would not cut her feet on the glass. He lifted the other foot in his warm hand and she watched with a bitter ache in her heart while he performed the tender task yet again. When her feet were shod, he stood and nodded for them to take her. She walked toward the men, suddenly not caring what happened to her.

"Make sure she has anything she wants," Trevallyan said stonily.

Greeves nodded.

Without looking back, Ravenna let him lead her away.

⊗

Ravenna walked across the straw-covered floor and stared into the void of darkness beyond the iron bars. With tears dried to her cheeks, she marveled at the fragility of love. It was so easily crushed. It could lie dying at one's feet long before it even had a chance to bloom. In a matter of weeks, Niall had taken her from intrigue to hate to unashamed confessions of love.

And now back to hate again.

She'd been down in the dungeon for two days. He had come to see her only once. O'Malley was jailed somewhere in the darkness to her left. At night—or was it day? without the sun she had no sense of time —she could hear Sean shuffle about in his cell. But it was a distant sound, and there were moments—or hours? time flew by or stood still depending upon the mood—that she feared the sounds were made by rats.

During Trevallyan's visit, they'd spoken hardly a word. As if to humor her, or patronize her, he gave her paper, pen, and ink, and told her to write. An extra lantern was passed through the bars so that she might read. Before he'd left, his hand reached through the iron cage and cupped the back of her head. He brought her close to the bars, and he'd kissed her mouth, the kiss made more aching because of the cruel bars that separated them.

She had wept then and begged him to release her. He'd refused. His only vow had been to clear her bad name.

And the hate that she thought was gone came back.

Depressed as she had never been before, she turned away from the bars and sat on her pallet. She should write, she told herself. Writing would take her to another place. Writing would help her escape. But she couldn't summon the will to do it. Until she became angry. He would never be able to take away her writing. Her novel was her one breath of freedom, and she would see it published, and damn Trevallyan, who had told her it couldn't be done.

She turned up the lanterns and placed a sheet of paper on the mahogany lap-desk that Greeves had sent down. Touching the swirled glass tip of her pen into a fine French blue ink, she continued the saga of Aidan and Skya.

Dawn came slowly in the deep woods, first with the twitter of larks and thrush, then with the howl of a roving wild peacock. Golden hinds with their sweet spotted young wandered to the brook to drink when the first gray light of a new morn reached down through the thick canopy of hazel trees. Finally yellow flags of sunshine dotted the forest floor and melted the mists, regally hailing the virgin day. This was the moment that Skya opened her eyes.

Aidan lay against her on the pallet, his heart beating strong and sure against her back. His skin warmed her, his muscular embrace assured her. She looked down at the rough wool blanket that covered them and at their still-clasped hands lying in the curve of her waist. She could not let him go. It was impossible now. The lonely years ahead of her would prove too painful now that she'd known what it was like to lie in such bliss. If he had never come to her, she might have endured. Now she had no choice but to keep him.

She turned her head, desiring to watch him sleep. To her shock, she found his blue eyes open and trained on her.

She said nothing. Words would seem trite compared with what she wanted to say to him, to give him. Instead, she smiled softly and placed a kiss on his beard-roughened cheek.

" 'Tis this day I'm going to leave you," he whispered gently.

She tightened her clasp on his hand. "If you go, I shall turn you back into a troll."

He kissed her, stealing her breath. He drank deeply, and when their lips parted, she mourned.

"You've got to understand. I must return. My father is not young. When he is gone, I will be king. Without me, anarchy will destroy the kingdom. And perhaps take your father's kingdom as well."

"You've always made war on my people. You've wanted their kingdom all along. You'll not make me believe otherwise."

With his head resting on his arm, he played with the fan of her gold tresses. Softly, he said, "I'm leaving this morning. I was not raised to hide in the woods in a mud-thatched cottage with a witch. I was raised to be a king, and a king I must be."

"But I can't let you go," she said, her lips trembling with tears. She hugged him close, crushing her bosom against his. "Stay with me and be my love."

"I can't." His hard features softened as he looked at the girl clinging to his chest. He stroked her hair and whispered, "I did not ask to become lost in these woods, nor to be turned into a troll and live beneath that bridge. I've hated you and this miserable time I've spent here." He bade her raise her gaze to his, then he said, "But I will not say it was all bad because that would be a lie. Our times spent such as now will remain sweet in my memory. Your spells are strong, witch, but I fear the spell of your womanliness has proved stronger."

"Then don't leave me. Don't you see? I'll die from the loneliness," she whispered, silent tears trailing down her cheeks.

"Then return to your father."

"I can't. I'm an outcast. My return to the castle will only hurt him. Besides, he may be your father's captive by now. Shall I return only to find a place beside him in your dungeon?"

He turned his gaze away. His resolve seemed as hard as the muscles that gridded his belly.

"Please. . . . stay. . . ." she said, stroking his cheek.

He sat up and he pulled her with him by their clasped hands. She knelt between his long, heavy legs that dangled over the edge of the pallet and he embraced her, running his hand down the length of her hair. She thought he might kiss her so she tilted her face up toward his. Slowly he bent his head downward until her eyes fluttered closed in anticipation. Then he wrought his cruelty.

He grabbed her free hand and pulled his own from her grasp. Before she had even opened her eyes, he had clasped her own hands together and was wrapping a thick leather cord around them to keep them that way.

"Don't," she choked, unable to believe what he had done.

"I must," he rasped, unable to meet her wounded gaze.

"I'll die if you leave me. I'll die. . . ." The words were spoken in the barest of whispers, as if her strength, her will to live, were even now being sapped away.

"I must go," he said, pulling on his linen small clothes he found in a crude oaken chest by the pallet. He then laced on leather braies and pulled on his purple velvet tunic heavily embroidered in gold with the king's crown and crest. His mail, he left behind. Too cumbersome, no doubt, and he could have the king's smithy make him more, overnight, if necessary, even if it meant calling all the peasants of Clancullen to work on it.

She stared at him, so handsome in the morning light, so royal in his rich clothes. Stumbling from the pallet, unmindful of her nudity, she tried to follow him, but he pulled her back and lashed her clasped hands to a corner of the pallet.

"Don't leave me like this. I'll die . . . I'll die." She wept into the straw ticking that formed her pallet.

He stared down at her, her loveliness and grief clearly moving him. But, as a king who is forced to sacrifice his own desires for others', he covered her with the wool blanket and whispered, "I'll send someone to free you."

"Would you have another be my company when I have known only you?" she cried softly.

"No. I would stay and be with you. But only if I could . . . and—I—cannot." His last words were laced with anguish. He looked down upon her weeping figure, then closed his eyes as if willing himself to do what he must.

He left the cottage without looking back, forcing his eyes to be blind to her tears, forcing his ears to grow deaf to her sobs.

He was born a king, and a king he must be.

Chapter 28

F ATHER NOLAN arrived in the hall of the castle, his two palsied hands not as deft as Greeves's single one when it came to removing his black, rain-spattered cloak.

Greeves bowed to the priest. "It seems you only venture here in fierce weather, Father."

"I find I'm only called in fierce weather." Father Nolan smiled. His teeth were nigh all missing, an occurrence not unusual for countrymen even much younger than himself.

"He's in the library." Greeves watched the priest with troubled blue eyes. He didn't seem to know what to say.

Father Nolan helped him. "You haven't seen such trouble since London, have you, my son?"

Greeves's mouth formed a tight line. He nodded in agreement. "The master . . . he's not himself anymore. Help him, Father. We don't know what else to do."

The priest's gaze shifted to the ominously closed library doors. "Has he taken to the drink?"

"No." Greeves walked with the priest across the flagstone, the priest's blackthorn tapping an unsteady echo along the hall's granite walls. "He doesn't seem to find interest in anything. He just broods and asks about . . . her."

They stopped in front of the carved doors. Greeves seemed uncomfortable with leaving the priest alone.

Father Nolan put his hand on the butler's shoulder. He smiled a weary smile. "I've faced greater lions than this one. Just tell me, is there a decanter of sherry in there? I think *I* might like to imbibe, given the circumstances." Upon Greeves's nod, he said, "Leave us be."

Greeves opened the door for the priest. A growl sounded within, but Father Nolan ignored it. Greeves took off in such a hurry, the priest thought he was anxious to seek the sherry himself.

Father Nolan had never seen a man become so dissipated in so short a time. Niall Trevallyan was not as he remembered. The man who sat in an armchair staring inconsolably into the fire had the beginnings of ruin etched into every line on his face. His jaw was scruffy, covered with a rough dark-gold beard and his eyes, when they chanced to turn in the priest's direction, possessed an uncivilized anger. Even his clothes were not as Father Nolan recalled. Instead of the finely tailored frock coats and jackets of thick, sporting corduroy, Trevallyan wore only rumpled trousers that looked in sore need of an iron, and a wrinkled linen shirt long past salvation. The boots on his feet were tarnished with rust-colored mud. He'd been walking his land. No doubt the sorry state of the potato crop had lent him little comfort.

"I've come with bad news, my lord," the priest said uneasily. "I fear 'twill be no balm for your tormented soul."

"What more could go wrong." The words were spoken in a low monotone, more as a statement than as a question. Trevallyan didn't even bother to look up.

The father rested his weary bones in a nearby chair and placed his blackthorn across his lap. "I've heard Ravenna grows thin these past few days. You've been cruel to her. You know she had nothing to do with the fire."

Trevallyan said nothing.

"So, why, my son," Father Nolan asked gently, "why do you keep her still in that dungeon?"

Trevallyan ran a hand through his hair, a gesture of agony. "If I release her, I'll lose her. She'd already run from me the night of the ball."

"But you treat her like a prisoner. Three days you've kept her down in that dungeon. Surely you know—"

"Yes, yes, damn you!" Niall's gaze pinned the priest. "Sean O'Malley told me as much. She had nothing to do with the fire. I know that. I've always known that."

"Then why do you keep her?"

"Because I want her, and I'll have her." His voice was a harsh whisper. "And because I love her."

"If you love her, release her."

"Are you daft, man?" Trevallyan rose and leaned his forearms on the marble mantel. "Weren't you the one to tell me of the *geis*? Whether it was foolishness or not, 'tis come true. I gave her everything I could think of and she threw it all back at me in the cruelest manner possible. I've lost. My life, this county, is in ruins because I could not win her love. But I'll still have her. She's mine, and I won't let her go."

"Is that why you mourn in this library—because you mourn your life and County Lir?"

Father Nolan would be forever haunted by the look in Trevallyan's eyes.

Niall turned away from the priest, and with words full of despair, he said, "I went to see her after O'Malley's confession." He paused. The words seemed difficult. "She slapped my face, and she wept, and she told me of the hatred she held for me within her heart. I should have let her go then. I knew the battle was hopeless. But I found I could not. *I could not.* I love her and I need her. And I'd rather she take a knife and plunge it in my sorry heart than watch her run from me and be gone forever."

"My son, my son," the father murmured, his own heart wrenching for Trevallyan's tortured soul.

"I cannot free her. Don't ask it of me." Niall went to the window. Father Nolan cringed as Trevallyan pushed aside the lace curtain and gazed upon the yellow, dying fields that seemed only there to mock him.

"My lord," the priest began gently, "the *geis* could not be fulfilled. It's

over. We must now accept that. You and your money, they can help
this impoverished county, but nothing will summon Ravenna's love if
she cannot do it herself. Let her go, my son. You've gone too far with
this. Making her a prisoner will only harden her heart further toward
you."

"Don't ask it," Niall bit out.

"I must ask it. Grania is ill and not long for this world. If Ravenna
despises you now, my son, think about her hatred when she finds you
refused to let her be by her grandmother's side while she lay dying."

Niall could take no more, not of the fields that seemed to scorn him,
nor of the girl whose hatred cut right into his soul. He took one long,
last look at the land, then, without warning, he slammed his fist into
the windowpane, as if trying desperately to erase what he saw there.

"Don't ask it, Father. She's all I have left," he growled, ignoring his
hand that was now etched with bloody lacerations from the broken
pane.

"I would not ask it if it were not imperative. Grania is near death and
she calls for Ravenna. You must let her go, my lord. You must, even
though 'twill break your heart and shatter your spirit. The *geis* has won.
The war is lost. Let her go."

Trevallyan stood staring mutely at the fields that he could not van-
quish. He crossed his arms over his chest, grinding his own red blood
in a smear over his heart. Slowly, his eyes lowered and his shoulders
seemed weighted with unimaginable despair. The priest had never seen
such abject hopelessness in all his ninety years.

"She will no longer eat, Father. They take her food and she sends it
back untouched." The words were filled with agony.

Father Nolan hated what he had to say. "My son," he began, "don't
you see the absurdity of this? If the only way to keep your love near
you is to hold her prisoner in your dungeon, then indeed all *is* lost. You
must surrender her, Niall, you must."

"I don't want her thin and unhappy." Trevallyan ran the hand
through his hair once more, hardly noticing the blood. "I only wanted
her love."

" 'Twill work to save your soul if you release her."

"No," Niall answered, his eyes glistening with hard, unshed tears. "Nothing will save my soul now. Nothing."

"Cleanse yourself, Niall. Go down to your dungeon and confess your sins to your prisoner. Tell her of your pride and your greed." The priest's voice lowered to a reverent whisper. "Tell her of your need to be ruled by your mind, only to see yourself toppled by your heart. . . ."

Trevallyan dropped his head into his bloodied hands.

If he wept, Father Nolan could not tell.

"Grania awaits her granddaughter, my lord." The priest stood, his face a picture of anguish. "I'll tell her Ravenna will come shortly."

Greeves entered with the sherry. The priest nodded for him to escort him out, but before Father Nolan left, he turned back to Trevallyan, respectfully averting his gaze from the despairing figure.

"I see a place at heaven's gate for you, my lord," he whispered. "Keep that in mind when you talk to her."

Niall said nothing.

※

Lantern light filtered down the stone staircase, rousing Ravenna from a light sleep. She'd been dreaming of devils and love and treachery. It was a relief to open her eyes.

A dark figure came into view, walking into the circle of light. She tried to hide the catch of tears in her voice but couldn't. It was Trevallyan.

"Does it amuse you to stare at me through these bars like I'm a captive lioness?" She turned away from him, not bothering to hide her disgust.

Then she heard the rusty scrape of the key in the lock.

Slowly, almost painfully, the key was turned and the screeching metal door opened wide. She thought he would enter, but he only stood aside in the shadows, mutely waiting for her to depart.

Her surprise was almost palpable. She had almost lost hope of ever going free because she knew better than most Trevallyan's iron will.

"You're letting me go free?" she gasped, not quite believing it.

Though foolish of her to question her fortune—she should flee and
never look back—she was perplexed by his surrender.

"You're not guilty of any crime. You know O'Malley cleared your
name. I've no reason to hold you." His words were nothing but a rasp.

Scrambling in the near darkness, she hastily gathered the pages of
her novel, all the while giving him a wild-eyed stare. She knew she
must hurry; she didn't know when his mercurial mood might swing in
the other direction and she would find the barred door slammed closed
once again.

Cautiously, she stepped outside the cell and edged against the slimy
wall, almost as if she were afraid of him. After all he'd put her through,
she knew it would be stupid to trust him. He was a madman. It was
only prudent to proceed with caution.

He didn't make any motion to stop her. He stood silently, not
moving, only watching, his eyes filled with shadow and anguish.

She turned to run up the dungeon's slippery stairway. There was
nothing he could have said to make her pause. Nothing except the
words he uttered.

"Go to Grania. She's ill."

Dread gripped her insides, and she whipped around to look at him.
It couldn't be true what he had said, but somehow she knew it was.
Grania was dying, and even now it might be too late.

Her world shattered. Her hatred for Trevallyan solidified. He had not
only held her prisoner but now he had taken precious time away from
Grania. Time she could never regain. Choking on a sob, she glared at
him, revealing all her loathing for him in one baleful glance.

"Go. Do not tarry here."

Silently, she began to weep. The past three days had been more than
she could bear. Now Grania was dying. Everything she loved had been
taken from her. Even her last days with her grandmother.

"I will never forgive you for this, do you hear? Never." She wiped the
tears that streamed down her cheeks. She dared defy him now because
she knew he would not stop her. Even he wouldn't be so cruel as to
keep her from Grania's deathbed. "I'll hate you until it's my turn to
die!" she spat, almost enjoying her cruelty for the release it gave her.

"Hate me," he answered quietly, his emotion-ravaged face in half-shadow. "Perhaps 'tis deserved."

She paused. His response was unexpected. Valiantly, she tried to rein in her tears and make sense of him, but her tears fell like rain, out of reach of her will.

"Ravenna, in the years to come, when you pass by the ruins of this castle, know the master sits inside, thinking of you, consumed by you." He swallowed and stepped into the circle of lantern light. From the staircase, she could see the hopelessness in his eyes. "Tell Grania before she dies, that it's over. The *geis* has won. There will be no union between peer and commoner in Lir to keep the peace. Instead, the Trevallyans have been destroyed."

She stared down at him, hardly believing her ears.

"And tell her I've paid well and good for the lands the Trevallyans took from the Gael."

She didn't know what to say. His voice was still defiant and strong, but his words spoke of defeat.

"And tell her . . ."—his voice lowered to a whisper—"tell her I've made my peace with you. I've lied to you and manipulated you, but no more." His words grew harsh as if he were forcing them out. "Finn Byrne was your father, Ravenna. I kept the fact from you because I couldn't bear to give you such power. But I give it to you now. You need only tell Lord Cinaeth who your mother was. He'll know then, without a doubt, you're Finn Byrne's daughter."

The hot tears in her eyes turned to ice. Fury lodged like a cold ball in her chest. She couldn't believe what he'd just said. He'd kept the most important thing in her life a secret only so that she would be that much more under his influence. If she hadn't been overwhelmed by Grania's impending death, she might have run down the steps and pummeled him.

"I loathe you." She regretted the word for *loathe* wasn't strong enough for the emotion she suddenly felt.

"I know." His expression was bitter, without hope, and yet contrite. "I valued all the wrong things and I spurned what I could not understand. But—" His voice seemed to catch. He ignored it and continued. "But I see now there is no value in a mind that ignores the pleadings of the heart. You say I could never treat you as my equal, Ravenna, but now I truly know that you're not my equal, but better than I am. You and all those in this county I've called fools. I didn't have enough respect for any other powers except my own. I didn't understand what everyone was trying to tell me. The powers that rule destiny are too great for any man's intellect, but what we all seem to misjudge are the little powers—the little powers that finally topple a Goliath. Remember this, Ravenna. Remember it forever: The *geis* did not bring me to my knees." He spoke in a reverent, anguished whisper. *"You* did."

She stared at him through frozen tears. Her emotions were too tangled to make sense of what he said. She wanted to run. To see her grandmother before it was too late. To extricate herself from his web, finally and forever.

"Justice has been served then," she whispered to his dark, brooding figure. Suddenly unable to hear anymore, she picked up her skirts and ran to the top of the stair, her hands reaching in the darkness for the door that would set her free.

Chapter 29

RAVENNA, PALE and thin, watched as the physician packed his black leather satchel.

"She's not a young woman, Ravenna. She can't even tell me when she was born. I've given her some laudanum to make her more comfortable. It's not long now. Be quiet with your words and gentle with your weeping. 'Tis time for her to go to a better place."

Ravenna nodded and wiped her wet cheeks with the back of her hand. It seemed she'd been crying for weeks, but it seemed, too, that there was more grief in her world than for which she had tears.

"How—how much do I owe you?" she asked, walking the old man to the door.

"Trevallyan will pay me."

"Damn him, he will not!" she cursed, not caring what the doctor thought of her. But then, despondently, she realized that all the money she had in the world had come from him anyway.

"I'll send a bill then." The doctor raised her chin and looked into her eyes. "Say good-bye to her now, Ravenna. And assure her you'll be taken care of. She worries about you so."

"I'll be all right."

"If you need me, send the O'Shea boy."

"Yes," she whispered, hardly able to utter the word.

Softly, she closed the door. Upstairs, Grania was breathing her last. It took all Ravenna's strength to mount the black oak staircase to the bedroom.

"I'm here, Grandmother." She walked to the bed draped in fresh white linen. Fiona had come from the castle to care for Grania in her final hours, and Ravenna had left her downstairs to knit in the kitchen with a small frown on her face as they waited for the inevitable.

Ravenna clasped the dear, gnarled hand that peeked out from the sheets. Grania's eyes were closed, but Ravenna knew she was alert.

"You've been at the castle all this time?" Grania rasped, her breath almost gone.

"Aye," Ravenna whispered, tears streaming down her face. She lowered her cheek to the twisted, aged hand. It was warm, and her heart ached to make it stay that way.

"Tre-vallyan?" Grania seemed to claw for breath.

"He . . ." Ravenna's eyes grew dark. "He is well."

Grania took a long moment to compose herself. Her breathing softened. Her speech became strangely lucid. "Do you love him?"

Ravenna looked away, her eyes sparkling with tears. The answer eluded her. Grania wanted her to be taken care of, and the old woman believed Trevallyan was the man to do it. But Ravenna didn't need taking care of. She had her novel, and there was always Dublin. Surely she would find work in Dublin.

"Grania, I—" She bit her lip. The truth seemed inappropriate now, even cruel, but lying to her, telling her that she loved a man she did not was impossible.

"Ravenna?"

Closing her eyes, Ravenna felt as if her heart were being torn in two. No matter how hard she tried, she couldn't find the right path to take.

"He's been so cruel. . . ."

"Have . . . you . . . never . . . been . . . cruel?"

"Yes," Ravenna whispered. Her teardrops splotched her grand-mother's pristine linens.

"Does . . . he . . . love . . ." Grania struggled, as if invisible hands were closing in on her throat. Sobbing silently, Ravenna watched her grandmother's face contort with pain.

Unable to take more, Ravenna brought her lips to Grania's hand that was already wet with her tears. "He loves me, Grania. Fear not," she sobbed. "I know he loves me."

With tear-blurred vision, Ravenna took a last look at her grand-mother. Grania opened her eyes for one brief second, then a strange peace seemed to pass over her like a translucent shroud. Silence came where there had been labored breathing. The old woman's face lifted heavenward and in death, her wrinkles seemed to fall away. Ravenna could almost see the handsome woman she had once been, the one who now had a former lover's hand to spirit her away to the other side.

Ravenna wept quietly at the side of the bed—for how long, she didn't know.

"Child, child, come down and sit with me in the kitchen. We'll send for the undertaker."

In her haze of grief and loss, Ravenna felt Fiona's hand stroke her hair.

"Come away, child. She's gone. Let her go."

Ravenna wept, unable to release Grania's hand. "She's all I had. All I ever had."

"Don't, child. Let her go. She cannot be comfortin' you now."

Ravenna shook her head, her grief engulfing her like thick, black smoke. It was hours more before anyone could take her from Grania's side.

There was no wake for Grania. She was buried in the public grave-yard where paupers and beggars and those not of an established faith were put to rest. It rained, but not steadily; instead the weather came in restless bursts of wind and calm, sun and showers.

The group that said farewell was a small one. Fiona was there, dressed in her Sunday best, a netting of black around her face. Father Nolan, thwarting his bishop, said the final words, along with a gentle, if obligatory, admonishment for Grania's life being lived outside the Church. Her tears petrified within her heart, Ravenna watched as the four boys who worked for the gravedigger lowered the pine coffin into the earth.

Afterward, no one spoke. Words were useless. With a pat to her hand, a hug to her shoulders, the others departed and left Ravenna alone beside the grave.

At the side of the road, Fiona fretted to the priest. "Her heart's broke, the poor dear. She's built a fortress around herself, that one. With Grania gone, I fear she'll never let another one close."

Father Nolan looked toward the graveyard, a frown on his careworn face. Old Grania was gone; it was time to think of his own death, not long in coming. But he could not take his thoughts or his eyes from the girl. Ravenna stood in silhouette at the gravesite, the wind blowing her gown, the same old blue gown she'd worn to Peter Maguire's funeral. She appeared as abandoned as a soul could be, and yet . . .

A man stepped from a copse of trees, a black silk hat solemnly in hand. The father hadn't noticed the Trevallyan carriage stop down the lane, nor had he seen Trevallyan disembark from it.

Holding his breath, Patrick Nolan watched Ravenna raise her head. She turned to look at the figure behind her. Trevallyan stopped. He did not step forward.

A century seemed to pass as Ravenna and Trevallyan locked gazes. The priest felt Fiona step next to him in the hope of a better view. Even the wind ceased to blow while the two lovers stared.

But then the scene fractured.

No one could miss Ravenna's cold demeanor. Nor could they miss the proud Trevallyan fury that passed across the man's kingly face. Trevallyan nodded his head as if in prayer for the soul who had departed. Then he slowly, achingly, turned and walked away.

In despair, Father Nolan watched Ravenna bow her head as if in great pain. The tears that had not come during the funeral came now in great wretched sobs. The priest felt his heart twist in his chest. Murmuring as if unconscious, he said, "A fortress. Yes. God save us all."

Chapter 30

THE NOVEL was finished.

Ravenna hugged the pages to her chest as she took the long walk into Lir from her cottage. The wind blew, whipping at the edges of her manuscript, unleashing locks of her black hair from the pins, but it felt good to breathe the salt air. She'd been cloistered in the cottage for two weeks, living off the coins she'd found in Grania's mattress. Painstakingly she'd spent her days copying her manuscript. Now she was ready to post it.

Giving it a kiss for good luck, she opened the iron latch-door of McCarty's dry goods store and set the manuscript on the counter, but the old wattle and daub building was empty. Mr. McCarty was nowhere in sight, but this was not unusual, for the old man liked to have tea with Father Nolan of an afternoon, and he simply left the door to the store open so that people could take what they liked and leave the money on the counter.

Penning a note to attach to the manuscript, she left tuppence and asked that the remainder be put down on Grania's bill.

Then she penned the name of the man in Dublin that Trevallyan had claimed to know, and the address of the publishing concern.

The wind came in gusts so strong the building seemed to tremble. A shuffling noise drew her gaze to one corner of the empty mercantile, but she discounted it as the shutter being pulled against its iron latches.

Finished, she wiped the pen with her handkerchief and then stuffed it inside the tight sleeve of her gown. She was about to leave when the strange noise sounded again, but this time more to the left of where she had heard it before.

"Is someone there?" she called, a chill running down her spine.

A crash and the sound of glass breaking came from the corner.

Stepping around the counter, she gasped at the form of old man McCarty bound and gagged on the floor. He turned his head to give her an imploring look. She ran to him and pulled the rag from his mouth.

"Who—who has done this?" she cried, her fingers slipping at the tight knots on his wrist. Old McCarty's hair seemed a shade whiter from the shock of his ordeal.

" 'Twas the boy-os. T'ey come in here with kerchiefs hiding their faces and took all me stock. Lanterns, whiskey, everything. . . ."

She helped him to his feet, disbelief slackening her features. "Do you have a guess as to who they were?"

"Nay, tall lads. Big and strong. Alas, more of them than me."

She sat the thin, quivering man beside his stove and tossed in a brick of turf to fire it up.

"You'd better tell Trevallyan he's not much time. T'ese lads are especially bad ones." McCarty rambled while she scrounged for a kettle to make him some tea. "T'ere's been talk of the boy-os taking the castle to retrieve O'Malley. T'ey've got all they need now to do it. Even the men who arose in '98 did no such wickedness as to steal from their own."

She couldn't hold back the sudden rush of anxiety. "He'll hold them off. I've no doubt of that," she said more for herself than for him.

"T'ey'll lynch him, is what t'ey'll be doin'. I saw it once over to County Down. T'ey took the master and hung him right in front of the Big House."

Ravenna's own hands began to tremble. For two weeks she had forced herself not to think of Niall. Now, though it might take her last strength, she particularly didn't want to do it.

Agitated, she looked around at the store, finally noticing the empty shelves. The boy-os had been so neat, she might never have noticed their theft.

"Father Nolan should be able to find them and get some sense into their heads," she said. "Such madness. Thieving from you to get to Trevallyan."

"The priest has no hold over them. The Church condemns them, so they go their own way."

"Liam McCarty, what have you done to your store?" Mrs. McCarty stood at the door, a basket of tatting hooked to her arm, her gaze astounded.

"T'ey've taken it all!" McCarty shouted, near on the verge of tears.

"Trevallyan will make it right. He won't allow this," Ravenna whispered, hating to even speak the name. Hating the way worry gnawed at her insides, hating what that worry signified.

"Aye, but no' if he's stretched."

Ravenna didn't answer. She couldn't. Instead she did her best to help McCarty regain his calm while he told his wife all the awful details. Ravenna then made them a pot of strong tea, and when there was nothing else to be done for them, she departed, promising to check on them in the morning.

The walk back to the cottage was dark and ominous. Storm clouds built against the eastern horizon, creating sheets of gray with no delineation of sea and sky. The hazel trees shook like hands imploring the heavens. Ravenna felt herself trembling as well. When she got to the cottage, she could not light the candles fast enough.

She hated him, she told herself as she stared out her mullioned window, watching the daylight seep from the land. The boy-os hated Trevallyan, too, but they wished him dead. And they would see him dead, if they were not compelled to stop.

She rubbed her forehead, agitated, yet uncertain. There seemed nothing to do about the situation. Certainly she must take a note to Niall and warn him—that much she would do for any mortal being—

but it was a useless gesture. Trevallyan presumably already knew the dangers, and her warning would be weak and vague. It wouldn't do him any good other than confirm what he already knew. They wanted O'Malley back. They would do anything they could to get him freed. They might have even killed Trevallyan for *her,* if she had not been set free.

The knowledge weighed heavily on her shoulders. She was only concerned about Trevallyan, she told herself, as any good person would be concerned by hearing such news.

So then why did her heart pound in her chest at the thought of them entering the castle? And why did her soul cry out at the picture of Niall strung up by his neck?   .

Her hand shook as she placed her fingers over her mouth. A strange, powerful emotion she had thought was dead, believed murdered by cruelty and possession, was being reborn. She did not love him, she told herself, forcing herself to picture again the dungeon, feeling her hatred grow like a child in her womb.

But it was said hatred was akin to love, and now she wondered if it was not so. The tender moments came flooding back to her stronger than the picture of the dungeon: of him watching her while she told him the story of Aidan and Skya, his eyes warm and content in the firelight; of him lying beside her in the barn near Hensey, tickling her with a piece of straw; of him shaking his fist at the *geis* and at the pitiful land that had betrayed him. He'd given her sweet, illicit pleasure, and she'd taken it because she wanted it, from him, only from him. She lived her life outside the Catholic Church and, according to Father Nolan, was hell-bound anyway, as were her mother, grandmother, and Finn Byrne, so hell was where she had wanted to go. And she had told herself that each time she'd been drawn helplessly into Trevallyan's arms and into his bed.

Yet his cruelty the past weeks could not be forgiven in a moment, she thought, feeling the flames of anger rise inside her. But the direness of the situation seemed to tamp down her fury. When she thought of him being lynched, she knew she must stop it. He didn't deserve it. Even a mere acquaintance of Lord Trevallyan's knew he was a good man, a strong man. The trouble between them arose, no doubt, because she, Ravenna, was not just a mere acquaintance of the master's, as life should have led her to be. Instead, there had been the *geis* and circumstance. And now she knew Niall deeper than probably anyone. And that gave him the ability to snap her emotions in two.

But, still, he was a good man, a strong man.

He loved her and she knew it.

God save her. And she now knew she loved him too.

A tear dripped down one cheek as she was struck by the force of her realization. She loved Trevallyan. With all his sins and grace, she loved him. For her love was not weak, as she had imagined, easily crushed by wrongdoing. It was strong and enduring and it did not relinquish easily. With even a bud still left in her heart, it could bloom again and form the mightiest of trees.

Sorrowfully, she realized she had not been able to give Grania the reassurances the old woman had desired, and remorse was like a bitter taste in her mouth. But deep down, she wondered if Grania hadn't known anyway. Perhaps her grandmother had indeed been a witch. Grania had always known things others did not. She'd known about Finn Byrne's death and his and Brilliana's immortal love for each other. And now Ravenna wondered if she hadn't known about this. She had died peacefully and without regret. Grania could tell Trevallyan had been her granddaughter's lover just by listening to the softness of her voice when she spoke of him. So she must have been able to see into her heart as well, and understand what Ravenna could not.

Until now.

She wiped her eyes and grabbed her old black shawl, stumbling in the darkness of the cottage. Evening had long since come while she'd been immersed in her thoughts, and now she didn't know what time it was—early or late. It would take her a good while to walk to the castle, but she would go there now, no matter the inappropriateness of the hour. She must find Niall. She had to warn him of the treachery around him. She had to talk to him. Their problems were great—there was still her anger and his abuse of his powers, almost insurmountable obstacles—but she wanted him to know that she loved him. She would not sacrifice herself to him, nor would she allow him to take her over, but she loved him, and she knew instinctively that he needed to hear it.

⊗

The bell in the clock of the tower room rang twelve times. Greeves had long since retired; even the sculleries had gone to bed. Scarred and blackened with soot, Trevallyan Castle was still, as if listening for the reassurance of midnight silence.

Yet one lone candle still burned. High in the tower room, someone was awake, brooding and drinking, his mind, his soul, obsessed.

Trevallyan put down his glass and stared at the seat opposite him, the one that was new and unworn; the one that mocked him. He stared until his gaze seemed to penetrate the leather and pierce its core. In his mind, she was there, her black hair fanned across the arm, her sweetly curved lips parted in slumber. The rightness of the scene gave life to his imaginings. She'd been born to the chair. It had been built for her. The injustice of her absence was unbearable.

He ached to reach out and run his hand along its smooth back, as if, futilely, to feel again the residual warmth of the woman who had once sat in it. But he didn't reach out his hand. He already knew the cold-ness that would meet his touch. The chair was only emptiness and leather.

As his thoughts were only shadows and despair.

The creak of the door should have turned his head. A visitor at this hour was unheard of. Even Greeves knew better than to disturb him in his apartment when it was late and when the candle burned long into the wee hours of the morn. But Trevallyan did not look up. The foot-steps did not interest him enough to acknowledge the intruder's pres-ence. Scorn cut deep into his features upon the sound of every motion. Only when the intruder paused, did Trevallyan deign to speak.

"What took you so long. The servants trip you up? I confess I expected you earlier."

"It don't do to rush these things. They only get botched."

Trevallyan finally looked up. His upper lip curled in a derisive smile as he gazed full upon his visitor. "So, here you've found me. At last." His gaze held wrath and fury. "Come to kill me, MacCumhal?"

Malachi stepped in front of the small fire still smoldering at the hearth. A pistol was in his hand. "Aye," he whispered hotly, and put it to Trevallyan's temple.

"That's rich." Trevallyan sneered. "Where are the rest of them? Downstairs, testing the oak limbs?"

"Come down the tower with me. You know what we want. Just do it."

"I won't release O'Malley."

"It's your life if you don't." Hysteria skirted the edges of his voice.

Trevallyan gave him a baleful stare, his gaze scorning the pistol and the one who held it. "You stand there, MacCumhal, trying to look like such a brave man, but you aren't one. You're a coward. Your hand is trembling. And the conviction that I've seen on O'Malley's face is wavering on yours."

Trevallyan stood.

Malachi, almost against his will, stepped back. "I've come to take you to Sean or to the tree. Choose now. They'll be growin' impatient down at the oak." His gaze hardened.

Niall laughed, a dark, harsh sound that echoed down the stone stairwell. He pinned Malachi with his gaze and began to stalk him. "MacCumhal, tell me," he taunted, stepping around his chair, "I want to know: Are you with the boy-os, or are you not?" He thumped his chest. "Do you feel the cause in your heart, or do you not?"

"I feel it, me bloody lord, I feel it." Malachi cocked the pistol. "Me own da was shot down to defend the likes of you." He looked around the room that was so sumptuous and foreign to his world. "You and your kind, you've taken everything. We have nothing."

"What have you come for, really, MacCumhal? Is it just for Sean, or is it just for the rebellion, or is it for you?" Acid dripped from every word.

"For me," MacCumhal announced, hatred in his eyes. "For her," he whispered.

"Ah, finally the truth."

"You had no business to take her from me," Malachi cried. "She was meant for the likes of me, not you. And you lured her away."

"And now you itch for me to tell you that I won't release Sean O'Malley. You can see me swing then. You can get her back, can't you?"

"Yes. Yes," Malachi whispered, anguish on his face.

"But I'm not going to tell you where O'Malley is. I'm not going to give him up. He's a criminal, as you are. He'll pay for his crimes."

"You're a bloody fool then, me lord."

"Aye, but better that than an inept felon. The only thing you're useful for, MacCumhal, would be as a messenger to send for death."

Enraged, Malachi rushed toward Trevallyan. He put the gun to Niall's temple once more, but to his surprise, Trevallyan didn't flinch. He almost seemed to relish the pistol there.

"Go ahead. Do it. You've always wanted to. Why, you've dreamed of this moment," Niall taunted in low tones.

"You're bloody mad, is what. I've got a gun to your head, man, don't you see that?" Malachi cried, beads of sweat popping on his freckled brow.

"I see it," Trevallyan hissed, not blinking.

"Do you want me to blow your brains out?"

"No, I want you and the lads downstairs to leave me alone."

"Not without O'Malley. Tell me where he is."

"I won't. So what else do you want?" Trevallyan smiled, the humor never reaching his eyes. "Do you want my land? It's worthless. My castle? You've already burned half of it. So now is it money? Her?"

"I want everything, Trevallyan. I want all that you hold dear." Malachi brutally pushed the point of the gun into Trevallyan's head.

Trevallyan only wrapped his hand around the barrel and kept it there. "If you've come for all I hold dear, then you're the fool, MacCumhal." He gnashed his teeth, his expression darkening. He violently shoved the gun away and slammed Malachi against the marble mantel. "Don't you see?" he spat, not seeming to care that Malachi put the pistol once more to his head. "Don't you get it?" He stared at Malachi as if in disbelief of the man's stupidity. "You're too late. *I've nothing left.*"

Malachi swallowed.

The men stood in a death grip, unmoving.

"Aye, hold him, Malachi! Hold him!" A man entered the chamber, a pistol in his hand also. Then another man came in, and yet another. They converged upon Trevallyan like crows to corn.

"Will you release Sean O'Malley? Do you tell us where he is, or do you get twisted?" one of the men drilled at Trevallyan.

Niall shoved against the lock-hold the men had on him, but he didn't seem to possess the passion to battle it. The light was long dead in his eyes and had been ever since that day at the graveyard; one could almost wonder if he didn't secretly yearn for the end the men promised. Still, instincts were hard to repress. When the men dragged him across the antechamber, he fought the entire way.

"Give us Sean O'Malley or 'tis death to you, Trevallyan," a man shouted, hitting him in the head.

"Then 'tis death," Trevallyan cursed as they blindfolded him, tied his hands, and shoved him toward the long, spiral stair that led to the oak.

Chapter 31

THE NIGHT was cold; the wind stung like needles, but the rain had yet to come from behind the Sorra Hills. With hands bound behind him, and eyes covered with a black blindfold, Trevallyan stumbled forward, ever closer to the noose that danced in the harsh breeze. Around him, men spoke in low, nervous whispers that got swept away in the wind. A horse whinnied, one no doubt stolen from the Trevallyan stables. A fitting end, Niall thought, to be hung from the back of one's own steed.

"Get him up there!" A voice cried out, and Niall was hoisted atop the horse. Without sight or touch, he didn't know which horse it was.

And probably never would.

"Trevallyan!" one of his captors shouted from the ground. "We give you one last chance to bring us Sean O'Malley. Tell us where he is and we'll be merciful."

Niall said nothing. He didn't fight the scratchy rope that was lowered over his head and slung around his neck; he didn't whine or beg; rather, he seemed reflective, as if he already wondered about the other side.

"I can't say I'm disappointed, Trevallyan," he heard Malachi say at his flank. "You have nothin' now. Finally you're bein' brought down to size."

"Covet what I have, MacCumhal. Covet it, and know that I pray you get it."

"Is that your revenge, me lord?" Malachi snorted. "A fine revenge to wish me riches and castles and land."

"I'd trade it all for what you've had."

Disparagingly, he asked, "And what would that be?"

"What she has given you. . . ." Trevallyan grew silent. Bitterly, he said, ". . . one genuine smile, one carefree moment of friendship. I'd give up everything for that."

Irrational anger rose to the surface. Fiercely, Malachi said, "Farewell, Trevallyan. I'm glad you won't be interferin' no more."

Niall felt men bumping against the horse. The steed was nervous in the wind, and someone held down its head. They didn't want to risk it bolting before they were ready. Ready to take a man's life.

"I love her, and I want her back," he heard Malachi murmur defiantly, his voice strangely mangled with emotion.

Niall turned his head in his direction, ignoring the catch of the rope at his throat. In a lordly voice, he said, "You love her, MacCumhal? But would you die for her?"

Malachi didn't answer.

Niall released a cynical laugh. "Coward."

"Damn you, Trevallyan," Malachi spat. "Love her in death if you must, for you never loved her in life, I'll not believe it. There's no love in your foul Ascendency heart."

"I loved her and love her still." The words were harsh, mournful, difficult. "And I prove it," Niall said quietly. With finality. "Because I'm not here to die for her. I'm here to die just for the ground she walks upon."

❀

Ravenna pounded at the castle door, despairing at the late hour. No one answered, and it was becoming clear that no one would. All the servants were in bed, and deaf to her pleas to open the door.

The wind cut into her. She hugged the shawl close. There was no other choice but to go around the ruins and try to enter the castle through the kitchens. Trevallyan was still awake, she knew it, because even from the castle road, she could see the light burning steadily in the tower.

"Bloody hell," she cursed, and gave the door one last pounding. The stiff breeze whipped at her gown, sending chills through her body. It was harvest weather. Cold and unsettling.

She skirted the fortress of the castle, feeling like a beggar trying to acquire a ha'penny from an unwilling nobleman. If the kitchen door was latched, as she suspected it would be during these uncertain times, then she would simply have to return to her cottage and come back in the morning.

The charred crossbeams of the ruins appeared like a skeleton clawing to reach the night sky. She didn't want to even look at them for they signified too much strife and hatred, but she was forced to as she circled around the castle. The keep was in view and, around that, the kitchen. Heartening, she quickened her step.

She rounded the keep, saying a silent prayer for the kitchen door to be unlatched. So encumbered by her thoughts, she at first didn't see the lights, the flickering radiance of torches in a copse.

But then she spied them, and fear came like an icy blast of wind through her soul. She stared at the lights and knew there was only one thing they could signify.

Her entire body began to shake. It was an illicit gathering of men in the woods.

⚯

"Trevallyan, we hang you in the revered name of Daniel O'Connell and Home Rule. What say you in your defense?"

Steady atop the horse, Trevallyan remained silent, obviously scorning the tribunal the men felt compelled to carry out.

"All right," the man said, watching him with an expression of be-grudging respect, "let your silence be a testament to your guilt. Hang, Englishman, and know that whom you ruled, will one day rule."

"I'm an Irishman," Trevallyan growled. "Take it to your graves that you killed one of your own . . . and let the remembrance of it haunt you the rest of your days."

"Enough." A man stepped from the dozen who circled the tree. With him, he carried a lantern that rocked in the wind and sent terrifying shadows streaming across their victim's blindfolded face. "We hang you, Trevallyan, because of the sins of your ancestors. Join them. Go in peace." He raised his arm. The man who gripped the horse's bridle watched in dread anticipation for the signal to release the animal and send Trevallyan to his death. All held their breaths. The lantern swung in the breeze, the creak of its brass handle like the screams of the damned.

"Untie him," a command came from their midst.

All looked in the direction of the traitor. All except Trevallyan, who in the wind could not hear the commotion on the ground.

The traitor was a woman, a beautiful woman, her head and shoulders wrapped in a worn black shawl.

"Leave here, Ravenna. You cannot save his life." Malachi stepped forward and tried to pull her back, but she flung aside his arms and stepped forward to the leader.

"This is wrong." She looked around at the faces of the men she knew from her childhood. "Patrick O'Donovan—Tim O'Shea—Michael O'Flaherty—don't you see? If you hang him, you must hang me also."

The horse neighed and stamped its foot. Donovan, the man holding him, had trouble keeping him still.

"Free him!" Ravenna cried out, terrified that the horse would break and Niall would be lost.

Brutally, she was taken aside. The leader, Michael O'Flaherty shook her and said, "You cannot help him. Why have you come here, girl?"

She stared at Michael, a new understanding blooming within her. Solemnly, she gazed at Niall, so far away beneath the oak, his life hanging by a paltry length of twisted hemp. "I've come because of a geis," she said quietly, "and because of what I now know in my heart."

She looked up at O'Flaherty. "I love him, and I won't leave until you free him," she said, the conviction on her face turning it into a mask of marble.

"Go home. Don't get involved in this. You can do nothing for him. He is lost," Michael told her.

"Nay," she said quietly, "he is not lost. Because I love him. And I wish for him to be my husband. I thought I could never give him what he wanted because I believed deep down that there was nothing I had worth giving. And I believed he would never need me." She grasped O'Flaherty's arm. "But he does need me. You all need me. Without me, he is apart from us. With me, he is one of us. Our marriage will end this strife and bring peace back to Lir."

"You expect a lot from your marriage. Too much, I fear," Michael said contemptuously.

"I do not expect. I know. What say you, Michael, are you to murder my own dearest love?"

O'Flaherty didn't answer.

Malachi, who stood at her side, shook his head in despair. Angrily, he made for Trevallyan as if he would hang him himself.

"Malachi!" Ravenna said, running to him. "You must understand, it was never you and I. Killing him won't change how I feel. You must accept it. I beg of you, go to Galway, and make your life again."

Slowly, Malachi's steps seemed to grow weary. Bit by bit he seemed to surrender his hell-bent vengeance as if finally accepting what he'd feared all along. Hanging his head, he whispered, "Don't say 'tis over."

"Yes, it is over. And be glad," she encouraged, taking his hand and squeezing it. "Go to Galway and find a pretty woman and make her your wife. Be glad, Malachi, as I am glad."

She turned to all the men and pleaded, "Go home and forget this night as I hope to forget it. It's over. Murdering Trevallyan would mean murdering our beloved Lir."

"He's teh cause of our troubles," a man shouted angrily from the rear, "and yet you're comin' here fightin' to spare his life."

"Yes!" she whispered, her dark, tear-filled eyes imploring the man. "We need Trevallyan. He is a good and generous man and will help us thwart the scourge that has beset our crops. Would you have Lir resemble Munster? I hear the dead are so many there that they block the roads." She stared at them, defying them to deny her words. When they had no reply, she softly began again. "The Ascendency is not the sole cause of our blight. Lord Trevallyan didn't make this famine, but he can help eliminate it. Trevallyan has fulfilled his *geis;* let him reap the rewards. Lir will get better, and he will set things right again." She looked around at the men's faces, some she knew, one she even loved. "I've come here to beg. I love him. Please, set him free. Don't destroy me as you would him."

The men shuffled about, avoiding her pain-filled gaze. They whispered amongst themselves until finally Michael O'Flaherty walked to the horse.

"Don't," she implored, knowing Trevallyan's life was now in his hands.

O'Flaherty seemed torn. She could see he ached to carry out his plans, but she could see, too, his conscience. He was not a bad man. He was just another victim of a cause gone astray.

"I beg of you." It was the barest whisper. But it seemed the most effective. Michael O'Flaherty looked deep into her eyes, and his shoulders slumped in defeat.

"Let Lord Trevallyan go," he said to Donovan, his voice filled with frustration.

"But you can't!" a man cried out, shaking his fist.

"I said, free Trevallyan," O'Flaherty commanded, flicking his gaze to Donovan, the man who held the horse.

"God bless you. God bless you," Ravenna sobbed, weak with relief.

The men watched her tears in begrudging silence. The noose was slipped from Trevallyan's neck. Still blindfolded, and ignorant of the battle that had occurred around him, he seemed surprised at his reprieve.

Ravenna took the horse's bridle from Donovan. Without speaking a word, she waited until the men had disappeared into the shadows of the woods, bound for home. She would keep their identities secret, and they knew it. The next time she saw them on the road to Lir or in the mercantile, she would be as pleasant to them as if this night were nothing but a bad dream.

"What goes on here?" Trevallyan said, slipping to the ground.

A rain began to fall and mixed with her tears. Without untying his blindfold or his hands, she stood on tiptoe and placed a kiss on his hard mouth.

"I thought we could never be as equals. But now that I have my power, I choose you to be my husband. Will you marry me, Lord Trevallyan?"

He leaned into her embrace, a groan of inexpressible relief rumbling from his chest. Finding her mouth as if by instinct, he kissed her deeply in the rain.

He'd found salvation at last.

EPILOGUE

Lughnasa

I gaze with delight
As the flock of cranes take flight
Into the blue skies.
The dream cherished in my heart
Since my boyhood has come true.

CROWN PRINCE NARUHITO

Waka

AVENNA RAN down the sweeping lawn of Trevallyan Castle all the while crying, "At last! At last! It has come!"

Trevallyan leaned against the same oak tree that one year earlier had almost brought him death. He'd been surveying the four fields of Lir that spread out beneath where the castle stood. The feeling it brought was good. The *ogham* stone still stood sentinel over Lir's fortunes, but for the first time in years, no potatoes grew in its fields. Instead, sheep grazed along the rocky coast; flax, pale and dry, waved in the breeze that kicked up from the Irish Sea, ready for harvest. Corn grew in one lot, turnips and cabbage in another. Lir was saved.

"Whoa, me girl. Quit your running. Do you want to shake our babe right from you?" He caught his wife by the waist and placed his hand possessively upon her swelling belly.

"It's here!" she said, her eyes ablaze with excitement.

"Your book? 'Tis finally arrived?" He tried to take the red leather-bound volume from her, but she snatched it from his hold.

"Nay. Sit. I want to read you the last chapter. You never did know what became of Skya and Aidan."

He lowered himself and sat against the oak, pulling her onto his lap. She opened the gilt-edged book and placed a kiss on his mouth. Closing his eyes, he seemed immersed in deep pleasure: the sound of his wife's voice as she read.

The wind howled, and the rain shook the tiny cottage that sat deep in the Woods of Hawthorn. Inside, a woman who had no more tears to weep lay quietly with her hands tied to a corner of her pallet.

Skya prayed for death. The loneliness had become too much. If she could not live among men, then she would die alone, cursing the gift that had long ago saved her sisters from the dragon.

She lay facing the packed-mud wall of her cottage, unwilling to move; unwilling to even attempt to free herself. She had loved him, and he had abandoned her, as she had always feared he would if she freed him. Now she must accept it, and rather than do that, she willed death to come and sit at her pallet; to take her by the hand and bring her to a better place.

A gust of wind rattled the batten door, shook the latch, and burst it open. Rain sheeted inside, spraying her, but she paid it no mind. Her thoughts were too filled with dark fantasies for her to even bother to look up. List-lessly, she stared at the wall, the wet spot beneath her cheek where her tears had fallen for two days now turned cold and clammy against her face.

She closed her eyes and dreamed of laughter and warm hands. As if she willed it, she almost felt a strong hand on her wrist slowly unwinding her bounds.

Hesitant, afraid that her reverie would disappear should she look up, she fearfully opened her eyes. The touch that she had imagined was real. A man was untying her, but he could not save her. Only Aidan and his love could save her.

"Go away," she cried, turning back to the wall, not even caring how the man had found her.

"I have gone away. Now I've returned."

Slowly, as if terrified she was dreaming, she turned toward her savior.

It was Aidan, rain slick on his hair and face, his handsome embroidered bliaud dark with water. Gravely he worked on the knots that held her wrists.

"Why . . . ?" she whispered, fresh tears, these of hope and cautious joy, filling her azure eyes.

"A witch's tears haunt like no other," he answered, unable to look at her.

"Is that the only reason?"

He freed her and took her in his arms. He was cold and wet, but she didn't care, she clung to him.

"I tried to flee. I almost got to Clancullen. But then I turned around. My will was no longer my own to command. I was driven by my heart instead." He took her hand, the one that made magic, and laced his fingers with her own. "I have only one question."

"And—and what is that?" she whispered, not daring to believe her fortune.

"I want to bring you back to your father. Your people will accept you if you are a means to peace. Our kingdoms have fought for centuries, but no more. I want to marry you and unite our families. Still, I must know: Will I be vexed with children like you?"

She looked at him through her tears. "If they are like me, will you banish them?"

His handsome face turned stern. Pondering the question, he wrapped her in a blanket as if trying to keep himself from temptation until the wedding night. Once he held her again, he whispered, "Nay, I fear I must keep them, for banishment would only cause their mother grief. You see, she cast a spell upon me and stole my heart. I am forever in her power."

His hand lifted to her cheek and brushed away the tears.

Then he sealed his fate with a kiss.

Ravenna closed the book and turned her head to look at Trevallyan. He smiled down at her, his still-youthful and handsome face filled with pride.

"I thought you would get it published. Tell me, is it causing a sensation?"

"Indeed," she whispered. "The publisher wrote to me and told me they cannot print enough of them. 'Tis causing quite a scandal, for it has become quite popular with the ladies, and their husbands don't approve."

"And they're buying it anyway, no doubt."

"Of course. They don't want to read as men, they want to read as women."

He took the scarlet leather-bound volume from her hands to study it further and he was unable to hide his surprise. Running his fingers across the gilt-embossed lettering on the cover, he read, *"From Out of the Mist: Tales from Ireland* by Finn Byrne Raven."

She lowered her gaze, still stung by the old resentment. "They wouldn't publish it if I insisted on a woman's name. 'Tis all right for a man to write so explicitly of love, but not a woman, they told me. So I took my father's name, as a tribute."

He held her face in his hands and stared down at her. They locked gazes, and he whispered, pride entwined with every word, "Someday they'll know it was you who wrote this. They'll know it was Lady Ravenna Trevallyan, the child of the ninth viscount of Cinaeth."

She smiled and kissed him. He reached for more. She gave it.

Settling back into his arms again, she said, "He loved her, you know. My father. Even with Lord Cinaeth's tales of Finn Byrne's deathly confession, I was still unsure. Then I found a letter to Brilliana among his things at Cinaeth Castle. 'Twas tragically never sent. It was addressed simply to Hawthorn Cottage, County Lir." She caressed her softly rounded belly, content and yet sad. "In the letter, he speaks of his happiness about the babe. He wanted me to be a girl, one who looked just like her mother. Then he spoke of his love for Brilliana and his hopes for the future. I do not think I could read it again, for 'tis too distressing to think of what might have been, yet I'm glad I read it once. I'm glad to know she was loved."

He said nothing. They were man and wife now. They shared everything. His silence was commiseration and she knew it.

Sighing, she looked out beneath her at the bountiful fields of Lir. Almost unconsciously, she asked, "Was the *geis* ever true?"

"Perhaps." Trevallyan rested his chin upon the crown of her head and gazed at the lush fields. "But I wonder in my doddering old age what truth really is. If people believe strongly enough in something, it becomes true in their own minds, and that may be the only truth we know."

"I'd like to believe it now." She glanced down at her hand. The three rings of the gimmal were united on her hand and had been ever since the wedding. It was bittersweet to think of it. The rings interlocked so finely that they appeared now as one; Trevallyan's was there, and her own, and the heart-carved ring of old Griffen Rooney's. The old gravedigger had held the middle ring ever since his childhood. He had given her the ring during the ceremony and told her he had guarded her heart all his life. She nearly wept to think of it now, for after the wedding, Griffen had retired to his room in the castle. In the morning, they found him dead. It was as if he had been living only to fulfill a task and with that task completed, he'd found his peace.

"I'd like to believe all the powers of this earth brought me to your side," she whispered.

"I would have found you anyway. Even in spite of all the powers of this earth." His voice was strong with conviction.

"You would have?" She looked up at him.

Gravely he nodded his head. "I looked for you all my life. So what purpose was my life, if not to find you?"

"I love you," she said, emotion catching her voice.

"I sold my soul to hear those words." He looked deep into her eyes. "You must never stop saying them."

She promised.